TERRIBLE PRAISE

BOOK ONE
THE REDAMANCY SERIES

LARA HAYES

BELLA
B O O K S

2018

Bella Books, Inc.
P.O. Box 10543
Tallahassee, FL 32302

Printed in the United States of America on acid-free paper.

First Bella Books Edition 2018

Editor: Cath Walker

Cover Design: Lara Hayes
Cover Designer: Judith Fellows

ISBN: 978-1-59493-597-8

On Being Unalone, Delaney Nolan for Vela Magazine
Source/credit: (http://velamag.com/on-being-unalone/)

Now I am safe from strange men, but nobody praises me. I need this terrible praise and I do not want to need this terrible, terrible praise.

-Delaney Nolan, *On Being Unalone*

Redamancy-noun: The act of loving in return.

Acknowledgments

This story might not have been told without Carolyn Cruse's constant encouragement and enthusiasm, her helpful notes and our countless late night discussions over the years. Similarly, thank you to Vera and Jordan Hayes for their endless support. Thank you to Jessica Hayes for sharing her expertise, and to Claudia Wilson who helped with pronunciation. Thank you to Dana Piccoli for sound advice, friendship, and more than one much needed push.

Thank you to my loves Megan Evans, Jackie (JK) Willett, and Nick Lutz for always listening to my stories. Also: Robby and Mandy Olivam, Nick Davenport, Matt Willett, Seth Miller, Lizzy Carraway, John Beechem, Kelly Shiflet, Sarah Maddox, John James, Jasmin Chen, James Willett, Erin Fuhrman, Veda Chapman, Jennifer Chapman, Bobby Evans, Angie Evans, Rodney Conard, Jimmy Buchanan, and Stephen Savage.

Lastly, thank you to my amazing editor Cath Walker, and everyone at Bella Books, but especially Jessica Hill.

Dedication

For my mother and brother

I
Meeting Minutes

By the time the elevator chimes its arrival, my senses are already muddled. My head feels lighter than it has in a long while and I struggle to focus. My eyes are drawn to the scalding bright white fluorescents behind the brassy redheaded receptionist. Our quarterly meeting is conducted face-to-face, and has always been my burden. Trusted associates though they may be, it takes every ounce of discipline to remain civil and controlled.

"Good evening, Opes and Sons. How may I direct your call?" The red hold lights blink incessantly in a never-ending queue of incoming calls. "One moment please."

I flex my hands to conceal their tremble, and place my palms flat against the corner of the black marble desk as I wait for Rachel to acknowledge me.

"Good evening Ms. Radu," she says. "Mr. Opes is finishing with another client. I'll tell him you've arrived."

Rachel keeps her head down as she rushes to say in person what could be relayed by phone. She reconsiders her haste and hesitates with one hand poised on the glass corner of the entryway.

"Can I get you anything?" she asks, courteous to a fault.

"No. Thank you, Rachel."

"Please have a seat while you wait. Mr. Opes will see you shortly."

Rachel vanishes and I indulge in a brief stretch, permitting myself to lean against the lip of her desk. If I sit, the urge to sleep will triple and it will take noticeable effort to stand again. One must appear infallible inside these walls, so I settle on presenting an impatient façade.

I can hear Rachel's hushed nervous whispers bouncing off the granite tiles. She does not want to return to her domain to count the tense minutes as they pass in my quiet company.

Her heels click toward me and I raise my head. She keeps her chin down and stares at my feet.

"Mr. Opes offers his sincerest apologies, Ms. Radu." Her voice is a soft but shaky melody to my ears. "He will collect you in a moment."

I nod and take to pacing by the far wall, granting her the distance we both know she prefers. I appreciate Rachel's apprehension. She is smarter than her predecessors, always keeping the bright emerald of her eyes hidden from the black of mine. She does not trust me so much as to fix her gaze on my dark sunglasses, though I doubt very much she could explain why. Perhaps her Irish forebears are to blame for filling her head with absurd superstitions.

Yet I can smell her fear—sharp and acidic—as she pretends to correct her lurid eye shadow in a small round compact she keeps on her desk. Rachel has never said a word of it aloud, but my reflection in the mirror startles her every single time. A smile tugs at the corner of my mouth as Andrew Opes appears in the lobby, hurrying his last client into the elevator. A fellow investor by the look of him.

Andrew does not trouble himself with small talk. Not while I have been made to wait, yet again.

Andrew Opes is an intolerable creature with a puffed chest and a perpetual strut. If only he had kept some of his hair after the age of thirty, or been born tall and broad-shouldered. If Andrew were not a slave to the drink, as indicated by the blood vessels webbing down the bridge of his nose, perhaps he would make for better company. He is not the hardened businessman his father was, though he tries desperately to dress the part.

He wipes his palms against the front of his wool trousers and offers his hand. "Kathryn, so good to see you." His warm clammy paws close over my cool fingers.

"Andy. A pleasure."

"Andrew, please. No one calls me that anymore." I suspect he knows that I insist upon the name to taunt him. A friendly jab at his transparent persona.

"Forgive me, Andrew. Old habits." I put more emphasis on the last line than I should in front of Rachel, whose heart is pounding like a trapped hare's. Andrew nods and clasps his empty hands, certain that I will repeat the taunt.

"Please, after you." Andrew waves me through the glass partition and down the hall to his office, slipping silently in step behind me. His door is open, as are the blinds. My steps falter, as he breezes around my body and heads for the bar in the corner.

The effects of the evening sun bouncing off the wall of windows and spilling out against the dark wood of his desk are dizzying. This is his small revenge. Andrew offers me a drink that he knows will be declined. His fingers curl around a scotch.

My fingers knot into fists as I watch the setting sun drown in brilliant pink hues behind the tops of lesser buildings that frame the view of his penthouse suite. I remove my jacket and hang it on the rack beside his door.

Andrew's father, Robert Opes, had kept a separate staff and smaller office in the dark basement of this building as a courtesy and a sign of respect to our family. For many years, he served as a loyal steward, managing our affairs. Robert was the face of Fane's amassed wealth, and a true ally in every sense of the word. However, Andrew has spread himself out against the sky in this sun-drenched office, as a way of saying he does not need us when we both know that his enterprise, his father's legacy would topple without our patronage. Andrew's hubris is the sole reason my meeting schedule has been altered from biannually to quarterly, and Fane is wise to doubt Andrew's competence. I suppose, were I in My Lord's position, I too would charge a trustworthy servant like me to be my eyes and ears.

"Would you prefer the blinds closed?" Andrew gestures with a wide-open hand. A small, disdainful laugh escapes me as I walk around the side of his desk ahead of him, and take his seat for myself.

"Andy, I would not dream of troubling you with my preferences. Shall we get down to business?" I settle comfortably in his over-sized chair, back to the window and flirt with the idea of propping my heels on the corner of his desk. He downs the last of his scotch, his hostility visible only in the single finger he taps against the glass clutched in his fist. Andrew has more restraint than I credit him for, just not very much.

"Of course," he says.

Andrew freshens up his glass and sets it carelessly on the table while he explains to me—as he does every quarter—how profitable the year has been for us. His verbose, self-aggrandizing yammering is of little interest as I review the numbers for myself. The glowing portrait he paints seems to correlate with the figures Rachel has printed for my visit. I question every quarter whether my abhorrence of him as a person warrants the skepticism I feel toward him as a businessman. I cut short his gloating ramble about the genius, if not underhanded plays he has made for the sake of my family's fortune.

"Another strong finish it seems." I lean back in the chair and Andrew takes a celebratory sip of his second scotch. "And yet again, I see no report on the Caymans." Undoubtedly the largest single account Andrew has managed for a decade, and the one which fluctuates the most. The account my family transfers from on a monthly basis. Anonymity, after all, is expensive.

I tap the tip of my black fingernail expectantly on his desk. Andrew sets his drink down and leans back in his chair, his hands folded neatly over his swollen belly.

"Well, for the sake of your time, I haven't included details of every account. Just the usual summary."

The sun's grip around my brain lessens with every passing moment and I feel more at home in my own skin, less like a passenger locked in a vehicle I cannot control. I slowly remove the sturdy black frames of my Wayfarers, and toss the sunglasses on the mountainous stack of papers towering between us. A familiar burn settles at the back of my eyes as they adjust, a single flame that flares and chokes. When my vision clears, Andrew looks quickly away and clears his throat.

"Thank you, Andrew." It is easier now in the dim twilight to focus my eyes on his. He meets my stare with great reluctance.

"Your concern for me with these meetings is touching. But I assure you…" I lean across his desk and flash a threatening smile. "Time is not as precious a commodity to me as it is to you."

His boisterous veneer subdued, Andrew apologizes with something approaching sincerity. "I will have Rachel arrange the figures for us immediately," he offers. I wave my hand in dismissal. "Tell me the quarter is a success on all fronts and I shall believe you, Andrew." He brightens and takes another slow gulp of his scotch. I reach for the family photo on the corner of his desk and watch his entire body coil. I hold his family in my right hand and trace his daughter's face with my index finger. "Christine has grown quite lovely."

Andrew stands abruptly and snatches the portrait from my hand, looking once over his beloved child's face before he returns the photo to his desk. "I will have the figures sent to you first thing tomorrow morning, Kathryn. I am confident you will be pleased with them."

After a few quick signatures, I reach for my sunglasses and stand on firm feet. Andrew adjusts his paisley-print tie and I take hold of his sweaty hand in a brief but strong shake.

"I am positive you would not give me cause to question your performance." I walk around the side of his desk and sweep my jacket from its place on the coat rack, casting it over one shoulder. "After all, you would not want to jeopardize Christine's college tuition. It is nearly that time, is it not?"

Andrew wraps his hand around the back of his chair and does not conceal the hate in his eyes. "Yes. This coming fall."

"They grow up so fast." I slip my arms into the satin-lined sleeves of my coat as I dig my words, like fingers, into his bleeding wound. "Good evening, Andy."

My dark glasses are fixed to my face before I pass the receptionist's desk. There is no need to scare the competent help more than I already have.

"A pleasure as always, Rachel," I toss the social nicety over my shoulder as I step into the waiting elevator.

"Until next quarter, Ms. Radu."

Rachel is standing behind her desk, and I do not miss her small sigh of relief as the steel doors close between us. I can practically feel her crossing herself.

Good girl.

The cool of the basement-level parking garage settles around my aching skull like a salve. A sojourn in daylight is as physically devastating as a marathon sprint on the surface of the sun, but every moment grows more tolerable as I reach the sanctity of my black Mercedes parked in the space reserved for *special clients*.

I crawl across the black leather interior of the backseat—not trusting myself behind the wheel—fighting with the sleeves of my jacket as I fling it to the floor. The second I settle on my right side, exhaustion hits me full force and I pound my fist against the floorboard. The burning in my eyes makes it difficult to keep them open and as I roll onto my back I pinch the bridge of my nose, which does nothing to quiet the screaming in my brain—as though colors themselves have sound.

There was a time before all this bureaucracy. Many blissful years before we had to trouble ourselves with keeping up appearances, or force ourselves aboveground in the daylight hours, when we were feared and revered in equal measure. A time when men like Andrew kept their eyes on their feet while they spoke, much the way Rachel operates today. A time when it was considered a slight to turn your back, and people backed carefully from the room thanking us for our patronage and generosity. I would have been well within my rights in those days—nay expected—to leave a man like Andrew pinned to the surface of his own desk with a letter opener, for so much as a misspoken utterance. In moments of his regular abject arrogance, my first instinct is still to reach for my saber. Even after all these years, I feel naked without its grounding weight knocking flatly against my hip. A simpler time, and one I find myself missing more with every passing year.

I shut my eyes as the dull thud in my temples joins the sharp roar of the blinding world.

* * *

I wake with a start, bolt upright in my car. An untimely sleep is a great danger, and I rip the back door open more forcefully than I should. The steel gives a slight protest in my palm as I slam it shut behind me. The air is cool and the sun has set completely. The wind carries with it the stamp of the hour: perfumes too honeyed and cloyingly sweet for office hours, the half-eaten remnants of discarded meals, evening flowers unfurled even in this concrete playground, all of which confirm that I have wasted several hours. I slide into the driver's seat and settle the key in the ignition. The dashboard clock illuminates: nine fifty-three p.m. I let my head fall back against the headrest. The hour is later than I would like, but there is still time to feed.

My impromptu slumber has steadied my nerves and my headache is manageable, but I am too weak for a proper hunt. I will need to meet with Fane when I return home, and he will want an overview of his financials. Fane will also need to eat. Business matters always leave him frustrated and peckish. With a weary sigh, I throw the car into drive and make my way to the only sure fare I have in such circumstances.

* * *

Emergency rooms are always bustling, and I prefer to enter a hospital there among the crowd. Window shopping, my brother calls it, taking inventory of the produce. The sick, the bleeding, the junkie frauds presenting with a myriad of fabricated symptoms in the hope that they will land a new physician. Someone who will not recognize them. But I do. I can smell their organs spoiling in their bodies, spot their dancing, nervous legs scuffing up the tiles.

Once, the easiest marks to take were the drunkards, stumbling home down darkened alleyways convinced that they were saving themselves steps, inebriated to the point that self-preservation was little more than the motor reflexes propelling them forward. Now there are all manner of mind-altering substances, the new science of intoxication.

Aware of security cameras in every corner I keep close to the stark white wall until the tiles underfoot gather into a blue and green mosaic in the center of the ground floor. There is a helpful map beside the elevator bank, detailing the wards. Long-Term Acute Care: Fourth Floor. The elevator opens and a nurse in green scrubs stops texting and looks up from her mobile. I adjust my sunglasses to suggest concealed tears and expend an empty sigh.

"Which floor?" she asks.

"Four, please." I affect a tremble and lean heavily against the handrail.

Our ride is a quiet one. I keep my eyes to the ground, my head turned away from the red blinking light of the camera above the control panel, the all-seeing eye in this brave new world. When the elevator dings, I step around my fellow passenger to disembark and the nurse gives my shoulder a companionable pat.

"Hang in there," she whispers. I watch her sad empathetic smile until the doors close between us, letting my mouth twitch just enough to appease her.

The nurses station in the center of the room is manned by a skeleton crew too weary to take note of me. I slip quietly along the deserted halls searching for a darkened room. I find several, but each with at least one friend or family member slumbering stiffly in an uncomfortable chair. Despite all measures to counteract it, the ward reeks of death, disease, disinfectant, and human refuse. How any creature could heal in a place like this is beyond me.

Then I see him.

Alone in the last room on the hall. No nurses fussing with his monitors. No visitor sleeping half-slumped at his feet. I take the chart off the wall and slink inside. Protected from prying eyes, I remove my sunglasses and tuck them in the pocket of my waistcoat. I strip off my jacket, draping it across the arm of a green plastic recliner tucked in the corner. The light above the sink near his bed buzzes like an insect. I switch it off and return to the door. The hall is completely empty.

"Just the two of us." I smile at his warm, sleeping body and twist the lock. My eyes welcome the dark, soaking it in, and focus without pain for the first time in hours. I retrieve his chart from the end of the bed, and flip through the notes.

"William Moore, twenty-eight years old. Multiple gunshot wounds." Chart in hand, I walk around the side of the bed and silence the beeping machines. His body makes no protest as he rests comfortably in a morphine-induced slumber. "Traces of methamphetamines in your blood on admission." William's soft blond hair sticks to the side of his face. "Your poor mother."

The most endearing thing about humanity is its collective recklessness. With lives and hearts and bodies so fragile, one would think they would take more care to guard themselves against calamity and yet, the opposite is true. Human beings run headlong into danger, butting at the walls of their precarious existence with soft, fleshy skulls until life breaks in half and submits to them, or as in William's case, they to it. I sweep his long sweaty unkempt mane away from his neck and tilt his head to the side. The blood surging in his veins calls to me, a part of him slowly becoming aware of the threat. I place my hand over his pounding heart and feel it gallop.

My lips graze his ear. "It does not hurt for very long."

I wrap my hand around the back of his head and lift him away from the pillow. William grimaces in his sleep as I open my mouth and close my lips over the warm, thin skin of his neck. My perpetually white fangs descend from the ruby bed of my gums, and sink into his pitifully unprotected jugular as effortlessly as twin blades.

Everything stops.

Silence replaces the beeping monitors in neighboring rooms, the polluted stench that has ensnared my nostrils finally abates, and everything that William is, or was, or might have been comes flooding into my mouth—carried to the core of me by a crimson tide. His last coherent thoughts come to life through his blood, and play out behind my eyes. I see his parents' eager faces at some school recital. William's crushing self-loathing as he watched his graduating class walk into the next phase of their lives without him. William when he held his stillborn son in his arms for the first and last time, dripping with birth fluids.

William's body jerks in my arms and I hold him flush against me—careful not to jostle him, mindful not to spill a drop—and when the swoon hits me the wave sweeps William along with it. His body stills, I close my eyes and there is only this: the slowing of his weak heart and the waking of my own as he rushes inside, filling the empty, echoing chambers of my heart with warmth—with life.

Reluctantly, I pull away before I have ended him. Holding his head in my hand, I bring my left wrist to my lips and score the skin. I place my weeping wound against the two perfect holes in his neck and the skin beneath awakens. William's skin soaks up the offering and his flesh begins to mend. I keep count of the seconds as they trickle past and slowly pull my wrist away as the matching set of puncture wounds shrink to pinholes before they disappear completely.

I take an indulgent moment to clean my wrist with my tongue and savor the last few drops of William that I find mingling with my own blood. Finally fed, finally whole again and sprightly with new strength, I retrieve a towel and a washbasin from the small en-suite bathroom. I resume my place at the side of the bed, and William's body—noticeably lighter—rolls limply toward me.

"Live to fight another day, my son."

I wet the rag and scrub the dried blood from his neck. He will not die tonight, but he will soon from the various traumas his body has sustained, as well as the significant blood loss. The darkness has him now. I cannot help but think his family will be better for it, assuming he has any left.

I tuck William back into bed exactly as he was when I found him, and make quick work of washing my own face in the bathroom. I hide the rag in the medical waste bin and empty the washbasin into the sink, watching the pink water swirl once around the drain and disappear. I take a last look in the mirror, pleased with the blush William's blood has lent to my normally sunken cheeks, and tuck the ends of my gray silk blouse back into place. I delight in the sensation of William rushing through my veins and remove an errant piece of lint from the leg of my dark trousers. Now that I feel better it is a shame that there was no time for a proper hunt.

I grab my black blazer, settle it around me and reach for my sunglasses, but against my better judgment I do not fix them to my face. A feed always leaves me feeling invincible and besides, the hour is far too late to walk around in them inconspicuously. The interaction with the nurse in the elevator had been quick thinking on my part, and thankfully dimwitted on hers.

The hall is blessedly vacant. I take one step toward the emergency exit before a voice stops me in my tracks. Hushed and frantic, a young woman caught on the losing end of a heated debate. Her impassioned pleas reach me from the open door of a small waiting room, one of those ill-lit oubliettes with horribly upholstered chairs and sticky end tables strewn with last year's magazines. Her desperation is palpable, and I linger in the hall edging closer to the doorway than I should, snatching at the threads of half a phone conversation.

"Mother…"

The downside of a feed is that there is no such thing as *enough*. I always crave more, and this girl sounds so small, so furious, so full of life I cannot turn myself away.

"Mother, please. She is trying to help you." I press my spine against the wall beside the open door and listen.

"No. Don't you dare!"

"Mother."

"Mom..."

"Lis—no you listen to me. I'll be home soon, okay?" Her weary sigh reaches my waiting ears, and the weight of her exhaustion threatens my freshly procured vibrancy. "If you don't want to eat it, don't. I'll make you something when I get there."

"I am not taking her side."

"Mother. Don't you hang—" The abrupt end of the argument leaves her cursing. All the frustration melts away into silent agony, so potent I can taste the sorrow welling up inside of her. Her breath comes in shallow bursts as she steels herself against threatening sobs. I glance toward the red glow of the emergency exit and attempt to smother my own raging senses. I only manage to take two steps toward the stairs.

"Hello?"

My fists clench and my muscles tighten, preparing for a sprint. I do not need to be seen here. I am poised to run, ready to vanish, but instead I find the starved snarl melting from my features. I turn around with soft, understanding eyes and bowed shoulders. A different kind of seduction and one I do not often employ.

"I did not intend to disturb you."

The girl answers my apology with a terse nod. "You're fine," she says. "I shouldn't be in here anyway." She shoves her mobile into the loose pocket of her scrubs. "I was just leaving."

I walk toward her. "Please, not on my account." I make my way to the end table beside which she sits ramrod straight in the corner chair. Her hands grip the wooden armrests with white-knuckled frustration as I present her with a box of tissues. Clearly taking offense, she locks me in her stare and cocks her head.

"No thank you." She watches me set the offering aside like the lowering of a loaded pistol, and her reaction is so harsh and unwarranted that I find myself questioning what I know of strangers, and socially acceptable behavior. I turn to leave before either of us can begin again, but the girl continues in a softer tone. "There's almost never anyone in this room," she states. "It's no excuse. I shouldn't be using it for personal calls."

Not an apology, but certainly an attempt at civility. I take the chair opposite her, my eyes on the open door, compelled to linger a moment longer. There is much loneliness in this world, easy to forget when you are moored on your own island. The girl lets her head drop back against the bubbling ivory wallpaper, resigned to my presence and unable to resume her duties. She shuts her eyes and tries to steady her uneven breath. I seize the opportunity to examine her in earnest.

Dark hair, richer than chestnut, hangs well past her shoulders in soft, twisting waves. The long line of her neck, graceful, almost regal. Her skin is warmed by some far-removed ethnicity, making her neither fair nor tawny. She has a strong chin, faintly cleft, and a clearly defined jaw though her face is too soft to be square. I want to hold that chin in my hand and admire her closely for as long as I can before she screams. They always scream.

"Are you visiting someone?" she asks through her own distraction, picking at the tissue box. She does not look at me, I suspect too angry with herself. I fold my hands and rest my elbows against my knees, hunting for a response that will satisfy her curiosity and endear me to her in some way.

"My mother…"

It certainly gets her attention. She regards me with thoughtful eyes. The silence stretches out and she rises from her seat to settle wearily into the chair next to me. The shift in her mood and our proximity is sudden, not exactly predictable, but then, this method never is. Trust takes time, and we have so very little. I listen for the steps of potential witnesses and calculate the distance between this hospital and the Carrington Funeral Home. Regretfully, I admit that I cannot dispose of her body before Derek closes for the night, and yet I make no move to leave.

"Why was she admitted?" the girl inquires with a soft voice, mellowed by genuine concern. Details, of course. She is a medical professional. This is becoming tedious as well as reckless. Someone will be making the rounds soon. They will find the quickly chilling body of William Moore and take notice of his silenced machines. Still, I maintain character.

"An infection in the blood." The girl's interested brown eyes run across my face as I search for the word. "Sepsis," I supply, and I swear I detect an edge of skepticism in her carefully controlled expression.

"How long has she been here?" She shifts her legs toward me, craning closer in her seat, and my limbs respond in kind to match her posture, until I realize she is straining for a closer look at my eyes. "The hospital, I mean. We don't have a septic patient on this floor." A coolly delivered statement of fact. Naturally she knows the ailments of every patient in her rotation. I should have covered my eyes and kept walking. The last thing I need to worry about is concealing the body of a night nurse who noticed too much.

"A few days now." I do not meet her heavy glare, instead turning away in my chair and straightening my coat to say with small gestures that I must take my leave.

"Is she conscious?" she presses, brushing a hand over the crook of my arm. Not to stop me, merely to slow me down as she angles closer to catch my eyes, which should be the last thing anyone sees.

"No." I reach for the sunglasses in my coat pocket and stand up. The girl follows suit, the youthful expanse of her brow furrowed in thought. I have already moved to the open door when my curiosity gets the better of me. "Your mother…" I begin. The girl uncrosses her arms and shoves her hands into her pockets. "Is it dementia?" My young friend offers no reply, and I slip the sunglasses back into my coat prepared to coax the answer from her if I must.

"Parkinson's Disease with dementia," she relents in a faintly bitter and clinically dispassionate voice. "Some days…" the girl swallows thickly, "are worse than others, cognitively."

I do look upon her now—I cannot help myself. Even in that awful pale blue uniform she is quite beautiful. I recognize her anger, the fury over her own impotence, and glance out into the hall. No footsteps. No sound at all but the beating of her heart. I could have her. I could leave her body in the stairwell and retreat unobserved. But that would mean retiring this location for a long while, and where would that leave the rest of my family when they are in need? Soft fingers on my face startle me from my musings as she tilts my chin toward her. The fact that I did not anticipate the touch troubles me.

"Your pupils are completely dilated," she observes. "Are you taking any medication?" Those large brown eyes narrow as she stares deeply into mine. She is too observant for her own good. I close my hand over hers and fix her in my stare. Her fingers flex against my chin, just once, and then she sighs, wavers slightly like she means to pull away. Lost to our surroundings, to all the burdens of her heart and mind, her hand hangs limp in my grasp and a blank stare is all that she can muster. She looks younger this way, untroubled, almost happy. When I leave this place, she will remember me as nothing more than the most beautiful stranger she has ever encountered. I revel in the knowledge longer than I should. I push harder than I should.

"What is your name?" I ask, brushing her hair back around the shell of her ear. She smiles warmly.

"Elizabeth." She leans into my hand, inches her body closer. The heat of her flushed skin is overwhelming.

"That is a beautiful name."

Elizabeth, more in control than she should be in this state under my influence, asks for my name in return, much to my surprise.

"Stela." The truth tumbles from my mouth without a second thought, not a moment's hesitation. For a second neither of us can move, Elizabeth beguiled into blissful silence, and I, mute with horror. That name is not mine to give. Furthermore, it carries a grossly unfair burden for someone with so much sadness strung around her heart. I know nothing of this woman aside from what I gleaned from a private conversation I was not invited to hear in the first place.

"Stela," she repeats with a wide smile that reaches her eyes and crinkles the skin at each corner. Those five letters wrap tightly around her tongue—she seems so pleased to receive them—curl their claws into the walls of her heart, and the deed is done. I lean forward because I can do no more damage than I have, and press a kiss to her warm blushing cheek. Elizabeth closes her eyes at the contact, and when I pull away to admire her face once more, her stare is heated by the desire coursing through her.

"Goodnight, Elizabeth." I release her hand and take a step back. There is no trace of her icy exterior. She grins like a schoolgirl and I find myself returning that smile. For a while her troubles will be lost to her as she sits under the veil my stare has drawn around her mind. Perhaps when she awakens fully the world will seem less grim. It almost sounds like chivalry that way, but there is no altruism at work tonight. I want to see her again.

"Goodnight, Stela," she whispers as I turn away and slip down the hall to the exit.

The stairs pass beneath my feet in blur—a fury of unspent energy—my movements too swift for the human eye. I shoulder my way out of a fire exit on the rear of the building and into the deserted parking lot, stopping only once to bring my fist hard against a lone steel Dumpster. The force of that blow sends the receptacle skidding over the asphalt on locked wheels, where it collides in an echoing crash with the concrete base of a streetlamp.

My Mercedes lights up when I press the key fob in my pocket, and for the second time this evening I pull the handle harder than necessary. The door makes a sharp scream, threatening to separate from its hinges as I hurl myself inside and collapse with my forearms braced atop the wheel.

I lean back in the driver's seat and I catch my reflection in the rearview mirror. The blood has already begun to slow inside me and my pallor is fast returning. My fingertips cool quickly against the steering wheel. Vacant black eyes stare resolutely back at me from the mirror, haloed with a feline sheen from the stark light of the parking lot lamps. I close them against the weight of my own foolishness.

"What are you doing?"

I hang my head at my own inability to answer the simplest of questions and contemplate returning to the vibrating hospital ward to hunt the girl down. I am not in the habit of operating without a plan, and I certainly do not like to leave loose ends. But I make no move to exit my vehicle. I slide my key into the ignition, fully aware that I will have to deal with this woman soon enough. Soon but not now.

Tonight, I need to meet with Fane and review the affairs of the day. I must have my thoughts organized. He cannot know of this. He cannot know how rash I've been. How wildly trapped I feel in a service that has always been my heart's only joy, unquestioning for centuries that to be his hand, his confidant, his loyal and humble servant was my life's purpose. But when the role assigned to me changed from bloodshed to banking, so too did my enthusiasm for service. A century of monotony ensued.

"This too shall pass," I murmur, and they are more than comforting words. A prayer of sorts, to return to the life I loved, to the warrior I was. Anything but the endless errands that comprise and consume my waking hours. But this is the world we live in now and I must crush this growing cynicism, this feeling of walking in a slumber when I am wide awake. I need to stop asking myself every evening when I rise why I bother. It is vain. Worse, it is traitorous, and I am neither of those things.

I chastise myself once more and whip my vehicle onto the black expanse of the whistling highway. I am certain that Elizabeth is a mistake that will keep for another night.

* * *

I park my car beneath the lazily strobing lights of the parking garage that sits atop my family home. Outside, the city begins to awaken. I hear the faint patter of weary feet dragging over buckling floors in windowless apartments. Is my drudgery so different? A century ago, the question would never have occurred to me.

The sweltering blush of the first rays of a new dawn threaten the black ocean of the horizon. I enter the passcode on a hatch that conceals the service entrance, slinking down beneath the pavement of a city so changed I scarcely remember its beginnings. With a wheezing, pneumatic sigh, the hatch shuts firmly above my head as I leave this world to the living for a few precious hours and slide down the steel ladder into the dank embrace of the tunnels below.

These underground service tunnels had fallen completely out of public memory. It was not until the nineties, when a construction company broke a retaining wall, flooding downtown Chicago, that the city realized the underground wasn't a myth. The old tracks remain largely intact, a smaller set, heavily rusted, once used for freight carts. Pipes—water and electric—laced into the ceiling above, and warped cables dead center, running straight through. There is no breeze in the stale air, only the distant rumbling of the L, and though the moniker is short for "elevated", the subterranean sections of the train are near enough to rattle our walls.

"What on earth kept you?" Lydia paces the entrance to Fane's chamber like a caged beast, her arms flying out in such fierce exasperation that I am uncertain whether she means to strike or embrace me. Thankfully, she does neither. She runs a soothing hand down the length of her long black hair, pushing it back from her oval face and the wide obsidian eyes we share. When I do not reply, she cocks her head curiously, both hands firmly mounted on her hips as if to bar my passage.

"Is he resting?" I ask, stepping up against her. She flinches—predictably—and I reach around her body for the gilded handle of his chamber door, but she does not step aside.

"No one rests until his Stela is safely at his feet," she chides. Lydia cannot insult me by ridiculing my fealty because it is fact, and this relentless jealousy is precisely the emotion that drives her further from Fane's good graces.

She has always been weak-minded and I tired of her petty taunts ages ago. However, I do feel a pang of guilt that my carelessness has kept the whole household awake. Lydia senses this and grows bolder.

"One evening in the sun is clearly too much for you in your old age," she delights. "If you are unable to complete a simple errand in a timely manner, perhaps I will bear the burden of next quarter's meeting." She brings her face near to mine as I count the ways I could end her pitiful existence, but the faint mark on the skin of her neck suggests that Fane has already fed at least once tonight. The relief that he may not need very much from me improves my mood considerably.

"You will move. Or I will move you." I swipe a hand between us, brushing the front of her white sweater, and Lydia all but jumps to one side of the hallway. I smile knowingly as she mutters empty slander and rushes into Fane's chamber ahead of me, announcing my arrival to our Prince.

"My Lord, Stela has returned." She infuses those words with the rancor of one child tattling on another, and kneels in the entryway. Lydia has loved Fane from the moment she was named. There is no space in her heart for anyone else.

Fane sits in his chair, the mirrored skylight at the epicenter of his suite open to receive the only trickles of sunlight that ever reach this lair. The small corridor built into the tunnels above his head glistens as the first rays break and bathe the crown of his head in gold. "Thank you, Lydia, that will be all." He waves her out of the room with the back of his hand, not even a smile to dismiss her. "Rest now," he commands. Lydia pouts and turns with a flutter of indignation, sure to let her shoulder collide with mine as she retreats.

My jaw clenches and only the hearty laughter of my Lord pulls me back from the brink of altercation.

"Tell me, my dove. How can petulance exist in a being that has witnessed whole empires turn to rubble before her very eyes?"

I kneel beside his chair and bow my head, ashamed that her tantrums have any effect on me at all. "Lydia's or mine, my Lord?" He curls his hand to cup my chin and lifts my face to his. Despite the pain it causes me, I look upon his sun-struck face to find a gentle smile settled on his lips. "Lydia, of course." He runs his thumb along my jaw, and I answer his smile with my own.

"Come," he says. "Sit beside me a while. I will not keep you long. You have a very good reason for having made me wait."

I stand on fatigue-stiffened knees and skirt the edges of stolen light that embrace him, to sit on the weathered lounge to his left. My head droops on my shoulders and with marked reluctance I fight to maintain eye contact. The gossamer strands of his pale golden hair are fire to my weary eyes, but the iridescent blue of his impatiently await my full attention. His muscles are tense, plainly visible in the stark glow of the sun reflected down upon him. They twist upon themselves in his shoulders, across his wide chest. The periwinkle veins that stitch him together beneath a single protective layer of flesh, web down his flexing forearms.

Not for the first time I note his very magnificence, the ethereal qualities that have always made him beautiful to me—his single layer of near indestructible skin, his fiercely magnetic, impossibly bright eyes—are why he cannot show his face aboveground and must entrust his children to oversee his affairs. Once more I am ashamed of my own folly, my ingratitude, and so I say nothing.

"I do so miss the sun." A genuine lament. He tilts his face up to the light just as the sun passes, and the beam that ensconces him ascends back to heaven. My eyes immediately welcome the reprieve, and as it happens every morning, my Lord stands with a heavy heart and covers himself with his robe. "Tell me," he says, tying the emerald silk sash firmly about his waist, "how does your Andrew fair this quarter?"

"He is not *my Andrew*, my Lord."

Fane chuckles. "Of course. But even still?"

"He is well, my Lord. He sends his respect and good tidings." My spirits rise as they normally do in Fane's presence and I find my footing in the conversation, the trifles of my evening momentarily removed.

"I preferred entrusting our affairs to his father's capable hands," he remarks, absently rubbing the fabric of his gown between his thumb and forefinger.

"As did I, my Lord." I reach for the report folded in my coat pocket. "But despite Andrew's wanting personality, it seems he makes an adequate substitute." I present Fane with the summary and his fevered, strong hand brushes my cool fingers. He reviews the numbers for himself.

"And the state of the Caymans?" he inquires and begins to pace.

"I found that curious, my Lord. We have seen no formal documentation specific to that account for over a year now." He stands very still in the center of the room, staring at the papers, searching for something. "But Rachel will have the figures sent to me before sundown."

Fane's demeanor lightens and, pleased with my diligence, he trails a hand across my shoulders as he steps around the lounge to deposit the report on his writing desk. He will give it to Darius this evening, so that it may be properly recorded.

"Very good," he says, joining me once again in the sitting area. He slips gracefully into the ebony arms of his enormous chair, a throne to any person of normal stature. "And on the off chance that the findings are bleak, there is a silver lining. You may finally have the good fortune to put an end to that horrid little man, after all." We share a laugh at Andrew's expense, and I shake the notion away before it becomes irresistible.

"I would not give Christine the satisfaction of an easy reason to terminate our relationship with her family's enterprise and forsake the legacy she stands to inherit," I confess, and pace along the window-like panels that line the front of his chamber. Floor-to-ceiling screens, blocked like lattice, illuminated this evening with an obnoxiously green forest-scape. A powerfully calming illusion, to be sure, but an illusion none the less, and one made all the more obvious by the fact that Fane never uses the accompanying soundtracks. The wind that rushes over the tall grass, between the leaves, and the specks of quick darting avian life are disconcertingly mute. He says the quiet helps him think.

"Ah, Christine," my Lord sighs. "How has she grown?" Fane comes to stand beside me with crossed arms and more than a little teasing in his tone.

"She has grown lovely. She leaves for university this fall." I stare at my boots and the glistening floorboards, thinking of the way I used a daughter's place in her father's heart against him today—a necessary evil—and push the fleeting emotion aside before Fane can sense it, unsettled that I should be anything but pleased with my methods, effective as they were.

"Well, then we will just have to tolerate Andrew for a moment longer."

I shift my weight from foot to foot, marveling in the strain of each muscle, my body pleading for sleep. Beside me, Fane flexes his shoulders.

"My dove," he laments. "I promise you, he will one day meet his end by your hand." Fane brushes his fingers against the small of my back, beneath the edge of my blouse.

"If it pleases you, my Lord." I place my hand over his, and Fane's smile pulls his upper lip up over his shining teeth.

"What pleases me is what pleases you, Stela." His warm hand splays across my skin. "Do I not always grant you that which you desire?"

I close my eyes and push the deepest dissatisfactions of my soul just out of his reach. "Always, my Lord."

Fane tenses, his familiar touch held rigid and firm. "And what of this late hour?" he presses. The edge of his voice has sharpened with renewed curiosity, and he no longer distracts himself with the calming projection cast upon the windows. I can feel his eyes digging their way down to the truth, burrowing into my temple. I cannot avoid their depths for very long.

"I fell asleep." I give him half the truth I hold and hope to fabricate the rest as I go. My hands are clasped in front of me like the child I am, and though I do not turn to face him, I keep my body relaxed—prepared to be turned by force if it suits him. Deeper he searches, pushing his way to my heart, rolling the words over in his mind and weighing them carefully. The words ring true, and the sincerity of my confession was not contrived in the least, nor is my embarrassment.

"You fell asleep," he repeats in a slow, deliberate voice. He seems neither pleased nor disappointed. Finally, the grip on my mind loosens, like the unexpected slacking of a noose. Fane breaks his stare and once again resumes his seat, tapping his lips with a pensive finger. I collect myself quickly, careful not to show my relief through any physical display, and turn around.

Fane beckons me closer. I cautiously take his hand in mine, filling my mind with nothing but the panic I felt when I awoke in the backseat of my vehicle, focusing my thoughts entirely on that moment. Fane cradles my hand in his, raises his clear blue eyes to mine, and makes a final push for the truth.

I answer him with a push of my own, sending all the anger I harbor for myself hurdling to the surface of my wayward thoughts, and I funnel that fury into a single memory: the moment I ripped open the backseat door and took my first inhale of the cool night air. Fane's lips press lightly against my knuckles, his thumb soothing the skin of my wrist with gentle ministrations.

"Falling asleep outside these walls is a very dangerous thing," he warns.

"Yes, my Lord."

"And falling asleep at our servant's doorstep...even more so."

I hold my body stiff against the threat of the impending lecture.

"Perhaps I belabor you too greatly with responsibilities that should be mine," he says. I reach for him and place my hand along the side of his smooth face.

"To labor in your service is what I desire most in this world."

For a moment Fane is content, his eyes bright and untroubled. He looks every bit the happy youth his ageless body suggests.

"Get thee to bed, my dove." Fane turns his face into my hand, and places a kiss to my palm. "You have had a trying night."

"As have you. I loathe to give you cause for concern." I run my fingers through his fine gold hair. "Have you eaten, my Lord?"

Fane closes his eyes and shakes his head. "Enough," he smiles. "If the mood strikes me I will call for someone I have taxed less."

Exhausted by the sheer force it takes to thwart his searching stare as well as my own ridiculous antics, I bow my head and take my leave of him before he can change his mind. A little too gratefully, a hair too fast, and my obvious relief does not go unnoticed. Fane grabs me by the wrist, and pulls so frightfully hard that I bend backward over the arm of his chair and fall into his lap. He is not smiling anymore.

"Would you leave me without a taste when I will be so many hours without your company?" He poses a question that is not a question at all. When I attempt to arrange myself gracefully in his arms he holds me closer and leans his body forward until there is nothing to push against but him, which he knows full well I will not do.

"No, my Lord." It was foolish to think I would leave this meeting without thorough inquiry. Foolish to believe I had completely dispelled his skepticism.

Fane's hand cradles the back of my head as he brings my mouth to his. "Good girl," he whispers against my open mouth. His teeth graze my lower lip and, as blood floods my mouth, we taste the iron left over from William Moore. Fane lingers in the blood, coaxing it into his own mouth with a firm tongue. I see my victim's face, I hear the chorus of his monitoring machines, the stench of bleach, the sweat long since dried on William's body. I hold that image as tightly as I can and think only of Mr. Moore. The weight of his body in my arms, the memories he showed me—I offer them up to Fane and wrap my arms around his shoulders until he finishes.

"Until tonight, my Stela." He brushes the last rivulet of blood from my bottom lip and his grip falls slack around my body. I rise from his embrace without grace, wavering slightly on unsettled feet. I smooth the front of my blouse, and retrieve my jacket.

"Until tonight, my Lord." I genuflect—a proper exit—remembering my place, and wait to be dismissed by a nod that takes noticeably longer to receive.

When my freedom has been granted, I depart with marked humility and retreat quickly to the safety of the hall. Nothing stirs in the darkness, the rest of my family long since retired. I slip inside the narrow ironwood corridor that barricades Fane's chamber from the tunnels outside, headed for my dormitory, crawling silently. Only one light remains in the narrow enclosure, the intentional, unnavigable darkness—the candle perched above my hatch. The air in the tunnel smells of the snuffed-out day, my charred and flickering wick mingling with the dry air as I lift the wooden hatch and drop into my darkened suite.

The sconces dotted along the hall serve more as aesthetics to appease Fane than anything else. Everything in the fashion of his long-abandoned home in Braşov. I flip the light switch on the wall, and from the oak-concealed control panel choose a night surf scene for my windows. The small speakers mounted in every corner wake to life with the soft lapping of waves, and the glassy cry of gulls. The windowscapes were Darius's idea, installed several years ago in every dormitory as a distraction. An inspired notion from my most curious sibling. My brother Bård procured the contractors, I procured the funds for materials and guaranteed discretion, while another of my family, Crogher, was in charge of overseeing the installation. The contractors, of course, proved painfully capable and inquisitive. They were handled, and their bodies were given to the hounds.

I throw my jacket over the arm of my sofa and fling myself across the expanse, imagining the salt from the spray and the cool seaside breeze tangled in my hair. I am tired, far more so than I have been in a great while, but I am positive that sleep is still hours away. I lay my face against the distressed leather upholstery and before I start searching for her, will myself to sleep. One defiant eye opens and falls upon the sleek steel casing of my laptop glinting in the light—a playful taunt. With a frustrated growl, I sit up and settle my feet on the floor. I know how all of this will end.

South Bayside Hospital's internal records are easier to access than I anticipated and within minutes I find exactly what I should not have gone looking for in the first place: Elizabeth Dumas. Twenty-six. A degree in nursing from Claremont—the accelerated program—but prior to that, enrolled in a dual degree in Medicine and Medical Science from the University of Michigan. Two published articles on stem cell research, the last with a footnote indicating that Ms. Dumas was headed for Johns Hopkins the following fall for their prestigious Medical Scientist Training Program. Obviously, she never went to Baltimore.

An older article on her talent as a violinist when Elizabeth was in high school. A photograph of her when she was very young, standing beside her mother, Claire Dumas, with her instrument raised proudly for the camera. A wide smile on her round face, her mother's hand clasped around her shoulder. Mrs. Dumas shows none of her daughter's exuberance, her mouth set in a hard line, a severe beauty with perfectly manicured nails, dressed in an immaculately tailored navy suit A late pregnancy, it seems, from Claire's intentionally variegated gray hair.

A single photograph in a public newsletter from 2002, and then nothing. No further scholarly articles. Not so much as a résumé floating in the ether. No record of Elizabeth on any social media. The silence is enticing. One moment Elizabeth was a precocious, budding talent, gifted in mind and musical ability, full of promise, and the next moment she was gone. The lack of information is intensely irritating as I rub my temples, and close the lid of my laptop.

There is no great mystery here. She is a woman like any other. Perhaps the pressure of school caused the abrupt discontinuance of further education, or nursing was simply her heart's passion. I shake away the pointless musings and undress, throwing my garments into the fireplace. I can incinerate them tomorrow.

I feel cheated somehow, like Elizabeth has reached out and closed a door in my face. My thoughts circle her as I climb into bed and drift into a fitful sleep.

* * *

Standing on the shore of the Danube in Moldavia, the earth begins to drum beneath my feet. The wind whips my clothes tight around my body as the tide surges against the shore, cool water frothing between my small pink toes. Behind me, a lone figure looms atop the grassy mound, beckoning me back, waving skinny arms high above her head. She calls out, but the words are lost to the breeze. I scramble up the hillside, tugging on long grass with my small fists as my feet struggle to find foothold in the black dirt and sand.

At the summit, I see my mother bent before me. Her dark, curling black locks strike her flushed cheeks. She fusses over my wind-swept hair and wraps me in a warm wool cloak, licking the tattered edge of her own soiled dress to scrub the dirt from my face and hands. I pull away from her and she clicks her tongue, sweeping me up in her arms and taking off in a sprint toward the village. From over my mother's shoulder, I see the river bob with whitecaps. The drumming has become a thunderous drone, and fearing a storm, I wrap my arms tightly around her neck. The vast gray sky has only a thin covering of clouds that the sun will burn through soon, and the rain is a fine mist that collects in tiny droplets on my lashes.

My mother pushes us through a large crowd where everyone waits, but no one speaks, and sets me down to stand beside her.

She frets over my appearance again, she holds my hands in a firm grip, speaking with some urgency. The drumming echoes in my ears, drowning out her voice and I try to pay attention to her, but I cannot make out the words. She turns me around and holds my back flush against the front of her legs as the first emerald banner peeks up from the valley.

There appears one rider charging down the hill. And then there are ten. And then there are many. I want to turn and run but my mother fixes me to the spot. I settle for placing my hands over hers, pressed against my chest like a living shield. The horsemen encircle the great crowd, all of them on black horses save one. They part before my mother and me, making way for him to ride into their ranks and dismount.

His steed is white, double the size of any I have ever seen, and his armor—bright and silver like all the others—is draped with emerald cloth. He dismounts and stands beside his horse, patting its thick neck and watching us closely. As he removes his helmet the only sound is that of my own startled gasp. I have never seen another with hair the color of mine. Pale and gleaming, a finer yellow than that of his horse's mane. His eyes are so light a blue that the sky itself appears sickly in contrast.

Another horseman rides into the crowd behind him, quickly coming to his side. My mother's fingers tighten on my chest as the second horseman takes a quick glance around the crowd and settles on her face. He does not remove his helmet. Only two black eyes can be seen, nothing more of his face. He gestures to my mother and then to me. The Lord says something under his breath to his companion, and with the cuff of his armored hand strikes the second horseman across his helmeted cheek. The masked man falls to one knee and shakes himself, blood dripping from beneath his visor. Without another word, he stands and mounts his black steed, riding off alone.

The pale-eyed Lord approaches my mother on foot. He removes one metal glove and offers a veined, blood-red hand. My mother's fingers wrap around my wrist as she extends my trembling arm to this beguiling stranger. I struggle away, but my mother pushes me forward. His huge palm swallows my wrist and he kneels to get a better look at me. My chest heaves under the force of my own broken sobs and frantic breathing, but as the stranger stares into my eyes the world grows quiet and soft.

The Lord picks me up and carries me to his horse. When he releases my wrist, I miss his touch immediately, and with one hand on the reins I reach for him as he returns to my mother. He places a hand on her shoulder, whispers something, and my mother falls to the ground in tears.

Mounting behind me, the Lord wraps one arm around my waist. My mother sobs into the earth, crying out to us, but once again her words are lost. A beautiful melody fills every fiber of my being in this Lord's embrace and drowns out everything else, every care I have ever carried.

The horse beneath us rears as we turn to leave, and I notice a figure standing at the edge of the crowd. She is dressed in a drooping blue shirt, too long for her torso. Her legs and arms, naked in the unseasonable chill, are covered with goose flesh, and her long chestnut hair billows out behind her in the breeze. She covers her mouth with her hands, trembling with tears. All the calm leaves me, fresh panic seizing my nubile young heart, as my Lord speaks low in my ear.

I sit bolt upright in the dark, my fine covers a mess between my tangled legs as I kick them down the length of my four-poster bed. I go quickly to my washroom, splashing the cold water against my face and neck. I grip the sides of the marble sink and take in my disheveled reflection as the water runs in rivers down my chest. Fane's voice echoes in my mind, requesting an audience.

For hundreds of years and in a dozen countries, I have had that dream. The memory of the day my mother presented me to Fane. But never in all my long life has it ended with anything other than Fane's arm closing around me as we rode off toward Braşov.

The panic was not mine. The fear was not mine.

They were Elizabeth's.

I dress myself quickly, and leave my chambers to answer my Lord's call.

II
A Pale Horse

For five nights straight, I've had the same dream.

Standing on a foreign shore, I watch a pale-skinned girl play beside the water's edge. I make my way toward her and she scurries up the side of a hill with more agility than me. My movements are comically slow, like the dust wants to shackle my feet. I try to retrace the child's small steps in the sandy black soil, but my legs sink and by the time I reach the top I have to pull my waist free from this smothering hold. I sit for a moment at the top of hill, trying to catch my breath. The world around me is a beautiful green tapestry, rolling from one foothill to the next, dotted with wildflowers I can't name.

The girl is a speck of brown against a lush and vibrant background, growing fainter by the moment. My panic for this child can't be explained, and I run after her to warn her, but when I reach the crowd I'm too late. The man has the girl in his arms, on his white horse—a monstrously large beast, animal and rider both—stamping its feet in the long grass, but the child's face is so serene. Whatever her fate, she has already made peace with it and though the outcome is a mystery to me, this is not something I can accept. Her mother's broken-hearted wailing brings tears to my eyes. Her mother shouts the same broken plea repeatedly in a language that is familiar but nothing I understand. Latin bones, to be sure, a romance language, but what is the accent? The girl notices me as the man turns his horse to leave. I think to call out to her, but I don't know her name.

"Elizabeth?"

My mother has been calling to me for the last ten minutes, shrieking from the foot of the stairs.

"I'm coming."

I plant my feet on the floor and take a slow, deep breath. Even in the calm light of day I can still feel the dread when I saw that child's tiny body fall into the man's huge arms as his horse reared. I hold my head in my heads and run my fingers back through sweaty hair.

"Elizabeth," my mother's wail echoing through the whole house. "This is an emergency."

I doubt that. With the weary sigh of the perpetually fatigued, I reach for my cell phone on the nightstand. Seven a.m. She had better be bleeding. I push my limbs through last night's hastily discarded scrubs and make my way downstairs.

Mother's velour-clad ass is sticking out of the refrigerator. I'm not entirely sure what she's looking for, but it clearly wasn't hiding in the carton of smashed eggs oozing onto the floor. The kitchen cabinet doors are ajar, bowls and plates pushed around inside. On the counter, each ceramic jar has had its lid removed, their contents tossed.

"Mom?" I stagger toward the coffeepot. "Mother?" She continues her assault, focusing her efforts on the freezer and will not answer me. I start the first pot of coffee, for what I already know will be a three-pot day and take a seat on the counter.

"Elizabeth, we have chairs." My mother waves me down with an impatient hand, and I move to a stool at the oak island behind her.

"You said there was an emergency, so, where is it?"

"Well that is what I would like to know." My mother turns with a face full of shaky makeup. I stifle a groan and humor her.

"What are you looking for, Mother?"

"My car keys, Elizabeth. Don't play dumb with me, you're a lousy actress." She punctuates her displeasure by stomping her slipper-clad foot, and I can tell the soft thud is less gratifying than she anticipated. She's sure to slam the freezer door to reinforce her rage.

So, a bad day then.

"Ma…" She blatantly ignores me. "Mother." She crosses her arms with a scathing stare. "Two things: One, I don't accept jabs about my acting abilities before I've had my morning coffee. Two, I have your keys. We talked about this."

My mother scoffs with a flutter of her shaky hands and pointedly procures her cup of coffee before the pot has finished brewing. Apologies are still a long way off.

"Elizabeth, please. You were terrible in that play," she responds, resolutely ignoring any suggestion that she has forgotten our discussion about driving. "What was the name of it?"

"The Tempest."

"Yes, that's the one. You were horrible, all long gaping silences and stilted dialog. That's not an insult, dear, it's a fact. Now, I have to get to the gym."

I walk around my fuming mother and pour my coffee. I set my mug down in front of her and clasp my hands. "I was sixteen."

"Age is hardly an excuse for poor performance," she says with a disapproving tut. I laugh in spite of myself, which only infuriates her.

"I didn't call you down here to laugh at me, Elizabeth," she warns. "I am late for my appointment with Luke. So, be a dear and fetch my keys." Returned is the honey-tone as she waves me on with a commanding hand. The graceful gesture is cut short by an ill-timed tremor, and she wraps her fingers firmly around her mug. Decreased mobility, moments of rigidity, loss of orientation and coordination, we were prepared for all that with her Parkinson's. But dementia as well? The diagnosis was terrifying.

Mother taps her overgrown French tips against the granite countertop. It's far too early to have this argument for the fiftieth time. I take a sip of coffee and instantly feel more myself.

"Mother," I begin, and her face hardens like she already knows I mean to refuse her. "You haven't had an appointment with Luke in ten years." No discernible reaction. "He started his own company in San Francisco with his partner Adam. Remember?"

Mother takes a deep breath, holding the air captive and for a moment I worry that this is a new type of tantrum. She exhales slowly through her nose. "Elizabeth, I don't know what you're playing at," she almost sounds amused, "but I saw Luke last week. Like I have seen him every Tuesday for the last six years." Her eyes shine, the same way they always do when she catches me in a lie. Few things please her more than being right.

"Yes," I agree. "You saw Luke every Tuesday, and the occasional Thursday for six years, until about ten years ago." The irritation is there, of course it is, but I keep my own anger and confusion just out of reach.

My mother wavers in the small ways to which I'm growing accustomed. A slackening of her tense jaw and she settles in her seat like she means to stay there. Her eyes seem to take in the kitchen for the first time, the unfortunate mess. Fear and uncertainty are foreign emotions to her. She's so thin in that stained jumpsuit, it hangs on the protruding bones of her too-sharp shoulders. I lay a consoling hand on hers, but she quickly pulls away, tucking both hands neatly in her lap.

"What day is it, Mom?"

"Tuesday!" she snaps. "Or have you been listening to me at all?" The tremble is there, threatening the tight, pale line of her thin lips.

"No. The full date, Mother." I keep my voice as gentle as I can.

She runs over me with a skeptical eye, and purses her lips. She doesn't answer. Lost time is becoming increasingly frequent, but no less troubling for either of us. She takes a loud, undignified slurp of her coffee, and remains unnervingly silent. Her fingers push the magazines strewn atop the island into even stacks and perfectly matched corners.

"When Luke left town, you had a big party for him here." I don't know if the context will help. She gets so angry with herself, and we're both much more comfortable with that rage being directed at me. "We spent three hours in Nordstrom because you wanted to find him the perfect tie." An unwitting smile spreads across my lips. "You said 'a man needs a strong tie if he's going to be taken seriously.' Do you remember that?" I can't check the hope, or the pleading tone, clogging my voice.

Mother tilts her chin, considering, and I know from that distant look she recalls something about that day. "We got back to the car and that bald guy in the Volvo dinged your driver's side door right in front of you. He tried to lie about it. I thought you were going to kill that poor man." I laugh again, I can't help it. A warm laugh at the memory of my mother in her prime, filled with righteous indignation and wholly without fear.

"Served him right," she sniffs. "Lying to my face like that. I have eyes." She smiles a little herself, but I can tell this has upset her deeply. I hate mornings like this. Days, weeks like this. I hate this disease.

When I was young, my parents were invincible. I believed in their superhuman strength and intelligence right up until my father passed, but not even his death could convince me of my mother's mortality. She was unshakable, energetic, and independent. She didn't crack, even widowed at forty-six and suddenly a single parent. My mother wept silently, only once, at the burial, and then it was business as usual. Recitals for me, meetings at the country club, fundraisers for the impoverished. She never missed a beat. Not once in her sixty years and now this. It's like staring at a stranger.

"I know I'm a poor substitute for Luke," I offer with a tentative grin. She doesn't seize the opening for a well-timed jibe. "But how 'bout we finish our coffee and walk along the pier? I promise to annoy you as much as possible to ensure your heart rate stays up."

Mother exhales wearily and rolls her eyes. "A walk will have to suffice," she decides, pushing away from the island to begin the Herculean task of tidying the kitchen. "But please, I can't be seen with you like that, dear. Do something with your hair."

I drain the dregs of my cup, and rub my bleary eyes. "Yes, Mother."

* * *

As a child, I was thoroughly convinced that The Windy City possessed a magical air current all its own. A meteorological phenomenon, unique to my hometown and explainable by some science I didn't yet understand, but mystically localized none the less. I made the mistake of entrusting my awe to my mother, who promptly explained with an impatient snort that the name was derived from a fierce political debate. She chided me for my childishness—obviously displeased with my spectacular misunderstanding—and thought that was as good a time as any to clear up any lingering fantasies I might have about Santa Claus and the Easter Bunny, despite the fact that she had never lied to me about either one. I was ten, and that was the last time I ever made the mistake of sharing my enthusiasm with her—no matter the subject.

I'm more than a little surprised she agreed to walk with me to Navy Pier. My mother despises tourists and the general public alike. Perhaps this strange and sudden acquiescence to take a leisurely stroll through the bustling early morning crowd is yet another signal of her rapid decline. Do I make enough of an effort to ensure she is socializing? Is she getting adequate exercise with her nurse? Most days I find myself wishing that my mother was here to care for my mother, which could be a symptom of my own deteriorating mental health.

For much of the walk we say nothing. I'm too lost in my own worries and her attention is rapt by the strangers we push past in their smart suits, skirting the shiny facades of the mammoth buildings. Every couple hundred feet she bumps into someone. She either misjudges the space needed to circumvent collision, or more likely, her unsteady gait is to blame. I keep a firm hold on her elbow, worried that she might be mistaken for a feeble old woman on vacation and subsequently mugged. I suppose our walk might feel like a vacation of sorts to her. She drinks in the city the same way tourists do, although my mother has lived here all her life.

We don't walk along the pier. Even on a workday the foot traffic would be too heavy for her to navigate. It's a beautiful day with a soft, cool breeze floating in from the harbor, so we stroll down Lakefront Trail and I choose a bench beside the water away from the joyful squeals of children at play. Mother settles down beside me to watch the circling gulls as I shield my eyes with my hand and look out at the end of the pier jutting into Lake Michigan.

"Thinking of your father?"

I start in my seat and turn to my mother. She's struggling with the zipper of her black Windbreaker, caught on her tracksuit underneath. I place my hands over hers to help and she rolls her eyes, releasing an exhausted sigh.

"How did you know?" The fabric loosens around my fingers and the wind whips her light jacket out around her, billowing gently in the breeze. With blue-veined hands she immediately clenches the front of her coat, pulling it shut over her chest. I don't know why she wanted to unzip it in the first place, but I let it go. "He loved it here," she says. "He used to take you to the pier when you were a little girl."

I smile at her, but her focus stays fixed on the slow progression of a rust-encrusted tugboat creeping along the horizon. "I remember." My father and I came here often. I forced him to take me on the boat tours at least once a week, though he never complained. I was in love with the view of the skyline from the water, and my enchantment was all the reason he needed. I couldn't believe how large, how beautiful my hometown was, with its skyscrapers glinting like diamonds as the light trilled down their windows, spires like needles in a geometrical haystack, all of it man-made. The miraculous effort required to forge such a sprawl inspired me to believe anything was possible.

Mother purses her lips and nods, long and slow. Now is not the time to push her. She never mentions him anymore and the good days are becoming increasingly rare. This is all the time we have.

"Did you love him?" It sounds more like a plea than I intended. My heart gallops as I prepare for any number of plausible reactions from my eternally animated mother. She turns her head, and her eyes soften slightly when she reads the panic in mine.

"A long time ago." The papery skin of her palm pats me twice on the thigh and then withdraws, tugging the edges of her coat back into place. She surprises me when she tilts her gently bobbing head in consideration, parts her lips. "And on occasion when I would watch him with you."

I press on, because that is a more generous response than I anticipated. "Do you miss him?"

She makes a soft noise through her nose that is somewhere between somber and annoyed, but she doesn't look at me. She keeps her eyes on the endless expanse of blue and green, the indifferent tide, watching the waves roll in. "Sometimes," she concedes. "Not the way you miss him."

I turn toward her. "How then?" My leg leans against the back of the white park bench and I wrap my arms around my shin, resting my chin on my knee. The well-worn denim tickles my skin, but I remain motionless, entranced. She never talks about him. If she's willing to do so now she can have my full attention, even if she won't give me hers in return.

"Lately, I find myself wishing he was alive," she says breezily. "So that I would not have to burden you the way that I do."

"Mom…" I reach out to touch the sleeve of her coat. She leans away, which doesn't shock me in the least. I don't like to be touched when I'm feeling vulnerable, a trait I most certainly inherited from her. She's angry now, I can see it in the tilt of her chin—up and defiant—whether the irritation is directed at me or at him is really anyone's guess. And be that for his misdeeds or her own loneliness, I'll never know.

"A good father and a good husband are not the same thing, Elizabeth," she snaps. I drop my leg back to the ground and face the lake.

How can someone who is inches from me feel so much further away than the memory of a face I have not seen for fourteen years? I remember perfectly the way his stubble scratched my lips when I stood on tiptoe at his bedside and kissed his cheek. The delighted faces of the nursing staff when I fumbled my way through the first three minutes of Tchaikovsky's "Allegro Moderato" on my violin, the last thing I played for him. The chirping of the heart monitor growing uneven, longer between bursts before he flat-lined, is a chorus that sings between my ears to this day.

But I couldn't tell you the last time I hugged my mother.

"You never feel it," she whispers and I am more than reluctant to further any discourse between the two of us.

"Never feel what?"

"Age. Not really… You start to register its effects on your bones when the weather changes. And then the aches are there year-round. That registers, of course, don't misunderstand. But your heart doesn't change with your body. You're still the person you've always been. Exactly as you are now, with an old woman peering back at you in the mirror."

From the corner of my eye, I watch her for tears that will never fall. Her eyes mist, her jaw tightens as she swallows the pain of her own words, and I wish more than anything that she had kept them to herself. But something tells me if I remember nothing else my mother has said to me, I will remember this when the skin on the back of my hands grows thin, and the veins protrude on the surface. When the staircase in the home I stand to inherit—much sooner than expected—looks insurmountable, and my knees lock every time I bend, these words will ring in my mind the same as the concerto of my father's monitors do.

"I should have thrown myself in the harbor the moment I was diagnosed." She nods as though firmly agreeing with herself, morose and undeterred. It's too much honesty for one day, and far too melancholic for the lovely morning light.

"That's a bit melodramatic, don't you think?" I nudge her with my shoulder.

She smiles suddenly and laughs, a rare one with her head thrown back. She swats my sternum with bony fingers.

"You started us down the road of difficult discussions, Elizabeth. Don't begrudge the patient her sullen outlook when you're still bristling with youth."

A reluctant smile curls the corner of my lips, because I don't blame her. In her position, I might find the harbor a viable option too.

"'One should die proudly when it is no longer possible to live proudly,'" I quote. The words are readily familiar to her. She takes a moment to consider them.

"*Madame Butterfly?*" she ventures.

"Nietzsche."

"No, it was *Madame Butterfly*. I'm sure of it." She stands and zips her Windbreaker with ease. She's proud of herself, I'm proud of her too—impossible as she is—she still has her moments, and in those moments, she's the sharpest mind I've ever encountered despite the disease ravaging her brilliant brain.

"It's nearly the same line. In *Madame Butterfly*, it was: "'Those who cannot live with honor must die with honor.'"

She scoffs at my correction. "Peaches and pears, Elizabeth." An expression she picked up from my great aunt Nadine, another forbidden topic.

"Apples and oranges, Mother." I smother a grin when she fashions a contrived glare.

"Well, now you're just being rude."

I take her arm and we make our way back to the land of the living.

* * *

The ritual of rounds is comforting, even though the patients change regularly. Honestly, any time I can spend out of the house is a welcomed reprieve. In the afternoon, I leave my mother in Helen's capable hands. A fellow nurse who retired after thirty-six years with this hospital and quickly found that an idle life was not for her. Helen reached out to me after her four months of extensive travel—India, Greece, a whole month in China—and offered to give me a hand with Mother. The woman is a saint, and the money I pay her is hardly enough to fold, but she insists that Mrs. Dumas is not the most difficult patient she has had in her charge. I hope she never says that to my mother, as she does so love a challenge.

I review the patient log and see an all too familiar name, Richard Longfellow, fifty-two, massive stroke. He has yet to open his eyes, but the daughter refuses to give up hope. Cases like the Longfellow's show exactly what a poor a nurse I really am. I can't distance myself like the veterans. I struggle with their levity, their coping mechanism. Empathy is not something I can entertain one moment and shut down the next. I've always known that bedside nursing was not a great fit for me, but then my mother had her fall. It was the summer before I was set to move to Baltimore, and when she came out of surgery we were told that her undiagnosed Parkinson's was already quite advanced. I needed something stable and close to home. Nursing, I reasoned, would be my time in the trenches. That was four years ago.

This will be the third night in a row I've had to watch Ms. Longfellow hold vigil at her father's bedside, stroking his hair and weeping quietly. After the morning I've had, I just don't have it in me to face her. The pain of losing a father is something I know well, and don't care to feel again.

"James?"

My coworker raises his shaggy blond head, and slides his chair along the edge of the nurses station nearly colliding with my legs. I take a step back and he chuckles, swallowing a sizable bite of his wilted vending machine sandwich.

"Liz?" He smiles. I have asked him repeatedly not to call me that. Essentially an eight-year-old boy at heart, it's done nothing but spur him on. He's the same self-assured, self-obsessed, hopeless flirt that every woman has dated at least a half a dozen times before thirty. The fact that his endless pestering and youthful charm garner little to no response from me has recently made him double his efforts. In all fairness, if his reputation wasn't so well known, I might have succumbed to his relentless advances when I first started here.

"Would you take bed four-ten off my hands tonight?"

James squints, comically furrowing his brow and strokes the soft, faintly red stubble on his perfect jaw. "That depends..." He lets the condition linger in the air between us, but my nerves are raw from the long morning at home. I don't ask him what it depends upon. I raise my eyebrows and drop the clipboard on the counter between us, squishing his sad excuse for a dinner. He laughs openly at my unwillingness to play. "C'mon. What's in it for me if I do?"

I clasp my hands and rest my forearms on the Formica ledge of the desk. "I'll take four-twelve off your plate," I offer.

He leans forward in his seat. "I was thinking more along the lines of an extracurricular incentive," he stage whispers.

The line is completely played out and he knows it. Still, it's hard not to smile a little at his persistence. "I would think the Hippocratic Oath and simple camaraderie would be reason enough to help a friend."

"Oh, so we're friends now?" he teases, shaking the hair from his eyes with a flick of his neck. He's too pleased with himself. My scowl does nothing to temper his enthusiasm. "I can see how you would think that," he continues, "but as usual you overestimate my ethics and underestimate my attraction to you." James cracks his knuckles loudly and leans back in his chair.

I manage a heartfelt sneer and retrieve my discarded clipboard, resigning myself to another evening of Mr. Longfellow and his forlorn daughter.

"Besides," James shrugs, "can't give you four-twelve." He dusts the knee of his powder blue scrubs with a disinterested hand. "It's an empty bed."

I turn in my tracks and James grins, pleased to have kept my attention this long.

"William Moore? When was he released?"

"He wasn't. Died a few days ago." James pitches the last few bites of his dinner into the waste bin and pretends to organize the stacked folders in front of him.

I can't explain why I find this news unsettling, but something starts in my stomach and works its way through the rest of my body. Like a sudden chill without the cold, without a cause. "When, exactly?"

James leans back in his seat, hands clasped behind his head with a smile that says he's already won simply by inviting further questioning.

"Forget it," I mutter. I turn to take my leave a second time, but he relinquishes his chair and halts my progress with two warm hands on my shoulders.

"Wait—wait—wait…"

I shake his hands off and take a step back. He sighs.

"I'm on inventory tonight," he concedes. "You fill the supply order and I'll take four-ten off your hands. Fair?" I wait for a last-minute addendum, but James merely extends his hand to seal our bargain. We shake and trade clipboards.

"Thank you."

James winks and pushes past me to check in with the Longfellows. "What are *friends* for, Liz?"

The supply closet is a long, narrow room that sits in the center of the ward. The main entrance is through the breakroom behind the nurses station, but there's another door at the back that opens onto the hall. I take the long route, telling myself I want to avoid the bustle of the common area, the perpetual line at the coffeepot. I stop outside room four-twelve, lingering on the empty bed turned down awaiting a new patient, and glance to the emergency exit to my right. For a long while I stay fixed to that spot, uneasy, before I round the corner and seek out the waiting room across the hall.

It's hard to recall exactly what happened that night, and impossible to say why it suddenly matters. However, I do remember bits and pieces, looking in upon this dark little cove. I was on the phone arguing with my mother, which is nothing new, and I saw a woman I didn't recognize, headed for the back exit. I step inside the waiting room into the nearest chair.

I have the intense desire to leave, to close the door and never enter this room again. But a strange familiarity in the air keeps me there. It takes a moment for the memories to focus, as though I'm staring through a dirty lens. I close my eyes.

First, a dark silhouette, and then a shock of perfectly blond hair. We're roughly the same height, though she may have had an inch or so on me. Similar build, but there was something sunken in her face that lent an unhealthy thinness to the rest of her. I could sense her apprehension when I sat down beside her, like a change in air current. I know I tried to get a better look at her face, but she kept herself turned away in her seat. She succeeded in hiding most of herself behind the straight curtain of her hair until I stood in front of her.

Suddenly, the fog clears. The smooth firm skin of her jaw, the electric charge I felt when I held her face in my hand returns with such force that I open my eyes immediately and leap from my seat, staring down at the empty chair as though it's somehow to blame.

I stagger out into the hall, struggling to catch my breath, and count the gleaming floor tiles until two vacant black eyes appear in my memory—as close as they were that evening.

"Goodnight, Elizabeth," she had said over her shoulder, slinking through the emergency exit without another sound.

"Stela…" I whisper. Despite my discomfort, I sense the beginnings of a smile on my face. Her name is strangely intimate and oddly familiar. As though we know each other well, which is ridiculous, as I know we haven't met before. Unless you believe in reincarnation, which I do not. But this emotion is distinct, and one I've been feeling frequently the last few days without associating it with my unexpected visitor. It hits me hardest when I'm alone, usually in the fleeting moments before sleep. A sensation like being watched, minus the panic that should accompany such an intrusion.

From down the hall I hear Mrs. Whitley in four-eleven begin her nightly pledge of allegiance mixed with a few indistinct jokes from the staff, and the routine brings me back to the present with a shiver. Just like that, the sensation is gone. I look over the darkened doorway of Mr. Moore's vacant room once more before I slip inside the supply closet and seal myself away to fill the order.

* * *

Morning walks have become Mother's new favorite form of torture. Often rousing me at five or six in the morning when I have only slept for as many hours. She shuffles into my room and throws the curtains back, seemingly surprised every time the room fails to brighten. When I don't readily hop to my feet to greet the day she flicks on my bedside lamp and smacks the tops of my arms, cautioning that I will sleep my life away if I stay in bed.

"Honestly, look at your blankets." She frowns, yanking the duvet off me.

"Good morning to you too." I yawn.

"Elizabeth, it looks like you've been fighting with your bed."

I sit up stiffly and take in the disarray, rubbing my hand roughly over my face to scrub away the last vestiges of sleep. "Yeah, I haven't been sleeping well lately."

"Nightmares?" she scoffs. "Rubbish. You're too old for them, dear."

I throw my feet onto the floor and crack my neck. My mother makes a sound of disgust and stares disapprovingly at me.

"Something like that," I admit.

"Are they recurring?" she probes with folded, clinical hands. A dry laugh catches in my throat as I stand with a lazy stretch.

"Please don't psychoanalyze me, Mother. It's too early."

She harrumphs and totters down the hall calling after to me to get dressed. I make my way to the bathroom, bouncing more than once off the wall with my shoulder, and run a groggy hand over the wallpaper, feeling for the switch. The moment I flip on the light I turn with a start and press myself flat against the wall. My heart races as I stand clutching my chest.

I'm alone.

But for a second I swear there was someone behind me in the mirror. I curse under my breath at my sleep-deprived delirium as I wait for the shower to heat up. My reflection is exactly as disheveled as I feared. The bags under my eyes are a sickeningly deep purple. I inspect them with my face pressed against the glass until the mirror fogs over with steam.

"You shouldn't walk in the cold with wet hair," my mother admonishes over a steaming cup of black coffee in her shaking hands.

"It'll dry out before we leave," I assure her, and she places a hand up between us to say she's backing off as she returns to her morning paper. I grab my tablet and open CNN.

"Elizabeth…"

"Hmm?"

"You look terrible."

I smile around a large gulp of coffee. "Thank you, Mother."

"No, you do," she insists. "Worse than usual, dear. Are you well?"

I chuckle from behind my tablet, and set it aside. "Nothing a walk won't fix." I pat her bony hand, which she pulls away to fish her cell phone from the pocket of her robe. She moves so quickly I hear it ring before I can make any attempt to snatch it from her. "Mom it's six thirty. Who are you calling?"

"Dr. Gregg," she whispers around the fingers muffling the microphone.

"My pediatrician?"

"He's your doctor, Elizabeth, and a friend."

"He's retired, and I am an adult now," I snap, reaching over the island to grab the phone before anyone answers. Reluctantly, she hangs up, lips pursed. She stands slowly, a tremble passing through her legs, and wobbles to the sink to rinse her mug.

"You really should get more rest," she says, bracing herself against the sink. "Sleeplessness ages a woman, you know."

I tighten my grip around my own mug and force a smile. Homicide is never the answer.

* * *

Traffic is at a dead stop on Michigan Avenue this morning. Every third car seems to be laying on their horn as though the blame rests solely on the driver directly in front. My mother jumps every time. She's never been one for loud noises, one reason she gave me for never having a second child. One shrieking infant, she said, was enough. Some days even my violin practice was too much. I steer my steps closer to her and lay a hand on her shoulder, as much to comfort as to guide.

"Heathens," she seethes. "This is why we have public transportation."

My movements feel sluggish today, my muscles stiff. I lose track of my mother's one-sided conversation about the evolution of the Chicago Public Transit System and the invaluable role several of my forbearers played, as I try to recall the details of my dream last night. I really should start keeping a journal. They're so much harder to reconstruct once I've left the limbo of my bed. I remember that I was standing over Mother's bed. There was someone behind me, in the doorway. I was certain of the presence before I turned around.

A jarring boom rumbles down the sidewalk and my mother wraps her hand around my wrist. She looks up at me anxiously as I take her hand, and steady her by the elbow. The gridlock bubbles over to the pavement and foot traffic comes to an abrupt halt.

"I think we've walked enough today, Elizabeth." My mother has stopped in the center of the sidewalk, but then, so has everyone else. She keeps a firm grip on my hand, tugging me back in the direction we came. I chance a glance over my shoulder, aghast. All I can see is a pale, white mane peeking up over the heads of the pedestrians behind us. Then the eyes, large and black and empty. Oddly familiar. Terrifying. Before I understand exactly what's happening, and whether or not this is another nightmare, I'm on the ground beside a blue post box screaming with my arms raised, my eyes pressed shut.

"Whoa! Easy now…Easy…Steady now."

When I open my eyes, Mother has one hand pressed to the horse's neck and the other wrapped around a lock of its white mane. I sit on the pavement fighting for breath, my body drenched with sweat. A large man, equally winded, with a sun-kissed face and a dirty denim baseball cap comes rushing forward. He reaches out to take my hand, his face awash with concern.

"Are you all right, hon?" The rancher steadies me on my feet. "You poor thing. You look like you've seen a ghost." He slaps me between the shoulders and turns his attention to my mother. "Thank you so much ma'am," he gushes with an honest-to-goodness tip of his cap. "We're just passing through from a show, and Buck here hates a long haul like nothin' else."

Mother makes polite small talk with the flannel-clad southern gentleman as he wraps a bridle around the horse's head. Buck shakes his thick neck and chomps the bit back in his teeth. "He don't normally make such a fuss in his trailer. But it happened once or twice when he was young that he kicked his way loose."

"Magnificent animal," my mother praises. She strokes along the beast's broad pale nose as I stare into Buck's wide black eyes. I watch the horse rear as the rancher turns him around, morning sun streaming down his haunches. My whole body goes cold at the sight.

"Elizabeth?" My mother shakes me by the forearm. "Some equestrian you are. And after all the money we spent on riding lessons."

With difficulty, I pry my eyes from the fast-fading sight of the horse and back to my mother. "What?"

"Are you crying?" My mother recoils, pulling her hand away as though weakness is a virus she might catch. Her expression is a strange mix of concern and alarm. I shake my head emphatically, but touch my fingers to my cheeks. I'm more than a little startled when they come away damp.

"What's gotten into you?" she gasps, tugging at my sleeve to resume the walk home. My eyes remain fixed on the moisture glistening on my fingertips.

"I have no idea."

III
The New Deal

I cannot recall a time when I have enjoyed waiting for someone more than I do in this instance. The house is quiet, save the howling of two inbred Lhasa apsos locked in the cellar. I have been so patient, certain that he would betray us but without a crumb of evidence to prove it. Until now.

A small part of me thinks it was a brave thing to do. Foolish and ignorant, but brave.

Everything is as I would have it. The sound of his Bentley rumbling to a halt in his heated garage. His car keys ringing out against the marble counter in the kitchen where he discards them until morning. The falter of his confident steps as he regards the cries of his sniveling pups, trapped behind a locked door. Now he asks himself: *Did Christine lock the dogs in the basement? No. Olivia maybe? Impossible.*

The wretched creatures yap and nip at his heels when he frees them. I hear their clipped nails drumming along the hardwood floors, across the kitchen tile, up the carpeted staircase—tracking my scent through his home. They call to their beloved master when they trace me to his office. Their tiny paws pound the closed door, digging at the space between it and the floor, searching for a way inside.

His steps rush across the landing to his bedroom at the end of the hall. He rummages loudly through his belongings, slamming drawers until he finds his courage. I hear the cold steel click of a cocked hammer, and I can scarcely contain my anticipation. He chides the pups for their raucous whimpering and scoots their soft bodies to safety with his foot.

A hand on the door.

A deep breath.

A moment's valor.

He steps across the threshold with the pistol raised, and inches into his own darkened office. The light from the hall falls over my face and he finds me seated, once again, at his chair behind the desk. This time in his home with his personal records splayed in front of me.

"Good evening, Andy." I bare my teeth and the paste-like pallor of his normally ruddy face twists from a look of recognition into abject contempt. The gun shakes in his hand as he lowers it to his side, and flips the light on the wall with his elbow.

"What are you doing in my home?" His voice is a low growl, which might sound threatening were he a worthy adversary and not a traitorous servant.

I arch an incredulous brow. "*Your* home?" I throw the heels of my boots up on the corner of his elegant desk, lazily sweeping my hands around the room. "Andy, all that you have is ours."

He swallows firmly, rubbing a hand over his mouth and forehead to mop his own sweat. He closes the door behind him and walks to the front of the desk, his eyes scanning the folders strewn about.

"Why are you here?" he asks, tapping the barrel of the gun against the desk. I could not have wished for a better reaction than the one he is so generously providing. It is all that I hoped for and more, since the very first time I imagined this confrontation.

"Put that away, Andrew," I warn. "A weapon will not save you, and I find the presence of gun in a civil conversation quite rude."

The gun quivers in his grasp—his attempt to unnerve me having failed—and he lets it drop from his fingertips and clatter on the table. Andrew removes his suit jacket and with his last shred of dignity, settles perfectly straight in the chair across from me. To his credit, he outwardly appears as calm and composed as he would be walking into any negotiation. But there can be no compromise tonight. There is only one thing I want. I throw my feet down on the floor and he jerks in his seat, his hand shooting up to cover his neck, which he tries to play off as loosening his silk tie.

"Something to drink first?" I can hardly help myself, his panic is intoxicating and I want this to last. His fingers flex around the armrests when I rise and cross to the bar in the corner. The spread is arranged on a small glass cabinet, identical to the bar in his office.

Holstein and Beech, the old-money investment firm Andrew's great-great-grandfather, Harold Opes—then a mere banker—conquered through a takeover with the aid of his most affluent client, Fane, whom he knew as Stephen Radu. Harold was seduced by the promise of a fortune that would follow his family through the ages, and cement Harold's legacy. A firm handshake in those days was the whole of the transaction, and a bargain was struck. The Opes family gained Holstein and Beech, and we made good on our promise. Dealing directly with me, an heir from each generation retains control of the firm, which now bears the Opes name, and in return Fane's wealth is kept hidden in various shell companies and off-shore accounts. It has enjoyed steady growth for decades without incident. Which brings me back to the problem of Andrew Opes.

"Scotch is your preferred indulgence, is it not?" I ask, but I already know the answer. I drop a perfect cube of ice into a short glass, and pour two fingers of Johnny Walker Black Label. Andrew watches me silently, unable to look anywhere else as I run a slice of lemon around the lip of the glass and drop it gingerly into the amber liquid. I have studied Rachel so closely for so long, the preparation is automatic.

Andrew's blood rushes through his veins as I circle him, his pulse so loud I am almost faint with the promise of what will soon follow. I stand behind him and lean over his shoulder, settling the glass in his trembling hand. My fingers run up the tops of his weak arms as I pull away, and his body shakes with the slightest touch. I need a moment for myself before continuing, to gather my faculties and my control. It would be a shame to see all my meticulous planning spoiled by gluttony.

"Rachel sent details of the account in the Caymans," I bait. Andrew says nothing, but takes a long sip. I must credit his reserve. He barely blinks. His pulse, however, tells a different story. "Did you know that I keep a record of every statement you have ever given me filed away for safekeeping?" He nods slightly, to ensure I have been heard, but he seems to recognize that he can make no stronger defense than his continued silence. His eyes are distant, intentionally empty.

I reclaim my seat behind his desk and remove a folded envelope from my jacket pocket. "Lovely girl, Rachel. No excuses, no delays." I open the envelope and remove the documents I compiled for Fane earlier this evening. They detail balance, withdrawals and deposits into my Lord's second largest account. "Imagine my surprise when I discovered that the monthly balances appear to be repeating themselves, down to the cent, every two years."

I lift the packet to his eyes. Andrew takes the corner of one page with his free hand, running his eyes down the assorted balances, before he lets the paper float to the desk. He leans back in his seat, flicking his tie free from the front of his trousers and takes another long drink. His swollen belly puckers the buttons of his starched white Oxford.

"Tell me, Andrew, did you think you could hide this from me forever?" I flip open a folder of his personal finances, and turn them around to face him. Charges made to the Cayman's account, with his authorizing signature and expert forgeries of mine. Withdrawals of varying amounts, vacations, a summer villa in the south of France, a BMW for his wife Olivia, orthodonture for Christine. Every penny accounted for, but no credits toward the funds he liberated, no payment ledgers that I could find in the hours between Olivia leaving for yoga and Andrew returning home for the evening.

He parts his lips, about to speak, and raises his glass again looking me square in the eye. He brushes the knee of his trousers, scrubbing away a smudged paw print. My anger is beginning to get the better of me.

"Perhaps I have done a poor job of impressing upon you the severity of my allegations, Andy. Now would be a good time to speak." I tap the edge of the folder against the desk. Andrew finishes his drink and stares down into the melting ice, watching it clink against the glass as he swirls the cup, gathering the last droplets of scotch in the watery residue. Waste not, I suppose. His silence spreads out between us. When I think he will freeze me out completely, he straightens quickly in his chair, as though waking from an unpleasant dream.

"All that I have is yours," he reflects, speaking softly to himself. "All that I have."

Finally, a bit of progress. I lean forward and rest my chin upon my palm. There is a storm brewing inside this horrid little man as he begins to accept his fate. I am more than anxious for a glimpse behind the mask of polite indifference.

"What did you expect, Kathryn? What did the elusive Mr. Radu expect?" he asks with a scotch-sharpened tongue. I smile.

"Do go on, Andrew."

"Did you think you could purchase a family? That you could own me? Isn't that the purpose of this meeting?" His chest heaves, a dangerous glint burning bright behind his eyes. "When my dogs misbehave I tap their noses with my finger. They cry, they hide their faces, and they piss on the floor in submission. Is that what you expect me to do?" He tosses his glass across the table—drunk on his own fury—and folds his hands across his belly, settling back in his chair with a smug smile.

For the life of me, I cannot understand how the man could have so little concern for his own safety by speaking so openly about his betrayal. I walk around the desk, taking a seat on the edge of the table, my legs spread open on either side of him. The angle forces him to look up at my face. I lower my eyes to his and run my fingers up along his neck, holding his clammy jowls in my hands.

"Yes." I stroke his warm cheeks with my thumbs. "That is exactly what we thought."

Andrew's watery gray eyes blink rapidly, the rims bloodshot from a long day of imbibing. He makes a move to pull his face free, but I catch his head between my hands and keep his eyes on mine. Locked in my gaze, a single push for calm would be enough to strip the wind from his sails and leave him complacent, completely without fear. I do no such thing.

"That is exactly what we have done, Andrew. What we will continue to do. All that you have, *my friend*. Your daughter notwithstanding."

He rips his head free and spits upon my face, quaking in his seat. "Fuck you."

I sit up straight and wipe my cheek with the end of his silk tie. My fingers wind playfully around the noose at his neck, before I jerk him forward. The seat flies out from under him, leaving him on his knees at my feet. The tie constricts his circulation, his face bulging and bloated with blood.

"That was always the trouble with you," I sigh. "From the time you were a boy you were smug. Tell me, Andy. Are you smug now?" With every word I bring my face closer to his, inch by inch. "Exposed, clawing at your throat, kneeling before the thing you hate most in this world? The very thing that made you the man you are today?" I see the whites of his eyes and release him. Andrew grips the carpet with his nails, gulping down the air that fights its way into his lungs and coughing at the force of it. He sits back on his heels, staring up at me.

"Are you smug, Kathryn?" he challenges with a tilt of his head. The anger coursing through him makes him lose all sense of decorum. "I may be a pencil-pushing accountant. But you? You're nothing but a glorified errand boy."

My hand closes around his throat before I can think better of the act. Andrew is off the ground in an instant and prostrate on his desk, his fingers clawing at my hand, up my forearm. I have the presence of mind to watch my grip—firm enough to keep him trapped, but not so constricting that he should have the sweet luxury of fainting—and bring my lips to his ear.

"A message then," I whisper, "from our Master. As one errand boy to another." I lift my head and part my lips so Andrew can watch my fangs descend and finally see me for exactly what I am, affirming the stories he has been told.

The fleshy folds of his throat offer no protest, and I admit, I tear the skin back cruelly. He screams, of course, what else can he do? He kicks the sock clad heels of both feet against the back of my legs. I close my mouth over the wound, drinking loudly, my teeth driving deeper as I struggle to stop at taking only what is needed. His body jerks against the table, and soon the cursing, the shouting stops. Tears fall freely down his temple as all that he thought he owned slips away from him.

The blood always tells a story. This time, the unremarkable tale of Andrew's brief existence, rushing down my throat and playing on a reel behind my eyes. Andrew as a boy, no more than eight, running through the halls of Opes and Sons to his father's basement office where he sees me for the first time, sitting with a sly smile across the desk from Robert Opes. I ruffle his hair, and Andrew sneers at the touch of my cool hand—hurried out of the room by his father's secretary. I am there with him the first time he lays eyes on Olivia, a blushing schoolgirl in a lavender gown with a white carnation pinned to her breast. And finally, Christine, pink and slick in his arms. Her small, naked eyes opening to look upon her father's beaming face. But Christine does not stare into Andrew's eyes, she stares into mine. This frail creature, warm to the touch, curling in the crook of her father's arm. I feel her as clearly as I can feel him now. The sight of her ignites a fire in my chest.

I rip my face away with growl and blood gurgles in the back of Andrew's throat. I leave him rolling about on his back for a moment, clenching the wound in his hands while I straighten my black blouse. I walk over to the reflection in the darkened window, sweeping up my pale blond hair and tucking it back into place. I take a deep breath to extinguish the residual burn in my chest, tamping down the memory of Christine.

Behind me, Andrew falls to the ground, spitting and coughing up bright blood upon the floor. I kneel beside his head. The carpet hemorrhages around us in crimson pools. He weeps silently and grips his throat, the fear of death outweighing his self-importance so that he takes my hand and pleads for life with his eyes. His breaths grow deep and slow, the flush of panic licked away as the pallor of near exsanguination settles in his lips, and darkens the skin around his stricken eyes.

With marked reluctance, I tear the skin of my wrist and lament that I must part with even a single drop of what I have taken. I press my wrist against the wound, and his body stills as the skin begins to mend. He cannot move much. He can barely raise his head, although he tries. His recovery will be greatly hastened with my blood circulating in him—not that I expect his gratitude. I settle on both knees next to him as my own wound seals itself, and stare down at his face.

"I am glad we had this talk, Andrew." I take his limp hand in mine. "I trust it is one we will not need to have again."

His eyes widen and he manages a slow shake of his head. He pulls his hand away to run a cautious finger across his flesh that only moments before left him writhing in hopeless agony. "Excellent." I pat his chest and lean over him, stroking his shiny bald head. The good-natured gleam of my recent feed fades into deadly calm. "Because if I am forced to revisit this matter, I promise you, the pain I put you through just now will look like a blessing compared to what I do to your beloved Christine."

Andrew nods as vigorously as he is able. There will be bruising and discomfort, but he will live. He tries to sit upright, and flops back to the floor. I pat his head and stand up. With the incriminating ledger in hand, I retrieve my herringbone blazer from the back of the chair, and tuck the document away. I stand above him for a moment, poised to leave, content to let him cower.

"One more thing, Andrew. Mr. Radu demands a forty percent increase in the Caymans account by the end of the year."

The protest is there, thick on his tongue, but he thinks better of arguing. He licks his dry lips. "Consider it done," he says in a voice no more than a rustle even to my ears.

I walk over to the door and open it slightly. His frantic pups clamber atop one another and scamper over to him, licking the blood drying on his neck.

"See you next quarter, Andrew."

He musters something resembling a wave, bringing his hand up to push away the eager hounds. I close his office door behind me and leave the house very much as I found it, excluding the soiled carpet.

I make my way quickly around the block to my vehicle, concealed in the underbrush of an overgrown bike trail. Even now, in the peaceful night air that winds around my hair, I see Christine's infant face peering up at me with disarming calm. That force in my chest, seizing my empty lungs, burning up the back of my throat. I close my eyes and push the memory to the furthest corner of my mind.

I feel infected, poisoned by Andrew. Like a parasite has slithered through his blood and wormed its way into my heart. The image of his child leaves me raw and exposed. The utterly foreign sense of affection I had for Christine as an infant safe in her father's arms causes an intrusive unhelpful panic in me.

I focus on the sounds around me. Crickets sing in the tall grass. The sleepy sweep of swaying branches, the soft scurrying of rodents, the distant sounds of traffic in the city. I filter everything else out, all the noise in my head. And in that soothing din, a question comes unbidden, yet another invasion of my thoughts. Did Elizabeth feel intruded upon, panicked like this when she stared into my eyes?

The second my mind whispers her name my anger returns in full.

"Elizabeth." It was one thing to see her scrawny frame pulled into my dreams, to feel her fear as though it were my own. But this? To sense her presence with me on a hunt? To have her affections and humanity violate my mind in the middle of a feed?

I can almost sense her movements, buried deep inside the hospital. Bone-weary, and troubled, so far from me and yet, near enough at heart that I could reach out my hand and touch her. Close enough to crush, if the mood struck me. That conflict is more than I can handle this evening. Her emotions bleeding between my carefully constructed walls have stolen my peace.

Feeding is not a science, but a dance, an exchange between my victim and me. In the beginning, I was often moved to tears I could not shed by the flashes of a life lived, what might have been, what almost was, and all the promise of potential both realized and wasted. Over time the mind develops compartments, like callouses. Doors are shut, others are opened wide, and in the end, there is only blood.

What troubles me more than my incongruous compassion for the infant Christine is the guilt. I have always seen Andrew as an investment, as Fane's property. Never as a father belonging to his child. My contempt for him, the absolute vindication that comes with the taking of a life were taken from me tonight, and I cannot help but wonder what price I will pay next. This connection with Elizabeth was entirely my doing, invited the moment I gave my name. There is no escaping that truth, and only one way out of it that I can fathom. But Elizabeth is absolutely the last person I wish to see right now, and I recognize the cowardice for what it is, whether it belongs to me entirely or not.

I slide inside my vehicle and shut myself away. There is just enough time for a second hunt, a proper kill, one that will bring me the bliss that is rightfully mine. It should be Elizabeth's cold corpse in my trunk. I know this, even as I pull my car onto the empty road and drive toward the south end of the city.

* * *

I arrive at an old haunt in what was once the Irish district. A pub that has stood for nearly a hundred years, tucked between two darkened alleyways. The sort that blasts sterile electronic music on the weekends to lure the college crowd, and awful karaoke every other day. The walls are lined with framed pictures of the ale that coats the floor in a fresh wax. The stools are sprinkled with crushed peanut husks, and the only sound to rival the drunken screams of over-served patrons is the distracting clatter of billiards. Places like this are always so blessedly dim that no one notices the oddity of my iris-less eyes. So dark, in fact, that these very people will be unable to give an accurate description of the soon-to-be-departed when the police inevitably come calling—holding up photos of a single lost soul in a sea of so many self-involved ones.

The bartender casts a narrow-eyed glare in my direction. An older man, with a haggard face and steel-colored hair stiff as straw, pulled into a sloppy ponytail. He looks like an unattractive copy of my eldest brother, Bård. This man has seen—or believes he has— my kind before: well-dressed, clearly searching, always arriving alone and leaving with a gentleman on my arm. He ignores me, offering his services to several customers without another glance my way. Not that it matters. What I want is not a draft he has on tap.

The bartender continues his argument with his current customer who is furious that the machine dispensing prophylactics in the men's room has stolen his last quarter, at which point, the gruff barkeep chances a second look in my direction. His apparent disapproval is as comical as it is inaccurate. If I were a man he would welcome me, he would offer a brew on the house. And when I left on the arm of some undeniable beauty, he would tell stories of my conquest to his regulars and eagerly await my return. I should leave with a woman tonight, just to see his reaction.

I flick the empty carcass of a cracked shell across the top of the bar and it pings against a squat bottle of Knob Creek. I am looking for a brawl this evening. I want someone young, virile. Or older, perhaps, with a face as calloused as his hands. A man with a short fuse and a foul mouth who will curse, and try to crush my chest with his fists before I break his arms. I want a firm grip around my neck before I snap his back in two. Someone who will not go quietly into the abyss that awaits him.

Everyone has a preference.

I have siblings who love the seduction a woman requires. They live for the chase, the skill it takes to convince a woman to trust and forget the warnings that have been drilled into them since before they were old enough to speak in sentences. For me, those kills are too cerebral when they should be feral, and too pitiful when the target realizes in her final moments that her mother was right to fill her with such deep apprehension of the world.

My mark finds me before I find him, moving deliberately in my direction and pretending to chase the bartender with his order. He makes it so easy. I know when he settles on the stool next to mine with five dollars peeking from his shirt pocket that he is here alone, buying only for himself. He is not a regular. The hand he positions in front of my face has no ring, no pale indentation in the flesh either. He will not be slipping into the house, in the early morning hours, to crawl into bed beside a gently snoring wife. When he looks at me and finds my eyes already settled on his face he smirks, and turns his whole body to me. He keeps one elbow propped comfortably on the bar, feeling assured that tonight will play out exactly as he desires, that his luck has taken a turn.

He has no idea.

"Dennis," he shouts, holding his hand out to me. There is a moment of hesitation after I shake his hand, a noticeable silence on my part. I am wary of even supplying an alias anymore, and this simple exchange is just one more reminder of Elizabeth and what she holds. What I gave to her.

"Kathryn."

"Really? That's my mother's name." He smiles with nicotine-yellowed teeth and runs his fingers around the edges of his black beard. That is not his mother's name, and I wonder at the reason behind this lie. Perhaps to gain trust, establish a connection through coincidence. Whatever the motivation, he has used it before.

The bartender sticks his sweaty face between us.

"Rolling Rock, and whatever she's having," he yells over the ruckus into the barkeep's ear. The bartender does not ask my order, but he does wait for it.

"Nothing for me, thank you." I wave the old fellow off and turn in my seat toward Dennis. He seems puzzled by my lack of indulgence, and concerned that his chances may not be as strong as he hoped if I am sober.

"Not a big drinker?" he hedges, leaning in close to be heard without having to shout. Despite the clamor of our bustling surroundings, I could hear his heartbeat from the parking lot if I wished. But I stay near to him, enjoying his scent. Nicotine and motor oil, laced with beer.

"Something like that," I tease, speaking directly into his ear. My fingers toy with the frayed edges of his yellowed shirt. He leans back slightly with that same smirk and takes another lazy swig of ale.

"What do you do for a living?" he asks, emboldened by my casual touches. He rests his hand just above my knee. I am grateful that Andrew's blood on my pants has dried on the drive over. I hook my calf around the leg of his stool and pull him forward. He masks his surprise well as I stare up into his face.

"Investment banker." The secret to any lie is a healthy dose of the truth. "And what about you?"

Dennis slips off the stool to stand between my knees, peering down at me and seeming to enjoy it very much. He feels powerful, desired. I know he is a mechanic of some sort before he tries to over-complicate his job title. Choosing his words carefully to make himself sound like an expert in a specialized field, the effort is more sad than endearing.

Dennis wastes time with small talk. Where he grew up, why he moved to the city. As if I care. I lose myself in the beating of his heart, counting his long black eyelashes. I watch the jump of his carotid artery every time he swallows. He is a man aged well beyond his years, an ex-convict as indicated by his choice of tattoos, though he does not mention his incarceration. A hard life has peppered his temples prematurely with long white hairs.

There is an edge to his voice, a malice beneath each word that I cannot place. A strict mother he hates, a father who beat him. He has scars that curl like teeth on his knuckles, and he lies about the various engine parts that caused them when he catches me staring. His hands and arms are covered in thick, black hair. It peeks out from beneath the collar of his shirt too. His nose is strong, but badly misshapen, clearly broken more than once and never properly set. After much rambling on his part—and feigning interest on mine—Dennis swallows harshly and gathers his courage. He twines his fingers around a lock of my hair and pushes it over my shoulder.

"Do you wanna get out of here?" he husks. I smile up at him, and I know he senses something—a mischief that does not belong in a smile—but he is too aroused to worry about it.

"That is precisely what I want."

Noting that he does not step back when I stand up against him, I fish a folded bill from my pocket. I settle his tab, leaving a more than generous tip for the cantankerous bartender. When Dennis chances a look at the bill he makes a move to refuse the money, but I pull him along by the wrist behind me as we make our way to the exit.

With slightly more force than I should show, I push past the patrons blocking my way. The strength of my grip and my assertiveness vex Dennis, who tries and fails to drag his feet. Before we make it around the building to my vehicle his hand twists out of my hold, and I know he will push me against the crumbling wall of the tavern's exterior before he realizes it himself. He positions his body flush against mine and I allow the display of dominance, congratulating myself on another successful hunt. He is every bit the bully I suspected.

"What's your rush?" He runs his rough hand down the side of my face and over the top of my breast. I look up the alley toward the street. The city has grown quiet this evening, and apart from the smokers shuffling under the bar's awning, completely out of view, I cannot hear the footfall of pedestrians. In the distance, charged like static, is the familiar buzz of police radios already distracted by domestic violence and assorted gang activity. We are alone, Dennis and I, and if I do not have to mar my vehicle's interior with his dirty work boots, I see no reason why he should be alive for the drive ahead.

"No rush." I tilt my chin up and push my hips against him. He peers down into my eyes, taken aback by my forwardness and clearly uncertain as to whether he likes it or not. Regardless he brings his lips to mine, and his breath tastes like metal on my tongue.

"No?" he asks, grabbing the back of my thighs to hoist me up against the wall. "You always leave a forty-five-dollar tip on five?" He shoves me forcefully against the bricks. I do not grimace, or squeal in alarm, much to his dismay. His actions are met with my throaty laugh. I wrap my arms around his shoulders and flick his top lip with my tongue.

"Always."

A low groan rumbles in his barrel chest as he pushes his tongue unceremoniously into my mouth. I am content to receive him, for now, and tilt my head back as I tug at the hair on the back of his head. He drags his wet mouth down the skin of my neck, and another listen for would-be witnesses ends in blissful silence. I whisper his name into his ear, and trail my tongue against the black bristles covering his jaw. His pulse beats against my lips and I revel in the cadence, the steady rhythm with my mouth pressed against his throat, before I tear him open with my teeth. Dennis drops the arm that holds me, and my feet hit the asphalt with a thud. A firm hand over his mouth all but silences his enraged screams, and I keep him in place with an arm locked around his shoulders. He uses all his considerable weight to pull me away from the wall and throw me against it as hard as he can manage, my scalp splitting and just as quickly it mends.

Dennis is not so fortunate. The force of his own shove brings his forehead harshly against the brick and a flap of skin peels away from his skull. His knees quiver and begin to sink to the ground. I keep him locked against my body, looking for all the world like two lovers caught in a passionate embrace. The truth is there, swimming in his blood—his sordid past, his violent youth, his young face already cruel. I pay them as little mind as I can.

With a final volley of fortitude, Dennis brings his fist from around his back and slams it hard against my ribs. The first blow shatters three metacarpals, the second fractures his wrist and the third barely serves to jostle my footing. His weight settles in my arms, his hands fall limply at his sides as the blood that rushes with white heat begins to slow until, regrettably, the fount is all but a trickle past my teeth. I release my hand covering his mouth and true to form, Dennis's last breath is a string of broken obscenities.

My fangs recede into my gums and with a long-contented sigh I lean against the brick wall. Dennis's head drops against my shoulder and I bunch the front of his shirt in both hands to keep him from collapsing.

My revelry is short-lived. Pleased as I am to have a proper feed, we are exposed here. I wrap my arm around his waist and hit the trunk release on my key fob. I hold him just above the ground as we round the back of the building, a loyal girlfriend or a close acquaintance carrying a blacked-out drunk to his ride. But the parking lot is vacant, and I throw him over my shoulder. His mud-caked boots make a high-pitched squeak when I shove him feet first onto the rubber lining of my trunk. I attempt to rearrange his limbs twice to close the lid, forced to dislocate both his shoulders and his hips for the lock to catch.

With both hands resting on the closed compartment, I muse. If I picked smaller victims, I would not have this problem.

* * *

Carrington Funeral Home is a long drive, but my family has frequented this establishment for the last forty years. Derek Carrington, the proprietor, is a quick, efficient and above all, respectful young man. He speaks when spoken to, asks very few questions and the matter of the body is handled as smoothly as any other transaction.

The building is a sprawling fieldstone ranch, once the family home, sitting atop an immaculately maintained sprawling green lawn. Clover petals twinkle with dew as my headlights dance across the landscape. The parlor has seen no outward renovations since the early seventies—Loreen Carrington's hand-sewn avocado-colored drapes are still drawn over the boxy windows—asleep to all the world, but with extended office hours for us.

Derek, the only son, is standing at the back entrance with the usual brown paper parcel tucked under his arm. Sandy blond hair hangs in his eyes, his wide face drawn, his meaty shoulders hunched. Beside him is a dark-haired man, roughly Derek's age, whom I have never seen before. I check the messages on my mobile as I throw the vehicle into park, more than suspicious that I was not warned about the new help.

Derek steps out from the light of the open cellar door, ahead of his guest, and rushes across the pavement to greet me. He reaches out to take the handle of my driver's side door and I throw it openly quickly against him. His knuckles make an audible crack as I exit, and slam the door closed forcefully behind me. Derek holds his hand cupped to his chest, straightening his back, and with a trembling arm offers the package to me. I fling it behind me onto the roof of the car, tracking the movements of Mr. Carrington's mysterious companion as he joins us.

My eyes widen in the dark, swallowing the weak surrounding light so that I can see every detail of this man. He has slick brown hair combed back from his face, unshaven with at least three days' growth on his jaw. Unlike Derek he is not wearing the standard black rubber apron or the customary rubber gloves—rather, sleek, leather ones. His clothes are solid black and plain. A simple coat, a V-neck undershirt, dark denim jeans, black boots. He has the world-weary eyes of the unapologetically corrupt, and the crooked mouth of a criminal who has never been caught. Most unsettling, is that this man is not at all alarmed by me.

Derek motions to the unsavory individual to his left. "Kathryn, this is my associate, Mr. Collins."

I do not respond, nor does Mr. Collins. Derek's heartbeat echoes in my ears. After several moments of searching both their faces—the only flinch belonging to Mr. Carrington—I turn myself entirely toward Derek. "What is the meaning of this?"

Derek fumbles with a squint, genuinely puzzled by my abrasiveness. "Meaning of what? Mr. Collins'? Didn't Birgir tell you?"

Birgir, my brother Bård, keeps all manner of company. But he is nowhere to be seen. "Tell me what?"

Derek offers a nervous smile to Mr. Collins, who stands motionless with arms crossed. The mortician rubs the back of his own neck with a rubber-clad hand, and the elbow length gloves squeak against the skin. "Mr. Collins will be handling the remains," he clarifies.

"Handling?" I tilt my head, and step closer.

"Yes. He'll dispose of them this evening."

I smile and my teeth glint in the reflection of Derek's large dark eyes.

"How, exactly?"

Mr. Collins bristles, uncrossing his arms. He fishes in his jacket pocket and withdraws a pack of Marlboros. The cigarette casts a red glow on Mr. Collins's cheeks and he exhales pointedly in my face. "Does it matter?" he asks with a disinterested shrug. His vocal cords have leathered from years of smoking, though he cannot be more than thirty-five. He has a low register, voice steady and surprisingly confident.

I turn to face him in time for his next directed exhale and brush the smoke aside with my fingers. I narrow my eyes at this dark figure, but he only flicks the ash from his cigarette.

"It matters a great deal to me that these remains are handled properly."

"So, you're a family member of the deceased?" Mr. Collins gestures down at the blood on my blouse with his smoldering cigarette.

I take a step closer to the dauntless Mr. Collins. "No—"

"Then I doubt it matters much."

My fists clench and my body lurches forward, but Derek is quick to position himself between us with raised hands.

"Please, Kathryn, this is all just a misunderstanding. I assumed that Birgir told you about the new arrangement. Mr. Collins will be picking up a few...deliveries...to lighten the considerable load on our crematory. That's all. He was contracted by your family, by Birgir, specifically."

Reluctantly, I straighten myself and adjust my jacket as Mr. Collins finishes the last of his cigarette, crushing the orange embers underfoot.

"So..." Collins shoves his leather-gloved hands in his coat pockets, and rocks onto the balls of his feet. "What'd you have for me this evening?"

My thumb finds the trunk release in my pocket, but my eyes never leave Collins's face. They track him to the back of the vehicle, where he tugs at the cuffs of his gloves and removes a small Dictaphone from his jacket pocket. He records his observations with the clinical detachment of a doctor, a detective...

"White male, identification indicates thirty-nine years old, hips and shoulders appear to be dislocated. Swelling in the right hand and wrist, laceration on the neck, blunt force trauma to the forehead. Can I get a blood type here?"

I walk around the side of the car and stand with my hands on my hips. Mr. Collins lifts the recorder to my lips, I knock his hand away and he nearly drops the device.

"O Negative."

Mr. Collins repeats this information, and pauses the recording. He resumes his examination of the corpse, dipping his head beneath the hood. One good slam of the lid would ease my troubles considerably.

"Everything appears to be order," Collins concludes. "Next time do me a favor," he points with his thumb to the wound on the victim's neck, "cover your tracks before you drop him off. Keep the damage to a minimum or we'll never move the product."

With that, Collins takes the legs and hoists the lower half of the body free, leaving Derek to wrangle the head and shoulders. Together they shuffle across the darkened parking lot in a slow side step of a dance, to an unmarked black van that I must admit, I had not noticed. A thick white cloud tumbles from the refrigerated interior when they swing the back door open. Mr. Collins takes a moment to clear the door of limbs—too many for a single victim, clearly the table scraps of Bård's and Lydia's meals have already been collected. The presence of their kills steadies me. Collins guides Dennis's body inside while Derek pushes.

Mr. Collins shakes Derek's hand and turns to look at me only once before climbing into the driver's seat. The tires screech across the blacktop in a puff of smoke, weighed down with a heavy load, and I watch the taillights disappear down the side of the building. My mind is flooded with concern for the fate of its incriminating cargo, racing through scenarios as mundane as a routine traffic stop.

"Kathryn," Derek calls breathlessly. "Come inside and get cleaned up." He waves me through the cellar door, and disappears into the harsh glare of the embalming room. I retrieve the parcel from the roof of my car and follow.

The heat from the open furnace is smothering as I strip off the evening's attire and cast it in. The hollow lights overhead gleam along the surface of an empty embalming table and dance in the reflections of several glass beakers, and a discarded syringe in the large metal sink. Derek drops a clear plastic bag on top of my clothing—all the identification Dennis was carrying—and pushes a button on the side of the cremator, sealing the steel door of the furnace.

I arrange myself quickly in the corner of the room where Derek keeps a small partition—presumably to protect our modesty, if we had any, but more likely to protect his own. In the parcel I find the usual attire for the trip home: snug black thermal, dark jeans, flat boots. Fleetingly, I remind myself to thank Lydia for the pains she takes to keep all of us presentable, and then I remind myself of Lydia, and the thought of praising her causes me physical discomfort.

Derek averts his eyes when I emerge, clearly nervous to be alone with me as angry as I am, and pretends to clean his instruments in the sink. I retrieve my mobile and keys from the foot of the embalming table.

"Will there be anything else?" he asks, in a small, cautious voice, breaking his own self-imposed silence.

"We shall see." I hover in the doorway with one foot on the highest stair, the other firmly planted in the outside world, anxious to return home and confront Bård regarding this unexpected change to our established routine. Derek's shoulders slump in response, his head twisted at a sharp angle to regard my face though my silhouette is darkened by the shadow of the door.

"Kathryn, again, I didn't know you didn't know."

"I believe you."

Out in the parking lot, the gentle whispers of a warm night rush up to embrace me, but it does little to ease my troubled thoughts. Who is this Mr. Collins? Why would Bård leave me to fumble my way through this new arrangement? My brother is always so diligent, and his loyalty to Fane—to the family—is beyond question.

* * *

I quickly make my way down the dark wood–paneled corridor to Bård's chamber—positioned opposite my own. The slight groan of the floor beneath my feet is my only introduction as the hatch overhead closes. Bård stands in the center of his comfortable suite, not fifteen feet away, his back turned and his attention focused elsewhere. Despite my brother's enviable physique, not even his wide shoulders are enough to obscure the edges of Fane, reclining comfortably on the sofa.

"Stela," my Lord greets. "So good of you to join us. I trust you met the new help?"

I take a respectful knee at the sound of his rich and welcoming voice. "Yes, my Lord. Mr. Collins is why I am come."

"I have no doubt." He smiles. "And unannounced. You owe Bård an apology, my dove."

Finally acknowledged, Bård is free to face me with a cursory glance over one shoulder, careful to show as little of his back as possible to Fane. I take up residence beside my brother who smacks the space between my shoulder blades playfully but with such force I have to take a step to compensate. I grit my teeth and Bård offers me a blinding white smile, combing a stray lock of white hair back into the neat bun at the base of his neck. The skin around his black eyes crinkles with patronizing delight, and mingles with the deep lines etched into his forehead. My considerable years aside, I will always be a child in his eyes.

"My apologies to you both for this intrusion."

Fane responds with a good-natured laugh as he rises from the sofa and walks over to embrace me. The silk of Fane's emerald shirt pressed against my cheek hides most of my face, but not before I notice Bård's expression shift into apprehension as though I am about to be crushed. Bård does not enjoy the same relationship I have with our Lord, though the affection that passes between them is frequent and freely exchanged. My brother has been my protector as far back as I can remember, and if there be any cause for discord between these two it is born of Bård's thinly concealed concern and the unspoken implication that Fane would ever cause me harm.

Fane holds me at arm's length by the biceps. "I planned to make my way to you before sunrise." He strokes the side of my face with the back of his fingers. "We have much to discuss. But come, be seated with us." He releases his hold, and I am ushered forward between their towering bodies. Bård smiles again and stands beside Fane, with his hand outstretched toward the sitting area in clear invitation. Indeed, my brother is so pleased by my visit that I doubt my own motivations for dropping in on him. He must have believed I knew about Collins. Bård would never leave me so under prepared, and I am not in the habit of questioning my elders.

Though my brother and I share a similar station in life, his age affords him a superior position in the hierarchy. He has been so long in Fane's service, and with that comes enlightenment, a kind of mental evolution for any human-born Strigoi, or vampire as the English say. Such a crude term for a life so special. He put away selfish musings, egotistical pursuits and pointless guilt centuries ago. I was so certain I had done the same, but my recent misstep with Elizabeth was motivated by blatant self-interest. I am quick to bury her name inside my heart, behind the fortress that protects my private thoughts from Fane's all-seeing eyes.

Bård settles in the high-backed elk bone chair opposite the sofa, and I take a seat beside Fane. My Lord rests his arm around my shoulders, pulling me close, and picks up the thread of their earlier conversation. Not surprisingly, they were discussing their newest business partner.

"We can expect thirty-five percent of Mr. Collins's profits," Bård reports with absolute modesty.

With iridescent fingertips, Fane plucks and straightens the cuff of his charcoal pants. "I believe that number can be increased. But Stela will discuss the rate with Andrew next quarter, once he has had a chance to trend the profits." Fane turns as if only just remembering my presence beside him. "I trust henceforth, Andrew will be a vigilant and dedicated ally." His mouth curls up at the corners with the meager beginnings of a smile.

I look to their faces, waiting for some clue to fill in the gaps. Both men are placid, expectant but patient. Their silence is remarkably unhelpful and Bård grows uneasy the longer it takes me to answer Fane.

"Profits from what?"

My brother raises his bushy white brows, settling his ankle on his knee with both hands folded neatly in his lap. He schools his surprise, looking every bit the fine, Scandinavian gentleman he is, watching Fane closely.

"Stela?" Fane leans away from me to search my face. Too soon I sense the familiar pressure, prickling and warm as his eyes peer into mine and then behind them. "From the sales, of course." His answer is hardly helpful, but his shock at having to explain himself and Bård's obvious surprise over my ignorance, make one thing abundantly clear: both men assume that this topic is as familiar to me as it is to them. I realize quite suddenly that I have missed some crucial detail, with which I am no doubt deeply involved. Perhaps it was discussed at a family conference. I curse the distraction of Elizabeth. Once turned, a Strigoi rarely forgets. The life that came before eternity fades, but the days, years after—memories sharpened by new eyes—remain, untouched.

I try to relax my expression and my mind, while Fane's crystalline eyes, like icy fingers, comb through my thoughts, and if he senses some resistance on my part I will have to explain more than I am able. Bård's eyes shift back and forth between our faces before settling on mine. He knows that I am lost.

"You hate change, Stela." To my complete shock Bård laughs, a full, deep sound like thunder rolling between hills, effectively derailing the conversation. "Of course she recalls our discussions, my Lord." He smacks Fane conspiratorially on the knee as he stands. Fane's gaze is broken at the unexpected contact, and he turns with a start in Bård's direction. That deadly focus, Fane's singular stare is at once hooked into another being, releasing its drowning grip on my mind.

The relief comes like a rush of blood to my head and I follow Bård's gregarious lead, laughing at myself and bewildered by this act of kindness. Not because I do not care for my brother, or him for me, but because pitting himself between Fane and the object of his focus is a dangerous game. To distract Fane in his search of one's thoughts, one must shift the focus elsewhere, and that means drawing his attention. Who among us does not have something to hide?

"Quite right, my son." Fane stands and takes Bård's broad shoulders in both his hands, bending my brother forward to kiss the top of his pale head. "I will admit that when you first proposed this unconventional venture, I thought it grotesque to say the very least. Bold, even for you." He shakes my brother, and through the tight-lipped smile on Bård's face, I know Fane's grip is tighter than either let on. Fane is not fooled, good-humored though he may seem. I can sense him still, prying at the edges of me with a passing glance.

How long can I keep going like this? Eventually Fane will find a chink. He will slither inside me and find the dark endless ocean of melancholy I seek to hide from him. Once he has waded through the blackness, he will uncover all the other little secrets walled up inside of me. Elizabeth being only one. At the very least, I suspect it will break his heart to know that I have lost my way, that my faith in him has been compromised. That the misery of my monotonous nights has become more than I can bear. At worst, he will see my unhappiness as treason.

Fane releases Bård from his outwardly affectionate grip, betrayed by Bård's sudden rebound and his decisive step backward. Eyes bright and furious, Fane smiles at me from over his shoulder. He knows already that I hide things, but he is biding his time. Perhaps, he does not want to believe it. He stalks past the elk bone chair, dragging his hand over the crude, worn stitching to stand before the large window display at the end of the room. The image projected on his screens is a mountain lake in Skarstad, Norway—Bård calls it a portrait of home.

Fane crosses his arms over his barrel chest, taking in the scenery as though he has never seen that lake before. I shift my weight on the sofa, unsure if I should go to him. Bård notices my small movements and puts a hand out, warning me to remain seated. My brother leans back against his bedpost, pressing his spine against the wood but standing straight. He keeps his arms tightly to his sides, his black eyes fixed on Fane. What must the subjects of Fane's lands have thought when my formidable brother first crossed the Balkans all those centuries ago, seeking asylum from the angry mob of villagers his unchecked appetite orphaned? Was he a beautiful walking image of Odin with the youthful vigor of Thor? Did they mistake him for a god?

"Human beings..." Fane drawls, flexing his thick arms. "They are carcasses, waste, even as they live and breathe. No surprise they would be willing to purchase their own dead. And for what? For bones, tissue. For scraps." He cranes his head in consideration. "Perhaps an old woman's prayer for a new hip will be granted tomorrow, or a burn victim will receive a skin graft...because we are as we are. And the lives we take now will change lives. Does that not make us the very definition of infinity?" Fane turns slowly around, his face a mask of contempt, tempered with quiet contemplation that softens his eyes and full lips. I force a smile, because it is expected and I am certain that behind me, Bård does the same.

"Well said, my Lord. Infinite."

Fane extends an expectant hand. "Stela, come. I have grown weary of Bård's room." I rise without a second thought. "Let us discuss the events of the day in my chambers."

"My Lord," Bård begins bravely, foolishly. "If I may keep your Stela this evening. I would like her opinion of Mr. Collins's conduct and demeanor. An evaluation from a source I trust to be critical as well as keen." I can sense my brother close behind me. He curls his large, dry hand over my forearm, pulling me back gently and away from Fane's proffered palm. There is malice behind those pale blue eyes as they brush along Bård's resolute smile, but a compliment to Fane's protégé is a compliment to his good taste. And he has never been one to refuse a compliment.

"Very well," my Lord concedes with a gracious nod. He comes to stand in front of me, pausing before he takes his leave. "Tomorrow, I expect a full account of your confrontation with Andrew." He cups the side of my face in his warm hand, and strokes my cheek with his thumb. A practiced gesture, and one that does not wake the sluggish beating of my heart the way it used to. "I want yours to be the first face I see."

"And yours the first I see, my Lord—" I barely finish the sentence. Fane covers my mouth with his own and firm, insistent fingers cradle the back of my head, pulling me close and out of Bård's reach. His passion is clear, as clear as his dominion though why he would seek to prove such an uncontested point to Bård is beyond me. My brother has never shown any interest in me beyond that of a second, a captain to his lieutenant, and jealousy is a lesser emotion. A vice for mortals. A hurdle for the turned Strigoi, unfitting for a Moroi. After all, what reason could a god have to be jealous of his creations?

Fane pulls his cradling hand away and the kiss ends so abruptly I stumble back into my brother. Bård does not budge, his body braces mine like brick wall and I straighten myself against him, markedly embarrassed. Fane has disappeared before my toes have joined my heels on the floor.

Bård steps back and takes Fane's place on the sofa. "Have a seat, Stela." He pats the space beside him with a large, white paw. A gentle entreaty twisted round his words and posture.

"I have sat long enough, thank you."

"That was not a request." He has never been one to make demands, certainly not of me. I do as he asks without further protest, sitting further from him than I had with Fane, comfortably and as an equal.

"I did not care for your associate," I admit.

Bård smiles and leans back with both hands once again folded patiently in his lap. He gives a small shrug. "What is there to like? The man is a scoundrel of the lowest form. An opportunist, a petty thief and a criminal. I did not keep you to discuss Mr. Collins."

I turn in my seat, curling a leg underneath me. I do not ask why he kept me from Fane's suite, though I want to know. A gift is not something to be questioned.

"You truly have no memory of our conversation?" he asks in his quiet baritone.

I cannot look him in the eye, but shake my head and fold my empty hands.

"We discussed Mr. Collins nearly a fortnight past. Having been silent facilitators in the arms trade, the drug trade for so long, human…produce…was a logical step. I should say, Fane and I discussed this venture. You sat in our presence as silent and distracted as you are now."

His face is as troubled as his voice. More than once I have questioned my brother's boundless concern for me, his unfathomable kindness. He has absolutely nothing to gain by delaying my debrief with our Lord. He did so all the same, for my sake. I turn away from him and rest my elbows on my knees. I hold my head in my hands, searching for a reason, but there is nothing I can safely admit. The memory is there, as Bård suspected it would be. I do recall attending the round table discussion, naturally. But what I remember in place of what was said, are the thoughts that drove me to such spectacular distraction. Namely, the dream I was pulled into the morning prior, which has occupied my thoughts ever since.

I was sitting on a low-lying floral print lounge, in a brightly lit and immaculately arranged living room. Despite the late hour— the early morning light flooding over the floor—I was not fatigued.

Upon standing I realized that the room was familiar to me, and though I was alone the presence of another was curiously strong. I could smell her everywhere, and it was her distinct scent that pulled me from the living room down the expanse of an eerily dark hallway. She stood at the end of the hall, before a white door that was slightly ajar and stole inside like a thief.

I walked up behind her. Each step closer was an assault upon my senses. The sweet reek of decay and human illness hung heavy in the air, souring everything else, and I stopped myself from breathing.

Elizabeth's chestnut hair spilled over her shoulders, cascading freely down her back. Her head was haloed in the light from an open window on the far wall. She did not turn to look at me, though I could sense that she was aware of my presence. Elizabeth stood motionless, towering over a sleeping form stretched out on the bed in front of her. I wondered how she could stand to be so close to the body's sickeningly sweet odor.

Clustered in every available corner were monitors and machines, I recognized the heart monitor immediately, and the room seemed strung together by a multitude of brightly colored wires darting from device to bedridden patient. Some machines buzzed like insects, and others chirped like songbirds. The body I recognized as Claire Dumas was wrapped in a lovely, checkered quilt.

Claire's gray hair was plastered to her satin pillowcase with sweat, and gripping a second pillow, Elizabeth hovered over her. I knew what she was considering. I took a step inside the room and watched as Elizabeth's proud shoulders slumped in defeat. Softly, she whispered to me: "You shouldn't be here."

I grew still, waiting for her to continue. She did not.

"You brought me here, Elizabeth."

She cast her head over her shoulder. There were deep, purple circles under her eyes, made all the more striking by her solid black dress. A mourning gown, thin and modestly cut that ended just below her knees. In her heart was the thickest despair I have ever felt, deeper even than my own melancholy. The weight of her sadness stopped my approach. She spared me a weak smile.

Elizabeth stared down at her mother's resting face. She placed her hand at the top of Claire's head and bending down at the waist, bestowed a gentle kiss to her furrowed brow. Slowly, she straightened and bunched the pillow tightly in her fists. I thought to stop her, but what is an old woman to me? And the moment was intimate somehow.

With a sudden cry like a whimper that gathered into a roar, she plunged the pillow over her mother's face, sobbing and repeating over, and over "I'm sorry," as Claire's ragged nails dug into the milky skin of Elizabeth's wrists. The struggle was prolonged until, finally, Claire dropped her hands and I did not need the wailing monitors to tell me she had passed. Elizabeth fell weeping atop her mother's chest, the pillow still in place, and curled her fingers into the shoulders of Claire's soiled nightgown.

I closed the distance between us and with my hands around her upper arms, lifted Elizabeth away from the corpse and turned her to face me. I was bewitched for a moment. I have witnessed many deaths—I caused most of them—but this heartbreak was something I had never seen, but was certain I recognized.

Elizabeth's warm, soft eyes peered into my own and she quieted in my arms as recognition began to smooth her features. She licked the salt from her lips and blinked her tears back. Apprehension pulled her body taut as a bow in my hands.

"I know you." Her eyes darted over my face and I released her.

I stepped around Elizabeth and took the pillow from her mother's face. Claire was a portrait of peace and dignity, so serene I found myself smiling down at her. I turned away and swept aside Elizabeth's hair clinging to blotched cheeks, curling it back behind her ear. She leaned into my touch, just as she had the night we met.

"So Elizabeth, this is what you dream of…"

"Stela?"

Bård taps the back of my hand with a brush of his long fingers, and startles me back to life. I remain cautiously mute, staring him down as though facing a stranger. We are at an impasse, he and I. I cannot admit the cause of my detachment, and he can offer me no further protection than he already has.

"What does Mr. Collins do with bodies?"

Bård shakes his head with a forced and humorless laugh. He is not accustomed to repeating himself. "He will auction what he can to the highest bidder. It is a flourishing underground industry. Medical implants made from body parts from the dead—bones, skin, ligaments, tissues that do not decay readily. Some of them may be sold to medical institutions, research laboratories, and so forth. Supply cannot keep up with demand, so corners are cut."

A weary laugh rumbles up my throat, having finally been made to understand what Fane meant when he said: "spare parts."

"Stela," Bård warns, placing his hand on my knee. "Whatever is behind this distraction. Whatever you are hiding from him…"

He need not finish, I already know how that sentence ends. Whatever you are hiding from him is not worth the repercussions. I have told myself the very same, every single night, for longer than I care to claim. For years, when the dissatisfaction I harbored for this meager existence was no more than a faint ache in my chest. When the lust for battle was so keen as to drown my persistent hunger. How I long to wander this earth freely once more, in Fane's service. To conquer in his name.

The easy part will be killing Elizabeth, but that will merely right a single wrong. Crushing my own damnable pride is another matter entirely.

I stand and make my way under the hatch in Bård's chamber, establishing a healthy distance before I address him again.

"Thank you for this evening, Brother." I bow my head in gratitude, my legs coiled and ready to pounce for the exit in the ceiling.

Bård rises, but does not approach. He rests his shoulder against his bedpost and crosses his willowy arms. His answering smile is a remorseful, deflated thing. "I will not distract him again, Stela."

"I would never ask."

IV
Disturbance

"Lie down, please."

Karen graciously holds the back of my gown closed as I hop up on the table. The sterile paper cover crackles under my hands like Christmas morning as I clench my bare legs, and sweep them up off the floor. In the dimly lit observation window, Arthur glances up from the monitor and gives me an uncomfortable smile from behind the glass. Immediately, I regret choosing a specialist from within my limited circle.

Karen guides me down into the horseshoe-shaped headrest. With gentle fingers she straightens my floral hospital gown, pulling the modest covering down to just above my knees.

"Ready?" she asks.

I nod, certain that my voice will crack if I speak. She pats my arm and locks the table into position. I hear the soft thud of her clogs retreat across the yellowed linoleum, and the door settling on its hinges seems to suck the last breath of comfort from the room.

All I can see from my prone position is the bright, white gleam of the harsh fluorescents, and the soft, molded plastic of the scanner closing in around me.

"Elizabeth, try to lie perfectly still." Arthur's firm voice slices through the quiet—clinical and impersonal. "The first pass will be conducted without contrast. I may ask you to hold your breath."

I know the drill, but he's obligated to give me a blow-by-blow of the procedure. It makes me feel like a patient—which, I am—and my powerlessness only exacerbates my fear of what he might find. I give him a thumbs-up from the table and his hearty chuckle warms the sterile lab.

"Here we go," he says.

The room darkens and the only sound is the machine, loud enough to drown out my pounding heart. I hold my breath without being told to do so, as though any moment the MRI will rain poison on my face. The scanner knocks and hums.

Have I overreacted?

When I was a child and my mother would take me to the doctor, but however minor the ailment, it would inevitably improve the moment I sat down in the waiting room. I always felt so guilty for having wasted everyone's time. I have a similar feeling now, enveloped in the cool embrace of the lab that Arthur had to pull strings to reserve on such short notice.

This morning I woke with a start from a fresh round of increasingly vivid nightmares convinced I was not alone in my room. The unmistakable stench of fresh blood had clotted the air…

I release a slow, steady exhale and fight the urge to fidget. The molded plastic obscuring my field of vision makes the room seem so manageable and contained. No space for fleeting faces. No dark corners to conceal…something. Someone. The sense of security this near-entombment brings me after weeks of unrest is both upsetting and infuriating.

"Very good, Elizabeth," Arthur needlessly praises. "Karen will be coming in now to administer the contrast."

"Straighten your arm for me." Karen's bright shock of orange hair and green eyes are a welcome sight, and I roll my arm to expose the IV strapped to my arm. Karen injects the contrast and I am assaulted by a metallic taste at the back of my throat that quickly conjures the taste of blood again.

What if he doesn't find anything? How do I explain it all then? The odors, the dreams, the visions, the feeling of being watched and followed? As terrifying as it would be to see a lesion on the scans, mental illness is also… I don't know which diagnosis scares me more.

Arthur is silent this round, which only underscores my fears. I hold my breath again and wish for something I can fight with pills, or a small benign tumor. Worst-case scenario: a "one-and-done" surgery. But please, a clear diagnosis of something with low to moderate severity. Temporal lobe seizures would be good.

Last week I was washing dishes after work. Mother had lately been particularly awful to Helen, and I insisted she leave the chore for me. Gliding as silently as I could from cabinet to cabinet, stacking pots and pans and plates I looked up from the sink and froze with a colander in my hands. Outside my kitchen window, for as far as I could see, was a foam-swept tide brushing against a beach. The foam fizzled over smooth, round pebbles, scrubbing the shore clean. The sky was weighed down by heavy stagnant clouds, and the stillness was broken by screeching gulls that I could hear and see as plainly as the machine that holds me now. The hallucination was accompanied by something that wasn't the beach at all. Something old, musty, a cross between a library and a cathedral fogged with incense. I could smell the earth—soil dampened by fresh rain. I stepped back and dropped the colander against the ceramic tiles.

My mother's voice came crashing down the hall, screaming about the late hour. I steadied myself and called back an apology. Shaking and unsettled, I picked up the colander, and when I faced the window all that greeted me was the predictable dark disrupted by the sudden glare of the motion light above the back patio. The light flicked off a minute later, shrouding my mother's azaleas in shadow. I let the water out of the sink and stood watching the suds gurgle down the drain.

On the back porch, the night breeze pulled the ends of my hair up around my neck, and beyond my suspicion that I wasn't alone, everything was exactly as it should be. I called Arthur the next morning and made today's appointment.

* * *

"There's nothing physically wrong with you."

Dr. Arthur Richmond, neurologist and friend sits across from me, hands firmly folded. He drums his fingers on top of my results—a final percussive flourish—perfectly satisfied with himself, understandably content with the findings.

I knew it was coming. I could see it in his eyes before the second scan began. A clean bill of health should be a blessing to any sound mind, but then again, my sanity is the reason for this expedited consultation. With a sigh that Arthur mistakes for relief, I draw forward in my seat. Tearfully, I plead with him to understand what I'm too frightened to say, and Arthur's pacifying smile vanishes when he sees my turmoil. He turns in his chair, facing the windows along the wall to give me a moment to collect myself.

"You must have missed something," I whisper. Arthur clears his throat diplomatically, and braces himself for what I'm sure would be a rallying pep talk.

"Elizabeth," he employs a softer, beseeching tone. "There are no abnormalities in your scans or labs. Your blood work was normal, hormone levels are stable. Hell, even your blood pressure is excellent. We'll need to wait for serology for various pathogens, but I'm not expecting anything at all." There is an air of genuine amusement simmering beneath his obvious concern. He's more used to delivering tragic news.

I walk over to the windows of his bright, cheerful office and take in the well-manicured view. A Japanese maple curls in the center of the path below, and I swear I can hear the leaves brushing against themselves in the breeze. "How do you explain the symptoms?" I challenge. "Auditory, olfactory and visual hallucinations?"

He purses his lips, taps his index finger against his tightly closed mouth. "May I speak plainly?"

"Of course." I lean back against the window, watching the sun spill across my shoulders and rub my arms, more for comfort than heat. The rays of the setting sun and the warmth radiating from the glass seep into the fabric of my navy cardigan. Arthur runs a hand over his naked pink scalp.

"I believe, from what you've told me of this…face you're seeing, the smells, the sounds are all very real…to you." He regards me with shy eyes and gentle tact. I'm grateful.

Face, he said. I hadn't considered the specificity of my delusions. It *is* a particular, familiar face and that makes the hallucinations all the more peculiar. If I closed my eyes now, she would be there, burned into the back of my eyelids. The sharp chin and nose. The parted lips. She would be so close I would feel the ghost of her blond hair tickling my cheeks, and those eyes—black, but not vacant—that seem to follow me everywhere.

Maybe that's why I let this go unchecked for so long, stayed silent about the sensation. In a way, I sometimes welcome the attention, the feeling of being admired from afar. Of course, that's not always the case. I often feel her presence at inopportune times, and there is an underlying aggression that terrifies me.

"Elizabeth, you know I have the utmost respect for you."

I do, and he does.

"You need to talk to someone."

I nod and walk back over to his desk, gripping the empty chair facing him—too anxious to sit and too nervous to stand without holding on to something. A sudden calm washes over me, a finality that seemed miles away moments ago, and with it a grim acceptance. I have railed against it since the first nightmare of that lonely little girl standing on the beach, and the first whiff of drying blood. Back when the shadows I saw were confined to darkened corners, and the deserted hall beside room four-twelve.

"Psychosis," I admit. Arthur sighs wearily, scratching the silver stubble on his jaw.

"Fatigue!" he bellows, dropping his elbows on the desk. "Hallucinations brought on by extreme emotional distress and fatigue. You're exhausted." He presses his short square thumbs into his eye sockets. "There could be several causes that are not evident in the scan and blood work. You'll need to speak with a psychiatrist."

He's right, the matter must be dealt with, and quickly before it gets worse. Before word spreads.

"Do you have a referral for me?"

Arthur looks positively pleased. "A colleague of mine, Dr. Kimberly Sharp. She's expecting your call. She's excellent. I wouldn't entrust your wellbeing to anyone else," he assures with a proud smile.

"Thank you, Arthur." I extend my hand, but he won't take it. Instead, he stands and walks around the side of the desk to embrace me. I've never been one for outward displays of physical affection, in fact, I have to fight the urge to fidget, but the gesture warms my heart. His small brown eyes are so serious I distract myself by finding constellations in the age spots that dot his bald head.

"For what it's worth, of the two of us, you're the only one entertaining the possibility of psychosis."

I offer him a crooked smile. "So, your recommendation that I seek professional help is what? A legality?"

"A precaution." Arthur pats my arms, and shoves his large knuckled hands into the pockets of his tweed blazer. "Call Dr. Sharp. In the meantime, my advice to you is to sleep, Elizabeth. Lay off the caffeine. You know as well as I do it will only exaggerate your symptoms. And for god sakes, get out of the house. Go do something just for you. Go out with people your own age. Your mother has a perfectly capable nurse. They can manage an evening without your company."

We both know I won't, just as we both know his advice is sound. So, there's really no point in arguing. "Thank you again."

"Give my best to Claire."

I pull the door closed between us, leaving Arthur to tidy his office and finish up for the evening. There, in the empty hall leading to reception, an inexplicable lightness settles over me. Our mutual concerns seem suddenly preposterous. The rush of relief carries me swiftly to the waiting room, modern and resplendent in the soft glow of the nearly set sun, and I stand in the spreading shadows pooling over the cheap carpet, brushing the business card in my pants pocket with my thumb.

"Ms. Dumas, do you need to make a follow-up appointment?"

I start and turn around to Arthur's receptionist, whom I have also kept after hours. I can hear everything: the subtle shift of the receptionist's feet against the floor, and the cool air from the vents—swirling around my ankles—droning on in an endless yawn, the steady drum of her heartbeat.

"No..." I push the psychiatrist's card deeper into my pocket. "I don't."

My oddly cheerful mood lingers as I leave the neurology wing and enter the main lobby on the first floor. My shift began five and half hours ago, and I warned Sylvia, the head nurse, that I would be late tonight. I stop at the greeter's station and reach over the desk, dialing pound four on the lobby phone. I've never been absent a day in my life, and a perverse thrill runs through me when the phone begins to ring.

"Long-term care, James speaking."

"James, it's Elizabeth."

"Liz, you okay? Your shift started—"

"I know, I'm late. Listen, I won't be coming in tonight." There's a muffled shift, like James is covering the receiver, or cradling it close.

"Is everything all right?" He asks in a low, soft voice and I wish he would tease or flirt instead. "Your mom?"

"She's fine," I snap. "I'm not feeling well."

"Yeah, sure." He placates, lingering on the phone. "I—hope you feel better. We'll see you tomorrow."

My heart races. I don't have anywhere to be, and when was the last time that happened? Mother has Helen, and the hospital— always short-staffed—will get through an evening without my help.

What am I doing? I feel fine, better than fine, excellent. I have a clean bill of health, which is surely the cause of this uncharacteristic laissez-faire approach to work. Why am I so nervous? And how is it possible to feel both utterly carefree, and riddled with anxiety? My eyes fall to the clock mounted above the east entrance doors: seven forty-nine p.m. Hospitals are a black hole—existing beyond the bounds of time—and in this building it's always midday.

The purple twilight is a bruise beyond the glass doors, voluptuous pinks bleeding into plum and darkening fast. The noise of the city is relentless, but not unwelcome. There's still moderate traffic in the parking lot.

Just as I reach the stairs the Red Line trundles off, whizzing down the rails without me, but the next train is only ten minutes out. I shuffle back across the platform, and I realize I'm completely alone up here.

Admittedly, I rarely take the L at this hour. I usually leave for work a little before two in the afternoon, and ride back from the metro just past eleven, sometimes later. But I can't recall waiting alone on the platform. It's odd and unsettling, and were it not for the steady, bumper-to-bumper traffic in the streets below, I could almost convince myself I'm the lone survivor of an apocalyptic event.

I'm losing my mind.

I feel exposed up here with the open tracks in front of me and the bare railings to my back. The yellow lights swaying overhead, and apart from my own breathing, the thin rustle of litter and old concert posters flapping in the cool night air are the only sounds.

Even the cluttered streets below seem beyond my reach, and all the calm I felt in Arthur's office, the ease with which I left him, the childish thrill of calling off work for a night to myself, wither and die under the sickly glow of the flickering lamps.

I don't remember choosing to call out of work, or why that was such an attractive idea in the first place, but I do recall debating whether or not to march back upstairs despite my conversation with James. I don't remember deciding to leave the main lobby, either. I now crave the smooth tile floors, the recycled air, the secure confinement of the hospital.

I fumble in the depths of my black Birkin, fruitlessly hunting for my phone. I hastily make my way to the edge of the platform craning my head for the train. I can just see the headlights. My watch face catches the glare just enough to read the time: eight-eleven p.m. Any minute now.

I shove my chilled hands in my pants pockets, forgetting Dr. Sharp's business card until the corner slices the skin between the knuckles of my index and middle finger. From behind, I hear a languorous sigh, relieved, the sound someone makes sliding into a warm bath. There's no one else on the platform. All the same, I sense an approach, and the hair on my arms and at the nape of my neck stands on end. Tachycardia sets in, my heart hammers against the walls of my chest cavity like it means to punch through my ribs. I would run, but there's absolutely nothing to run from.

And where would you go? The whisper is horridly clear, a lascivious, distinctly female voice—mocking, on the verge of delighted laughter.

"I know you..."

My purse slides off my shoulder and drops to the ground. I can't move. I can't even summon the will to scream. A tremble moves through my body, from the soles of my feet to the top of my head. Someone presses themselves flush against my back, standing so indecently close it's as though there are two of me. Adrenaline surges through my veins, twitching in my wrists, behind my kneecaps. My body reacts of its own volition bending back against a kind of fixed heat like a cat preening in the sun. A sharp breeze whips around my legs forcing me to stretch the sleeves of my sweater. The space behind me isn't warm at all, it's charged—the lingering electricity of another.

Firm hands spread across my shoulders, slip down my spine and rest upon my hips, tugging me into place. The hands reach out and cover mine. Every nerve-ending rejoices in the touch of someone who simply is not there. An aching emptiness sweeps through me—my brain sounding an alarm, urging for flight—as though I've felt this touch many times, and don't care to be parted from it ever again. The scent finds me, and is it orchid or lilac? Beneath the bouquet, a musty mix of damp soil and incense. The same smell I noticed in my kitchen, the night before I called Arthur.

A scream builds in my throat, pushing against my soft palate, filling my mouth, and every muscle in my body constricts.

And then…nothing. A dreamy sedation spreads through me, warm, euphoric, morphine without the drowsiness, as arms I can't see wrap themselves around my waist. The scream thins to nothing, released on a long exhalation, and my protest slides back down my throat.

The invisible hands move, spreading themselves against my hips. They smooth one shoulder down and run along my arm—guiding me, positioning me—and I lean down to retrieve my purse. White lights glimmer along the tracks as the train clunks and rattles down the rails. My feet shuffle forward—pushed or pulled, I can't tell which—until I'm standing at the edge of the platform, staring down at the quivering tracks.

Show me.

Gentle fingers trace abstract patterns up the side of my neck, around my ear and my eyes drift closed. The indescribable calm is made all the more unnatural by my own thunderous pulse.

I slip my hand into my pocket and withdraw Dr. Sharp's card, raising it up to the light. The hand moves up the outside of my thigh, climbs the edge of my torso, and a strong grip holds both my arms. I stare at the business card as though I've never seen it before, as though it materialized by magic in my hand. A nervous laugh spills out of my mouth and shakes me so hard I take a compensating step as the sleek body of the train barrels forward—not two feet from my face.

The card is taken in a single rush of air, sucked into the vacuum of the train. A thin sliver of eggshell-colored cardboard, fluttering once, flips over and sweeps out of sight as the train grinds to a halt with a serpentine hiss.

I'm still laughing when the compartment doors swish open, and a small, elderly black woman with stooped shoulders and a pink knitted cap regards me suspiciously as she steps wide of me to exit the train. She casts a concerned glance over her shoulder and the invisible hand pushes against the small of my back, directing me onto the car. It disappears the instant my hand closes around the metal railing. My laugh drowns in my chest, curdles and twists into a dry, tearless sob. I clutch the rail with both hands and turn around to face the doors. The old woman's pink hat is the only visible part of her, sinking down the stairs to the street below. Beyond that spot of color, the platform is completely vacant. A single sheet of crumpled paper stirs against the ground and swirls once in a gust of wind as the train trundles off.

* * *

Looming above the dark strip of street, our brownstone is dormant when I reach the stoop. The chocolate brick, the bay windows—strapped with wrought iron on the first floor—and black shutters seem unwelcoming. I press my ear to the oak door, listening for sounds of life inside—Helen in the kitchen, or Mother in the living room—but find none. My hands are shaking so violently it takes three attempts to fit my key into the lock. Finally, on the third try—palms slick with sweat—the heavy door creaks open seconds before I lapse into a full-blown panic attack. The entryway sucks me inside with a greedy breath and I fall back against the door, wrestling the deadbolt back into place.

Panting, I slide down to the hardwood floor, balanced on the balls of my feet, and hang my head between my knees. I swoon and my vision swims. I press my eyes shut and focus on my breathing. Slow, purposeful breaths, timed by the ticking on the grandfather clock in the formal living room. I check my pulse after two minutes of forced meditation and finding it steady, pull myself up from the floor.

The reception area is not ground zero for a mental breakdown. My mother's antiseptic decor never bothered me much before, but in the throes of this panic, the lack of personal touches stings like a slap in the face. Mother doesn't do comforting. But this whitewashed calling card of a living area, trussed and dressed like a *Better Homes and Gardens* spread is strangely insulting.

I slip out of my flat shoes and arrange them unobtrusively by the door.

"Mother?" My voice rings out over the first floor, bouncing off walls, and dancing across the ceramic tiles in the kitchen. Silence rushes up to greet me. No Mother, no Helen.

Is it too much to ask that I find her at home, waiting for me? I drop my purse and with resigned sigh, and recognize my anger as misplaced fear.

The kitchen feels better, though the tiles are always cold under my toes no matter the temperature. I press the back of my fingers against the half-emptied coffeepot, which obviously hasn't been heated since this morning. My drained mug sits on the counter top, exactly as I left it. I pour the hours-old coffee into the cup and heat it in the microwave.

Seated at the center island, I wrap my hands around the mug. A small, careful sip trickles past my lips and chases the chill of dread from my bones. Doctor's orders about caffeine be damned.

In the reassuringly familiar environment, I replay the events on the subway platform with as much objectivity as I can muster. It is less like a memory and more like a movie. Something removed, something to be watched not felt, or smelled, or touched, or lived. But I was touched, and that's noteworthy. What's worse, I was complacent. No that's the wrong word. Apathetic? Complicit?

Sedate.

Settled on a suitable descriptor, the memory unfolds as though my brain was waiting for permission, or a magic word. The sensation is vivid, disarmingly so, and my heartbeat quickens. There was someone behind me, against me. Thighs pressed to the back of mine, fingers trailing up my neck. I had wanted to run, and at the same time I desired nothing more than to stay exactly as I was. Unable to reconcile the two urges, I stood there with muscles coiled, my fright mounting with every non-action, the inner conflict paralytic.

My hands tighten around my coffee as though being pressed, molded, moved by another. That voice in my ear, close, intentionally intimate. *Show me.* And I did. I knew exactly what she wanted without further explanation or—oh god—the business card.

The stool clatters to the floor behind me as I dig in both pockets, turning the seams inside out. Were it not for the simple fact that the card has disappeared I could almost chalk the whole evening up to an elaborate fantasy, not a break with reality. I sprint into the living room and empty my entire purse in the middle of the entryway. The floor is a curious mosaic of lip liners, and eye pencils, tampons, a compact, a hair brush, three bottles of hand sanitizer, a lip gloss, a lip stick, my cell phone—I knew it was in there somewhere—and my open wallet. I rifle through the upturned purse once more, and coming away empty-handed, fling the soft Italian leather against the door.

I can see it in my hand, in Arthur's hand. I took it from him, and tucked it in my pocket. And then I took it out again…I watched the train carry it away.

What was the name? The Doctor?

This is ridiculous.

I fall against the door and kick a tube of concealer clear across the living room. A staccato pulse throbs in my temples. I've never had a migraine before but I've never been this exhausted, either. That's all this is, exhaustion, Arthur said as much. He wasn't worried. Mother has always said I worry too much. But I can picture the card perfectly. The thin black border, slightly raised. The unassuming eggshell card stock, even the darkish threads running through. But the name just isn't there. The lapse is so specific it's as though that single detail was removed with surgical precision.

I take a deep, measured breath and let it out slowly. Tomorrow, I'll call Arthur. Tell him I lost the card, I washed it in my pants. Accidents happen. Hell, he'll probably insist upon setting the appointment himself.

I resolve to clean up the foyer and start on the dishes after a nice hot shower. On the second floor I seal myself inside the bathroom, thumb hovering thoughtfully over the lock. No menacing shadows when I threw open the door. No fleeting faces in the mirror. I forgo the lock and turn on the shower, but that strange sensation moves through me the moment I begin to undress—a sudden shyness I can't reason away, or account for—alone in a room with just one entrance. I don't remove my underwear until I'm standing under the stream in the shower.

The scalding water runs in skinny rivers down my legs and I release a sigh that has been building for weeks. The water pools over my eyelids, trickles down my neck, not quite the brush of fingers, but reminiscent none the less. I am not crazy. I'm exhausted, defeated, miserable, but not insane. I repeat the words like a mantra, until the water turns cold. I shut the shower off just in time to hear my mother's pounding, ungainly steps thundering up the staircase. With only enough time to throw a towel around myself, my mother flings the door open.

"She's up here!" Mother calls over her shoulder to Helen, who I can hear stomping around downstairs. "She's *fine*." I immediately regret the mess I left in the hall and what it must have looked like to them. They came home late to find my belongings scattered across the floor, but no sign of me, having no reason to expect me for hours.

"Mother, I—" She doesn't let me finish. Her hand comes out of nowhere in a movement so fluid you'd swear she's had years of practice, and she brings it sharp and flat against my cheek. One minute I was staring at her, and the next, I'm looking at my own reflection, watching the tears swell. I keep my eyes on the mirror.

"Do you have any idea what was going through my head?"

She doesn't shout. She's beyond shouting. My mother is at her most dangerous when she cannot muster the energy it takes to scream. Her mouth is a hairbreadth from my ear, and in the mirror, it looks as though she's leaning in to kiss my reddened cheek. I take a step back and raise to my full height. I hold my towel shut in steady hands as Mother regards me with furious green eyes.

Helen edges into view, standing in the open door, clutching my purse. She surveys the scene in half a second and notes the palpable tension. Helen turns toward my bedroom and pulls the bathroom door shut behind her, disappearing without a word.

I step around my mother and retrieve my robe, letting the towel drop to my feet once my back is covered. Standing in the center of the room Mother sways slightly, expectant hands high on her hips, her mouth set in a thin line. I bend down to pick up my towel and blot the ends of my wet hair. The muscles in my back pull tight across my spine, winding me like a clock. Outrage, and the threat of violence, turning my legs and arms to metal as I remind myself not to react. She may not even realize what she's done.

A smell like rust tangles in my nostrils, and I grip the towel tighter in my hands. My body shakes, my vision darkens and a black wall rises between rationality and the bizarre. My mother—

still furious—fumes behind me, her eyes wide in a mix of fear and alarm, seeking me out in the mirror.

"I want you to listen to me very carefully." My lips move in the mirror, but the voice is nothing I recognize and my mother rears her head back at the tone. My words tangle. I hold my neck with one hand to strangle myself into silence. "If you ever put your hands on her again, be that in anger or in love, I will break your arms."

My mother's lips part, falling slack. Whether the use of the third person, the steely delivery or the blatant threat, she's stunned into muteness. My grip tightens around my throat, the skin of my cheeks and ears glowing red. I don't know if I'm trying to stifle the threat, or choke myself before I can harm her. I am not a violent person, but the image of my only parent crumpled on the floor at my feet will not abate.

"Do you understand me?" Despite the constriction, my voice is steady and calm. I turn to face my mother, my arms falling to my sides. But it's as though I'm staring at an inconsequential stranger. Mother's eyes mist as she clenches her jaw. The space between us is full of everything she wants to say, but I swear her fear of me in this moment has a smell—acidic, an acrid stench like dried sweat. To my surprise, she nods her head, cradling her elbows in her hands protectively and retreats from the bathroom.

My muscles unfurl as soon as she closes the door behind her and I bend forward over the sink, keeping myself upright with my palms braced on the counter.

Once I've regained my composure, I step into the darkened hall and escape to the safety of my bedroom. I find Helen sitting on the foot of my bed with my purse draped across her lap. Just beyond the rounded edges of her ample hips, is a smooth black case resting on my white duvet. My violin, the bow and the crushed green velvet covering pulled back. I look from the case to Helen and back again, but she is locked in thoughtful silence.

There's no way she placed the instrument on the bed, and more to the point, why would she? I can't even remember which trunk I packed it in before I left for college. I step cautiously into the room for a closer look, my heart pounding—pushing against the soon-to-be bruises around my throat that I made with my own hand.

It's a long, black case with brass buckles, the edges worn with age and rubbed smooth. The violin is a family heirloom, and belonged to my mother's father who I never knew. Did Mother put it here? When? My mother can hold a grudge for years, and she never forgave me for quitting my lessons. But I can't imagine she would venture into the attic by herself. And Helen would never allow her up there.

"I thought you might want your purse." Helen lifts the bag slowly, and that blank stare has shifted to focus on my face. The imprint on my cheekbone from Mother's slap is just a pinkish ripple under my left eye. But Helen's hands twitch around my purse strap, resisting the urge to triage. With no small effort, I turn away from the violin and school my features into a mask of gratitude.

"Thank you. You didn't have to clean up my mess." I take the purse from her outstretched hand and set it down on the dresser. She pats the empty stretch of bed beside her. Warily, I oblige, and push the case aside. I'm almost afraid to touch the instrument, and regard its sudden appearance with as much suspicion as I would a Ouija board. Maybe the damn thing is possessed and seeking revenge for years of neglect. Anything is possible.

"I didn't know you played," Helen states when my eyes have lingered too long on the violin, and the silence has escalated from awkward to fraught.

"I don't. I haven't played for a very long time."

Helen pats my folded hands, giving my fingers an affectionate squeeze. "Well, then I'm glad you're taking it up again." It takes all my effort not to shudder.

This has to be some kind of joke. The scents, the sounds, the face, the dreams, and now my violin. I get the distinct impression that someone is testing me, trying to ascertain just how much it takes to break me.

"Elizabeth?" Helen brushes a few tangled strands of wet hair behind my ear. I don't move, or acknowledge her gentle touch. She's waiting for me to breakdown, but that won't happen. Meanwhile, I'm searching for a well of anger that has disappeared. I can't touch the rage I felt in the bathroom. I can't call it into being and wrap that thick, dark blanket around my shoulders.

"I know you're angry," Helen ventures. "I know that more than that, you're hurt."

"Hurt?"

Helen scrunches her sparingly wrinkled face into a disapproving frown, and lightly brushes her cold fingertips over my tender cheekbone. I stand up quickly, tightening my robe, and spare her a dismissive wave.

"She was upset." I clutch the top of my robe closed. "I left a mess, and it worried her. I can only imagine what you two must have thought."

"Violent outbursts are not uncommon at this stage." Helen knots her gnarled, arthritic fingers in her lap. She cranes her neck to catch my eye and the silver hair that dusts her closely cropped head twinkles against her dark scalp.

"I know." I tilt my head and wait for the words she's working so hard to avoid.

"And before today?" she probes. "When was the last time your mother hit you?"

"Summer before sixth grade," I answer reflexively. "She caught me kissing a neighbor behind the azaleas in the backyard." Honestly, I can count the number of times on one hand my mother has even raised her voice to me. She was never one for loud or large displays of approval or disapproval. The memory of that stolen, summer kiss makes me smile privately. My skinned knees pressed in the dirt, Ashley's warm palm on my cheek. Mother swatted the back of my head all the way into the kitchen.

Helen unfolds her warped fingers, and lifts her empty hands as though the answer is written on her palms and all I have to do is read what's already there.

"And that doesn't strike you as odd?" she presses in the concerned but dispassionate voice of any true healer.

"Hell no," I huff. "If I caught my daughter with someone she barely knew—"

"Elizabeth," she reprimands, straightening her bowed back. She scratches her head. "I'm talking about the episode in the bathroom." My face clouds over, and when I refuse to answer Helen stands. She takes my shoulders and levels me with prodding, dark eyes. Once again, I step away, lifting my chin as I go. Daring her to say it, to finally push the argument we've skirted every other week for the last three months.

"You're not sleeping," she accuses. "You look exhausted, and this isn't the first time your mother has lashed out."

"What are you talking about?"

"She's been aggressive lately with me too. For about a month now. I didn't want to worry you." Helen gives a long, weary sigh, holding her lower back in her hands. "Some days she's fine. She's her normal, impossible to please, but still surprisingly conversational self."

My fingers flex and curl into fists. How does keeping this secret help anyone? If she'd told me, I wouldn't have been blindsided in the bathroom. "She's never hit me," Helen intones gravely. "But she has started throwing things, occasionally. Knocking things over. She's quick to apologize."

"Mother doesn't apologize."

"Well, no. But Claire does excuse herself, or rather, she excuses her illness. I guess I just take that as an apology, and clean up the mess."

Half a smile spreads across my lips. Helen has learned to translate the unspoken. It's probably why she's lasted this long.

"It's time to think about what's best for both of you," she says.

There it is. I nod, crossing my arms over my chest. Helen, knowing exactly what that stance means, parts her full lips, prepared to console and cajole me toward the "inevitable."

"Perhaps." I turn back to my dresser and open my purse, digging around for my checkbook. Helen goes quiet behind me, nervously shifting her weight. "But that will be a decision I make with my mother when the time comes." The sound of the check tearing is the loudest thing in the whole house. In my extended hand, I hold out her severance pay. She's done enough, more than anyone else in my life, and while she's right—I am exhausted—her own exhaustion is equally obvious. This isn't her fight. Not anymore.

"Elizabeth, please. Put that away." She tries to push my hand aside, but I catch her wrist and curl her fingers around the crisp paper. She refuses with a stiff shake of the head. "You don't have to do this alone."

"I'm not alone." I hold her hands firmly in mine, the check crumpling in our shared grip. "You've been a wonderful help to me. A true friend. But we do not require your services any longer."

Helen stares dejectedly at check. Her work here is done, she's officially a lady of leisure once more, and something tells me that after nearly a year spent chasing the whims of Claire Dumas, retirement will stick this time around. She couldn't quit. She would never willingly abandon a patient or a friend, no matter how hard the going. She needed an out. She needed permission to walk away.

"You'll call if there's anything I can do?"

I smile warmly, but say nothing. We both know I won't.

Helen grabs my elbows and crushes me in her strong arms. Rigid in her emotional embrace, I let the moment linger and fight the urge to pull away. She needs to show how deeply she cares. She expends a long exhalation over my shoulder, and the sound more than her touch, conveys the extent of her grief, her reluctance to leave. I pat the space between her shoulder blades and withdraw, incapable of meeting her eyes.

She folds the check in half, tucks it in her back pocket and disappears through my bedroom door. I listen to her swift, sure steps on the stairs, and then their steady cadence across the living room floor. The front door opens, and all is still for a few torturous seconds, until I hear her flip the lock and pull it closed.

I sink down on the edge of my mattress. A part of me believed she'd never make it over the threshold. She isn't coming back this time and my decision weighs heavily. My mother's care is truly my responsibility, and mine alone. I'll have to scale back my hours, if not quit my job entirely.

The violin shines in the light of my bedside lamp. I stretch across the mattress, drawing close to her with all the hesitancy of long-parted lover. I drag the tips of my fingers up the strings, tracing her elegant neck. The strings are too dry to play, but she hums under my touch. I lift the glittering bodice from the green velvet interior and the instrument is as ageless and polished as I remember. The bow speaks to me of long forgotten glories, of solace and comfort, of triumphs and incredible loss. The muscles in my arms and hands remember her weight, my fingers itching to play. But I've put those fantasies to bed, and there's no point in revisiting past failures tonight.

I retrieve my cell phone from my bag, set it in the docking station on the nightstand and hit play. The first crisp notes of Tchaikovsky's "Allegro Moderato" swell new life into the room, inviting bittersweet memories and opening closed wounds.

I take the instrument in my hand, but leave the bow on the bed and push the white curtains back from the windows. With the chin rest in place, I stand facing the sleeping city, the fingers of my left hand darting up and down the neck, and my empty right hand sweeping over the bridge. I feel a bit foolish at first, miming a piece I had once mastered. The silliness is forgotten in favor of the escape, and for eighteen minutes I stand at the window letting my muscles remember and relearn. I hesitate briefly at the sound of footsteps somewhere in the house, but don't stop to close my parted robe or chase the persistent ghosts away.

* * *

The room is cloaked with such dense shadow that when I notice him hesitating in the doorway, I bolt upright in bed and clutch the white sheets to my chest. Silently, he steps over the threshold, and my heart races when I hear the doorknob snick closed in his hand. I can't discern more than a silhouette until he's standing over the foot of my bed. His dirty blond mop gives him away, and even in the utter blackness I can tell he's smiling.

Only the faint rustling sound of his starched blue scrubs falling in a soft pile on the floor. He walks up the length of the bed and the light from the open curtain shines around the sharp edges of him. Self-conscious, I let the sheet slip from under my arms and pool around my waist. I'm suddenly painfully aware of my hands, and can't decide what to do with them. Every movement feels awkward and unnatural. He senses this and sits on the edge of the bed.

The mattress dips beneath his weight. He takes my hands from their fitful nest in my lap and brings his dry lips to my open palms. My body leans into his touch, and I run my hands along the stubble that dusts his jaw, brushing my fingers over the bristly hairs on the back of his neck. I should ask him to leave, but it's been so long since I've felt the weight of another person. James dips his head in the crook of my neck and I tilt my head back in mute acquiescence. He litters the length of my collarbone with rough kisses, while strong fingers press into the small of my back, guiding me down against the mattress.

Warm and pliant under his rushed caress, my body glories in the sensations. His hands rake down the ripples of my ribs, wrap roughly around the backs of my thighs. For all his eager entitlement, his tongue burns a hot trail up the length of my chest and hesitates above my lips, as though this is the line, and here he needs permission. I dig my fingers into the finely muscled shoulders and close the space between our bodies to fit my mouth to his. Ragged breath and the clumsy knock of teeth, we pull at each other's skin searching for a way inside. We find a rhythm and settle there, the anxious fumbling little more than a memory, and handle one another with a sudden familiarity.

Chapped lips become soft against mine, no longer filled with the haste to conquer but content to learn. Everything slows and I shudder at the change of pace, snaking my arms around his waist—slightly smaller than I'd imagined. The shudder of excitement gradually turns to chill as I pull my hands across the finely arched spine to a swath of soft hair hanging just past the shoulders. I push hard against the chest that covers mine, tearing my mouth away.

We don't move. I'm not sure I can. She has one hand wrapped around my right wrist, and the other planted on the bed beside my head to brace herself above me. Wide, black eyes bore into mine. She doesn't blink, she doesn't appear to move at all, but I feel the thigh pressed between my legs slide away in retreat.

"Wait." My voice sounds strange, a distant echo. Not half as odd as my actions.

I hook the back of her thigh in the curve of my calf and because she can't be moved, I slide myself back down against her leg. She's as still as a statue staring down at me, no outward indications of life, or want, or tenderness, suspended in vague curiosity above me. Hesitantly, I lift my head to hers, not bothering to wonder why, and part my lips against her mouth. She remains deathly still, eyes wide. It frightens me to be so near to them, magnetic in their depths, and as cavernous and unwelcoming as staring down into a dark well.

I focus on the precise angle of her jaw, the sloping symmetry of her strong nose, the planes of her face completely smooth and unblemished. Not even the crooked etching of a wrinkle in her stern brow. She remains so utterly motionless that I'm not certain she's real.

Gently, I press my lips to hers again. They remain fixed in a firm line, and just before I pull away she presses back delicately. It paints both our faces with surprise, and as the realization washes over me that the ivory cast above me is alive, the hand that holds my wrist clenches like a vise. A growl, almost canine, rumbles in her chest and with one swift pull she brings my arm across my chest, pinning my body into place.

I close my eyes and scream, kicking my legs and pushing the darkness of the deep night away from my face, until I wake to find myself sitting in bed with arms outstretched in front of me.

My body is coated with cold sweat. I don't fall back to sleep, certain she would find me again if I risked a few more hours' rest. Around dawn the rain picks up. The droplets on the windowpane paint a murky watercolor of the cobalt sky and rooftops.

I sit in bed replaying the dream until the panic wears off, and of all the nightmares that have plagued my recent weeks this one stands alone for lack of ambiguity. Dreaming of James was no great shock. It's perfectly normal to be attracted to someone because they are attracted to you, or make you feel desirable. The key is not to act on it. But the silence, the stillness, her tepid body—neither hot nor cold—and the floral scent of her hair are all so easily recalled, that I watch the skin of my wrist for the blossom of bruise that isn't coming.

Dreams are not fact. Sex is a spectrum. I believe this and a hundred other things any evolved, well-educated, scientifically-minded woman of today does. I just don't find either fact very comforting right now. Not because I dreamed of a woman in my bed, and not for the first time, but because something about *this* woman feels inescapable, and appropriate.

Are these the sort of things Dr. Richmond expects me to discuss with a psychiatrist? Could there be anything more humiliating?

"And how do you feel about that?"

"Why do you think you feel that way?"

Next, having to defend my artfully manicured response to a stranger's cameo in my dreams to ensure it sounds miles away from internalized homophobia which I do not have. To be told what? To be made to admit what? That there's nothing wrong with an erotic dream, no matter the sexual identity expressed therein? I know that much already.

Was it erotic? I suppose it was. She was naked, I was naked, and I pressed myself against her. I put my lips to hers.

Why did I do that?

Yes, it was erotic. But without sounding crazy, how would I convey that what felt wrong about the dream was how right she felt?

Sunrise finds me as beleaguered by my own musings as I am by this unwavering fatigue. I shuffle to the window just in time to watch the streetlights flicker off, one by one down the block. Each dying light solidifies my decision. I will not talk to some stranger about these nightmares. I'm not a child. The waking dreams, the fleeting shadows are a result of my complete exhaustion. Arthur said as much. I will heed his prescription to the best of my ability and sleep, lay off the caffeine—perhaps—for a few weeks and do something for myself. Time away from my troubles might lead to a good night's rest, and from there, hopefully, a rebound. As he said, my mother can weather a night without my company.

Helen…

I'd nearly forgotten about Helen's hasty termination. I draw my discarded robe over my shoulders and tie it shut. A pot of coffee will smooth the edges, and lubricate this tricky conversation with Mother. Caffeine abstinence will have to commence tomorrow.

I stop in front of the mirror. The violet bags beneath my eyes remain alarmingly bright, my features sunken and dull. But the bruise on my cheek is no larger than my thumbnail, and it seems I didn't squeeze my throat as roughly as I'd thought. My violin case slumbers innocently under the mirror, perched on the top of my dresser. I run my fingers over the closed case and my wrist twinges, as though someone is still holding me in place.

* * *

"You're up early." Mother lumbers briskly through the kitchen, still clad in her silk nightgown with matching mules, thudding softly against the tile. Her eyes are downcast, in anger or shame, it's hard to say. She stands beside me with a full mug, leaning heavily against the island, quietly refusing to sit. Every inch of her is poised for an argument I haven't the strength to revisit.

"I didn't sleep much last night."

"Yes, I heard you playing." Mother raises her brows, taking a delicate sip from her cup. "It wasn't awful."

Itzhak Perlman would be pleased to know that Mother finds his undeniable talent adequate. It seems a shame to waste such an underhanded compliment. "It felt good to play."

She snatches up the Arts and Entertainment section of my morning paper and settles across from me on her stool. She pretends to read for a while, the paper rustling delicately in her quivering hands. "You should play more often," she suggests with as much disinterest as she can muster. "Talent is a gift. Skill is a muscle. It must be exercised before it atrophies."

I discard the science section and retrieve my coffee mug eagerly. She isn't going to ice me out after all. She's going to pretend it never happened, thank god. "I was surprised by how crisp you sounded." She takes another sip and folds the paper in half. "It's good to know your ability hasn't completely withered."

I know what it meant to her, raising a prodigy. I know what my success would have meant to my grandfather. She was never more proud than I when I played a solo, or won a competition. "Thank you, Mother." I can barely shape the words. A genuine compliment from her is rare enough, but before seven in the morning? That is unprecedented.

The corner of her mouth quirks into a quick, fleeting smile, and she is visibly pleased that her olive branch was readily accepted. She quits her charade of the morning paper and tosses the Arts section lightly on the pile between us.

"I'm thinking of redecorating my bedroom," she announces. The triumphant, if not abrupt change of topic is welcome, and I turn slightly in my seat.

"What were you thinking?"

"Something bright, but not obnoxious." She flutters a wonderfully steady hand between us, her movements stronger, and more controlled today than they were last night. "Something tasteful, understated, without the dreadful use of pastels. You know I hate them."

"They remind you of Easter."

"And must it be springtime year-round for a room to be considered inviting or cheerful? I hardly think so." I agree with a grin, and offer to take her shopping.

"Don't trouble yourself." She waves the offer away. "There must be some distraction if I'm to whittle away the hours with Helen."

She states it so benignly, I wonder if she heard us last night and the whole morning is her long game—devised to ensnare the truth. But she couldn't possibly know. She was already locked in her bedroom by then. I consider a lie, but what would I say? I can't leave her waiting by the door, purse in hand, for Helen to arrive. I take another fortifying drink, and gather my resolve.

"Helen won't be coming back."

Mother tilts her head as though I've slipped into an unfamiliar language. She doesn't ask me to repeat myself. Instead, she fixes me in a narrow-eyed glare and waits.

"We had a disagreement. I don't believe she's a good fit for us anymore."

"For me," she corrects.

A blush threatens my cheeks. I will not get angry. I will not. "For you. I don't believe she's a good fit for you."

"And I have absolutely no say in the matter of my care?"

I stifle a groan, and gnaw anxiously at the corner of my mouth. "Mother, I was under the distinct impression you didn't like Helen very much."

"Well, that's hardly the point, now is it? I don't like anyone very much. Most days I barely like you."

My hands clench around my empty mug, and stare out past her into the empty hall. She's baiting me, but for the life of me I can't understand where the sudden loyalty to a woman she tormented daily is coming from. "There was an argument. Helen and I fell on opposing sides, and I asked her to leave."

"An argument about my care?"

"Yes, Mother. As in all things, it was about you." The bite in my tone does not go unnoticed.

"Oh no, dear," she checks me swiftly with staggering assuredness, and one stern finger raised in defiance. "This argument, this decision made entirely without my consent and on my behalf, was all about you."

I stand abruptly, using the excuse of my empty cup to put some distance between us. The mug pounds sharply against the sink. "Is that what bothers you? That your Power of Attorney made a decision without your input?"

Mother isn't derailed. "Anything decided for me without my input bothers me a great deal."

Scrubbing my face with my hands, I stand in front of her, all my hostility painted in place, forever playing directly into her hand. She keeps her aggravation in check, rolling it around on her tongue to savor the taste. "A lady never shouts in an argument," she told me once. "Raised voices show weakness." I thrust an accusing finger in her face before I can think twice about it. "You hated Helen. You hated the idea of a nurse. You threatened her job on a weekly basis. I gave you *exactly* what you wanted."

"What I want is not to need a nurse, or care, or you. That is what I want. I want to be able to come and go as I please, without stumbling, without tremors, without lapses in my memory. That is what I want. I want to live my life on my terms. I resented Helen, but I was grateful to her for her service. For the illusion of independence. Which you would know, had you ever bothered to ask. What am I to do now, Elizabeth? Sit at home and knit?" she nearly spits the words through her clenched teeth.

I don't know what infuriates me more, the absolute sense she's making, or the kick her logic delivers to my own wounded ego. "Don't I sit and wait for you, Mother? Haven't I sacrificed everything to be here with you?" The second the words leave my mouth, self-preservation tries in vain to blame the outburst on my profound lack of sleep. Regardless, it's the one thing you never say to a dependent, no matter how impossible they are.

Mother smiles and stares down at her long elegant hands. I can practically hear her counting to calm herself. A storm rages in us both.

"Who asked you to be here? Will you never tire of blaming me for your life?"

"You didn't have to ask. You called and I came home from college, like you knew I would. I packed up everything to brave this with you. I shelved my ambition, my goals, my plans to care for you. And you can barely manage a kind word."

Mother stands and washes her mug carefully, setting it gently on the counter to dry. Her every action is an unspoken criticism. She gazes out the window overlooking the backyard which is still in dusky shadows. Knowing I'm wrong isn't the same as admitting she's right, but she would take a victory lap either way.

"And then there was Dominic."

I haven't spoken his name, or even thought of him since it ended, so I don't know why it feels like playing a winning card. It's a low blow, even for me, and I'm vaguely sickened by my own implication that my carelessly mishandled ex-fiancé is somehow her fault. He was the kindest man I've ever known, and he loved me beyond reason. She never even met him, and that's on me. I didn't think she'd be won over by a communications major with a white smile and perfectly black hair who laughed too hard, and too often.

"Please," she dismisses. "That wasn't love. It was escapism." She doesn't know how right she is. Or maybe she does. Dom and I were all too eager to build a new life. It was the heady rush of orphans who've never been of much use or consequence to anyone. "If you were serious about that boy you wouldn't have left him. You've always been stubborn. You get that from me. It's easily my least favorite thing about you."

"And with a blessing like that, who wouldn't marry him?"

Her stiff shoulders slump, but it isn't an admission of defeat. She faces me again and doesn't seek to hide her unmitigated disappointment. It's the same expression she wore when I told her I didn't want to pursue music any longer. The same expression as when I told her I was engaged. Dom was simple and I adored that about him, as well as the uncomplicated way he adored me back. When I returned his ring, he sat in my dorm room, on the edge of my narrow twin mattress and wept openly for three hours, begging me to let him come to Chicago and help. To stay with him, or to let him stay with me.

"Elizabeth," she begins, hands clasped firmly in front of her. "By your own account, I have failed as a wife, a mother, and am now too feeble of mind and body to look after myself. Yet still you persist in blaming me for your own shortcomings." She takes a purposeful step forward. "I won't have it. The hardest thing in this world, for any woman, is to be your own person. Facing your failures and refusing to accept them? That's step one."

She reaches behind herself and dries her hands with a clean rag, as though wiping my weakness away.

"So, you want another nurse?"

Mother crows at my rebuttal, stopping in front me with the pitying stare.

"Have a good day at work, dear." She pats my cheek, and wanders down the hall.

* * *

I should have called in sick again, but honestly, I have no idea what came over me yesterday, and I can't justify another evening at home when there is work to be done. Not to mention, it's anyone's guess how much longer I'll be able to keep this job, and after this morning I'd much rather deal with the comatose and infirm. I've been running on autopilot in a distracted daze for most of my shift checking charts, vitals, and drips.

The altercation with Mother plays on a loop in my head. I absolutely blamed her for my failed engagement, but if I'd loved Dom I wouldn't have let her opinion of him matter. And I did make the decision to terminate Helen without consulting her first, despite the fact that it directly affects her. I have put the weight of my unfulfilled dreams on her illness, which is probably the most selfish thing a child can do.

I could have found a way to keep studying, and Dom would have married me no matter where we lived. But I'd hit a wall months before that fateful phone call led me back to Mother's doorstep. It's a terrible thing to realize that the life you've been building doesn't interest you. Not the science—that has always moved me—and academia was hardly a struggle. I was gifted in that respect, but something about the life I envisioned had soured by senior year.

The title of Doctor still thrills me, if only for the respect it demands. I let my cynicism get the best of me. After all, my father was treated by the finest doctors in the state, the very practitioners he dutifully protected from the occasional malpractice suit. Consequently, my mother has countless medical contacts who can treat her symptoms, but they can't save her life.

I spend half my shift pulling myself back to the present and focusing on what I can control, while reassuring my more observant coworkers than I'm no longer ill. Stomach bug, a twenty-four-hour virus. I'm sure they know a lie when they hear one, but I have a spotless track record. I'm a model employee. I was a model student once too.

There's a new face in room four-twelve. Mr. Greer. Several patients have come and gone through that door over the last few weeks, and thankfully Mr. Greer is none of my concern tonight. That small forgotten corner of our wing frightens me beyond reason. Every time I pass the room, the stench of dried blood plagues me.

Last week, I was certain that I felt a presence lingering in the door, but when I turned around I was alone—exactly as expected considering the hour. I turned just in time for a rush of air to sweep across my cheek, and watched in silent apprehension as the emergency exit drifted closed. Remembering it now makes my blood run cold, and I find myself absently stroking the skin of my wrist. The place her fingers fit around so perfectly, before she pinned me down. I haven't been able to shake the memory of her touch all day.

Frustrated by my own paranoia, I busy myself. Whatever I can put my hands on I rearrange to keep occupied. I refuse to continue with this ridiculous notion that a woman I met once, and briefly at that, has made it her mission in life to lurk behind my closed shower curtain, just around the corner, directly behind me, in the hall, on the subway platform, or is inexplicably planting violins to garner my attention.

The absurdity causes me to break out with hysterical laughter. James asks in his dry prodding way, what I find so hilarious about Post-it notes. I manage to get a hold of myself. "You wouldn't believe me if I told you. Or worse, you'd think there was something seriously wrong with me."

"Now you have to tell me." He folds his arms resolutely across his chest, his feet crossed at the ankle, content to linger in my space until I'm forced to confess.

"Do you ever catch yourself daydreaming about something so absurd, you just can't help but laugh?"

He cocks his head like a confused puppy, but the sly smile on his lips tells me that the taunt is forthcoming. "Yes…" he manages thoughtfully. "That is a common thing we human beings do. Laugh at ourselves."

I swat his thigh with an empty folder, and turn my attention back to the pens I've begun sorting by color and size.

"Lighten up," he urges. "I was just messing with you. Tell me what you were thinking about that had you laughing like that."

"Not happening."

He whips the chair out from behind his legs and drops backward in the seat with his arms draped over the headrest. "Three guesses, and if I'm right you are bound by decency to tell me."

Irritated, but mildly amused by the simple fact that he could not possibly guess, I indulge him. For once. "Only three. And if you're wrong, you leave me to my OCD."

"Scouts' honor." He raises the three-finger salute.

"*You* were a Boy Scout?"

"Eagle Scout," he corrects, scratching the stubble on his chin and squinting his eyes in thought. "You were thinking about my ass."

"No."

James rubs his hands together and closes his eyes, like a carnival fortune teller. He strokes his temples in slow circles, and a begrudging smile threatens my scowl.

"You were picturing me naked."

"James," I admonish. "How devastated would you be if I, or any woman, were picturing you naked and laughing hysterically?"

He raises two defensive hands. "You're right. That would be tragic. Let me think…" He drops his hands to his knees and meditates for a moment.

"One guess left," I warn.

"Silence, please. I need to concentrate."

He does have a certain charm. I can see why so many of my colleagues have fallen victim to his smile. James knows the childish flirting works, because it's worked his whole life. And I have pictured him naked—he's not wrong about that.

What would he say if I told him that I dreamed of him last night? That I brought him into my bed and reveled in the weight of his body against mine? I nearly lose myself to the memory as I stare at him, still miming deep concentration. His strong hands wrapped around my thighs. His breath hot in my ear. My arms closing around his smooth waist. Fingers dancing up the notches of her spine. Tangling my hands in soft blond hair, and bringing our mouths close but not touching. Black eyes hovering above me, consuming, entitled, freezing my actions, muting my thoughts. The whisper of my name falling from her lips and—

"I got it!" James announces with a clap. The sound is as jarring as a defibrillator to the chest. My face remains a mask of polite inquiry and genuine surprise. "You were thinking about letting me take you out tomorrow night," he says.

At first, I can't say much of anything. My breathing has picked up, and I'm certain he can see the blush blooming up my neck. "Yes." I unfold my arms and clasp my hands resignedly in my lap. "That's exactly what I was thinking."

His smile falls away. "Seriously?"

I clear my throat and force an airiness I do not feel. "Seriously."

"Just like that?" He asks with eyes too shrewd for his welcoming face. "After, what? A year of asking?" He's at a loss, and stands with his hands on his waist.

"Forget it." Flustered with my own stupidity, I resume my abandoned task of sorting supplies. "Forget I said anything."

"No—I," he stammers. "Listen…you just surprised me, is all."

I spare him a stiff smile over my shoulder and a casual shrug.

"Pick you up at eight?" he offers.

I cannot imagine anything more exhausting than my day off with my furious, impaired mother, followed by a meal with this man. "Sounds great."

James responds with a firm nod, and it clearly takes all his composure not to fist pump the air. He struts a little too triumphantly down the hall toward his neglected patients.

* * *

This is the most I've ever overreacted in my life.

An overtly sexual dream about a woman in my bed is not a reason to go out with a man I find barely tolerable on a good day. Or any man for that matter. Clearly, this is cause to spend an evening at a lesbian bar, or resurrect the dating profile I deleted six months ago and change my orientation to "questioning."

The problem isn't that I'm curious about women, or being attracted to them. That's not new. The problem is *this* woman. I can't get rid of her. She's everywhere. She's in my head, my dreams, she's like a second skin around me all day. Sometimes, I hear her voice, see her as plainly as my own reflection—if only for an instant. I know the way she smells. I've exchanged all of five words with this person—none of which I recall. It's an alarmingly unhealthy preoccupation because it doesn't make sense. She's familiar to me in a way I can't fully comprehend, and I swear I can feel her, like twins on opposite ends of the earth claim to know when the other is injured or in pain.

Instead of picking up my phone and telling James that this is a mistake: "I'm not feeling well." "I have a prior commitment," "I have grossly underestimated my attraction to the fairer sex,"—I'm pacing the length of my bedroom in my underwear with every article of clothing I own strewn across my bed. I pick up the twice-discarded black Armani dress and hold it up in the mirror. It's safe, classic, and I have completely forgotten what people wear on dates. The neckline is lower than I would like, scooped, nothing drastic. Full sleeves, and the hem hits tastefully below mid-thigh without being somber.

Shoes are a much easier decision as I have no idea where he's taking me. Flats in a crisis.

I make one final appraisal of the finished product, and I'm reasonably pleased with the results. The foundation smeared over my dark circles reveals only the faintest trace of lavender. With the pad of my index finger, I blend the crease of my eyelids once more to mute the shadow. Overall, I look more like a woman running late for an interview than an evening out. But as in all things, I do my level best.

With a weary sigh, I retrieve my clutch from the top drawer of my nightstand and move softly and swiftly down the stairs, as sure-footed as a burglar. I could cartwheel to the front door if I felt so moved. Mother has confined herself to her bedroom since yesterday, appearing only when she's hungry. She'd never ask where I'm headed. Not when there's an impasse to maintain. I leave a note on the island just in case.

Something close to excitement swells within me the moment I step out into the murky evening. The humidity is unseasonable, and a fine sheen of dew glistens on the sidewalk. James flashes the headlights on his Civic, and to my surprise he's out of the front seat in a flash, holding the passenger door open before I can protest. I've never seen him in anything but scrubs. He cleans up well: expensive loafers, dark chinos, a crisp lavender shirt. I smile at the effort, and his unexpected chivalry.

"Elizabeth, you look amazing," he remarks seriously, settling his hands at ten and two on the wheel. It's like prom night all over again.

"Thank you. For the compliment, and for not calling me Liz."

"I thought you'd like that." He winks, and revs the engine the superfluous way men do before whipping the car back onto the road. The rearview mirror clouds with exhaust, leaving my mother and my responsibilities behind.

* * *

James is both charming and inquisitive, without appearing pushy or overzealous. He's a good listener, a fair sport and slightly self-deprecating which is a surprise. He's extremely pleasant to talk to, even asks about my mother, but in a roundabout way that is casual enough to be easily dismissed in case it's a sore subject. Mother almost always is, and with practiced ease James redirects the conversation to his own quirky parents.

I'd forgotten how enjoyable it can be to talk about the past with someone, to laugh in public. By the time the meal is finished my ribs ache, and I can't push away the nostalgia it engenders. I'd blame it on the balmy evening air, but we're indoors.

When James suggests an after dinner drink, I agree without having to be coerced which emboldens him. As we leave the restaurant he takes my hand and keeps me close. I should have foreseen the venue. It's much more the atmosphere I envisioned for someone as playful and gregarious as James, and couldn't be a worse choice for me. But I suspected the moment we sat down that he was uncomfortable in the upscale restaurant.

Thunderous music quakes the pavement from at least a block away. The bouncer opens a dreary door, and dizzying lights slice through the crowd in green and blue beams that make my head spin. I haven't stepped inside a club in years.

Like a scalpel James cuts through the throbbing crush of bodies, shaking hands, and screaming introductions that drown in the bedlam. He changes our trajectory and veers off to the bar. He yells his order at the bartender, his fingers held up in a V to indicate shots for both of us. I tug on his sleeve and wave a hand in his face, telling him I don't want one. He smiles, and hugs me around the shoulders in a friendly embrace. Reduced to lip-reading does nothing to dull James's enthusiasm when he hands me a squat glass of tequila.

"Shots," he yells, clinking our glasses.

"Bad idea! No." My protest would sound more convincing if I wasn't laughing and could actually be heard.

"Good idea!" He nods. "Yes!" Our speech has been reduced to single syllables. He sets up lime and salt. "You've done this before, right?" Pressed directly to my ear, I can hear him fine.

"I'm reserved, James, not sheltered," I respond, drawing as close to him as I can with a barstool between us.

He settles the lime in my hand and licks the side of my index finger, sprinkling it with salt. I'd be lying if I said the contact was less than enjoyable. "Good to know," he shouts, and with a countdown we lick the salt from each other's hands and set our throats ablaze with alcohol. The blistering heat makes my eyes water, and I forget the lime until I see him bite into his. The acid forces my body into submission, and my vision quickly clears. My stomach swims immediately, and James balks at my tolerance, or lack thereof. He warns me not to throw up in his car. When I shove his shoulder, he kisses my cheek.

After three shots, a seemingly endless screaming match, and quite a bit of pushing, James pulls me through the horde and out onto the dance floor. The music isn't unbearable anymore, and the bass thumps pleasantly in my chest. James is an adept lead, guiding my hips with steady hands as the songs bleed one onto the next, in a cacophonous, electric symphony.

The longer we're out here, moving against each other, the more convinced I become that the last four years of my life have been a lie. I'm young. I have my whole life ahead of me. Under the right circumstances, I might even be fun. With each song, James manages to draw closer. We don't shout anymore, everything we need to say we communicate through touch, and when the beat drops to a low rumble he turns my back to him. I feel his lips part, breath heavy in my hair, against the side of my neck. I close my eyes and rest my hand on the back of his head as his lips brush below my ear.

Elizabeth.

My name rings out more clearly than the bass thumping in the floorboards—firm and chastising—but I can't make out the source.

Definitely not James, who is still distracting himself by nibbling at my jaw. It's impossible to see in this strobing half-light. I squint into the crowd, pulling away from my dance partner. The lights overhead drop in red streams that bathe her rancorous face.

Stela is standing to my left, not fifteen feet away, stoic against the pulsing bodies that claw at her like they're worshipping some Grecian divinity. In the mere seconds it takes for my eyes to adjust, to lock on her obsidian eyes, a chilling certainty washes over me: she is visible only because she wants to be seen. A terror unequal to anything I've ever known floods my system with adrenaline and dread so potent I launch myself out of James's arms.

Without a single glance in either his direction or hers, I bulldoze through the heart of the inferno. I see nothing but my own hands and feet, pushing at the damp flesh of scantily clad strangers, stepping on toes. *Get to the door. Get out.* I don't turn or slow to apologize, despite the curses of bruised clubbers. She's moving in time with me, toward me, and closing the insignificant gap with ease—I'm sure of it. But I will not check to see if she's really there, or if I've finally snapped. For the first time since this nightmare began, I pray for the latter.

By dumb luck, I find the door and fling myself against the barrel belly of the bouncer. He brushes me away like an insect, dismissing my frantic cries as the frenetic ramblings of a tweaked customer. He places his large paw against the small of my back and shoves me outside. I don't attempt to explain my situation again, there isn't time. I run as fast as I can, thinking oddly that flats were a smart choice. I zip past the shadowed faces of couples enjoying a night in the city, lovers on bus stop benches, distracted pedestrians arguing over cabs until the scenery changes into homeless women pushing carts, and dirty old men leaning in darkened doorways.

Rounding the corner, I slip between two weathered buildings. My back is drenched with sweat, and the bricks feel cool. I peek my head back out onto the street, certain she'll be waiting on the other side of the wall. But the city is still.

I let my head thud back against the brick wall. She isn't there. She never was. Slowly, my breathing returns to normal, and when I notice the persistent sounds of sirens, I reach for my phone. First, to figure out how far I am from the nearest train, and second, to text James that I was ill and had to leave. I have never heard the sound of a gun being cocked at my head, but it's a sound my body seems to recognize on instinct. I drop my eyes to my feet, and freeze without waiting for instruction.

"Purse and phone. Now."

I offer up my belongings in two trembling hands, but I resist the urge to look. "Please. I haven't seen anything."

"No?" A hand snatches my last ties to civilization, and a pair of dingy sneakers settle directly in front of me. There's a faint rustle of fabric as he drops my cell into his front pocket, and tucks my clutch in the waist of his jeans. "Look at you." He whistles. "All dressed up." Grimy fingers pluck at the front of my dress, just above my navel. "Lemme guess. You had a fight with the boyfriend and decided to walk home."

"You have what you want. I can't call the police. Couldn't give them a description of you if I did." I don't know how my voice remains steady.

The man wraps his fist in my hair and yanks my head back. I open my mouth to scream, but he pushes the barrel of the gun past my lips. He's young, early thirties, with a face as pockmarked as the bricks behind me. His lips are cracked and peeling in salty flakes. Hazel eyes, bloodshot and bulging. Greasy hair tucked into a knitted cap. His breath is foul.

"Scream and I will fucking shoot you. Nod your head."

Tears roll over my eyelids. I nod and he moves closer, greedily inhaling his fistful of my hair. I turn away, searching the dimly lit alley for something, anything I can use against him. His body presses against me, one hand settled at my waist as the gun slides out of my mouth leaving a trail of spit along my cheek. His hand is gone from my body as suddenly as it arrived. He's ripped away from me in a rush of wind, and a single gunshot rings through the air—shattering the sickening quiet.

Her back is to me, and she has both arms wrapped around my assailant. He tries to kick at the air. She hoists him skyward, his arms trapped at his sides, and his spine snaps in a series of sharp clicks. She throws him facefirst into the brick wall and his skull makes an audible crack as his knees crumble to the ground. The gun slips through his limp fingers and drops to the pavement with a feeble clatter.

She grabs him by the hair and twists his neck up to her mouth. The wet sound of his flesh tearing in her teeth has me screaming.

I scream until I can't hear anything else, until I'm faint from the force of my own expelled air and my legs buckle beneath me into a pool of warm, fresh blood. She drops the body and it smacks against the ground.

I touch my fingers to the blood around my knees, on my calves, my dress, and realize belatedly that the blood is mine. I try to check my pulse, but my left arm hangs limp at my side—a gush of blood oozing from my bicep. The pain is immediate, white-hot and searing. I cover the wound with my right hand, unable to scream anymore.

Stela stands over me, blood dripping down her chin. Only half her face is visible from the streetlight on the corner, and she is a portrait of indifference.

"He shot me." I lift my crimson-stained hand to her in starry-eyed amazement before my vision tilts the landscape, and paints the whole city black.

V
Preludes

She folds forward in half—bent perfectly at the waist, like a child's paper doll—her hands at her sides, forehead resting on her knees. Before I can resist, I savor the air with an unnecessary breath to taste the ripe life still pulsing down her punctured arm. My hands curl at my sides and I turn away from her to evict the seductive scent from my lungs.

What to do with them now? Two bodies, my car blocks away and beyond, a crowd. It would be impossible to carry them both unnoticed such a distance. A single street camera in an intersection, or a night shift worker standing at a window would mean my head. Worse, we could attract the scrupulous gaze of an upstanding police officer—be there any left in this city whose silence my brother has not ensured—out on a routine patrol.

Why could this guy not have satisfied himself with just a robbery? I stare down at his motionless heap of bones and soft meat, and raise my leg to strike him with my heel. I stop just short of his ribcage. Another bruise is one more damnable piece of evidence. "Acquired post mortem" on the autopsy report, and the police would suspect the kill was personal. Which it was.

"Ridiculous." I lift my head to the stars. It was utter foolishness to intervene. The sky is dense with thick clouds of black and blue exhaust, the pollution rife and stagnant in the humid air. A world in decay, inundated with senseless violence, and dressed in faux opulence. This city reeks of their waste. Animals, as my Lord said. Cruel, ruthless, dishonorable, and spoiled.

I take a handkerchief from my blazer and scrub my mouth and chin clean, forcing myself to look upon her. Elizabeth's face is barely turned toward the street, smoothed as though in sleep. I stare down at her would-be attacker. I could reduce him to nothing more than a stain on the pavement. Instead, I strip his carcass of the belt and retrieve Elizabeth's mobile and purse from his pants.

I kneel beside her, mindful of the enticing, black pool curling out from under her legs. The blood is thick but quick to push its way free from the shell of her skin, and my head swims at the thought of finishing her here. There would be peace in the act, for both of us. Her sleep would be endless, and I would be free of her scattered thoughts throughout my day. A return to the silence, as dense as the stillness that swims around us now.

Silence.

I hear nothing from her. No runaway thoughts, or fears, or hopes. I jerk her injured limb toward me, and the bullet glistens against the bone like a bronzed pearl. My blood will be of no use to her until it is removed, lest the bullet be sealed inside her forever. If it were my own wound, I would tear the flesh with my fingers, and pry the shrapnel loose like a shucked oyster. But she is weak and chilling fast. I rip the sleeve of her gown at the shoulder and strip the compromised limb, using the fabric to soak up the blood and make a tourniquet of her attacker's belt.

Elizabeth's head rolls back when I lift her upright. I puncture my wrist with my teeth and open her mouth, rubbing her neck to move the blood down her throat. The offering is enough to make her pulse quicken, which bodes well for the drive ahead. I lean her back against the brick and her chin drops down to her chest, as lifelessly as before.

Standing over the discarded young ruffian, I roll him on his back with the toe of my boot and smear a few drops of my blood over the gash in his throat. The blood circles the flowering flesh and disappears inside a new layer of skin. I do the best I can with such limited time. I wrap the gun in his cold fingers, and hope the injuries to his face and spine, the single defensive shot fired, and the smattering of Elizabeth's blood on the wall are enough to suggest gang violence. And should some ambitious medical examiner see fit to draw attention to his unexplainable blood loss, I trust Bård's associates to bury both the inquiry and inquisitor.

Elizabeth weighs nothing in my arms. I cradle her head close to keep her neck from breaking as I run down long deserted service roads to my car several blocks away. All the while, the beating of her heart grows fainter, more erratic. I lay her gently in the passenger seat, pulling the seat belt across her lap.

My keys are in the ignition before I can properly seat myself, and Elizabeth's torso peels away from the window as I whip the vehicle across four lanes of heavy traffic. Her head knocks against my shoulder, her face upturned. I chance one hand from the wheel and push a damp strand of blood-soaked hair from her cheek. Her peaceful face fills me with dread. I press the back of my fingers to her chest, just above her heart. Her skin is cooler than mine.

* * *

Mr. Collins's van is absent from the parking lot when we arrive at Carrington's. If there were a god I should thank it for this small mercy. The last thing I need is for our newest associate to mention my stray to Bård.

Derek's lone figure in the dingy light of the basement door is a welcome sight. I whip the car so close to his legs that he takes a leap back over the threshold.

"Get inside," I demand before I have opened the driver's side door. "Now." He stumbles indoors with his hands raised above his head and I heave Elizabeth's body from the front seat, following close at his heels.

"Kathryn…what—"

"Bolt the door."

Derek does as he is told, and I lay Elizabeth's chilled body on the embalming table as softly as on a marital bed. He takes a moment to understand that I do not deposit her by accident, gaze darting from the table to the cremator. He rushes to my side and makes a quick evaluation. I have always appreciated his haste.

There is the faintest hint of blush lingering in her lips and cheek. I would not expect any mortal to notice, were it not their business to deal in death.

"She's alive?" he gasps, covering his mouth as if to capture the words before they can reach me. I rip the makeshift bandage from her bicep.

"She is very near death. Fetch pliers, a rag, and a bowl."

Derek freezes. He eyes me suspiciously, the fear blanching his handsome face, and the unspoken *why* hangs heavily between us.

"Do not make me repeat myself," I warn. "I am in no mood." Poor manners to address an ally so harshly, but Derek responds well to clear instruction. He grabs what I need, and sets the basin beside her head.

"Leave us," I command. "Stand outside until I retrieve you."

"Why are you doing this?" He asks, standing by the door, unable to help himself. His chest heaves and falls with heavy panting breaths. I bat the bright overhead lamp away from Elizabeth. I can see the bullet just as well without it, and the stark light makes her look as though she already has one foot firmly planted in the grave.

"She is an innocent," I reply, and the sentiment is as ill-conceived as this entire evening. I do not believe in the word any more than I believe in hell. In fact, I cannot recall a time when I have applied the term to anyone. But Derek looks upon her with compassion which bleeds to confusion when he finds my face again. He marches out, settling the door closed behind him.

The bullet shimmers defiantly. I hold the flesh of her arm apart with my fingers and bring the pliers down. The bone makes a sharp crack when I pluck the mangled metal from its twisted crater. I check her face for pain, but Elizabeth is beyond that now—blissfully unaware. The world kept locked away behind her heavy, ashen lids. The bullet rattles once against the lid of the trash can, and falls to the bottom with an impotent thump.

Rushed by her deathly repose, I dig through drawers until I find a syringe large enough to deliver the last gift I intend to give this woman. I shove the needle heedlessly into the icy blue vein darting down my forearm—visible only because of my recent feed—and fill the vial to capacity. More care is needed with Elizabeth, and I inject her above and below the bullet's entry point, watching the skin pucker in response. The exposed bone splinters into place, polishing itself smooth. I do not savor the process, fascinating as it is, before plunging the needle down through her breastplate and emptying the rest of the blood into her heart.

Elizabeth rears up off the table with a gasp like that of the recently drowned, and a wet cough rattles her heaving chest. Her eyes are wild, flitting about the gloomy room. Her unscathed right arm swings frantically, her hand groping the empty air for something to hold on to. I remain bent over her wounded arm as the last slivers of exposed flesh repair. The wound will heal completely in a day or so, as a bullet wound is much more severe than a bite. She will scar. She knots a startlingly strong fist in the front of my blouse and stares up at me, mute from exhaustion and predictably terrified.

Elizabeth's eyes show a hundred emotions, only a handful of which I can decipher, and not a single one resembling gratitude. Fear, of course, but anger too, pressing her lips into a thin and unforgiving line. Her brow—so undisturbed moments ago—is ridged with confusion. She parts her lips to speak and I pry her fingers from my shirt, placing her arm at her side.

I walk over to the sink and fill the washbasin with warm water. When I resume my place beside her, the fight for life has all but exhausted Elizabeth, and she has fallen back against the table. I tear the soiled dress from her torso and slip it off her weakened frame. Her heart thunders, one strong arm lashing out to knock me away, and though the rest of her is too weak to offer much protest, every inch of her tenses in alarm. I press my hand down against her sternum.

"Calm yourself." I wet the rag and lift it to her eyes. She locks her jaw and ragged breaths steam from flared nostrils—she intends to do nothing of the sort. Even my fixed stare is no match for her outrage—an alarming development in its own right—my blood within her acting as a potent antidote to my gaze.

Left with few options, and dangerously short on time, I test our tenuous link. *Elizabeth.* The name moves through her, as it moves through me. Still rigid under my hands, she relents her physical protest, confounded into momentary submission. Whatever this is, she feels it too. With the warm rag I wipe away the blood that has dried in ruby streaks down the length of her body. She relaxes somewhat into the welcomed heat, watching me closely, a thousand objections rushing through her mind, which is louder and clearer than either of us would like.

I gather the tattered remnants of her black dress and my own ruined coat, her head rolling around the table after me, eyes never leaving my face. Elizabeth grips the edges of the table as I open the furnace door, convinced I mean to throw her inside. Which is exactly what I should do, what I seriously consider doing as I pitch each article of clothing into the fire. Her unspoken suspicion is oddly offensive in light of the trouble I have taken to ensure her safety. But she is wise not to trust.

Beside the cellar door rests not one, but three brown paper packages all stacked neatly together and penned in Lydia's elegant script. One marked Birgir for my brother Bård, the other Dilay for the woman herself, and the last package labeled Kathryn—a potent reminder that my siblings could arrive at any moment with fresh kills in tow. With renewed haste, I snatch my clean clothes and stand over Elizabeth, shredding the wrapping to reveal a fresh set of jeans and a plain black shirt.

"We must hurry," I say, hooking the denim around her feet. "The others are coming." Her eyes seek mine and I sense that some part of her knows the truth of it all already. She lets me slide the clothing up her bare legs, suddenly much more amenable to my aid. Her good arm instinctively covers her breasts, despite the presence of her undergarments. There is something Boticellian in her modesty as I pull the waistband up over her hips. I lift her shoulders to slip the shirt around her back, and she holds that arm over her chest until the last possible moment—a portrait of Venus in my arms.

"Have you the strength to stand?"

Elizabeth lifts her chin at the challenge and I finish buttoning her blouse. I wrap my arms around her waist and pull her forward against me onto two unsteady legs. I take a step back to clear away the last vestiges of our visit. She takes two firm steps behind me and collapses facefirst into my shoulder. I turn as carefully as I can and lift Elizabeth into my arms as her eyes roll back. She is alive, but what strength my blood bought her has gone. Her face is fevered, slightly damp with sweat and pressed into the crook of my neck.

I swing through the basement door, carting Elizabeth into the parking lot. Derek scrambles up off the curb, and opens the passenger side door. I deposit her gently in the passenger seat, tucking her limbs tight to her body and seal her inside the car.

"Where are you taking her?" Derek's voice startles me, and I whip around in his direction with shoulders squared for a fight. He raises his empty hands again and takes a step back into the looming shadows of the building. I relax my stance, and walk around the front of the car.

"Home."

"You know this woman?"

Poor fellow. Derek sees his folly when I turn on him. His eyes wash with fear so fresh, I can taste it in the balmy night air. He cannot be left to report this, neither can he be killed.

I seize him swiftly by the biceps. Derek struggles in my grasp, but unlike Elizabeth now—and as any mortal would without the protection of our blood—he succumbs immediately to my stare.

Each and every time Fane has reached into the recesses of my mind, I felt a stirring of instinct, an awakening I have become adept at ignoring. I recognized the ability in myself and yearned to test my limits, to wield it for myself.

Derek's mind unfurls before my eyes, and the evening spreads out around us, like a map studded with photographs. I wade through the images, scattered in disarray, until I stumble into a space that holds the story of my comings and goings tonight. Some pictures are sharp and defined, some darkened and overexposed—clouded with terror. One by one I reach in and pluck them from the tethers that string them all together. The tethers snap like finishing line, and drift away from him. Every likeness of Elizabeth, her face, her wound, is stripped from the halls of his memory, and only a handful of my own face remains.

When I release Derek, he wears the same dazed expression that Elizabeth had during our first meeting. He stares blankly, blinking slowly as though lost, removed from himself. The swoon should pass quickly. I clasp him firmly on the shoulder and begin talking about nothing in particular: proper disposal of a body, my dislike of Collins, my gratitude to him and my esteem of his long-deceased parents. Derek catches a few of these words, parroting them back to me in a desperate attempt to find his footing in the conversation.

Pride rises in me. It seems that Fane is not the only being gifted with this power to alter others' thoughts and memory, though I would have bet my life that such an insight was reserved for the Moroi alone. And through this new skill, can I secure for myself a kind of freedom? Certain now of how Fane sees my thoughts, should I not be able to control what he sees?

"Get inside, my friend. Birgir and Dilay will arrive shortly, no doubt." Derek nods his head and stumbling once on the curb, hobbles inside with his hands out to steady him.

Light-headed, and reeling from the exertion, I plant myself behind the wheel and roll down the driver's side window to welcome the night air. Beside me, Elizabeth snores softly, her head slumped back against the seat.

A pleased smile curls the corner of my lips. Perhaps she is a secret I can keep for a while longer. The desire to keep her close, to keep her safe is disconcerting. I had not realized that it was concern for her wellbeing and not simple bloodlust that has been fueling my actions these past few weeks. And why her? Why should this woman be any different?

Elizabeth's blood is caked on my fingers. I release the steering wheel and pull two fingers into my mouth, letting my tongue dance around them briefly. Her distinct taste hits the roof of my mouth, renewing my fury, and I strangle the moan that threatens to rip its way through my chest.

"I should have let him kill you."

* * *

This is not my first visit to her home, but it is the first time I have entered through the patio door. Carrying Elizabeth in my arms I step into the pristine kitchen and slide the door closed behind us, careful not to rouse her from sleep as I make my way toward the stairs. A strange compulsion keeps me from mounting the staircase straight away, and instead, I find myself standing at the threshold of her living room, exactly the room I found myself in when her dream bled into mine.

My sure steps, as even and delicate as they are, still cause the faintest creak in the hardwood floor. Elizabeth's body stirs against me and she pulls her injured arm close to her chest. Sleep licks the wrinkles from the corners of her eyes and I hold her closer, standing at the mouth of a dark hallway. At the top of it, behind the closed door, Elizabeth's mother snores loudly. I can picture the room perfectly, Claire's position on the bed, Elizabeth standing above her. The black mourning gown, her loose hair spilling down her back as she seals a pillow over her mother's face. Was the dream a metaphor, or repressed desire? I could fancy a guess, but I suspect that only the heart beating beside my own will ever know the truth.

Upstairs, the faintest whispers of girlhood ghost about the bedroom: photographs of young smiling faces, a few gilded statues on a dust-laden shelf heralding her early triumphs. I place Elizabeth on the meticulous bedclothes, and miss the intoxicating heat of her the moment we part.

My blood-stained hands and soiled shirt offer me a temporary distraction, and I move about the room for a change of clothes. Not surprisingly the drawers are stuffed with her uniforms. I linger over a gray T-shirt. The garment is soft, an obvious favorite riddled with her scent. I pull the shirt on, staring at a picture of Elizabeth smiling brightly with her face pressed to the cheek of another young woman. They both hold violins in their raised hands. She looks happy, proud.

My reflection in her dressing mirror shows the shirt as a ridiculous choice, impossible to explain and certainly not an article Lydia would choose. I consider selecting another, but Elizabeth's scent envelopes me and it seems no more a choice than leaving the room before she wakes.

Elizabeth's violin catches my eye, the shimmering body gleaming in the lamplight. I run my stained fingers down the strings and feel the vibrations beneath my skin more clearly than I can hear them. I have never made the effort to learn to play an instrument though music interests me a great deal. I settle the lid of the case over the violin, casting a glance over my shoulder, but Elizabeth remains motionless.

The least I can do is allow her to rest in blissful ignorance for a few hours more. The world will be changed when she wakes, and what will I tell her? What will she ask of me? The answers are not mine to give when her reaction could jeopardize the safety of my entire family. Night wanes outside her window, and the deadly grip of sleep rises as the approach of the sun sinks its teeth into me. Soon the pull will be too great to resist without considerable pain, and the new day will evict me from her bedside. That is if my host doesn't do so first.

With a fitful sigh Elizabeth rolls over on her side, but the bruise on her left arm forces her on her back and traps her hand beneath her thigh. Quietly, I stand over her and adjust her arm. Her mouth relaxes, and her furrowed features grow soft. I sit on the edge of the mattress and listen to her steady breath, studying her. Purple bruises smeared below both eyes, and an ashen kiss to her cheeks. I would brush them off as symptoms of near exsanguination were it not for the fact that she is noticeably thinner, a haunted and troubled creature. I nearly reach out to trace those sharp cheekbones, stopping myself. I rise and walk to the foot of the bed, standing with my back pressed to the edge of her dresser, as far as I can get without leaving the room.

The dirt-freckled sole of one bare foot twitches. Her eyelids flutter, impossibly heavy as she wrestles herself awake. The eyes widen in shock. Lips, parted in sleep, spread open and fall slack. Her chest stutters as she downs great gulps of air, scurrying up the mattress until the headboard braces her. She would climb the wall to get away from me, if she were able.

"I did not expect you to stir so soon." I tilt my head, amused and curious to learn how much she remembers. Elizabeth scowls, keeping still, but with that same protective posture, the roaming stare, searching some means to defend herself. When nothing presents itself, she pulls her knees close to the chest and remains rigid with her back pressed to the headboard.

"Who *are* you?" Her voice is weak, dry, and the sound is little more than a rustle of breeze past her trembling lips. I could not guess how many times I have been asked that question. It never occurred to me to answer any of them truthfully.

"A sizeable question for this time of night." I push up off the top of her dresser and stand with crossed arms at the foot of the bed. "You know who I am." My name tumbles inside of her, caught in a tangle of panic. She sifts it to the surface, holds the name close. A grimace contorts her stricken face as the pain in her arm surfaces, as the adrenaline wanes.

"Stela."

My name is not new. I have lived as Stela for centuries. A gift from my Lord to last several lifetimes, longer even. For all these years, only my name on Fane's tongue moved me, as it should be. Until now. "You should have full use of your arm within a few days." I shove my hands into the pockets of my trousers, anything to keep from reaching out for her.

Elizabeth tugs at the top button of her blouse, pulling the collar away to assess her injury. When she realizes that a full evaluation will require removing her clothing, she desists and cradles the compromised limb to her chest. Her eyes narrow, she licks her chapped lips and mouths the shape of several words, none of which come to fruition. Swallowing audibly, she pulls her right hand through her hair and shakes it back over her shoulders, wincing.

"You're not going to kill me," she alleges. I would believe the confident bluff, but for her staccato pulse. She sets her mouth in a firm line, and I cannot help the answering smile that sweeps across my lips. I walk to the bedroom window and part the sheer curtains. The sun has begun to warp the horizon from black to plum. We have so little time.

"You would have let me die in that alley if that's what you wanted."

"Are you reassuring yourself? Or are you asking me a question?"

Elizabeth's head snaps back as though slapped. She recovers quickly, gracefully despite the anger leeching off her ebbing fear. I turn toward her and she wills her body not to shake.

"No one deserves what that man had in mind for you."

Mention of her brush with death mollifies her momentarily. Her eyes grow distant, no doubt replaying the horrors in vivid detail. Unconsciously, she rubs her arm and an ugly realization ghosts over her. She nearly died this evening, but was spared. Elizabeth's mouth quakes once before she bites her lip. She does not cry. "You killed him."

My only reply is the arch of an eyebrow. Between us Elizabeth's heart pistons, as loud as an engine, drowning out every inconsequential sound. To look at her, one would never know. A misplaced pride swells in my breast, though her discipline has nothing at all to do with me. I have never seen a human come to terms with the fantastic truth of this world and react with anything less than abject horror—providing they were in their right mind, of course. I have skulked in shadows as they disinterred their loved ones and shoved stakes into freshly decomposing corpses. Flipped bodies face down in the grave. Drove twisted bits of iron through the eyelids, and severed the necks of their own children as they prayed.

Elizabeth takes a deep, fortifying breath. "What are you?" A better question, to be sure. Laced with the disgust I had been expecting.

"You know what I am."

Elizabeth shakes her head violently, as though physically expelling the thought from her mind. Denying the obvious. A sudden, anxious laugh spills out of her, not because of the brutality of what she has witnessed, but the sheer impossibility of it all. Her dauntless veneer slips, leaving her visibly shaken. She straightens her long neck, projecting a confidence we both know she does not feel.

"Are you going to kill me?" And this time, it is a question. One I cannot even begin to answer, and more abstruse than she realizes. Death, after all, is subjective.

I sit firmly on the edge of the bed with my hands clasped. She trembles, knotting her fingers in the crisp white sheets, but makes no move to run. I cannot undo what has been done. I cannot withdraw from her any more than I can expel her from my own heart. Though I have dreamed of this moment, I do not have the gall to tell her how this will end. A short answer is all I can offer in the way of peace; the conditions will have to be addressed when we have more time. If I am not accounted for before morning, Fane could force my siblings to come looking for me, and they would not be pleased to move about in the sun.

"No."

Elizabeth nods firmly, attempting to convince herself that she is safe, at least for now. She catches a rogue tear and relaxes back against the headboard, frightened but growing weary.

"Why are you doing this?" Scrutiny squares in her eyes. Her gaze moves down the side of my face and settles on her blood on my hands. I bring one leg up between us to face her and Elizabeth flinches. She promptly looks away. Repellent as my eyes may be, she can no more resist them than she can deprive herself of oxygen. She longs to linger in their shadow.

"I cannot justify my actions."

Elizabeth leans forward and the light of the bedside lamp cuts across her neck like the blade of a guillotine. I focus instead on the hinge of her jaw, tight with frustration. I linger on the cynical arch of her brow, and the warm, deep sepia of her eyes. A single, wavy curl falls in her face as she drifts closer, as though my reasoning is a whisper she cannot quite hear.

"What did you do to me?" The words knock sharply against her clenched teeth.

This time I am the one to look away. She is the only mortal I have ever marked for my own. Articulating that bond is more difficult than I imagined. How do you explain something at once so intrinsic, and yet so foreign without directly admitting that it was invoked irresponsibly in a single moment, and regretted immediately?

"Think of it as a door that swings open two ways." I turn to her completely, my legs folded to mirror her own, wrists resting on my shins. "The door that leads me to you opens fully and freely from my side. The door can be pushed open from your side as well, but only partially." Skeptical eyes search my face for sincerity—she is more frightened by the thought of being the brunt of a joke, than by the monster sitting on her bed—and some understanding I am not certain I can provide. What has happened to her is nothing practiced on my part. We are learning the subtleties together.

"A door?" The sarcasm drips heavily from her lips.

"I can think of no better way to describe it."

"I thought I was losing my mind. I had an MRI!" she snaps.

"Yes, that was an unfortunate surprise." With an aggravated huff, Elizabeth is up on her feet, pacing. She winces only once when she attempts to push herself from the bed with her injured arm. She holds it for a moment, pausing before resuming her brisk trail back and forth over the creaking floorboards.

"You were with me on the subway platform." Another accusation.

"In a sense."

"You took the business card out of my pocket."

"I merely suggested it. Impressed it upon you. You released the card of your own volition."

"Have you been stalking me?"

"Watching you."

"The violin?"

"Seemed a waste to keep such a fine instrument locked away."

Elizabeth halts, clasping both hands over her mouth. A scream builds inside of her, like wind caught in a sail. She swallows it back down, shaking from the effort. "This is my life," she says with dangerous calm. "Do you understand that?"

"Yes. And mine."

"What the *fuck* does that mean?" She stands above me with curled fists.

"It means that the door opens both ways. I have felt you with me, seen you in dreams, some mine, some yours." My patience has begun to thin, and her harsh tone is certainly no help. But I make every effort to remain calm, even if she cannot. Elizabeth has seen enough violence for one evening.

"*Felt* me? I've seen you, felt you, smelled you. Everywhere." Her voice rises steadily in pitch and volume with each word. "At work, at home, in my dreams. You drove me to the edges of my sanity."

"As you have said."

"I think it bears repeating!" She screams, stomping a foot to emphasize her distress. For a second neither of us moves, falling silent to listen for her mother. The unexpected quiet silences Elizabeth's bluster, and once again exhaustion softens her sharp edges. She sinks down beside me, and to my surprise, wraps pleading fingers around my wrist. Her touch is scalding and physical contact—no matter how chaste—is as dangerous as it is unwelcome at this juncture. My blood, moving through her veins, calls out to me. I savor the moment for as long as I possibly can, her elevated pulse beating in the pads of each fingertip.

"Please," she begs, tightening her hold. "Take it back." Her face is no longer a mask of contempt. "I didn't ask for this. I don't want it, whatever it is."

"I cannot change the past." My voice soft, and more troubling is my willingness to do or say anything and everything she desires.

"I'm not asking you to change the past," she explains in that same pleading way. "I'm asking you to stop."

"We are joined. That cannot be undone, Elizabeth."

"Joined?"

"I think we have discussed this matter enough for one evening." I attempt to extricate my hand, to stand, but she grips my shoulder and I relent. Beyond the window, unbeknownst to her, the sun has begun to hiss its imminent arrival in my ear. A burn buds at the back of my eyes, and I pinch the bridge of my nose to thwart the pain.

"You called it a door. *How* is there a door? *Why* is there a door?" Elizabeth's face seems to round itself in honest, open curiosity.

"Do you remember the evening at the hospital?"

"When we met? Vaguely." The corner of my mouth quirks into a crooked grin. Of course not.

"You were shouting into your mobile at your mother. The two of you were arguing when I discovered you." She nods thoughtfully, attempting to string together a few frayed images. "You noticed my eyes. Indeed, you sensed something disquieting about me the moment I entered. I could read it quite clearly."

"Yes." She swallows. "I remember." She seeks my eyes, sighing sweetly when I look upon her. Drawn to me, comforted. I grip the tops of my thighs to keep from touching her, and consider enthralling her a second time so that we might resume this conversation another evening. But I am as intrigued by my frankness as she is seduced by the absorption of knowledge. Honesty could prove as addictive as blood, and that is to say nothing of her rapt attention.

"There is a skill that we possess which renders a person unable to fully recall certain events."

"We?" she repeats, chin down and cheeks pale with fright.

"I have not finished. In the hospital, you were ensnared by my eyes, lulled into a black euphoria. The blackness was so heavy, the emotion so intense, you remember little else."

She blushes prettily. "That causes the door?" An upward inflection at the end of the question—a hint of disbelief.

"No, and yes. That causes you to open. But when the stare is broken, the door closes and you remain largely as you were before."

"Then how does my door open both ways? Why is it still open?" she hedges, suspicion coloring the tops of her cheeks. Perhaps a lie would have been better.

"You spoke," I reply. "I have never witnessed a mortal more self-possessed than you seemed to be. You asked for my name, and I gave it to you, which was irresponsible on my part. When the gaze was broken, you kept that name. I can hear it rattling around inside your heart even now."

"Let me get this straight…" She waves a dismissive and agitated hand.

"Hold your tongue if you intend to offer a witty rebuttal. It changes nothing, and frankly, your cynicism lessens you." I did not intend to raise my voice, but this woman has a rather infuriating way about her. The coming day bears down upon my senses, draining my limited patience frighteningly low.

Elizabeth has the decency to appear abashed, though she seems a breath away from defending herself. "Why should knowing your name change anything?" she asks earnestly.

"It changed everything," I lament. "When we are turned, reborn through blood, we are given that name by the one who owns us. I am bound to him by that name, and through the same principle, you are bound to me."

"For how long?" She ventures bravely, despite the quiver of her lips. Her eyes narrow to slits and her body radiates with barely repressed ire.

"The alternative is death," I respond dispassionately. "I leave that decision to you."

Elizabeth props one foot on the mattress, glaring at me, and rests her forearm on her knee. The decision is made more by her body language than anything else. Though, admittedly, it is not much of a choice. "You said there were others coming. You used the word 'we' just now. How many of you are there?"

"We are six in my family."

"Outside of your family?"

"We are many."

Her shoulders fall back against the headboard, and a breath whistles between pursed lips. She has begun to shiver, watching me closely. "Will they come for me?"

"They know nothing of you," I assure. "They will learn nothing from me."

The implications, the answers settle like a heavy meal, spoiling her appetite for truth. Her face appears aged from this conversation, drawn and pained.

"The person who named you," she hedges, watching the shadows that stretch along the floor. "Was he the man on the horse?"

At first, I have little idea what she means. But as I repeat the question thoughtfully to myself, I remember my own plaguing dream. The dream of my mother, the last time I saw her, and the day I met Fane. He claimed me as his ward then and there, and I never returned to my family or my village. I can picture Elizabeth on the edge of the crowd, the wind curling the edges of her nightshirt up around her thighs.

Elizabeth does not flinch away from me when I lean forward. She returns my interest unabashedly. I place my hand on the bed beside hers, so close my fingers warm from the heat of her. "How could you know that?"

Elizabeth shrugs indelicately and grimaces. "It felt that way in the dream. Like you belonged to him—like he thought you belonged to him."

She is a clever one, and her quick mind endears her to me rather unexpectedly. I reach across her folded limbs, brushing back the single strand of hair on her cheek. I half expect her to pull away from me, and I could not be pressed to say why I am compelled to remain so near to her, as torturous as this dance is. Elizabeth's unsteady breath rushes over my fingertips, but she remains still. I trace the shell of her ear with my thumb. She tolerates my momentary fixation, turning her head into my touch, and permits me to run my index finger along the tapering sweep of her eyebrow. She is a thing that feels, and reasons, and solves, and grows, and acts, and ages, and will inevitably end.

"Is knowing your name why I feel this way?" she beseeches.

The question rouses me from my morbid preoccupation over the misapplication of so much potential in so fragile a vessel. I pull my hand away, but linger beside her with a steadfast gaze. One she meets unreservedly.

"What way?" I probe, fascinated by how she will answer.

The tops of her cheeks and ears grow scarlet. Twice she beings to speak, only to stall. "Like you're all over me," she husks, seemingly against her will. "Even when you aren't touching me."

Elizabeth chases my touch as I rake my fingers through her hair, letting it sift through my tempered grip. When the last strands have slipped over my knuckles I withdraw, standing by her bed as she struggles to recover. She swallows thickly, the color bright in her cheeks and bare neck.

"The pull you feel is stronger now, because I have given you my blood." Her curiosity roused, the haze of lust begins to clear from her darkened eyes. "Stronger still because of our proximity, but I suspect that will dissipate."

"Suspect, but don't know?"

"No. I have never given any human the amount I have given you."

"Why give me your blood at all? Why not let me die?"

"I told you, the choice to live or die is yours."

Elizabeth slumps forward, resting her elbow on her thigh, her exhaustion defeating her curiosity. We are both bone-weary from the trials of a long night. "On what terms? What's in it for you?" she presses.

I cast a glance over my shoulder to measure the light spilling between the parted curtains. "The sun will be up soon. I should not be here when it arrives."

"You didn't answer my questions, and I have more."

"I am sure that you do. Some of which I may answer, and others I may not. But for now, I will have to bid you goodnight, Elizabeth." I tip my head cordially, twisting on my heel for the door.

"You have to come back," she demands. I halt my retreat in the doorway for one last look before we part.

"And why is that?"

"That's my favorite shirt," she retorts with complete seriousness. I cannot tell if it is a jest, or if she meant to say something else and lost her nerve. I pluck the front of the shirt in my fingers, as though the answer is encoded in the lettering. She stares at me expectantly, and finally looks away. "Goodnight, Stela," she says, though I doubt her intention to sleep.

I pull the bedroom door closed quietly behind me.

* * *

As I descend into my dormitory the rising sun swelters against the pavement overhead. Once inside, I lift Elizabeth's shirt over my torso and the haste to conceal this trace of her is thwarted by a low growl. Instinctively, I bare my fangs. Two sharp shark fin-like ears skate behind the back of my sofa. I will my snarl into submission before he can gauge my reaction and grow any more hostile. He reveals himself slowly, dragging his hind leg behind him as he edges his way into the open, his haunches slumped in pain, and tail curled between his legs.

"Erebus?" His ears perk, and the lights of my chamber brighten automatically as I step out from under the hatch. He does not rush to greet me, but drops in a crumpled heap at the foot of my bed. His face is tilted up in tempered glee, the tip of his tail flicking lazily in a meek greeting.

Carefully, I kneel beside his exposed belly and examine his wound. A pointed warning rumbles in his barrel chest as my hand hovers over the tear, matted with blood and coarse black fur. The wound has already sealed, but the shape is revealing—straight and deep—another inch or two and he would have lost the limb. I settle beside him and take his heavy head in my hands, placing it gently in my lap. Erebus whistles a whimper through his wet nose and relaxes against me, hooking a paw the size of a saucer around my leg. I stroke the spiny hairs between his downy ears, alarmed by his pronounced fatigue and the affectionate way he brushes his snout across my knees.

"I see he found his way back to you."

Fane is so surefooted that his approach is undetectable, even to me. Which leaves me with little time to brace myself and prepare for the bevy of questions that will undoubtedly follow. I am late, again, with nothing to show for it.

"What happened to him?" I do not meet Fane's insistent stare. He crosses the length of the room and perches on the arm of my sofa, his silken shirt parted down his chest, the lapels brushing his ruddy veined sternum.

"A transient in the tunnels nearly severed his hind leg. The rogue stabbed Macha twice in the chest before Erebus arrived."

"Where is Macha?"

"Bård and Crogher are with her. She will survive, but she was badly maimed."

"And the transient?"

"There was barely enough of him left to fill a thimble."

A fond smile spreads across my lips, and I scratch along Erebus's jaw in silent praise. His unblinking black eyes shift between Fane and myself. He has never cared for my Lord, and his body is tense in my arms. Aware that we are speaking of his heroism, Erebus draws up with his weight solely on his front paws, and positions his torso in front of me. His posture is distinctly protective, and his head—even seated—towers a half a foot above my crown.

Fane rises, and takes a single step toward me to fix his radiant blue eyes on Erebus. The hound stamps his foot between my legs, but has the good sense not to growl. Fane forces a smile that does not reach his eyes and resumes his place on the worn leather arm of the sofa. "He nearly ripped Bård's hand from his wrist when your brothers attempted to bandage the wound, so Crogher let him go. He was certain that Erebus would retreat to your quarters."

Gently, I rub the soft, long fur that falls in dark charcoal sheets down his chest. Erebus presses his long snout against the side of my head, shifting his weight uneasily. "He has not come to me for comfort in many years. He startled me."

"Your tardiness startled me, my dove." Fane wraps his thick hands around the leather armrest, but does not ask what kept me. He prefers an indirect approach when he is certain the answers will displease him.

"A long night's hunt."

"So, it would seem." He trails the words along in marked disbelief, and tilts his head expectantly.

I occupy myself entirely with comforting Erebus. Fane crouches by my splayed legs, his face a breath from mine as he glares venomously at my fearless protector. Erebus rears his head back, utterly silent as he pushes his chest out in defiant loyalty to his mistress. Fane's hand curls into a fist and I know he considers striking the animal. But Erebus is our most loyal and formidable hound, and Fane needs him fit to guard the tunnels.

"Mr. Collins reports that you failed to deliver a corpse to him this evening," Fane begins casually. He is tugging at the threads of my conscious, tracing the seams of memory with greedy hands. He pulls the affairs of my night taut like a sheet spread around our shared space. I see Elizabeth's face buried in my deeds, as clearly as if her likeness was projected upon a screen, and snatch the images from his sight, tucking them away. I leave behind memories of the cremator where I discarded our soiled clothes, an image of the embalming table before I laid Elizabeth down and Derek's timid face. I meet Fane's relentless scrutiny with feigned ignorance.

"I must have arrived too late for Mr. Collins, my Lord. Derek saw to the disposal of my feed." Hungrily, Fane picks over the scraps of event, turning them this way and that, but seeing no trace of misdeed he rocks back on his heels—granting me a momentary reprieve.

"And this feed that kept you so long from me?"

"She proved a difficult mark to win over, my Lord."

Fane has not finished his assault, but I cannot withstand another round. I turn to Erebus and busy myself with the tidying of his hackles, now raised in Fane's presence. Slowly, I slip the remnants of my remembered evening from Fane's grasp and fold them back on themselves, shutting him out as delicately as I can. Fane's frustration is palpable, the air itself is charged as he straightens and towers above me.

"You do not often hunt women," he remarks, and it is both observation and accusation.

"No, my Lord. Not often."   •

Fane makes his way beneath the hatch, moving idly, taking his time. He turns with a satisfied grin that shakes me to my core. "She must have been quite the prize for you to take a trophy." His smiling blue eyes trace the faded lettering across my breast, and I stare down at myself in a horror I can barely conceal. I hadn't removed Elizabeth's shirt. My jaw sets, and my composure returns, but Fane does not wait for my floundering explanation before taking his leave. Silence is all the answer he needs.

Acutely aware of my turmoil, Erebus holds me in place with a paw flung across my legs and another behind my back. He playfully pushes his long, narrow face between my crossed arms. I have not seen this behavior in him since he was very young. Despite my growing alarm the familiar gesture earns him a smile.

I retrieve my mobile from my pants pocket and type the letters emblazoned on my chest into the search bar. ISYM 2004: Illinois Summer Youth Music, a program for senior students. Elizabeth Dumas is among the list of attendees, so easily found that I grow cold with concern. All Fane has to do is search those letters. He will know she was a local. The year will give him an approximate age. And he will search, chances are he already has.

VI
Symbiosis

The clanging of curtain rings rips me from a fevered sleep, and my mother's disapproving scowl is the first thing I see.

"It's almost eleven," she warns, shuffling back over the threshold. The first words she's spared me since our argument in the kitchen about her ongoing care. I haven't slept this late since childhood, and that was due to a particularly vicious flu.

The bright white sun spills across the floor and drips down the walls with an optimistic glare. I close my eyes against the onslaught and roll over on my stomach with my head buried under my pillow, bracing for the impending hangover. Instead, the answering discomfort is sharp, specific, and not at all the malaise and nausea I'd expect from a night of heavy drinking. The pain is localized, radiating behind my eyes like two hot spikes pressing against the backs of my pupils. I squint into the late morning light. The ache in my skull has color and sound—a high pitched hissing I can't drown out.

Shielding my eyes, I shuffle toward the window and pull the drapes closed. Carefully, I take in the room. A bone-deep throb in my left arm halts any attempt to move. The ache gnaws my elbow with dull teeth, sending jolts to my fingertips and I cradle my forearm protectively. My mind swims as I find that the shirt I'm wearing isn't mine.

Inching in front of the mirror, I make slow one-handed progress with the shale-colored buttons, and shake off the shirt cautiously. I find exactly what I feared: a closed, angry wound bruised purple and green. The skin has already scarred, knotted and raised, a pucker in the middle of my bicep. I run my fingertip over the ridge and marvel that the skin itself is not hypersensitive—in fact the skin is completely healed. My mind floods with memories of the night before, memories I might have brushed off as psychotic, or a liquor-induced nightmare were if not for this parting gift.

"This isn't happening..."

Despite my limited mobility, I tear open every drawer looking for my damned ISYM T-shirt. Proof of a gunshot wound I can accept. Proof that Stela is real, that she was here in this room, that she...No. I can't accept that. Frantic, I upend my laundry basket on the bed. The shirt isn't anywhere.

I sink down onto the mattress and fall back into the heaped pile of my soiled work clothes. Stela wasn't a nightmare. She found me in the club, she killed that man. She stood at the foot of my bed and spoke to me. She sat beside me, so near I could note the absence of her breath between us as she traced the lines of my face. And I let her. I stared into those black eyes and leaned into every touch, pulled toward her, like the blood she gave me missed her terribly. The draw was so strong that every hair on my body stood on end and seemed to reach for her.

And what if I did? Reach for her? Will I end up like the man in the alley, my hands wrapped around my punctured jugular? Instinctively, I rub my neck.

A low buzzing brings me back to myself and I sit up, scanning the room for my cellphone. I find it exactly where it should be, on the nightstand. I crawl up the length of my bed, one-sided, scared to touch the device and half expecting to see a message from her when I do. Six missed calls and twice as many texts, all from James.

10:52 p.m.: Liz where you at?

11:07 p.m.: Come on, I'm not that bad a dance partner.

11:39 p.m.: Liz, where are you?

12:02 a.m.: Elizabeth this isn't funny.

03:31 a.m.: Please text me back. Tell me you're safe.

I text a hasty reply to confirm that I'm alive and will explain later, though I have no idea how.

Do I shower now? Do I brush my teeth, and put on makeup? Make breakfast? Go to work? How? Just the thought of stepping out into the hall feels like gambling with my life. And how do I hide something like this? That Stela has to remain a secret is a forgone conclusion, no one would believe me anyway. If I told someone—Mother, the authorities—I'd be committed, or tried for the murder of a man I'd never even met before last night. The worst part is that they'd be right, not about my being insane, but that it's my fault he's dead. I shouldn't have run off like that. She was after me, not him. Part of me welcomed her.

The curtains drift apart in the cool breeze but the glare still presses against my eyes, sharp, but less forcefully. Watching the curtains flutter, an eerie sensation ghosts over me, not quite a touch or an embrace. A calm follows on its heels, flowing through me in a soft rush and replaced by an inexplicable numbness—everything detached and automatic—but nothing I recognize. And then I'm on my feet, surveying the room for a clean shirt, putting one foot in front of the other and abstractly stunned by my resilience.

Closed in the bathroom as the mirror clouds with steam, I wonder briefly how I got there. This close, my reflection isn't what I expected. My pallor has regained a healthy glow and the skin around my eyes, though dark, is less sunken. A shower is exactly what I need.

I watch the water run down my body and pool onto the floor. I don't remember stepping out, or turning the shower off or scrubbing myself clean, but the ache is my arm is much less pronounced so the heat must have helped. I grab a towel and as I dry off, another symptom of last night's misadventure makes its presence known. At first, I'm convinced it's residual fear, an adrenal manifestation of stress. I picture Stela's face as she towered over me, the blood of that man coagulating on her chin. The memory is gruesome, but the panic is just beyond my reach. I recall the moment I sat up in bed and saw her standing there, black eyes and mussed hair, stained fingers. My heart raced then, but not the way it's galloping now. When she leaned over me, my pulse quickened. The blood rushing through my veins, calling her body into action, begging her to finish what she started. I was terrified.

Securing the towel under my arms, I hold two fingers to my wrist. My pulse is normal. I press the pad of my index and middle finger to my carotid, which is also steady. I hold the heel of my hand over my heart and expect to find it hammering, but no. There's an arrhythmia, a random beat every few seconds, like a shuffling step. For whatever reason this barely troubles me at all.

Downstairs, Mother pointedly pours the last cup of coffee from her morning pot into her own mug. There is no mug laid out for me. No breakfast. She keeps her back to me as she walks over to the kitchen table in front of the patio doors, open to welcome the breeze. The chill wraps around my ankles. I retrieve my mug from the cupboard and start a fresh pot of coffee. I don't take my seat beside her at the table. I have the distinct feeling that it's her territory today and I'm not welcome. Out the back door, beyond the privacy fence, a dense line of heavy storm clouds push their way across the otherwise cerulean sky, shading my mother's immaculate emerald lawn.

Would Mother have me committed if I confided in her? She flips through the pages of this month's *Vogue*, sipping cold coffee, stalwart in her resolve to ignore me.

"Mother." That's as far as I get. I know I need to tell her, someone, anyone. I brush my fingers against my lips, as though they're being moved and molded by invisible hands.

Then there's a carton of eggs in my hand, olive oil sizzling to life in a frying pan.

Breakfast. Right...Sure.

Mother, immune to my inner chaos, responds with a drawn sigh, sliced in half by the quick, aggressive flipping of a page. She knows how much her silence unsettles me, her relentless criticism is the white noise of my life.

Everything seems so unreal. It's like I never left my bed this morning, and I'm watching a woman who looks and sounds like me get my mother's breakfast. Two eggs over medium, fresh strawberries, and two pieces of turkey bacon burned to a cinder. I cross No Man's Land and drop the plate on top of the open article she's pretending to read.

"Cute, Elizabeth."

"Don't let it get cold." I pour myself a bowl of granola as she taps her fork against the side of her plate.

"These eggs are overdone."

Bowl in hand I curl up cross-legged in the chair to irritate her with my *heathen posture*. "Overdone is how you take all your meals, Mother." I'm not even angry with her.

"Helen always made them over easy," she baits. "One must adapt to survive."

"Any other symptoms of Stockholm Syndrome I should be aware of?"

She breaks a strip of charred bacon between her frail fingers and I can see the effort she makes not to smile. "None that come readily to mind, dear." Mother returns to her magazine, poking her eggs in distaste and taking small miserable bites. Round one to me this morning.

When she stands to place her dish in the sink she staggers toward her left side. There is a noticeable lack of grace in the way she steadies herself against the table to lower herself carefully back into the chair. I correct my own posture, planting my feet on the floor and push my seat up to the table. In between small mechanical bites, my concern gets the better of me. "Something happen to your knee?"

"No."

My breakfast bowl becomes the most interesting thing in the room, because I honestly don't remember deciding on granola. I wasn't particularly hungry this morning either, but the bowl is almost empty. Mother stares out across the patio, taking inventory of her azaleas. Gardening is just one passion that fell by the wayside when she was diagnosed.

"You're favoring your left side."

A scowl distorts my mother's face, aging her ten years. She's near enough to touch, but as unreachable as ever. "May I see your knee, Mother?" The angry lines dig ditches across her forehead, but I keep my attention focused on her leg she twists out from under the kitchen table. She parts the bottom of her robe to reveal an ugly black bruise covering the entire kneecap. My hand lingers in the air above her leg, fingers curling into a fist that lands in my lap. "What happened?"

"Nothing," she snipes, pulling the robe closed. "I slipped in the bath."

"Does it hurt? Have you iced it?" I get as far as the freezer door, but her vicious laugh is enough to curb my incessant need to fix.

"Some good that degree has done you. Yes, it hurts. Yes, I've iced it. I'm sick, Elizabeth, not simple."

I must be some special kind of damaged, because her barbs are a balm compared to her stony silence. I lean against the sink, one hand holding the countertop. She's deteriorating. "I'm going to hire another nurse."

My mother answers with a sigh that sounds like a hundred dreams abandoned all at once. She pushes herself away from the table, the legs of her chair scraping sharply over the tiles. Shuffling, she lands beside the island, directly across from me and crosses her arms over her robe, whipping a wayward strand of hair back into place with a flick of her bobbing head. My mother, so commanding that even her hair is frightened of her. And yet, her body has grown clumsy and awkward. This is not the first time she's fallen, but she believes that I count the accident in the bath as such. Like I haven't noticed the bruises on her forearms, or the one on her temple she's caked with concealer. These little accidents happened under Helen's careful eye too. Why doesn't that help?

"I'm sure you'll do exactly as you like," she says. "But if you think I'm going to allow a stranger to watch me bathe perhaps we should take you for e—examination."

The retort is clunky and we both know it, lacking her usual punch and poise. She fumbled for the word and I don't think *examination* was the term she was fishing for. Sometimes what she begins to say isn't what she intended at all.

What will I do when she can't even string a proper insult together? This isn't a fight she can win, and that is the only first here. Some mornings it's a fight just to breathe around her, the weight of her disease is more than I can bear. I want to say something reassuring, give her an out, sweep that clumsy sentence under the rug and pretend I haven't noticed. When did I turn away from her?

"I have to get ready for work." Cold and careless, and painfully indifferent. One foot after the other, all the way up the stairs without a look back.

What am I doing?

* * *

The whole morning is a blur. Waking, showering, cooking, eating, Mother. I remember walking away from her, but I don't recall dressing. Readying my face in the mirror, I caught myself humming midway through a tune I've never heard before. I left the house without my lunch. Mother had retreated to her bedroom before I left.

I'm standing on the subway platform, swaying dreamily on my feet. A cautionary glance confirms that I'm correctly dressed for work, phone in hand, purse hanging from my shoulder with a light jacket to ward off the chill. My heart thumps irregularly, just as it had this morning in the bathroom. Did I run to catch the L? My cheeks are cool to the touch, not flush from exertion.

On the train, I put my headphones in and turn the volume up loudly, disregarding the disgruntled utterances of the older woman seated beside me. It's rude, but I don't want to think. Not about Stela, not about James and how I'm going to explain myself, and especially not about my mother.

I thought it was a nightmare, even as it was happening. I'd been so convinced. I joked with Stela about stealing my clothes. Then I woke up and I could still sense her presence in the room, before I ever saw my scar. In the clear light of day, the truth was as impossible to dismiss as it was to believe.

How is Stela possible? Did she leave that man in the alley, or cover her tracks? There has to be a system for her existence to be a secret. What does she do with the bodies? I cringe at the thought, and scan the vacant faces of my fellow commuters for clues. Eyes on their phones, a few glued to their book, each person pointedly avoiding human interaction.

We are six in my family. We are many.

How many times has a patient of mine been a victim of hers? Only once that I know of, and I'm more than a little surprised by my certainty. She killed William Moore, room four-twelve. The night we met was the night his vitals dipped, and when the morning shift found him, his leads had been disconnected, the machines silenced.

Is this a habit? Does she frequent hospitals? My hospital? How can no one know about this? How can they not see?

Maybe it's always been this way, the ill plucked right out from under our noses, and we were too self-involved to piece the puzzle together. Too preoccupied, and too righteous, thoroughly enamored of our own superiority.

The train rattles along the rails as it barrels deeper into the city. I tremble in my seat for an entirely different reason.

My stethoscope is the first thing I retrieve from my locker. I wait for the last of the morning shift to disembark for home, and my fellow second shift to suit up and set out. The flat face of the instrument is cold against my chest. I hold my breath and listen. Every third beat it strays, a rogue flutter in the background, knocking around aimlessly and noticeably more quiet, empty as an echo. It could be any number of things. Arrhythmia is common post-surgery, though I'm not sure my arm qualifies as surgery and anesthesia was certainly no factor. Electrolyte imbalance is highly possible.

I hear my name and slam my locker door with a start. James stands at the edge of the lockers, blocking the aisle.

I rip the stethoscope from my ears, and wrap it casually around my neck.

"What are you doing?"

"Nothing." I fling my purse over my shoulder. "Hi." It isn't eloquent, but I'm genuinely relieved to see him standing there. Safe, and sound, and wholly pissed off.

"Hi? That's all you've got? Hi?" He stands expectantly in front of me with his hands on his hips, boxing me in. The closer he inches, the more his proximity irritates me. But James has always been one of those people, a personal space invader. "What happened to you last night?" He reaches out to take my hand, his worry clear in his gentle touch. A dark impulse flickers behind my eyes and fades before I can name it. "You scared the shit out of me."

James leans in close, brushing his fingertips over my jaw. I straighten up, shoulders square. The impulse returns, stronger than before and reckless to boot. My fingers ball into a fist with his hand still wrapped around them, and this does not go unnoticed. James withdraws his touch, but he doesn't step back, and suddenly the woodsy scent of his cologne is the only thing I notice.

Stela...

Her presence is so pronounced that she might as well be standing between us, effective as a brick wall and infinitely more dangerous. She's been with me all morning, *suggesting*, as she called it. Pulling my strings, plucking me from my bed, soothing my worries, and most importantly stilling my tongue. I could almost consider it a kindness had the motivation behind it been my fixing mother's breakfast. But this is something else, personal, uncalled for and unwarranted interference.

She's terrified of what I might do, what I could say.

"I got sick," I say by way of explanation. James deserves more than that, but unsurprisingly, I can't forge more than those three simple words. I can only imagine how frightening my sudden disappearance was for him. Last night certainly scared the hell out of me. The need to comfort James is far outweighed by the urge to physically hurt him.

James leans heavily against the neighboring locker, his arms resolutely crossed. Bloodshot eyes and fresh stubble paint a picture of his sleepless night. "You got sick," he muses, clearly not biting. "And the first thing you did was throw your phone in the toilet?"

My concern for him is as real as my hatred, both bubbling up inside of me independent of each other. The latter is distinctly Stela. "No. I got sick, and I remembered something." The words come readily now, supplied by a sure and steady hand. Unstoppable.

"Remembered what?"

Shoulders back, feet apart, James doesn't move as I step over the bench in the middle of the aisle, tugged away from him by invisible hands. I'm not a puppet, I'm a human being, and last night happened to me. It's mine to tell if I'm so inclined. My indignation is something Stela can use, channel, and so she does. "I remembered that I'm not as much fun as you think I am."

James takes a step back. The words hit him like a smack in the mouth, and his lips part but nothing comes out. My eyes burn, cheeks flushed, and I must look as cruel as I feel. But the apology on the tip of my tongue never finds its way out of my mouth as I turn on my heel and saunter out the door.

Christ. I don't know how I missed it. Even my walk isn't mine.

At the nurses station, James slides up next to me for his assignment, eyeing me like a wounded and wary animal. He takes his leave as quickly as he can, and we don't resume our conversation. He doesn't have the nerve, and I don't blame him.

She's isolating me.

She can't do this. I hold the words close to my heart, where I'm sure she can hear them. Despite the mounting disdain spreading through me like poison, I maintain a pleasant neutral expression. New patients arrive before the old patient's beds have cooled, rounds are made, bed pans are cleared, meals are served, families are consoled, people mourn and rejoice and pray and pound their fists against the vending machine. All familiar, but I am a stranger here, and yet no one seems to notice.

The more my fury grows, the less I can find the will to speak. Is it safer that way? Stela, are you worried I'll give something away? It scares you, doesn't it? Not being in control, and the vulnerability that goes along with it. I hope so. I hope you're terrified of me.

Beneath the sleeve of my scrubs, two gentle fingers brush up my right arm and draw delicate circles around the puckering edges of my new scar. My internal tirade grinds to a halt, but when I look down I see only my own hand tracing absent patterns on my skin. "Cute." I yank the sleeve of my shirt back down into place and pick up the chart I had placed at Mr. Dormer's motionless feet.

"What's cute?" Andrea, a new intern, has stopped changing the drip and stares at me incredulously.

I lift the chart to my face and attempt to appear entranced by it. I look to the heavily sedated body. "We're both allergic to hydrocodone."

Andrea nods slowly, her eyebrows knit as she hooks the new drip into place.

The moonlight wanes in the windows along the hall and shrinks to small silver pools that gleam up and down the white linoleum. I've become so alert to Stela's presence, she might as well be whispering in my ear. I leave ten minutes before the end of my shift and I don't stop moving until I've reached the elevator bank. I haven't even shed my scrubs.

The thought of taking the train is truly terrifying. Will she be standing on the platform waiting for me?

Stela isn't there. Only the whistling wind, and a turbulent sky. The night is charged with the electricity of an approaching storm, still miles away but sure to arrive by morning. I'm certain that Stela is bringing me to her. Now, in the dreary sinister light of the platform, seeing her would be a comfort.

My body recoils like a released spring. Stela has vanished, and only in her absence can I understand how firmly she had been holding me. My vision brightens as though floodlit. Those around me sharpen to such an astounding degree that I can see the pores on their tired faces. I can hear everything, the whispers, the weary breathing, the crinkle of crumbled bills and papers stuffed in pockets, and fingertips working phones as loud as the surf. Stela is still close at hand, but her attention is elsewhere.

Every stray, floating fleck of dust and debris shines like glitter in the air, and I reach out to touch a lingering cloud of dirt to see if the haze is as soft as it looks. The clarity is astounding, undeniably beautiful, like finding out I've been far-sighted all my life and handed my first pair of glasses.

My budding smile melts from my lips as an all-too-familiar odor seizes my senses and fills me from toe to top. Metallic and hot, thick bodied and slow moving. With the first involuntary swallow my body temperature soars, and my skin tingles with disgust so violent I barely shoulder my way to a nearby trash can before vomiting. Clammy with sweat, I lean my back against the wall and I focus on my breathing. I open my eyes, straining to adjust to the dark again. My whole body shudders while several onlookers shift their feet, faces twisted in my direction, silently daring me to step onto their car.

The world seems lonelier. Everything is returned to its unremarkable state. Wherever Stela is she is otherwise occupied.

The train arrives on time and I wrap my hands tightly around a standing rail toward the back of the car.

I can't live like this.

* * *

Our brownstone is hung with heavy shadows, and my mother's door is closed. I stand with my ear pressed against it. I never crawled in bed beside my mother, not even as a small child. It's surprising how strong the urge to seek that comfort is now.

Everything is still. I take a step back and stand in the long hall, staring out into the empty living room like the only living, breathing thing in the world. The house is different, strange somehow, although everything seems as it should be.

I bolt up to the second floor and rush into the safety of my bedroom, flipping on the light and closing the door. Folded neatly on my pillow is the shirt Stela commandeered the night before.

Cautiously, I make my way to the bed. Every corner of the room hums with her presence. I pick the garment up carefully and bring it to my nose. Lilac and incense, the scent fills me with warmth that I immediately resent, and I throw the shirt against my closet door. Stela is cheating me out of the confrontation she is wise enough to avoid.

I backtrack to the kitchen for a glass of water and a carving knife, carrying them both quietly upstairs. The full weight of my anxiety doesn't descend until I'm showered and ready for sleep. I lie awake, clutching the splintered handled of the carving knife beneath my pillow with both eyes trained on the closed door.

As terrified and angry as I am, there is no one else I can talk to about what is happening between us. Was she even aware of what she was doing? How could today have been anything but intentional? If her presence is frightening, her absence is twice as unsettling. There is no one to keep watch over my door. No one but Stela to keep the rest of her kind outside where they belong.

I must have dozed off, because awareness arrives quite suddenly. The hairs on the tops of my arms stand on end, and my brain fires a tingle of adrenaline. My muscles are sluggish with fatigue, but my fingers tighten around the handle of the carving knife. I shoot up in the bed, a faint sheen of sweat breaking out across my brow as the bedcovers pool around my waist in the faint glow from the window.

"A weapon is a rude greeting." Her outline is barely discernible between the parted curtains. My ragged breath fills the room and I lower the knife, unwilling to relinquish it completely. I can sense her movements like a change in air current though her steps are soundless. Her silhouette has vanished into the shadows.

"Where are you?" No sooner than I ask, the bedside light flicks on and I stifle a scream. Stela has not moved away from the curtains, leaning casually like she belongs here. I'm as angry in an instant as I have been all day. "Do you have any idea what time it is?"

She laughs, a whimsical sound too light and girlish for her. Her hair, resting just past her shoulders, is in straight blond plaits that curl faintly at the ends. She looks much the way she did when we first met. Immaculately dressed in an invitingly soft navy sweater and pressed herringbone slacks. The ensemble is a far cry from the T-shirt she stole, which seemed so garishly out of place.

"I know the hour, and you should be asleep."

"And you should be in a boardroom, negotiating the terms of a hostile takeover."

Stela turns from the window, her arms crossed lightly over her chest. Her legs slowly make their way toward me. The movement is precise, fluid as a dance, almost feline. "How do you mean?" she asks.

I gesture absently with the knife, still clutched in my right hand. "Aren't you a bit overdressed for an evening of skulking in the shadows?"

Stela doesn't falter, or smile. She tilts her chin, one sculpted eyebrow arched to the middle of her forehead. "I do not like to repeat myself, Elizabeth. The weapon. Put it down." Marble-faced, with an emotionless expression as hard as the rest of her, her black eyes fill every empty space inside me. I toss the knife carelessly on the nightstand as a breeze passes over my bare chest. My blush can't be controlled any more than the awkward fumbling for blankets can be avoided, or made graceful. Stela smirks and looks away.

"You used me."

"Pardon?"

I sit taller with the sheet bunched under my arms. "Don't," I warn, and Stela tilts her head. "I know it was you. You pulled me out of bed this morning, pushed me around. You made me say things…"

The muscles in her jaw clench and ripple with unshed tension. An instant later I'm curling my legs underneath me to make room for her before she sits on them. The bed barely dips beneath her added weight. She keeps her eyes on the window. What I can see of Stela's features are pained. She seems imbued with a bone-weariness. She drags a hand through her hair, immovable as stone beside me, radiating hostility.

"Would you rather I left you to spend the day in bed, wallowing in foreboding?"

"So, you were what? Doing me a favor?"

"It would not be the first time, Elizabeth." She insists upon my name. I can't tell if it's a joke the way she uses it, or something she enjoys saying. Stela turns and glances at my scarred arm. Her eyes find their way back to mine, and I can't tell who's pushing or pulling anymore. The sensation of meeting her stare is unlike anything I've ever experienced, a bit like drowning. Not in a romantic way, but smothering and all-consuming—black and breathless and disconcertingly addictive. I struggle to organize my thoughts and force myself to look down at my hands, rubbing them nervously in my lap.

"I don't need or want your assistance getting out of bed in the morning. You overstepped and you know it. You were cold to my mother, and you were worse to James."

Stela almost smiles at his name, and runs her tongue along her teeth. Which are normal, totally normal human teeth...

"James." His name sounds like a sigh and she faces me head on. There is in fact a bulge to her upper lip, a gentle protrusion. Undetectable to anyone who wasn't actively searching for concealed fangs. "Is he the reason for your vexation?"

"No, I—He deserved..."

"The truth?" Her eyes are comically wide, mocking, lips spreading into a genuinely amused smile, and it is the most condescending expression I've ever seen on anyone who is not my mother.

"I wasn't going to tell him the truth," I defend.

"No. You were not," she agrees. "So why should it matter what was said?"

I quell my fury, before I say something that might get me killed. "Stela. I'm a person. Not a toy."

"Yes. You are a human being." She nods long and slow, speaking much more softly than she has so far. "A human being who sustained a serious injury, and confronted a very unsettling truth that few have ever had the burden, or the opportunity to carry." Her hand finds my shin, gripping it gently. "You reacted far better than I would have guessed. And in the morning when the nightmare was still so raw, you were frightened. Which is understandable. But you had a job to do, and a mother to cook for, and a witness to appease, and I willed you onward. My aim was to aid you in those tasks, not to violate you."

Locked in Stela's patient focus, I struggle to maintain my indignation. When I try to gain a reprieve by breaking her gaze, I find that I can't. I'm not sure I want to. But the draw isn't something she forces, nor is it contrived the way the rest of my day has been. "You don't get to decide what I need. Please, don't do that again."

"Do not even flirt with the idea of telling another soul what you know," she warns, and I wonder how much of a liability I am to her. "Deal." I nod my head, and Stela shifts her eyes warily over the glinting blade on my nightstand. My mind reels the second she releases me from her stare, like a held breath finally released.

"Are you still afraid that I mean to cause you harm?"

"You're an anomaly, an unknown. That scares me. But the knowledge that you're not alone is what terrifies me."

She purses her lips and falls into a thoughtful silence. "There are no others here. Your heart is racing."

"I know. It's been erratic all day."

Stela closes her eyes and tilts her head toward me. She leans forward, a pleased smirk tugging at the corner of her mouth. "Not erratic," she says after a quiet eternity. "Merely an echo." Her eyes aren't as vacant when they open. There's a light in her face I haven't seen before that makes her appear younger, maybe even younger than me.

"An echo of what?"

"Of mine."

As though a dial has been turned up, the echo thunders in my chest, pounding in my ears every third heartbeat. The rush of my blood becomes audible, like a whirlpool locked inside. Stela's blood, surging in my veins. At the sound of her voice and as it had the night before, my body sings out to be closer to her. "The echo, it's because of the blood you gave me?"

"I suspect so, yes. But it will fade. Dress yourself," she instructs, walking to the window.

"Why?"

"To join me for a walk."

Outside, the moonless night is black as ink and under any other circumstances I would have refused. But I have so many questions and perhaps the fresh air will help. I inch out from beneath the sheet and Stela turns away and stares into her reflection in the windowpane.

"Elizabeth?"

"What?"

"Why were you there with him? At the club?"

I freeze. "Is it so unbelievable that I would go out dancing?"

"You are deflecting." I can hear her smile. She runs her long fingers affectionately between the creases of the drapes.

"To get away from you."

Stela turns on her heel and clearly the response is more honest than either of us anticipated. I smooth my jeans down into the cuffs of each boot and stand stiffly. "Why were you there?"

She closes the distance between us, her face smooth and severe, and placing the palm of her hand against the small of my back she ushers me into the darkened hallway.

"To feed."

* * *

The wind howls down Michigan Avenue and I tug the collar of my coat around my neck. Sharp as needles, the breeze is icy and I regret the decision to accompany her. Stela hasn't removed her hand from my back, or faltered a single step in the piercing chill.

"Are you cold?" It was rude of me not to offer her a jacket before we left. Stela answers with a bemused shake of her head and tilts her chin defiantly into the breeze to clear her tangled hair.

"The cold is not oppressive to me," she assures. "I am aware of temperature. I prefer to be warm, but our bodies do not suffer the effects the same way."

A block ahead four young men in oversized coats are taunting one another under a streetlight. Instinctively, I move closer to her and her hand wraps protectively around my waist. The irony isn't lost on me. The young thugs notice us, stepping from the curb into the street. With one murderous glance from Stela their catcalls die in their open mouths. We pass unchallenged and I stay beside her, expecting to her to remove her arm. She doesn't.

"What do you call yourself? Your kind?"

Stela steers our course to Buckingham Fountain, which will soon be shut off and drained to protect the pipes from freezing. She releases me from her embrace to sit on the edge of the pool and I miss the contact immediately. We stay close enough for our shoulders to brush, facing the city, and the streetlights shine in the surface of every window.

"Strigoi. An old word, from another life."

"Eastern European?" I know Latin roots when I hear them. The word has a certain elegance, at least the way she says it. A whimsical name for a frightening thing.

"Is that where you're from?"

Stela keeps her face forward, scanning the city Her reluctance to answer is a wall between us.

"I was born to a small village along the Danube, in Moldavia. Raised in Braşov."

"Romania?"

"Today, Romania. Transylvania during my formative years."

Her wariness is obvious, but I can't seem to help myself.

"When was that?"

Stela laughs openly, the same girlish giggle that filled my bedroom. Her fingers wrap a lock of unruly hair behind my ear without even a cursory glance in my direction. I could not guess at her age.

"A long time ago," she says on an empty breath.

When I was young my mother took me to the Art Institute every Sunday. Though nominally Presbyterian, those cultured outings were the closest we came to religion. The sculpture court was her favorite exhibit and one we visited together for many years. I didn't share Mother's enthusiasm for the cold, unchanging faces, but one piece I found particularly moving was *Truth* by Daniel French Chester. A classical sculpture of a woman partially draped, staring out into space with a mirror just inches from her face, looking down at the passersby in a state of perpetual remorse. Every time we passed that statue I braced myself for the inevitable crash the mirror would make against the marble floor, but it never came. Stela reminds me of her. Frozen in time, neither old nor young. In the right light, she could be in her early to mid-twenties. But facing her head on, without a hint of her carefree laugh, she's tired in a way that defies her physical body.

"You were with me on my feed earlier this evening," she says. There seems to be an insurmountable distance between us, even with her hair tickling my cheek. "That must have been unpleasant for you."

"There was a moment before the taste hit me when the platform lit up like the sun was shining and I could see everything. The faces of the people around me, the threads of their clothing, the dirt swirling in the air above us. For a second, it was beautiful."

Stela narrows her eyes and waits for me to continue, but what would be the point? We both know the end result was sickening.

"I had to replace the blood I gifted to you," she explains slowly, as though anticipating protest or interruption. "Hunting does not happen every night, as I suspect you know. In a few days, when I am compelled to feed again, the bond we share should have waned."

The bond of our blood but not our minds. Stela is going to feed, regardless of whether it's convenient for me. "I can handle what it was like before. When there was only the smell and the tinge of taste."

She's silent for a long while, with eyes like two polished onyx stones locked on my face. "You are strange," she remarks when I don't flinch under her unwavering attention.

"How am I strange?"

A smile pulls the corner of her mouth. "I seek to make amends for sickening you mere hours ago, and your only remark of the experience is the lovely view." She doesn't laugh at me, but I can hear the humor coloring her words. "I make a point of mentioning that I will continue to feed and you make no attempt to dissuade me?" She's on a roll now, working herself up and speaking rapidly. "You bore witness to my brutality in the alley last night, and here you are: unprotected, isolated, asking me where I hail from."

I cross my legs toward her and our shins brush. Stela straightens, and I lean forward with my hands folded diplomatically in my lap. A trick I learned from my mother. "What am I supposed to say, Stela? Get away from me? I begged you to remove yourself from my life and you told me it couldn't be done. Was that a lie?"

"No."

"I didn't think so." We regard each other silently for several uncomfortable moments. Stela stares back out at the city. "I know what you are, even if I didn't know what I should call you. I think I've known since the night we met. Any doubt I had disappeared when you saved my life. Whatever this is, this *bond*, it feels inextricable for me too. And I'm not going throw a fit and ask you to stop killing people, no matter how contemptuous I find murder, any sooner than I would ask an obligate carnivore to do the same. This is a biological imperative for you, yes?"

"Yes."

"Good, we understand each other then. Or, I understand the situation. But I would like your word on something."

She's inclines forward intently, elbows on her thighs, watching me as though I'm still holding that carving knife. This isn't her first negotiation. "Name your terms."

"You will not feed from my hospital, or in front of me under any circumstances." Stela tilts her head, running her eyes up and down my person. She hears what isn't said, but that's as close as I can get to asking that she stay. Being near her is the first time today that I've felt even remotely safe.

Before I understood what she was, when there was only the inkling that I was not completely insane and that someone was really following me, I sensed that it was more than just a single pursuer. Something much bigger and far more dangerous. Now I understand that I know next to nothing about what happens on these empty streets when I'm warm in my bed. To push Stela away with ultimatums would be suicide. And this creature, so polite, so convincingly female is intrigued by me for who knows what reason.

"That is a fair request," she says guardedly. Stela stands abruptly, extending her hand and helping me up. My legs are stiff with chill and I'm surprised to note that her fingers are as cold as mine. "And one I intend to honor, at all cost." Stela pulls me in step beside her and the shoulder of her sweater brushes my chin. It's the softest material I've ever felt—cashmere, of course—but finer than anything I've ever owned.

We move north toward home down roads and dark alleys I'd never risk. I reach for her hand and she surprises me by sparing my fingers a light, reassuring squeeze.

"Are you always this cold?" I ask, resisting the urge to hold her hand cupped in both of mine. Stela remains vigilant in her surveillance of the vacant street, the apprehension only visible in the tightening of her jaw.

"My skin takes the temperature of my surroundings. After a feed, I am as warm to the touch as any other living thing."

Cold-blooded then, like a reptile though I can't imagine she suns herself. The science of her is seductive. "I would ask about your reflection but I've already seen it. Any truth to crosses and holy water?"

Stela stops abruptly, and I keep walking until her hand, wrapped around my wrist, makes another step impossible. I know I've misspoken before I turn around. Her eyes glimmer around the edges with a silver sheen. The effect is as menacing as her pointed silence, which stretches on for an age.

"We will not speak of myths." She doesn't approach me. She stays exactly two steps back, and though we're roughly the same height there is something towering about the way she stands.

"Sorry. I was just curious."

Stela sighs pointedly. An audible declaration, but not of fatigue. Does she sleep? She must if she dreams. She takes a step forward and encloses my hand in both of hers.

"I know you are riddled with questions. You would be a fool not to want answers." She stares down at my hand in hers. "But this is new territory for both of us. I ask that you respect my apprehension in discussing these matters, for now. Our existence is built on deception. The answers you seek are truths I have never shared with any person."

I slip my fingers from her chilled palms and clutch my coat tightly as the brutal night rushes a gust of icy wind past my collar. Stela's grave expression softens with my obvious discomfort and she runs her index finger up my cheekbone. The temptation to lean into her touch is overwhelming. Stela's hand lingers in the space between us, as though she doesn't know what to do with it now. Self-consciousness looks awkward on anyone, but especially on her. She brushes her fingertips once against my elbow to usher me on, and we begin walking again under a dense silence.

She must be a capable hunter. Despite having witnessed her viciousness, my body responds to her with frantic desperation and I ache at the thought of her leaving me tonight. I'm not sure if that is a lingering side effect of the blood she gave me, or symptomatic of the space she's taken in my mind and made her own. Growing up as independent as I have, this connection to Stela is unsettling. All day I was furious at having been pushed around, coerced, but the second I laid eyes on her that anger withered in favor of this awful magnetism.

"I pushed you this evening," I admit. Stela regards me cautiously. "I won't apologize for that." I can sense her answering smile. "Trust is vital to any relationship. You've asked me to take you at your word, that I won't be harmed. I'm trying to trust you. You've been to my home. My work. You've seen my mother. You know me, Stela. But I only know what you show me of you, what you tell me. It's hard to trust something when you're kept in the dark."

Stela shakes her head, her loose hair obscuring her shadowed face. "You have not asked me to stop feeding. I will not ask you to stop questioning. This is who we are. What I want is your patience."

"That sounds fair to me."

By the time we reach my desolate street I'm overcome with exhaustion from this late night excursion. Should Stela's visits become a frequent occurrence, between her and my early bird mother, I'll never sleep.

My mother's stoop looms in the distance. Do we part with a hug? A kiss on the cheek? A handshake seems so impersonal after what we've been through together. She absolutely cannot accompany me upstairs. I'd never be able to rest with her perched beside my bedroom window.

These idle worries are quickly dispelled as Stela's hand pushes roughly against my spine. She smothers my protest with her palm and pushes me behind a flight of stairs three doors down from my own. I struggle to free my mouth, but I'm completely pinned between her body and the brick wall at my back. The fight all but leaves me when I notice the way her eyes narrow and focus on a single point, every muscle in her body clenched. She brushes her lips across my cheek, pushing the hair back from my ear with her nose.

"I do apologize," she whispers, eyes still straight ahead and unmoving. "I will uncover your mouth if you promise to be quiet."

I nod my head, and Stela slowly pulls her hand away with an encouraging, albeit pained smile. The concern in her dark eyes carries a heat all its own, and I can see my own mounting anxiety reflected there, like two round mirrors. She cups the side of my face, and the touch has the same protective inflection as when we encountered those young men on the street. It's enough to escalate my anxiousness into outright panic.

"Is it one of the others?"

Stela's face remains cautiously reserved and she straightens my jacket collar, smoothing the front of my wool lapels. A calm settles inside me. My body relaxes when Stela's does.

"Were it one of mine, we would be dead where we stand."

"Comforting. Thanks."

She guides me by the shoulders between two tall, narrow brownstones. The space between them is so slight I walk with my back pressed against the wall. Stela pushes me in front of her and slips after me in the dark, side-stepping at my heels. My hand reaches for hers instinctively the second I step out into the alley that runs behind my backyard, and she grasps my fingers eagerly. Stela leads and pulls me along after her, swift and silent.

We sprint beneath the shadows cast by my neighbors' privacy fences until we reach Mother's. The lock on the back gate has always caught and has to be wiggled, just so, before it gives. The warning is on the tip of my tongue when Stela swings wide the gate and shuts us inside my backyard with a familiarity that is both unnerving, and completely expected. Likewise, she makes quick and quiet work of the sliding glass door—which has opened with a screech my entire life—and shoves me unceremoniously into my own kitchen.

"Who's out there?"

She's nearly to the island when she whips her head in my direction, and the look on her face is enough to silence anyone. I shift closer to her, but she places a firm hand against my sternum to keep me in the shadows. I wait as Stela slinks over the tile toward the living room. As carefully as she moves, Stela remains tall, gliding between the shadows stretched from the pane of each window. She hooks the edge of one curtain with her finger and peers out onto the street. The light from above our stoop cuts like a blade across her white cheek.

"Collins," she hisses.

Stela drops the curtain back into place with a contemptible snarl. She charges into the kitchen. I've seen this look before, when I noticed her in the sea of writhing bodies at the club. She has a hand on the sliding glass door, and I grab hold of her shoulder, though I'm not entirely convinced that distracting her is in my best interest.

Without pause my wrist is caught in her iron grip, and she wheels around to face me without a spark of recognition in her twisted scowl. The blood drains from my face so quickly that the top of my scalp tingles, and I plant my free palm forbiddingly against her chest. A flicker of remorse flashes across her features and her grip loosens. She takes both my hands gently in hers, holding them in the limited space between us, stroking my knotted knuckles with her thumbs. I stare down at our fingers, astonished that they lace together so readily.

"Tell me what you saw."

"One of my family's associates is parked on the far side of your street."

"Why?"

"Reconnaissance. He would not send a human to harm you."

"He who?"

Her fingers tighten around mine and she brings them to her chest, cradling them close. There is a palpable fury clouding the air around us, and Stela's fight to direct that rage away from me lingers in her touch. "Elizabeth," she whispers, and my eyes snap to her face as though my name is a command. Maybe it is. "There is a man outside your home. He answers to two people in my family, and it won't have been my brother that sent him. I will deal with this matter."

I try to wrench my hands from her gentle grasp, and though she doesn't tighten her hold, neither will she release me. The harder I pull, the stiller she becomes, staring in that silent, beseeching way she has, until I have no choice but to relent and stop railing against her.

"I can't just sit inside all day. I have a job, Stela. A life."

She releases one of my hands to reach into the pocket of my coat for my cell phone. Her rummaging drags me a step closer and our knees brush. Stela either doesn't notice, or doesn't mind. The light from the screen casts an eerie blue glow across her pale cheeks. She flips the device around and shows me her newly added contact information.

"You will go about your day tomorrow as though this never happened, without a word to anyone, without a single thought of me. You will be followed, Elizabeth, as surely as the sun will rise. A dark-haired gentleman in a black van will note your every move. If he exits his vehicle, if he speaks to you or takes a single step in your direction, you will notify me immediately. Am I clear?"

Her number is programmed in my phone under S. The link to her is comforting, and for once this affair doesn't seem entirely one-sided.

"Who sent him here?"

She takes a step back, hands dropping limply to her sides and despite my earlier resistance, I immediately reach out for her straight shoulders. She abandons her retreat, and my thumbs find the shelf of her collarbones beneath the impossibly soft sweater. We linger for a tense moment, openly staring at each other, drifting back together.

"Fane," she says. "My Maker."

"How does he know about me? And why does it matter to him?"

"It is my sincere hope that he does not know about you yet. He merely suspects that you exist. He is certain that I am hiding something from him, and he has sent Mr. Collins to find out what that is." Her words are fraught and bitter. Moments ago, she was a feral thing, cagey and vengeful. Now she has an air of timidity. If something as strong as she is fears what will happen next, what can she possibly expect from me?

"I can't live like this." My mouth is a hairbreadth from hers, though I have no memory of leaning in. Stela reaches up with a trembling hand and her fingers slide up the back of my neck, tangling in my hair. The same hand that held me pinned against her, the same that flung a man against a wall as though he weighed nothing, is shaking.

"Neither can I," she confesses, lips brushing against mine. The words are weighted with heartbreaking sincerity. What must it be like? A life lived in darkness, a life dependent upon anonymity? What restrictions does she have, if simply giving her name to me could cause such havoc? Does she have any real freedom?

Our knees knock, mouths open and lips touching, though only my staccato breath and pounding heart can be heard. Her fingers tighten around the back of my head, at once pulling me closer and pushing us apart. I'm the first to close my eyes, and Stela is the first to step away. The absence of her registers before I have visual confirmation of the fact. I stand beside the open patio door, fingers pressed to my lips, still parted in preparation for a kiss I didn't know I wanted so badly.

The door groans when I slide it closed, as it should, as it always has when anyone other than Stela has touched it. I stand in the empty kitchen, watching the shadows skitter over the deck, and chase the sinking sensation in my gut all the way down to the cold, forbidding tiles beneath my feet.

VII
Renaissance

Mr. Collins has not strayed far from his vehicle in nearly five days. I may have underestimated his work ethic. He is getting her habits down before he risks confrontation. Under different circumstances, I would admire both his discretion and his dedication. I too have hunted a person of interest—dozens, in fact—but the terrain has been irrevocably altered. Bodies were once as common as vermin in the gutter. Surveillance these days demands a level of distance and discipline that is not for the impatient, or the impassioned.

Every evening, before I can glean a few precious hours of sleep, Elizabeth sends me a message detailing small changes to her route and routine. She rises later than he expects one day, and much earlier the next, keeping to the house in her off hours, and walking with her mother only on the busiest streets during the most congested time of day. But subterfuge is only half the battle. There is not a doubt in my mind when he readies his camera to capture the likeness of every tall blonde rounding the corner, or crossing the street, that Elizabeth is not the only one Collins has been sent to monitor. And what is worse, I am certain he was not sent merely to lurk. His actions are too meticulous. He is careful to leave no trace of himself, changing the position of his nondescript van, even the vehicle itself.

That very paranoia will be his undoing. The blindingly bright red Dodge he used to tail Elizabeth yesterday was his own private car. Andrew asked no questions when I gave him the license plate—fear is a potent motivator—and forwarded the request on to one of Opes and Sons' unlisted freelancers.

The answers were surprising. Mr. Collins's home is modest and neatly kept. Two small boys with their father's crooked mouth, criminal features softened by their mother's round blue eyes. I lingered over the glossy photo of their sharp little faces, considering the time it would take to leave their cold bodies tucked in bed for Collins to find. His wife prostrate on the narrow kitchen table, the blood pooling over the pockmarked linoleum beneath. Normally, I am not one for waste, but neither do I bother with empty threats. However, Mr. Collins is also a person of interest to Fane, and of course, to his benefactor Bård. Whatever mishap befalls the loathsome lackey must be subtle, and above all—untraceable.

Elizabeth has been a far better sport than I anticipated, but I imagine that when you are gambling with your life petty inconveniences are just that. Still, she has managed to sling her barbs, even while we are restricted to text, following my added instructions with a curt *good morning to you too*. More than once she has referred to me as her preferred stalker. I should take less pride in the title. Being, once again, annexed to the shadows of her life is a punishment in and of itself, but we cannot risk being photographed together.

I would believe the pang to be one-sided were it not for the way her striking eyes search the street, stopping only briefly on Collins's van. She can sense my proximity, though not as acutely as I can sense hers. She flashes a private grin from her stoop, she stands a bit taller, she walks with a long stride, and does not shrink away from the strangers on the sidewalk.

I have to sleep.

The hours are blending into one another, and a piercing shriek has taken root between my ears. Even the night has begun to blister my sun-leathered eyes, and I am no good to her this way. No use to anyone if I cannot think clearly. Daylight is extraordinarily draining, and despite my superior tolerance, I fear I cannot continue without rest for much longer. I have been careful to be present and accounted for every morning, disappearing through the service entrance Erebus uses to come and go from my quarters. But I have no way of knowing whether or not Fane is in the habit of checking in on his sleeping children.

The others will notice soon, assuming they have not already. I am not as quick, or as patient as I should be. Twice yesterday, I took the bait with Lydia—thinly veiled barbs about my apathy, hinted that I was not as adept with managing Fane's fortune as she. Which, as of late, has regrettably proved to be true, and I nearly went across the conference table in our meeting hall. My attack was halted by Fane's booming disapproval, accompanied by a heavy hand on my shoulder from Crogher—the least likely of my brood to intervene on anyone's behalf, providing they do not walk on all fours. Darius was all eyes, poor soul. He has never been one for outward displays of aggression. Indeed, it is a wonder he can feed himself at all. He gathered the month's statements into his ledger and scurried back to the sanctuary of his library.

Fane suggested that perhaps a change in station would reinvigorate my loyalties. Loyalties, not my strengths, not my abilities. Would it please me to keep the hounds for a year, to see to security and tend to the compound? That was the first time in my life Fane had questioned my allegiance, albeit indirectly. In retrospect, it had been a mistake to blame Bård for my financial oversights. And it was not entirely a lie. My brother has been lax in sending me the figures from our newest business venture with Collins.

"Yes, my dove," Fane said. "I am sure that he has. Bård has never had a mind for figures. Yet, Lydia, our faithful seamstress was able to provide documentation of profit. Are you challenging her reflection of the account?"

"No, my Lord."

"Good, because it is sound. The profit she quoted falls in line with my own projections." Fane has been checking my work. Another first. Did Lydia get a copy of the quarterly statements from him? Or Darius, perhaps? I could not protest with his unflinching stare upon me. He let me linger in silence, twisting on the hook for a while before he released me. "Come now, Stela. It would not be banishment. It was merely a suggestion. Besides, I doubt Crogher could be pried from his duties willingly."

I straightened in my seat and offered my humility, my sincerest apologies that my recent performance did not reflect my gratitude. Fane accepted all of this with a disinterested wave of his wide hand. "I trust this is not a conversation we will be forced to revisit, my dove," he said. "You will rouse yourself from your musings, and apply yourself fully to the tasks you are assigned."

I bowed and took my leave. Fane let me depart without a taste, without a kiss or a hand on my arm, or the promise that I would come to him at the evening's end. Did he hasten my exit to speed along the inevitable? Rushing me away so that I might be seen with Elizabeth, my treason caught red-handed by Collins, so that I may be proven the traitor Fane suspects, once and for all? Tending the compound was a threat, implying underground confinement. No one is more familiar with the integrity and the subtleties of our tunnels than Crogher.

Fane had been a great general. He was never impetuous—unless it served him somehow. His eyes never strayed from the goal. He is nothing if not patient.

Elizabeth is a powder blue smudge darting down the sidewalk, unforgivably late for her shift this afternoon. Typically, Mr. Collins is fast on her heels, taking service roads to reach the hospital long before she arrives, where he sits behind the wheel with a crossword puzzle in his gloved hands and waits for her shift to end. I usually accompany Elizabeth from afar, occupying a separate train car entirely, but close enough to hear her heart beating.

However, today Collins waits a full twenty minutes before setting off for the hospital, and I remain trapped on the neighboring corner—the blistering sun hot on my face—and my back pressed against the stone staircase of an adjacent stoop, staring down the street long after I lose sight of her.

The mobile in my pocket buzzes to life. Elizabeth has sent only a single question mark. I had been uncertain if she could sense my absence. But I have my answer. She may not know that I was kept by this uncharacteristic idleness in the deplorable Mr. Collins, but she is certain that I am not as near as she would like. I warn her to keep her wits about her for the remainder of the night. It is possible that Collins has kept me in place, so that another— sent in his stead—might watch Elizabeth unobserved, and without obstruction.

After an age, his engine rumbles to life. Collins's van is parked in the Emergency lot when I reach the hospital. This is the first evening he has beaten me to her, though I doubt he can be sure. I settle at the window in an abandoned office on the second floor to keep watch over him and reach out to Elizabeth with my mind, as easily as a finger pressed to a pulse point. She is troubled by the unexpected change in routine, but the gentle intrusion of my presence quietens her darker imaginings.

Twice a night Mr. Collins ventures into the building through the emergency ward to procure a cup of coffee, and tonight is no exception. This little expedition takes him exactly six and a half minutes. Tonight, he has been gone from my sight for ten. He could be wise to my tactics, and using them against me. Forcing me to intervene directly simply by changing his own timeline. I slink up the stairwell to Elizabeth's ward to make sure.

The fourth floor has few occupants this evening, and the staff have dwindled to match. Elizabeth is not at her station. I consider playing the part of a grieving daughter once more, searching for her father's nurse, but I am unfamiliar with Elizabeth's patients and it would not serve to draw unnecessary attention to her absence. Besides, her heartbeat echoes like distant thunder trapped in the elevator at the end of the hall, making its way back up the building with my precious cargo, and taking its sweet time.

With no choice but to wait, I linger in the doorway of a darkened room, ignoring the soft snores of the unconscious occupant at my back and watch a janitor flip and drag a gray mop along the polished tile. A doctor and a nurse march directly by, ensnared in some boisterous disagreement.

When the elevator doors open Elizabeth is a whirl of chestnut hair. Her eyes wide, her pulse erratic, clutching a thin manila folder to her chest. With her arms crossed, the edges of her angry scar are just visible beneath the cuff of her blue scrubs. The young man she favors, James, makes a joke about her sudden disappearance. Elizabeth mumbles something about a prank phone call and the smacks the folder down on the counter in front of him.

I slip further down the hall and return to the waiting room where I first encountered her. Sealed inside, I close my eyes and let her name fill my mind. Elizabeth senses my call, and her heart pounds louder than her shoes knocking down the hall. My name blooms against the roof of her mouth, but she swallows it back.

She opens the door barely wide enough to permit her body to slink across the threshold, and shuts it firmly behind her with a tremulous exhalation. She does not acknowledge my presence, but stands facing the closed door, collecting herself. Elizabeth turns on her heel, and I expect to be greeted with harsh words regarding this intrusion, or reprimanded for calling her away from her work. Instead, the scent of her hair engulfs me—citrus and cinnamon—as two thin arms tighten around my shoulders, and her racing heart presses against mine. With no chance to hunt before this unexpected embrace, my body goes rigid in her arms, reacting to such temptation when I haven't fed. Like anyone would, Elizabeth pulls away.

"He was here," she confirms with affected calm.

"He has been here every evening this week. Did he approach you?"

Elizabeth bides her time closing her eyes and pushing the dark, curling locks from her face. Twice she begins to answer me, and both times a tremor threatens the corner of her mouth. I loathe Collins for it.

"We got a request for a patient file, from Pathology. I answered the call, so I agreed to take it downstairs. It's been a slow night. The elevator stopped at the third floor and a man boarded with me. The pictures you sent…I didn't recognize him without his hat, but he was wearing the same jacket. Stela, I—he knew that I knew who he was. He stood right beside me, edged me into the corner, leering the whole time. There was nothing covert about it."

Elizabeth shivers, and I lead her over to the small sofa in the corner. I would give anything to have hunted before I began shadowing Collins, so that I could comfort her now the way she so clearly desires. Even her warm hands around my wrists are enticing. Gently, I move to free myself from her hold, but she tightens her grasp.

"What is it with you?" she snaps. "One second you're inventing excuses to touch me, but the minute I initiate physical contact you pull away?"

I have met few people quicker to anger than she is, myself included. Elizabeth is angered if she is afraid, if she is sad, and above all when she has been made to feel foolish. She is her mother's daughter completely, more so than she would like to think.

"I mean you no offense. I have not yet fed this evening, and it would be wise if you kept your distance until I have."

Elizabeth releases me and straightening her scrubs, moves quite obviously as near to the opposite armrest as she can. A nervous laugh escapes her lips before her hands can smother the sound, but she says nothing, eyes skirting the edges of the room as though she only just realized that she has effectively sealed herself inside with a deadly occupant. I had hoped we were beyond this distrust.

"Elizabeth, if my intent was to harm you, I would have done so weeks ago."

"But you want to, right? A part of you...that's what you're saying."

Reasoning with this woman is exhausting. If you raised a lion from a cub, it would be loyal to you. But if you starved that animal for days on end, deprived it of sleep, and then tried to hold it in your arms, would you blame the lion for attacking? We are all animals at our core, in the most basic sense. Another sharp scream builds at the base of my skull, and the muscles in my body constrict against the pain. I rub my temples, willing the discomfort to the back of my mind, focusing on the sounds of the hospital: the hum of the lights, the thrum of fingers against keyboards, and the drip of IVs. I reach inside my coat pocket and slip on my sunglasses.

"Please," I beg her. "Continue. Mr. Collins boarded the elevator, then what happened?"

"He lifted my shirtsleeve and asked about my scar."

"What did you tell him?"

She shrugs. "I just said it was an accident and pulled away. He laughed at me and stepped between me and the doors." Elizabeth fights off tears. "He lifted his shirt. There were three poorly sutured GSWs on his torso, fully healed. Old wounds. He said, 'yeah, these were accidents too.' And he winked at me, like we were friends." Her hands ball into white fists, and her shiver is one of disgust, not fear. "When the doors opened, I shoved him in the chest as hard as I could, and pushed past him, and he let me go. He was still laughing as the doors closed. He said my name. When I got to Pathology they told me no one had requested a file from the fourth floor."

I place my hand on her forearm, and Elizabeth relaxes under my touch. The roar in my head eases too, and I find myself wondering if some small part of this pain is due to my refusal to accept this woman's hold over me. And could I lose myself entirely in her warmth?

"I knew you were here," she whispers. Her eyes meet mine without hesitation. "The air changes the closer you are."

"In what way?"

She brushes her fingers over my arm. "I don't know," she admits. "Charged. Almost electric."

A pleased smirk steals across my lips and I run my palm over her shoulder blades. A sigh catches in her throat, and she turns away from me. The sensation that accompanies Elizabeth's proximity is similar—it simply exists, as she exists. Magnetic. The nearer she is the more influenced my environment becomes by her emotions. Now she is frightened, and alone. The chill of that fear reaches me before the sound of her quiet sob. I pull her shoulder back, but she refuses to look at me. I cup her chin in my hand and turn her face. Her cheeks are splotched with pink, and her rich brown eyes are red-rimmed and weary.

"Are you afraid?"

Elizabeth pulls her chin from my palm and reaches for a box of tissues.

"No. I mean, yes, of course I am. But it's everything. This man—Collins. My mother. You. This…" She gestures vaguely between our bodies, and crumples the tissue in her palm. "I'm not usually a crier."

"I know. I have a great many limitations, Elizabeth. But at least one of your problems is well within my area of expertise." We stand together, slowly, both exhausted. Elizabeth's lips are pressed in a firm line. "Stay in this room until I have gone. We should not be seen together."

Her small fist balls the edge of my emerald sweater in her clammy fingers. "What are you going to do?"

I slide my sunglasses down and stare into her hesitant eyes until her lids grow heavy, and her hand loosens its grip and falls into my waiting palm. She drifts closer to me, lulled by the promise of peace. I stare down at her hand, which seems so small. Collins has frightened her, intimidated her, stalked her, and no doubt intends to do much more than that. A possessiveness I have only ever felt for Fane rises in my chest, so swiftly I cannot obscure the malice that twists my features. Elizabeth snatches her hand away, and takes a step back.

"I am going to pay a visit to Mr. Collins."

* * *

Elizabeth's only reprieve the past week has been between the hours of one and four a.m. every other day when Mr. Collins abandons his surveillance and heads to the mortuary to collect the evening's bounty from Derek Carrington. Little good it does her, as her mother rises promptly at six every single morning. I waited in the shadows beside Elizabeth's brownstone until the sun threatened to rise and Mr. Collins drove off for a few precious hours of sleep.

My family hunts only those who will not be missed and our night is staggered to keep the number of disappearances to a minimum. Month after month, measured by the flesh of the dead. Year in, and year out. The task of obscuring the ever-mounting body count belongs to Bård, and I sometimes accompany him on the occasional meeting with lackeys in the mayor's office, the district attorney, a tight-knit brotherhood of veteran detectives who call themselves "The True Blue"—all corrupt—and the leaders of every local gang and crime syndicate. Money talks and through the tireless efforts of the Opes family as well as lucrative side ventures—like our arrangement with Collins—Fane has more than enough to make even the most damning surveillance footage vanish. Still, we are all expected to be discreet and careful.

Down by the docks, I watch the shadowed silhouettes of strong muscled bodies shuffle below. The whole outfit is finely tuned. Fishing trawlers having emptied their cargo have empty freezers, awaiting Collins's more sinister meat. The loadmasters do not speak aloud of the work, not even to each other.

I have spent the last few hours rifling through Mr. Collins's boathouse office. His records are as meticulous as they are vague. All written in the same indecipherable shorthand, similar to what I receive from Bård. Perhaps this is a code they developed together. Where on earth did my brother meet this man? Collins is cautious, to be sure.

The screaming ache behind my eyes dulls to a low roar in favor of a sharper sense. Mr. Collins's van rumbles to a halt at the top of the incline at precisely three thirty a.m. As always, he collects his cut, secured in a manila envelope in a drained diesel barrel. In anticipation of counting his booty, he whistles a half-forgotten melody, keys jingling between his fingers and boots assuredly crunching the gravel underfoot. But the lock on the boathouse door offers no resistance to his key, and his jaunty tune dies mid-whistle. He shuffles his feet, and from the shadows of his office I watch his cap-covered head twist into the night to scan his surroundings.

Fear has already begun to pickle his blood, and bitter is precisely the way I imagined he would taste. He slips the pistol from his waistband and steals into his office. Papers rustle beneath his feet, a whirlwind of mess spread across the floor. The acrid stench of human perspiration fills the air, and his pheromones carry me further and further away from myself. The thirst. Always the thirst. My throat, unbearably dry, constricts.

From the corner, in the deepest shadows and just in front of the barrel of his gun, the swoon of the hunt hits me like an inescapable tide. Heat—or the anticipation of it—licks its way from the tips of each finger, to the soles of my feet and curls between my ribs, my body spreading open on the inside.

The blaze rages through my veins as Collins fumbles a frantic hand along the wall, searching for the light switch, lowering his pistol in the process. All my distraction, the fatigue, the booming in my head, the sun-weary ache behind my eyes, the worry, the doubt over this treachery and Elizabeth—all of it burns to a cinder, and what is left is instinct.

One hand clamps over his gaping mouth, and the other twists the gun from his distracted grip. I push the cold steel barrel against the base of his skull, and all protest leaves his body until he is as stiff and still as the chilled corpses in his van. "Turn around."

Collins does not hesitate, and when he faces me his eyes are deceptively calm. His muscles tell a different story, taut and thrumming with unspent violence as he fights the futile impulse to retaliate. I press my face so close to his that our noses touch and my eyes stretch to fill my sockets, to swallow him whole. His muscles loosen, as though slipping into a warm bath, lips parted, mouth slack. My body shakes from the effort to restrain my hunger, to remain calm.

"Mr. Collins, I apologize for the mess."

Tears gather in his eyes as he stares back unblinking, mute.

"Does your wife know the nature of your business?"

He can only nod.

"Good man. Honesty is the foundation of a strong union."

Fat tears roll unfettered down his stubbled cheeks.

"You love your family, Mr. Collins. You want to protect them." Again, he nods. "Write a letter to your wife. Tell her to take the children and leave the city this very morning. She must call no one. Tell her to stay with someone she trusts, and not to return until you come to get her."

I back him against the desk, careful not to break eye contact until pen and paper are in his hands.

"Write to her. Something urgent, but nothing specific."

Reeling from the sedation of our encounter, Collins hastily scribbles his final correspondence. When he reaches the affectionate valediction, his penmanship steadies, and upon concluding the signature, he grips the pen as tightly as a blade. His right hand raises to plunge the pen into my breast, but I sidestep behind him with an arm around his waist.

He opens his mouth to scream—they always do—but my hand is already in place, closing his mouth, drawing the long neck back. The flesh erupts under my teeth, and the blood—molten in its slow-moving heat—crashes down my throat in a maelstrom of memory. The faces of his children, sweaty after play. His wife's soft body, limp and sated beneath him. Her trembling arms wrap around his neck as though it were my own, and my grip on Collins doubles. The spinal cord pops in that satisfying way that few will ever know. Gauzy flashes of life. The threads disintegrate as the blood slows, a warning of his imminent demise I ignore out of sheer contempt for this man.

I drink deeper than I have in years, to the bottom of him, to the base of the cup, until the memories drown and all that fills my mind is an unfathomable and impenetrable darkness. Mr. Collins takes his first wavering step out of my grasp and into cold oblivion, and I rear back, shoved to safety by death herself as the body crumples at my feet.

If there exists anything more ravenous than my kind, it is the vacuum that awaits us, and though I learned several lifetimes past that death has no interest in me, neither am I welcome in her realm. I press my palms to the top of his desk, powerless to stop the icy shiver that races down my spine, a cold that penetrates my bones despite the heat of his stolen blood.

A moment's meditation is required, a deliberate and sobering breath, and in my reflection Fane finds me. A familiar swell of gratitude washes over me, warm and honest, that my Lord saw fit to save me from such an impersonal fate, and blessed me with life eternal. However far I have fallen from his grace, the honor of being the only human from which Fane has ever fed, is mine.

The poison of my unclean, mortal blood which Fane took into himself was made extraordinary at great personal cost. For weeks he lay in bed, tainted by my humanity, writhing in pain. Strigoi blood, his nightly fare, could not cleanse him. The blood of a fellow Moroi was the only known antidote. And had a Moroi felt physical pain before, or was Fane the first? Did death keep him barred from the black beyond, hanging on the precipice between the living and the deceased by her crooked fingers?

Once he was restored Fane refused to speak of the experience.

Why turn me himself when any Strigoi under his command would have readily ushered me across the divide?

A low bellow gurgles from the depths of the trawler docked below. I set to work swapping Collins's clothes with mine, leaving his worn denim in place and looping my own emerald sweater down over his head and shoulders. I don his yellowed undershirt, his black Carhart jacket, stuffing the pockets with his identifiers: wedding ring, watch, wallet. I tuck my hair inside his cap as the boat cries its final warning.

Any one of the young men waiting to load the cargo could recognize his face. I kneel beside his head and remove the straight razor from my boot. The body is dry and barren as bone. A few shallow scores along the jaw, the forehead, the eyes, and the skin separates in my hand like the rotten peel of some exotic fruit. I have not scalped a man in centuries. I fold the flesh against itself and shove the evidence in the outermost pocket of my stolen coat.

I hoist Collins's horribly disfigured body into my arms, and shoulder him through the side door. The edge of the road is clotted with helpful shadows and at the top of the hill, I open the back of his van. Five bodies lie tangled in the cargo hold. Two with the ghastly pallor of the freshly exsanguinated, and three more riddled with bullet wounds. There is little time to wonder just how many other business partners Mr. Collins had as I flip one carcass on its side and shove Collins to the bottom of the stack.

At the foot of the incline, the young men stand shoulder to shoulder in a ready line. I whip the van around and slowly back down the dock. The crew smacks the side of vehicle and I throw it into park. With the engine running, three men lift the bodies into the night, as a fourth works to cast off the ship.

"What the hell were you doing up there, asshole?" a thickly bearded man asks familiarly. I throw a gloved hand over my shoulder and raise a middle finger. The crew cackles and continue to collect their bounty.

The gasps are audible when they reach for Collins's body, and the well-oiled machine grinds to an abrupt halt. A string of coarse words, the bearded man crosses himself, and I tighten my grip on the steering wheel, one hand waiting on the gear stick. The youngest among the crew mutters under his breath that this job is not worth it. The rear door slams and with a rap of hands against the back window, I throw the vehicle into drive.

My work here is not over. I hide the van behind the boathouse and reenter Collins's office.

I text a short message to Elizabeth that she can rest peacefully tonight and resume her usual routine in the morning.

Collins's letter to his wife is waiting on the desk. I secure it in the manila envelope he collected this evening, and empty the contents of the safe beneath the desk into a duffel bag hanging from the back of the door. Collins's personal effects cannot be delivered to his widow, of course. But in the morning, she will wake to a considerable sum and an odd note in bed beside her, where her husband should have been.

In an oil drum at the back of the building, I place the jacket with all its incriminating content and douse the evidence in petrol. There is just enough petrol left to deal with the van, but not here.

Sleep, when it finally descends upon me is fevered with visions. Mr. Collins standing behind his two young boys, pushing their curved backs high overhead on a rusted swing set. Their short legs kicking the air and behind them, Collins's skull shining in the bright morning light, bits of meat still clinging to his cheekbones, his mouth—all teeth—stretching on forever in ghastly, lipless amusement. And as the sun descends for the night and wakefulness returns to me, Collins is waiting at the foot of my bed, a motionless, fleeting shadow, while Erebus whines in a crumpled pile of spiny fur in the far corner of my chamber.

* * *

The waning evening hours are spent on the phone with Andrew, poring over Fane's finances to ensure I can answer any question, and that Lydia will never again be better versed in our financial state than I am. She has always had ideas above her station, and she has been after my position in Fane's heart and his affairs since the night she was made. Andy surprises me with his cordiality, his candor. To his eternal credit, my Lord was right about him. Pampered his entire privileged life, Andrew was lacking the proper motivation to serve our family well.

Fear is a great motivator, after all.

I am mindful to be seen about the compound, and careful not to hide myself in my room. Civil when I bid good evening to Lydia, warm when I greet my Lord. Crogher and I discuss the hounds, and Erebus's reclusiveness. I spar in the armory with Bård while Fane looks on from the hall with familiar amusement. I lose, of course. And though the right to move aboveground has never been denied me, I leave the compound as quietly as a thief, and exit my chambers through the service tunnel, instead of the hatch.

Elizabeth stands in a circle of blue-uniformed nurses beneath the overhang of the Emergency doors, dodging clouds of second-hand smoke. Hers is the only voice I can distinguish. Elizabeth's attention turns toward me gradually, whether I wish to be noticed or not. Brown eyes pitch across the parking lot as she shifts her bag to the other shoulder, and then she stops. She can sense my proximity, but she waits until her colleagues disperse. She does not approach my vehicle until the last has vanished from sight.

"What are you doing here?" she asks with her head craned through the open passenger side window. "Someone might notice." Without invitation Elizabeth tosses her purse to the floor and seats herself quickly, rolling up the tinted window.

"I came to drive you home. Unless you prefer to take the L."

She arches her brow, and grows still. Reluctantly, Elizabeth leans back against the leather with no reply apart from the eventual snap of her seat belt.

The sound of the engine as we drive is the only disturbance to the heavy silence, neither knowing where to start, or what to say. Elizabeth finds her voice in a tangle of traffic.

"Nice car." Her fingers trace the inlaid wood of the armrest, the stitching around the base of her seat.

"Thank you. You were less than complimentary the first time I drove you home."

"What?"

"The night you were wounded," I explain. "I carried you back to my car, and took you to a trusted ally. Mended you myself."

Unconsciously, Elizabeth rubs her left arm and the conversation drowns before it has really begun. She stares out her window at the familiar streets.

I find a park half a block from her door. One can never be too careful, and I am being anything but.

"Thank you."

"For?" I pull the keys from the ignition and tuck them in the pocket of my coat.

She twines the hair back round the shell of her ear, and keeps her eyes forward. "Not leaving me to bleed out, I guess. And for taking me home after."

"You needn't thank me. I am to blame for your injury."

Elizabeth appears poised to protest, but I exit the vehicle before she can continue. The soft thud of her thick-soled shoes echoes against the pavement as she rushes to catch up with me. To my surprise, the faint hairs on the back of her hand brush the back of mine in a hesitant dance. I turn my palm outward and her shy fingers entwine themselves in mine. We both stop walking, stalled in the middle of her deserted street. Blood thunders in her wrist, and the blossom of a blush spreads across her cheeks, flooding her full lips. Beneath our feet, the black street stretches out undisturbed, and if I am still, if I quiet the warnings in my mind, I can nearly convince myself that we are the only two beings left in the city.

The flashing high beams of an oncoming car break our shared trance and I pull Elizabeth roughly from harm's way, pushing her ahead of me down the short thruway between her brownstone and the next. Once more in the alleyway outside her fenced backyard, she tenses under my touch and digs her heels in. "Stop shoving me. I thought you said you took care of everything." She crosses her arms.

"I handled one threat, yes. It would be irresponsible to invite another."

The silver of the waxing moon spills down as she inches closer. "What did you do to him?"

"Elizabeth, please. Not here. If you will permit me to join you upstairs, I will explain."

"Is that real?" She tilts her head. "Do you need permission to enter?"

I do not mean to laugh at her, and instantly regret having invoked another glare. "My actions thus far should confirm that I do not."

"Right," she grouses as I pull open the back gate, and urge her ahead of me. To further illustrate the point, I silently let myself into the darkened kitchen a step ahead of her and lock the door behind us.

Once inside Elizabeth does not lead the way. "You can show yourself upstairs," she says with an intentionally flippant wave of her hand. "I need to check on my mother, jump in the shower. Won't take me long."

She is only marginally aware that the state of things has shifted, some tangible alteration to our connection. The new depth of our bond, though disquieting, is little shock to me. But then, murder is a contract. Once you have killed for someone, you belong to them.

Mounting the darkened stairs, I think of Fane and the legion of dead I have laid at his feet. Can one corpse alter the meaning of thousands? And how many masters can one serve? Is it possible to remain a loyal servant while serving yourself? And if not, to whom do I swear my allegiance? Taking Collins's life was yet another act of treason, far worse than my connection with Elizabeth. I regret it, but not enough to promise to avoid such measures with the spy that is sure to replace him.

Elizabeth is mine.

Shame washes over me, the conviction of my claim waning under the weight of a dozen implications. Her fragile frame tiptoes down the hall. I stand beside the parted curtains and scan the street below. But with a wide, gaping yawn, the city sprawls around us—wrapped in sleep—without a stir. The night is far less troubled than I.

"Is someone out there?" Elizabeth's damp hair glistens in the dark reflection of the glass. I do not turn.

"No. Not tonight."

"But you think that won't last." She pulls the front of her white, terry cloth robe tighter, and absently continues to towel dry her hair.

"Nothing lasts forever, Elizabeth. Not even peace."

"Says the person who I'm guessing can't die," she rejoins.

A small chuckle betrays my stony indifference, and I turn in her direction. "I never claimed to be invincible. I can die, of course. Just not as...organically as you."

"But you don't age," she posits.

"Are these more myths?"

Elizabeth's eyes darken, two smoldering coals in her humorless face. She drops the sodden towel on top of her dresser. She inches closer, pink toes budding against the polished floor, her ire perfectly obvious in each deliberate step. "Is that all you can give me?" she challenges, her voice deceptively reasonable. "Riddles? Answering my questions with more questions?"

"I told you before, we will not speak of peasant legends."

She stands before me, undaunted. I find myself pleased in a way I have no right to be. "If these *legends* irritate you so much, why not give me the truth?"

The truth.

Why not?

Several hundred years of firsthand experience, and sound reason. Years spent in hiding, hunting in the shadows. Centuries of last-minute relocation and upheaval.

Although she may have a point, I suppose. In all that time, it was the myths we ran from, not the truth. Never the truth.

"Fire. Beheading," I offer, though for the life of me I cannot say why. Elizabeth, who had turned her back to seek clean clothes, pauses with one hand on the open drawer. "Catastrophic blood loss can rob our bodies of the ability to regenerate, and leave us as open to assault as any other living thing. More so, in fact."

Elizabeth runs her tongue across her bottom lip, eyes wide in awe, and undeniably intrigued. "And aging?" she ventures.

"A disease to which I am immune."

The flick of her smile is just visible in the mirror.

"But I'm not," she whispers, as though to halt my slow approach. My hands, outstretched, unconsciously reaching for the curve of her hips. "So why would you go to all this trouble?"

For someone who will wither and die, she means. How many times have I asked myself the very same question? My hands fall flat at my sides, and Elizabeth stares at me from the mirror, motionless, holding her breath. She cannot know what she asks. Or how dangerously thin the line we walk grows with each encounter.

Everyone *thinks* they want to know how their story ends. Even I have speculated on my own. Far be it from me to tell her what I know, to give her the knowledge she almost begs for, and in so doing make it plain that soon she will have to choose. She can live a mortal life, forever intruded upon by this unwilling bond, and die a natural death. Or she can become something more, bonded to me by blood, bound to Fane by name. When the choice is forever with conditions, or decades with a catch, is it really a choice?

I trail the tips of my fingers up the cuff of her loose sleeves. Her desire is indistinguishable from my own, and perhaps the two are not separate at all, but one beast—two-headed—and growing stronger every wasted second. "You are not as tired today," I observe, nearer to her exposed ear than necessary. "I am glad of it."

"You told me to rest easy, and I did," she says, leaning back to be embraced. Eyes drifting closed, and so deliciously vulnerable.

"Would that you were always so adherent." I step back and with sharpened outrage she watches my steady retreat. Her curled fingers grip the lip of her dresser until I perch at the foot of her bed, waiting for her. Elizabeth's harsh swallow cannot be disguised.

Crossing her arms in that prim, forbidding way she has, Elizabeth stalks the edge of the room. She keeps as far from me as she can manage and steals my spot beside the bay window. "What did you do to him, Stela?"

"I killed him."

Elizabeth nods her head gravely, her arms wrapped around her waist. "Was he going to kill me?"

"By his own hand? I cannot say. And should it matter?" Elizabeth does not move. "It became clear that he would play some pivotal role in your execution. I have killed better men for less."

She finds my eyes from the safety of the windowpane, and though we have not spoken of the power of my direct gaze, Elizabeth appears to have an instinctual understanding. She gravitates to viewing me via reflective surfaces, and through those barriers she is protected, unreachable. "How did you do it?"

The wet weight of Collins's freshly peeled skin is a fresh memory, and it is a small mercy that Elizabeth appears to have no knowledge of the nightmares that plagued me. "That I will never tell you. As a courtesy."

Elizabeth purses her lips and turns around, leaning back against the glass. With the streetlights streaming in around her, she looks as though she flirts with the edge of an abyss. And perhaps she does.

"You know what thought keeps me awake at night?" she volunteers.

"I am sure they are numerous."

Elizabeth comes to stand between my bent knees. Even with her face tipped down, she avoids my eyes.

"If you can exist, what else is there?"

To my surprise, Elizabeth does not shy away from my touch. Instead, she allows herself to be guided by the wrists and gently settled at my side. "There are a great many wonders in this world," I begin, brushing a thick curl of hair behind her shoulder. "Be more specific."

Several times she hesitates, her fears utterly ridiculous. "Should I start sleeping with silver bullets?" She nearly laughs at herself. "Or do I need to bone up on my knowledge of the occult? Spells. Spirits. Exorcism? And is there some kind of FAQ? What to do when you've thoroughly pissed off the powers that be? *How to Navigate the Unexplainable? A Rational Woman's Guide to the Irrational World? Witches, and Everything You Need to Know About Hexes?*"

"Silver bullets?" I nudge her with my shoulder.

"Stela, if you're going to make fun of me, I'd rather you just leave."

She is suddenly sullen and exhausted, as though the mere act of giving voice to such folly has drained her completely. Without thinking, I reach out and sweep her hair aside, stroking the back of her neck with my thumb. A small sigh escapes her parted lips and though her expression remains furrowed, guarded, Elizabeth leans against my side. She takes hold of my free hand and draws it into her lap, a silent plea to give what answers I can, if only so she can sleep without fear.

"Werewolves were a misunderstanding. Like many superstitions. But there remains a grain of truth."

Elizabeth perks up, intrigued. "What truth? Which part?"

I turn to face her with both legs crossed on the mattress and she follows suit, bringing our knees together. Storytelling is an art I have never had occasion to perfect.

"A great many years ago, in a small village belonging to what is now the Swedish city of Västerås, a Strigoi was made in the worst possible way. His Maker drained this man of blood, but must have taken pity on him and let him drink from immortal veins. The man had no brood, or shelter, or master, and was abandoned before he was named. He was left to wake in the woods alone, freshly buried beneath a blanket of snow with the sunlight gleaming all around him. He suffered the same pain you felt the morning after you woke with my blood fresh in your veins, only a hundredfold worse.

"The man crawled on hands and knees to return home, every movement under the weight of the sun excruciating. His wife—a strong, kind woman—tended to him beside the hearth, where he collapsed for two days. She sent their only child, a son, back and forth from the village for drinking water. But no matter how many cups she raised to her husband's pale lips, his thirst could not be sated, and the man wailed, writhing in agony, begging for more.

"On the third day, he awakened as his wife leaned over him to lay a cool compress on his brow, and drape him with blankets she had warmed beside the fire."

Elizabeth leans forward, still clutching my hand. She tightens her grip just as I begin to reconstruct the story, to soften the sharp edges. As if to remind me, without speaking, that all she asks is the truth.

"I have often wondered, what kind of hell it must have been… to have your only son find you like that. Bent over his mother's lifeless body. For surely, he loved the boy, even then. Even as the blood ran down his chin. But he was feral, and the son fared no better than she."

I pause to take stock of Elizabeth. The air around us is curiously quiet. "Realizing what he had done, the man covered his family with the blankets and fled. For days he walked, deeper and deeper into the black forest, but he was not alone. The son's wolfhound, Bjorn, was close at his heels.

"In four days' time, the bloat of his family's blood had all but abandoned him. The thirst—which never abates—was sharper, and brighter than before, because now, you see, he knew exactly what he needed. Bereft, and encamped as far from his village as his body could carry him, he called to the wolfhound and fed from him.

When the beast stopped clawing at the man's face and chest, he paused. Bjorn whimpered in his lap, struggling for those last shallow breaths, and the man—being so recently human—was overcome with sorrow. He could not bear to see what he had done, and so he bent over the mutt, spilling his heartache into the coarse fur, lamenting all that he had lost.

And then there came the leathery pull of a long dry tongue that ran down the gashes at the man's neck, still healing slowly. When he pulled away, the hound tried to lift its head, his silver snout smeared with blood. He raised Bjorn's head in his hands, and with surprising strength the animal continued to lick his master's wounded chest.

The man recalled his own attack just days before, in those very woods, the horror he visited upon those most dear to him, and opened his own wrist with a hunting blade. The wolfhound lapped at it too, until the wound closed, and to the man's shock, the hole in the beast's throat began to close.

"They fed from one another in that same manner for a fortnight, during which time the man noticed that Bjorn had grown a least five inches in height. The dog was also more sprightly than he, and would often set out ahead of him, returning with live game for his master.

But one golden evening, the man awoke on the shore of the river Svartån with the beast nowhere to be found. For several hours, he walked in the moonlight, along the icy bank, following Bjorn's footprints in the snow, until finally, he found him. The beast had consumed an entire hunting party, save for one gangly young boy who screamed in pain and terror as Bjorn pulled his torn ravaged body down toward his master.

"All that time, although feeding from all manner of game, the man still experienced a crippling unslaked thirst. He praised the hound, and drank the offering without pity or remorse. Together, the pair continued in such a fashion for longer than the man could count. He would wake alone, in some desolate place, and he would follow the paw prints in the snow until he was reunited with Bjorn, who never emerged without an offering.

"But the hound was smarter than the man could know. His senses as sharp as ten wolves, and all too late the man realized that the wolf had brought them to the outskirts of another, smaller village. The man bolted into action, calling out to the dog. This time, Bjorn did not answer his master's call.

When the man reached the encampment he fell to his knees in despair. Just at the edge of the tree line, suspended between towering branches, was the empty weeping carcass of his faithful companion. But two armed villagers heard the anguished cries of the man, and approached the stranger, high up in the tree as he attempted to cut the ropes laced around the hound's great paws. The man dropped from the branches and attacked the larger of the party, while the other fled to alert his fellow villagers, pounding his fists against the mud walls of the surrounding huts, screaming *Varulv!*

"From that village, the legend spread of a hound the size of three wolves, drunk on human blood. And of the beast's master, or the man trapped inside the animal, who came to the village to wreak vengeance on the brave men who captured and killed the monster."

For once, Elizabeth does not repay my honesty with cynicism. In fact, she does not reply straightaway. She merely stares, open-mouthed, seemingly saddened by the tale. "What happened to the man?"

I sweep my thumb across her cheek, and smile as reassuringly as I can. "The man escaped the villagers, but he was alone for many years until he discovered more of his kind."

Her eyes narrow to slits, and it is clear the skeptic has returned before she utters a word. "Where did *you* hear this story? How do you know it's the truth?"

With a weary sigh, I stretch out across the mattress, raised on my elbows.

"When I was young, the only things that traveled any distance were plague or parable. My village elders used a similar tale to keep children from wandering in the woods after dark. And many years later, the man himself told me his side of things."

Elizabeth's face falls, lips turned ghostly pale and pressed tight as though fending off a scream. She wins this internal struggle—thankfully—and after a steadying breath she reclines alongside me, her head balanced in one hand. She watches me closely, unblinking, rolling the story over in her mind, picking it apart and digesting it piece by piece. She searches my face for a wry smile, something physical to confirm my falsehood.

"You know him?"

"Indeed. Quite well, and for some time now. He's my kinsman, Bård. The word means devil in old Scandinavian. Fane, my Maker, named him, claimed Bård as his own. But that was ages before my time. It was the story that first endeared Fane to Bård. We did not know that our blood had power over beasts and Fane was impressed, which is no small feat. Bård presented Fane with a male and a female pup to show his gratitude and fealty."

Elizabeth collapses with a theatrical thud and rolls over on her back, staring blankly at the ceiling. I tug the edges of her robe together where they have begun to part down her chest. She barely seems to notice.

"The Moroi, Fane's kind, are different. They were not made, but born of two Strigoi. They have special skills. For example, the ability to set fires with their minds." Elizabeth releases a quiet gasp. "You equated my presence, my nearness to you, to electricity. The sensation preceding these fires is similar, more volatile, obviously, and the heat can be detected by bystanders, as well as the intended target. The Moroi are the only creatures that prey on the Strigoi, my lot. They possess a force powerful enough to obliterate us, their closest competitors, with just a focused glare."

Elizabeth curls on her side, drawing her limbs close. Her chilled toes brush my shin. Perhaps it was unwise to tell her, in no uncertain terms, that there are things in this world far more formidable than I am.

"Fane. Your Maker is a Moroi?"

"The head of the family is always Moroi. They also have the power to name, to claim."

"And you've seen him do this? You've seen him set fires?"

"I have. But I do not wish to recount any such unpleasantness tonight."

She tightens under my casual touch, not because it is unwelcome. "Where is Fane from? Originally?" A change of tack, but as undeterred as ever.

"He is native to the Balkans."

"In your dream he was fair-skinned, with bright eyes. He looked more Nordic than Eastern European. Certainly, not Romani. He's too pale to be descended from folk who originated in Northern India."

"Have you done much reading on the migratory patterns of early tribes in fourteenth century Europe?" Her eyes narrow, body coiling for an argument. "The Moroi are all fair of feature, at least by the standards of their respective regions. So much so that in the light, you can see the purple casing of their muscles beneath the skin, trace the path of each vein. It is the reason Fane cannot move aboveground unnoticed."

Elizabeth gnaws thoughtfully on her bottom lip. "Is that why you're so pale?"

My shoulders shake from the force of another smothered laugh. She could not hope to understand the flattery she has heaped upon me, or the insult she has dealt my Lord by raising my station. "I was turned, not born. There's a vast difference. All I know of my past is that I was an anomaly, which was an omen in those days. I was the first child born to my village with blue eyes and blond hair. Hence the haste to rid the village of my presence. Fane taking me away was an alternative to drowning me in the river."

Elizabeth stares at me, grave and discomfortingly quiet, as though trying to imagine my dark eyes as they once were. She raises a hand between us, inches from my face, a finger hovering above my brow. She changes course, threading her fingers through her hair instead. "You said Bård means 'devil,'" she continues with forced airiness. "Are all your names equally revealing?"

"Stela in Romanian means 'star.' Fane so named me the night I was turned. He said that is what I was to him, his night star, his star pupil."

Elizabeth scoffs. "A stela is also a stone slab or pillar used for commemorative purposes." She raises a hand to her mouth as though the words might be swallowed unspoken. Her eyes glass over. The door between our minds must open both ways, because without a single word of acknowledgment from me, Elizabeth is fending off a frightful round of tears, like my pain is a part of her. "I don't know why I said that," she chokes, shaking her head savagely. "I didn't mean to do that."

"Names are powerful things. Sacred."

"I know," she assures.

She could not possibly. I stare impassively at the ceiling. It would be so easy to end this madness. A moment of shared bliss, and never another careless utterance. Never another betrayal to Fane. A clean slate, a new beginning.

The bed dips beneath me and Elizabeth leans up on her side. Her thin fingers brush across my forehead, sweeping stray hairs aside. She strokes my furrowed brow, her face contrite, and traces the line of my jaw. "I'm sorry. I hit a nerve. I hurt you."

"Turnabout is fair play, I suppose."

"Stela, look at me. Please." She turns me by the chin. She meets my eyes with fearless intensity. She opens herself, she lets me inside without a blink, without subterfuge. Her sorrow is rancid on my tongue. "Parents," she sighs, fidgeting with the collar of my shirt, "have a way of making their children feel like an extension of themselves. A means to achieve immortality."

"Our relationship is more complex than that." Elizabeth nods, blinking her dark brown eyes clear. "He is my Maker, not my parent. And immortality is his to dispense as he chooses."

Her fingers keep busy with the lines of my blouse, stroking, straightening. She smooths her hand over my collarbone. Eyelids heavy, but gaze steadfast, the pressure of Elizabeth's thigh between my legs is a surprise. Her robe has parted, leaving the limb exposed and warm against me—dizzying, even. She trails her fingertips over my lips, and in her touch are traces of all the objects those hands have held: countless cups of coffee, milled lavender soap, latex, Formica, iodine. I consider—against my better judgment— the flavors waiting on her tongue. Once entertained, the impulse is nearly impossible to ignore.

Further discourse could only serve to ruin what has already begun to unfold. I ghost the tips of my fingers up the back of her thigh and her lips part, hovering centimeters above mine. She tangles her delicate hand in the front of my blouse, shivering, uncertain as to whether she is frightened of me, or enamored, and probably too young to care. "This is a bad idea," she affirms in a whisper.

An undignified yelp escapes her when I flip our position, but she does not go without a fight. Elizabeth remains raised on her elbows, her back arched like the neck of a harp. "Without doubt." Her whisper is catching. I brush the hair from her eyes with a tenderness that surprises me. "This is the worst idea I have ever had."

Doe-eyed and uncharacteristically silent, her lips quiver into a smile. I cradle the back of her head in my palm and listen to her body. Her rigid frame is caught in a war of fight or flight. She lifts her head and the tendons in her neck bulge—a stark reminder of how ill-advised this illicit affair truly is—but her frantic, uneven breath rushes over my lips and I cannot deny either one of us any longer.

The second our mouths meet my own impulses wage a blitzkrieg. The taste of her tongue, her warmth amplified, her galloping heart wears my defenses so frightfully thin that every inch of my body shakes with restraint. I have lain with more mortals than I can count, and not one among them has ever lived to see the morning sun. But any warning bells are consumed in the blaze of her thundering blood.

Elizabeth pulls her mouth away with a drowning gasp, urging me closer with pleading hands, trembling uncontrollably as I oblige. I drag my hand down the side of her flushed face, the front of her robe, and wrap my fingers around the already loose belt. She neither moves nor speaks, panting, heavy eyes that dart back and forth between mine. Her intoxicating scent, the heat leaching into my bones is such distraction that my fingers fumble with the knotted fabric. She grins, clearly pleased with her effect on me. Her eyes press firmly shut as my hand charts the length of her exposed torso. I kiss her lips, the decadent cleft of her chin, and holding her neck in my hand I press my mouth to the middle of her throat.

Frightened, Elizabeth's palms press defensively against my breast in a sobering move for both of us. We remain locked in that position, Elizabeth blinking the lust from her eyes as I stroke the skin above her pounding heart. In a short eternity, her pulse steadies and those sharp eyes render me mute as her hands begin a journey all their own, down my abdomen, under the hem of my shirt. The effort to remain self-possessed is too much to bear.

"Elizabeth—"

"Don't."

She raises my shirt overhead—forgoing the meddlesome buttons altogether—and pulls my bare chest against hers, and there is nothing else. Nothing exists beyond her warm and welcoming limbs, her racing heart, the swift drum of her blood as it races beneath the skin, tapping like Morse code against my fingers.

Despite our best efforts, the skyline ignites with the mauve hues of the approaching sunrise. Elizabeth makes a disgruntled sound and twists onto her stomach, limbs flung out in every direction, as I quietly shrug into my trousers.

"Where are you going?" she groans into the bedclothes.

I drape my blouse across the foot of the bed and crawl alongside her. Surely, we can spare a moment before the inevitable. She bunches the sheets as she turns over, wrapping my neck in her weak arms and burying her face in my shoulder.

"I have to return home before sunrise." The tunnels will be empty, apart from the hounds, as will the corridors should I choose to take them. Perhaps it would be best to return with my head held high through the main gate, as though nothing were amiss. My siblings have all retired for the day, or will have by the time I join them. Fane, however, is another matter entirely.

Elizabeth protests, tightening her grasp and holding me close. She releases me reluctantly and I part with a kiss to her cheek, the corner of her mouth, though she is too exhausted to respond. She smiles sleepily under the attention, and I hastily retrieve my blouse, buttoning as I slip my feet back into my boots.

"Stela?" She rises on one arm, her hair tumbling over her face.

"Sleep. It is nearly dawn."

She flicks the hair from her eyes with an aggravated jerk of her head. "What was your name? Before?"

I hesitate on the last button and regard her timid face from over my right shoulder. Why should it matter now? So many lifetimes hence?

"I was called Ruxandra."

Elizabeth is careful not to move. Her eyes dip down, shift right—a memory.

"I heard your mother say it. In the dream, when Fane came to take you away."

"Did you? What else did you hear?"

She opens her mouth but utters no sound. Her pulse quickens, and through sheer force of will alone her eyes stay focused on mine, intent. "Nothing." She lowers herself back into bed with a tight smile. "Will I see you soon?"

I run my fingers along the top of her exposed foot. "Soon," I assure her. "Until then, Elizabeth."

She watches after me as I pull the door gently closed, and through the barrier I sense her eyes upon me still. I linger at the top of the stairs, listening to her breath as it grows deep and heavy, as first threads of sleep reclaim her. The dip of the mattress as her body goes slack.

Why should she lie about a dream?

VIII
Not With A Bang

Who can say how, or when it happened? Did I fall straightaway, in one sweeping rush from our first meeting? Or was it a series of small, innocuous concessions that built on the back of the other, until there was no space inside of me that hadn't been altered by Stela?

When we started, she was a fleeting shadow skirting the edge of my life. A half-remembered face lurking around every corner, waiting behind a closed door. Stela was the breath ghosting across my neck. The unexpected assault of lilac and earth. The tinge of iron that seemed to cling to her, like a droplet of rain at the tip of a petal.

Stela was always more than a figment, and she's more than a presence in my bed, or fingers brushing the small of my back, or lips that spread into a smile against the shell of my ear, on the inside of my thigh. I can taste her as I exhale, feel her skin pressed against mine, even clothed. I wear proof of her existence in the goose bumps that bloom down my arms in the middle of the day. I can picture her so vividly that I question whether I'm asleep or awake. And are those moments her dreams, or mine?

The fear hasn't left me, but it's astounding what I've grown accustomed to. I know the carmine stain on her lips means she's already fed, and she'll stay until I've fallen asleep. I know that the taste of blood will linger on her tongue, waiting to be shared. She won't hesitate to reach for me. And I know the vulgar shade of red, the too-sweet taste of her mouth will excite me in ways that sicken and shame me into silence.

She is heartbreakingly beautiful. It's hard to believe that I ever mistook her for a human being. She obscures everything when she's near, the whole world narrowing to a single point, with the absolute certainty that Stela is the only thing that matters.

That conviction is so strong it terrifies me.

I don't know if I dread these stolen evenings, or hold my breath waiting for her return. My body responds in a similar way, arching into her touch only to recoil just as quickly. Like teetering on the edge of the stairs with my crossed arms, waiting to be sucked down into darkness. Being with Stela is like falling, but the ground never rushes up to meet me.

There are peaceful moments. Time before and hours after, when our bodies are folded together and Stela fills the loaded quiet with colorful stories of villages long since dead. And we talk.

The night before last I was spent, and had wrapped myself around her body. My fingers traced the sharp lines of her collarbone, my leg draped casually across her hips. How is something so resilient, and in possession of such innate strength, still so soft?

"What drives you?" I asked, my cheek pressed against her shoulder.

"I have never viewed life as a choice. We live until we die. Had you asked me six months, or sixty years ago, I would have said loyalty." Stela grew solemn, her grip tightening around my midsection as though the topic frightened her.

"And now?" I whispered, worried that an ill-timed question would speed her departure.

Stela shifted, relinquishing her hold on me to lie on her side with her head propped in her pale hand. I doubt I'll ever grow accustomed to her eyes, the weight of her unwavering stare. I don't know what she sees when she looks at me, but I'm certain she sees more than I would ever willingly share.

"I continue because I am," she responded as though the question was ridiculous. "What motivates you?" she rejoined with a pleased smirk.

"The pursuit of happiness."

Stela arched her brow and fought valiantly against laughing. "The least you can do is repay my candor, Elizabeth."

"I used to think praise was enough. My father was generous with his. When he died, I craved it, terribly. But my mother has always believed that accomplishment is enough. I tried to believe it too." I saw no need to elaborate. Somehow, I knew she understood. A person cannot sustain themselves on accomplishments alone, something I had learned only when the validation stopped, after I'd come home and lost myself in the task of caring for my mother. Outside academia, I was lost. There were no awards, no competitions, and I realized that all my honors meant nothing to the rest of the world. And they were no longer a comfort to me either.

"I do not believe that any being capable of conscious thought is above accolades," Stela said, hand moving over my shoulder to cup the side of my neck. She drew her thumb down the edge of my jaw.

"Hope," I said. "I hope more now than I ever have. That this stagnancy is temporary. That I'm still meant for more."

Stela nodded gravely. "As do I." She spoke too softly for me to doubt her sincerity. Stela pushed me onto my back, her fingers finding the edges of the still-red scar on my bicep. She circled the raised ridge with her thumb before bowing her head to press her lips to the wound. The blood thundered under the new flesh, as though answering her call, like the blood she gave me the night I was injured remembered where it belonged and desperately wished to return. Sadness washed over Stela, and rushed through me as though it were my own. Stela has repeated that action many times: a hand on my arm, a finger tracing the raised skin with a forlorn expression.

Last night, after a horrendously long shift at the hospital, I came home to a mountain of dishes. Upstairs Stela was draped along the foot of my bed and as exhausted as I was, I couldn't bring myself to ask her to leave. I wasn't sure I wanted her go. My distraction lingered as I shed my scrubs, until Stela's hand ran lightly over my mangled arm.

"Do you regret what you are?" I said. Is Stela capable of remorse? She withdrew her touch and eyed me with suspicion.

"Only that I might have outlived my usefulness," she replied, still as stone. "That I have no place in this new world, or worse, that I cannot find contentment in what I have. Never that I was turned. Does that disappoint you?" she asked with an amused tilt of her head, as though the answer mattered little.

I honestly don't know what answer I'd been gunning for, or why. Stela has existed this way for ages, far longer than she lived as human. She has an unusual perspective of duty, and weirdly, what she believes to be a strict moral code. The cruelty, the bloodshed, the horror she's wreaked doesn't touch her. But I can't reconcile the Stela that kisses the ache from my arm, with the monster that has no doubt murdered thousands of unsuspecting people, and that is a problem for me.

I knew in that moment that she would never apologize for what she is, no matter the fallout. My distaste for her diet, though not directly voiced, dropped like an iron curtain between us. I marveled that of all the people I have ever known I am closer to Stela than any of them.

How much of that infatuation has to do with the physical reaction her proximity elicits? And are my feelings for her genuine, or is it chemical? In such moments, her eyes disgust me. Magnetic as they manage to be at all other times, they twist into empty pools. But I can only hold on to the disgust for as long as it takes her to coax me into the void, and I begin counting the seconds between the last time she touched me, and the next. Which is how we ended up facing each other, my body only half clothed, and then bare. We stood, silent, staring each other down, and then she was above me in bed. Everything in between is a blur.

It was late when Stela stirred. She lifted herself from the bed in a stretch as graceful as a pirouette. Her long limbs glowed faintly blue in the moonlight. She tumbled into the armchair. She'd spent hours with me and though she didn't say it, her departure from bed was an unspoken instruction for me to sleep while she kept watch. She draped her legs over the arm of the chair, and stared at the street below my window.

I lay down with my head at the foot of the bed so that I could watch her until I fell asleep, and pulled the blanket around my torso. Her body leaches the heat from mine until she's as warm to the touch as anyone else, and I'm left grasping for the comforter, a few degrees cooler than I should be.

Her face was obscured by the sharp cut of her hair, which gleamed like silver in the light. She looked like a porcelain doll, her skin polished and hard.

"Surely, it must intrigue you," she mused. "What would you give in exchange for everlasting life, Elizabeth?" I had no answer prepared, though I'd asked myself that question many times. Stela continued, as though she was asking herself the same thing. "What morals, what convictions would you compromise? Could you harm? Could you kill for it?" Had I scoffed at the question, Stela would have seen right through me. If I deflected with a joke, she would press.

"Why didn't I turn when you gave me your blood?" I asked, leaning up on my elbows.

She drew one foot down to the floor, and swiveled the chair to face me, crossing her legs again. She folded her hands against her bare belly, and with the light from my window shining in around her, her hair caught fire and the reflection illuminated the outer edges of her eyes.

"More is required to turn someone," she explained with a wave of her hand. "The blood must be cleansed, if you will. Had I also fed from you, had I taken your blood into myself, and then opened my veins to save you, well, I would not need to ask what you would give for eternity."

I stayed quiet. She was in a rare sharing mood. I didn't understand what had changed. "It is a dangerous dance for both parties," she continued, staring at the floor, though I knew this only because I could not sense the cloying presence of her eyes on my skin. "If I gave too much to you, the thirst would consume you, and I would descend into slumber. Akin to a coma. Likewise, should I drink too deeply from you, you would die," she trailed off "You would slither right out of my arms, and drown in the dark hereafter. I have never attempted to turn another."

I finally realized what Stela had been leading me toward all along. The implications took my breath away, and though I was still lying down the room rocked, as though a train had barreled through it. Dread, like icy fingers, ran from the base of my neck up to the top of my head. Drown in the dark hereafter…

Fearing and knowing are two completely different things.

"There's nothing after this life, is there?"

Stela didn't respond. I suppose there's no way to pacify someone as they reconcile their brevity of existence, as they struggle to accept that death is absolute. This was something I believed I'd made peace with, because there was always the possibility—however slim—that I was wrong. And that possibility is the reason people get out of bed in the morning. The sting of tears burned my dry, sleep-deprived eyes, but they were not for my inevitable end. They were for my mother, who I could not imagine slipping quietly into emptiness. They were for my father, who—if this is the truth—never watched me graduate, wasn't there when I was shipped off to college, and wouldn't be with me *in spirit* on my wedding day, because he simply *wasn't* anymore.

"Are you sure?" My voice was small.

Stela slipped out of her chair and lay in front of me, perfectly still and straight on the edge of the mattress. Her long fingers brushed my tear tracks dry, combed through my hair. "I can tell you only what I have seen," she said, "from my own death, and the death of the victims I followed to the end of their journeys. There was no bright light. No chorus of angels to sing them home. Only blackness."

Reflecting on all of this, it takes all the energy I have left to turn away from the blinding sunrise this morning and hunker down beneath my comforter, though I really should get up and check on Mother. Constant fatigue is nothing new for me, but the addition of heightened skin sensitivity is. I can hardly remember what eight hours of unbroken rest feels like. Acquaintances at work have commented, a few patients too. I've lost six pounds and the dark circles under my eyes have brightened to a frightening new shade of violet, tinged yellow at the edges. My wasted state is Mother's favorite breakfast topic.

"Elizabeth, the nineties may be in vogue again, but that doesn't mean Heroin Chic is a trend worth resurrecting."

"Please tell me it's depression and not drugs."

"Is this some sort of rebellion? Or are you conducting an elaborate social experiment?"

"For god's sake, Elizabeth, wash your hair or so help me I will drag you outside and hose you down like an animal."

I don't have the energy to spar with her, and that upsets her most. All her sharp wit, just wasted, and the best I can muster is: "What was that?" "Have you eaten?" "Of course, Mother. Of course."

The truth is it hurts to look at her. My heart breaks for the simple fact that none of it will matter when my mother draws her last breath.

Work is a different story. I find myself approaching patient care with near religious fervor, believing in the face of the most condemning diagnosis that I can wrestle these unwitting passengers back from the edge. My floor hasn't lost a patient in almost a week. I have been commended for my unwavering zeal as often as I have been questioned about my health. That is, by everyone but James. Twice he's cornered me at the nurses station, opened his mouth to speak only to shake himself as though he'd fallen asleep standing up, and both times he promptly disappeared for the remainder of my shift.

In the quiet moments, I imagine what the hospital could accomplish with just a few pints of Stela's blood on hand: bullet wounds and burns wiped away, bones setting themselves, muscles stitching themselves back together. But this is precisely the reason she maintains her anonymity. Humankind would want exactly three things with the Strigoi: to join, harvest, or eradicate them.

"Elizabeth!"

My mother's battle cry. I won't answer her. I don't have the strength to leave my bed before eight on my only day off. I barely have the energy for my early morning musings. My hand reaches out across the mussed sheets, but there is no one beside me. My mother calls again, louder this time, her voice echoing over every kitchen tile. I flip over onto my stomach and clamp a pillow over my head.

My mother's steps are slow and measured on the stairs, intentionally pronounced. The bed shakes as she stumbles into the room, throwing the curtains open.

"Go away, Mother. Sleeping."

She rips the pillow from my face and tosses it toward the dresser. "I won't have you lying about all day. Now get up. I'll start a fresh pot of coffee."

"In a little while, Mom, please. I'm exhausted."

"That's enough. I am taking you to the doctor, and I don't want to hear a single protest, Elizabeth. You can't keep moping about like this."

Squinting against the searing sunlight, I wave her away with an open hand. "I'm just tired."

My mother wraps a commanding hand around my left arm, which is still sensitive. I jerk the arm away with a curse and cover my scar.

"What is that?" she demands. "Are you injured?" She leans over me, attempting to pry my hand away. My completely misdirected anger boils over in an instant.

"Worry about your own goddamn health! I said I'm fine!"

I have never once sworn at my mother. Her expression steels over immediately, but not quickly enough to mask the pain. I grope the air for an apology, both of us stunned. Her hurt vanishes beneath her trademark indifference. She lifts her chin, presses her lips in a tight line, and there isn't a doubt in my mind that she will hold this outburst over me forever.

Mother turns sharply and storms out of the room, with my profuse apologies falling impotently at her heels. I hear it the moment my feet plant themselves on the floor—a missed footfall on the stairs. A single, staggered beat that has me out of bed in the breath before the ensuing crash.

"Mom!"

She's still falling when I reach the stairs, a tangled bouncing heap of sprawled limbs. The smack of skin against hardwood is sickening.

No.

No.

No.

My scream is so loud that its echo startles me into believing we're not alone in the house, and I turn, expecting the presence of another aghast onlooker. I take the stairs two at a time, but the damage is done. The blood has already begun to pool around her head forming a shallow red pond. I grab her shoulders and catch myself a second before I begin shaking her. Instead, I place a finger to her thready pulse. I fetch a clean towel and my cell phone. I leave the phone on speaker to keep pressure on the wound. The operator is a weary young woman with a child-like voice.

She attempts to lead me through triage, but I bark over my shoulder for her to be quiet. Mother is breathing, but that's all that can be said. She isn't conscious. She doesn't register my touch or my voice. I hold her head in line with her spine, in case she jerks awake and out of my hands. Blood seeps through the towel. The disembodied voice of the responder on the other end of the call assures me that help is on the way.

Fractured skull, probable spinal injury, subarachnoid hemorrhage, subdural hematoma, extradural hematoma.

She looks so small in her dressing gown.

"Please..." the operator stops spouting reassurances. "They have to hurry. I can't stop the bleeding."

"They're coming, Elizabeth." Did I give her my name? "Help is on the way."

"I yelled at her."

"You'll hear the sirens soon," the operator promises.

Low at first—like a fussy infant—the sound of sirens climbs up the block, the distant howl sharpening into shrill screams the closer they get.

"I can hear them," I manage between heaving sobs. "Mom? Mother? They're almost here. Please, stay with me."

Two EMTs charge across my mother's immaculate living room in a flash of stiff navy cotton and heavy black boots. I frown at their muddy trail on the Oriental rug. She'll be so displeased.

"Elizabeth, move." A short, stocky woman shoulders me back and cradles my mother's sticky head in her gloved hands. "Let us take care of her." Her partner, a tall, broad man, all shoulders, straightens Mother's limbs and prepares the spinal board. They work side by side as one four-armed beast. My mother's face only visible above their bowed backs, and further obscured by the oxygen mask.

"Can you tell us what happened?" The female technician never takes her eyes off my mother. The tall man fastens a neck brace.

"We had an argument. She was angry. Parkinson's. She isn't steady on her feet. It was too fast—she was going too fast. She missed the step. I heard, she was still falling when I got there. She didn't even cry out."

In unison they hoist my mother onto the gurney, thick black straps across her limp arms and legs. "Elizabeth, we have to move now." The technician turns and I recognize that she's Beth. The tall man, her partner, is Allen. We were friendly when I first started at the hospital, working in Emergency. Faces I have only ever seen at work, faces that do not belong in my mother's home.

"I'm coming with you." Beth spins to stop my first step. She shoves a forbidding, blue latex hand at my chest, which lingers in the air without touching. The blood makes her fingertips appear purple.

"Elizabeth," she swallows, fighting to maintain eye contact, "you're naked."

I look down. The blood is so thick on my knees and calves it's hard to believe it's not mine. My chest and arms and underwear are smeared with it.

"Get dressed. Meet us at the hospital. We have to take her now."

This would be mortifying if I could feel anything but horror. Beth and Allen depart as they arrived—in a rush through the front door, leaving a trail of blood behind. I stand at the closed door, peering through the curtains as they load my mother into the ambulance. Half the block has turned up, cell phones in hand. The second they shut the door on my mother, I collapse in violent sobs, heaving yellow bile all over my mother's ruined Persian rug.

* * *

Stela doesn't come the first night.

Hordes of attending physicians and nearly all my fellow nurses stop by to check in with us. They bring me coffee, new magazines not yet relegated to the waiting rooms, the heaviest disposable blankets in our arsenal, clean pillows from the On-Call rooms, food that I accept but don't eat.

Mother has a private suite—naturally—with a view of the harbor. Something she wouldn't appreciate awake or asleep. And Arthur checks in every hour, on the hour, though he can't be Arthur to me now. He is Dr. Richmond, acclaimed neurologist.

Mother is in surgery for hours. She has a fractured skull, two bulging discs, four broken ribs, compression fractures in vertebrae C three to six, an acute subdural hematoma that resulted in a stroke, and a shattered femur.

When they wheel her into recovery she's swollen and partially mummified in braces, sterile gauze, a full leg cast. Her face is so bruised she's nearly unrecognizable, and for a fleeting moment I fear that this isn't my mother at all—stranger mistakes have happened. But the broken body is wearing my mother's wedding ring.

I tilt the diamond toward the setting sun and bursts of square rainbows splatter across my face and chest. I am assured that the surgery was a success. There was a clot, but it has been successfully removed. The next seventy-two hours are critical. They will keep her in an induced coma. After that we can discuss further surgery, next steps.

Stela doesn't come the second night either, but around three p.m. a beautiful bouquet of white calla lilies is delivered without a card. The arrangement is too extravagant, and the flower choice too morbid to attribute to anyone else. While I admire a bloom, a shadow falls over the foot of my mother's bed. Helen's short strong figure in the doorway is a gift and a wound all at once. She's so many things: steady bracing arms, a warm heart, and a thorn that digs into my guilt. I don't deserve her comforting words, her optimism or her company, but she gives all three freely.

Helen spends the evening regaling me with stories of my mother, and the humorous tantrums Helen tolerated in private so as not to add to my growing list of troubles. She smiles fondly at her tormentor, as one would a co-conspirator.

"You didn't have to come."

Helen squeezes my forearm. I keep my fingers wrapped around my mother's wrist. Her steady pulse is soothing, the familiar throb that reminds me she hasn't left.

"Yes, I did." Helen nods. "She made a difficult patient, but when she wasn't busy testing boundaries she was a true friend." Helen speaks with such assurance and respect. I would call my mother many things: a mentor, a tyrant, a parent, a strict disciplinarian, an inspiration, but I would never consider her a friend. Not to me, or to anyone else.

The monitors chirp their slow lullaby and I take my mother's hand. She doesn't move. "I'm sorry."

Helen stands on stiff legs and kisses the crown of my head, wrapping her arms around my shaking shoulders to stifle my fresh round of tears. "Elizabeth, she was weak, unsteady on her feet. She could have fallen on my watch, and she did several times. You have nothing to apologize for."

I shake my head at her, and my own selfishness.

"You should go home," Helen suggests. "Sleep in your own bed, have a shower. I can stay with Claire tonight."

I straighten in my uncomfortable seat, and my back cracks so sharply that Helen grimaces. "Thank you, but I really can't leave her."

Helen rubs small circles between my shoulder blades and sighs. She finally checks the monitors. "I could run home for you," she offers. "Pick up a change of clothes, something to read, whatever you like."

"That's very kind, but I don't want you to—"

"Elizabeth, it's no trouble. I'm a blundering old retiree, with nothing but the morning paper waiting on me. Put me to work." She nudges me playfully, and I smile for the first time in days. Helen said the exact same thing to me a year ago when she first offered to give me a hand with Mother.

"That would be wonderful."

* * *

The walls are black as ink and the sticky linoleum under my bare feet stretches out in front of me, like a pale yellow street. The nurses station is strewn with papers and the computer monitors are blue-screened with scrolling white lines. The patient rooms are vacant, and the doors ajar. There isn't a soul left on the fourth floor.

The absolute silence is as unsettling as the dark. I know that I'm in danger, but I walk the echoing hall. The emergency exit glows a menacing red.

She's here. Close, but concealed. Why is she hiding? Why draw me deeper into this wasteland after her? The pull of her presence grows stronger with each step and the silence bears down upon me as though I'm sinking to a great depth. I open my mouth to call to her, but nothing happens. Beside me, room four-twelve radiates portent.

The hall is so dark that I'm amazed I made it this far in my journey. There are three open doors to choose from: four-twelve on the left, the waiting room to my right, and the exit in front of me. I am compelled to room four-twelve, though I know neither escape nor safety await me. The room itself sucks me inside with a greedy breath, and the door slams closed at my heels. She isn't here, but something else is waiting.

The air is sour, oddly stale. There is an unaccountable humidity, a permeating dampness, like a rancid sauna. My hands stretch out in front of me, groping for the wall or the bed, but before I can ground myself with either, my foot slides out from underneath me and I land sprawling on my back. The dampness isn't confined to the air. The floor is warm and wet, seeping through my clothes, soaking into my hair and coating my palms. The smell is everywhere at once, sharp and unmistakable. I slither backward on all fours, reaching for the door handle, screaming her name, but only a rush of breath escapes my lungs. The thick air closes around me, pressing down to seal me inside. I scramble to my feet, the door handle slipping between my slick fingers, and stumble back out into the hall.

Laughter—not mine—bubbling up from the bowels of the hospital. I slink toward the emergency exit and the flickering red confirms my fears. The blood is a deep purple on my hands and feet, black on my scrubs. I lunge for the exit, but my attempt to cross into the stairwell is rebuffed. The exit isn't real. A projection. I touch the surface of the screen, the edge of the door, and the image wrinkles around my fingers.

Behind me, the floor settles under foreign weight, and the next thing I register is a soft light spilling across the tile.

The waiting room door stands open with the small table lamps lit and inviting. I should be furious with her. I should be frightened, but I am so relieved not to be alone that I rush into the room. But I don't find Stela.

There is a man, tall and broad-shouldered, in a workman's coat and jeans. He's in the center of the room facing the wall, his back to the door. His black hair is slicked back, his fists downed with dark brown fur. I want to turn and run, but I can't. There's nowhere to go, and I understand that he's the one who brought me here—not Stela. Slowly he turns around. His face has bright crimson tendons and blue veins that curl around a mouth without lips—all pink gums and crooked teeth. The eyes are what hold me—lidless, naked, grotesquely wide. He doesn't move. He doesn't make a sound.

The waiting room door slams shut at my back.

All my panic culminates around the sound. I attack the closed door with all that I have, rattling the handle, pulling at the hinges. I pound the wood with my fists until the bones in my wrists splinter from the force of my frenzy. A fur-covered hand curls around my shoulder, and I find my voice long enough to release a scream that had been building inside of me my whole life.

"Elizabeth?" I have a fistful of Helen's polyester coat in my hand when I open my eyes. "Easy now…Hey now. You're all right. It's just me." The recliner that I've lived in for nearly three days sticks to my spine and the back of my legs, covered in cold sweat. A bead of perspiration trickles down my temple. Helen stares down at me tenderly.

Helen leaves my side to answer the door and explains away my outburst to a herd of concerned fellow nurses.

"Here. Have some water." My voice is harsh when I thank her. "That must have been some nightmare." Helen attempts a reassuring smile. "You wanna talk about it?"

"No. I don't."

Helen nods and slumps down on the foot of Mother's bed. "I brought you some clothes," she says, running a thumb over my folded shirts. "I couldn't find the pants you asked for, or the book, or your overnight bag for that matter."

My thundering pulse slows. I clear my throat. "It's fine. Thank you for bringing what you have."

Helen holds the bags tightly and won't meet my eyes. I pull the bags out of her hands. "It's late, Helen. You should go home. We'll be fine."

Bewildered she rises from the bed shakily, and fixes me with a peculiar stare. Helen braces herself with the foot of the bed, cinching the front of her coat closed. "Where did you say your mother fell?" It's a simple question.

"The stairs. I told you that."

Helen silently agrees, tapping her fingers against the molded guardrail of the bed. "The basement stairs?"

"The first-floor stairs, Helen. Why would she be in the basement?"

Helen moves around the side of the bed in a distracted daze, tugging the purse strap at her shoulder. "Did you clean before you came to the hospital?"

"What are you talking about?"

"There was no blood." Helen shrugs, what should be a casual gesture but there's no hiding her intense interest. "Not on the stairs. Not at the foot of the stairs."

No blood? I was covered in blood by the time the EMTs arrived. Am I still dreaming? Helen makes a show of examining my mother's sleeping face, straightening her blankets, and everything about this line of inquiry and her reluctance to leave suggests that she fears leaving Mother alone with me. There's only one plausible explanation. Someone cleaned up the blood. But she'd never believe me if I told her my theory.

"Helen, the only clear memory I have of the accident is that when the EMTs turned to take the gurney through the front door, I was standing in my living room in my underwear. I don't remember rushing to her, or calling 911, or showering, or getting dressed, or driving to the hospital, or—"

"Of course." Helen rounds the foot of the bed and squeezes my shoulders. "Oh baby, of course you don't." I lean forward and rest my head on her shoulder. Helen embraces me and pats my back. "Please, don't upset yourself. I was surprised, that's all. Everything was spic-and-span when I arrived, and part of the reason I volunteered to make that trip was to clean up, so you wouldn't have to. I couldn't find anything you asked me to bring. I didn't know if you'd made a trip home and forgotten about it, or what happened."

There's no safe response. Helen gives me one more fierce embrace and makes to leave. "You'll call if you need anything?"

I nod and gently steer her toward the hall. "I promise. Thank you for the clothes. And just being here." We stroll to the elevators, arm in arm. "I don't know where my mind is right now," I confess, waiting for the elevator to arrive. "Everything happened so fast."

Helen nudges me sympathetically. "I lost whole months to my husband's heart attack."

"That's exactly how I feel. Like the world is moving without me." Not even remotely true. It's as though I'm caught in a swift undercurrent that means to swallow me whole, and every breath is borrowed.

"It gets easier," she promises.

I place my hand on her back, ushering her onto the elevator. "Thank you again. For everything." Helen presses the button for the ground floor and winks at me as the doors close.

One full body exhalation is all I manage before a tidal wave of sensation threatens to knock me off my feet. I double my pace back down the hall.

I slip inside my mother's room. Only her long legs—heels crossed lazily at the ankle—are visible in the shadows.

She's resting on the window ledge, her back rod straight, pressed against the darkened glass. "Have you any idea how frightened I was?" she asks.

"How frightened *you* were?" I know that I'm angry with her, but just haven't had time to work out why. She gives me her undivided attention. That's all it ever takes. Her onyx eyes, accustomed to the dark, find mine and all that anger—the fear for my mother, the lonely hours waiting in this room before Helen arrived, the gruesome nightmare—evaporates. The magnetic hum of her proximity radiates in my marrow, and any thought I had about storming out of the room is as distant as it is ridiculous. She crosses the room.

A protest, somewhere. Stela's fingers skirt along my jaw, she cups my face in her hands carefully. Her lips brush against mine and any confrontation regarding her prolonged absence is swallowed by a fevered kiss. The very hand I thought would push her away, curls around the back of her head to keep her in place.

She opens her mouth to me and the tang of a recent feed sits heavily on her tongue. It hits the back of my throat with sobering force, and I'm trapped in my nightmare all over again. My body grows rigid in her arms and I place my palms on her chest, twisting away from her mouth. It would be wonderful if the taste of her mouth was the cause, but what horrifies me more than any nightmare ever will, is that I no longer seem to mind.

Stela's initial response is to press forward, her arms tightening around my waist and bowing me backward. This isn't the first time I've rebuffed her affection, and the simple fact that I can seems to both shock and irritate her. She releases me so suddenly that I stumble back against the door. When I regain my composure, Stela is standing at the foot of my mother's bed, absently flipping through her chart. "I see that you received my flowers." She replaces the clipboard, a tight smile stretched across her lips.

"Yes. They're beautiful. Stela, I—"

She clasps her hands firmly behind her back and steps away from my mother. "I have something for you," she whispers, pulling my overnight bag from behind the chair and setting it on the window ledge. She stands beside me as I unzip the leather satchel and pore over the contents. I find my ISYM T-shirt neatly folded, my favorite sweatpants, my toiletry bag bursting with sundries. Every item I asked Helen to bring is meticulously stacked in the very same bag she could not find.

Stela reaches around me to unzip the side compartment and the skin of her wrist brushes my forearm. My hair stands on end and without so much as a glance, I know that she's smiling. She lifts a gilded frame from the satchel's pocket and lays it in my hands. A portrait of Mother and me taken just after I won Nationals. Mother's hand on my shoulder, her sharp green eyes staring unflinching into the camera. Holding my violin up for the photographer I look as proud as I felt. Stela slips the frame from my grasp and places it on the nightstand, beside the flowers.

"I was right to bring it along," she surmises. "The flowers have done nothing to warm this dreadful space."

"They're funeral flowers."

"Pardon?"

"Calla lilies. You send them when someone has died."

"Hmm. Well, I have always been fond of them."

An awkward silence falls between us.

"Thank you for bringing my clothes. And the photo. That was very considerate."

"You are most welcome." Stela tosses a smile over her shoulder with a flick of her pale hair. "There were no signs that you had taken anything with you, and I venture to say that you have not strayed far from her side."

"How did you find us?"

"This would have been the first place I checked, regardless. But your neighbors have been talking about the accident for days." She brushes the back of her hand against my jaw and my body leans into her of its own accord.

"Helen went to the house to gather my things."

Stela flicks the plastic bag beside my satchel. "Yes, I see that." She curls her hand around my neck. I close my eyes and forfeit a shiver I can't conceal.

"She suspects something. She said the stairs were clean when she arrived."

Stela huffs, pulling me close. "Elizabeth, if this is your idea of gratitude—"

"Gratitude?" Once again, I place my palms against her chest. "Do you have any idea how that looks? What if the police want to inspect the fall? What if Helen tells them it was cleaned when I was supposed to be at my mother's side?"

Stela doesn't release me this time, she locks her arms around my waist. I've seen her angry before, but it hasn't been directed at me in weeks.

"What if she does? You did nothing wrong. There are troves of nurses to confirm your whereabouts. You have nothing to hide. And even if you did, I can handle the police."

"All we do is hide, Stela."

Her grip slackens and she grows solemn, silent. Stela rubs calming circles against the small of my back and gazes distractedly out the window at the vast city below, only inches away from me and yet, she might as well be on the other side of the glass. "I was sleeping when it happened," she says. "But a part of me is always aware of you. Such intense horror, like nothing I have ever felt before. I woke when it was still light, mad with fear that you had been injured, or worse. Then, everything stopped. You were quiet, beyond fear. I could glean no emotional cues. You must have been in shock.

"I let myself in through the kitchen door, unlocked, which was unusual and terribly disconcerting. I could smell the blood from the backyard, and confined in that house it was inescapable. Old, and drying quickly. I did not know whether it belonged to you or your mother until I was upon it."

I can sense the panic Stela felt as clearly as I remember my own. I press my forehead to hers. When my arms wrap around her shoulders, Stela skims her nose along the side of my neck. I don't push her away this time. Her mouth opens against my skin and she takes a deep lingering breath just below my ear.

"I did not want you to return home to such an unfortunate mess." Her low voice moves through every inch of me.

"I know. You meant no harm." I straddle two worlds: one with Stela, and one without. The latter is becoming as undesirable as it is infrequent. Stela slides her palm beneath my shirt, up my back to press between my shoulder blades. My body arches into her embrace.

"Why must you always rail against me?" she asks. "Analyze every utterance? Every compliment, every gesture?" There is a word of warning, just beyond my reach. A caveat hanging in the air, just on the periphery. But Stela's hands wrap around my thighs and she hoists me onto the window ledge. The glass is cold against my back as she traces my collarbone with her teeth. "Tell me it does not please you to see me," she taunts.

My head swims as her lips climb the column of my neck, dance along the edges of my jaw and come to rest teasingly light upon my own. Her lips parted, but not pressing. Her eyes are all that I can see, drowsy lids filled with bright shining dark. I open my mouth and my own lips quiver with every brush of skin. My legs lock around her waist and Stela falls into me willingly. The taste of blood is still there, tingling on her tongue, heating her skin. My nightmare is there too, conjured by the blood, the faceless man with his wide-reaching grin, but the fear is miles away. Life's turmoil is extinguished.

Without a word, Stela rips my T-shirt over my head, casting it over her shoulder and covering my front with hers. She pulls my hips forward so swiftly that my bare shoulders streak down the glass, and I gasp for the air I've forgotten to breathe. Her tinkling laugh fills my ears and wills my eyes open, but they don't land on Stela. My mother's face is deeply lined, slack-mouthed, but otherwise peaceful. Stela's fingers slip into the top of my jeans, and I catch her by the wrist.

"Wait." Stela tenses around me, every inch of her inflamed with the threat of rejection. "Stela, we can't. Not here."

Her hands release their hold and I slide off the ledge. Stela paces furiously, anger is radiating off her in waves. "Wait? We can't? Do you have any idea the risk I take every visit I grant you? Have you the slightest notion what would become of me if we were discovered?"

"Grant me?"

Stela twists on her heel and strangles the guardrail beside Mother's head. The metal groans in her grip as she leans over the bed. "Yes. Grant you. Everything I do is for you, Elizabeth. And for what?"

I steal a glance at the monitors. Mother's heartbeat remains steady. "I've been asking you that question from the beginning. For what, Stela?"

"It is not your place to question my motives."

My hand moves protectively over my mother's chest, as Stela bends further over the mattress. "What would happen to me if we were discovered? Did you ever stop to consider that?"

Stela releases the bed with a shove that forces the mattress against my legs, leaving the rail knotted and buckled in finger shaped ridges. She stalks to the end of the bed. She always seems so much taller when she's furious. "I killed Collins for you, did I not?"

Stela's anger is infectious and I face her head-on. "Killed him for me, maybe. But you tore his face off for yourself." It wasn't real until I said it out loud. The man in my nightmare, a fourth presence in the room, just barely recognizable. He was wearing the same oil-stained workman's jacket that Mr. Collins had on when he accosted me on the elevator. The same slicked black hair. Stela has no witty rebuttal. I seize the momentary lull to check my mother's heart monitor again. Stela grabs me firmly by the chin.

"She cannot hear us, Elizabeth." My hand flies up at her face before I realize my intention, and Stela catches me easily by the wrist. I swing my free hand at her head. Stela holds both my hands tight to her chest. "You only harm yourself," she warns. Tears run unbidden down my cheeks, obscuring my vision, and my desperate attempts to break free only increase Stela's hold on me.

"She can. She can hear me."

Stela softens, but she doesn't release me. She holds me in an inescapable embrace, pinning my hands in place against her chest. I struggle furiously against her body, which remains soft in its confinement. All I can manage is to turn myself away from her to face my mother's slumbering form. The monitors beep in time with my quiet sobs.

"Your mother no longer resides in that body."

"You don't know that."

"I do."

My muscles lock, my body trembling with rage. "Fix her." Stela runs a placating hand through my hair, but I tilt my head away from her touch.

"The damage is too great. This is beyond the ability of my blood."

When I twist in her embrace, the softness has returned to Stela's eyes. "You're lying."

Stela's gaze bores into me. It's oddly warm, like sinking into a hot bath. But my limbs remain chilled with dread.

"You know not what you ask. This is beyond a wound of the flesh. I could heal the body, but I cannot restore her mind. Where your mother is now, I cannot venture."

I thrum with unspent venom. Stela becomes the focus of every horrid thought I've ever had, the cause of every misfortune that's befallen me. "Isn't that convenient?" Stela doesn't bat an eye. "It's everything you wanted, right? To leave me just as alone and forgotten as you?"

"Elizabeth," she begins, drawing back. "I cannot undo the injustices you have suffered. And I cannot take this pain from you. But I would share it with you, if you let me. I would comfort you." She reaches out to take hold of my hands, but it's too soon. My anger is still so near. I push her hand away and lean over the bed to pull the sheet back up around my mother's shoulders. Fresh tears itch the tops of my cheeks.

"You can't comfort me. Please leave."

She places a hand on my hip while I fret over Mother, straightening wires and electrodes, pulling them off to the side so she won't get tangled when she wakes.

"Elizabeth—"

"I don't want to see you, Stela."

Stela has vanished before the pressure of her hand leaves my hip. Gone as silently as she arrived. A sinking sensation drops through my stomach, forcing me to sit before my legs buckle. A swoon, not unlike the first time I laid eyes on Stela, but reversed and made sickening. And then the sensation is gone.

I can't feel anything from her anymore.

IX

Consent

There are those who say that God never closes a door without opening a window. Of course, I know nothing of God or any benevolent, guiding force—excluding Fane. I imagine that such immaculate involvement would be a comfort to many, but I have no deity to blame for my troubles. No sympathetic All Mighty to right my wrongs.

Elizabeth is aware of my absence, which is not to say that she dwells on our separation the way that I do. The closed door between us is still a door with life on either side. When she thinks of this blockade—of me—she falters with nothing more than a missed step. I am a distraction she shakes off, resuming her duties as diligently as before. Would that I had her resilience, but I lack her conviction that there can be no other way. And to think, she considers me the cold, unfeeling one.

Still, this is all the peace that I can offer her, a stalemate. The petty errands of my day offer little distraction. I keep my meetings with Andrew. I accompany Bård on his dealings with local law enforcement and rival gangs though my brother hardly requires my protection. I have even taken to stalking the tunnels with

Erebus as it is the only way the hound will leave my chamber for any length of time.

I can check in on my darling, bitter girl whenever I so choose. And how could I keep away from her with so much left unsaid? With so many misunderstandings, so little between us resolved?

Suppose we could make amends, what then? Elizabeth and I would be right back where we started, hiding in the dark. How is that fair to her? She belongs to this world, she is product of her century. Too lovely for darkness and too strong to reach for it.

In the early hours, just before dawn, I sit at my desk with a stack of pristine parchment, tapping my pen. If I could only explain. If I had the words to make her understand. Can she sense my desire to fix this? Though she makes no outward acknowledgment, she is aware of my presence below her window, or as a shadowed figure on the street corner. Are the hours I spend recounting her in my mind likewise detectable?

She is right to hate me. I stole her silence, her oneness. I can shut her out, I can shut myself away, but I cannot take what happened back. I cannot make either of us whole again.

James visits her now in Claire's nursing home. First, he came with magazines and books. He hoped that she could read them to Claire, but it was no use. Poor fellow. What must he have thought of the visions I gave him? The nightmares, the panic I instilled if he so much as gazed in Elizabeth's direction. Would she be happy to know that it was my doing?

I think of them often, much more than I should. Elizabeth smiles openly at him over take out, which they consume together in her mother's kitchen, or in the depressing cafeteria. She smiles in his company much more frequently than she ever smiled in mine, though her eyes remain weary and red-rimmed.

James could build a life with her. He could make her a mother, a wife. Elizabeth would be a good parent. She could continue her academic pursuits. But would that please her? It pleases me to think of her poring over the American Journal of Medical Genetics with a toddler on her hip. The sun in her eyes, her chest shaking with an easy laugh. Yes, that is how I imagine her life, years from now, when she has finally buried her mother's ghost which I suspect will take much longer than handling her remains. When Elizabeth has buried me, perhaps in the attic, beside her violin.

Would that not be a most gratifying life? And do I love her enough to let her have it?

I hear her rushed footsteps echo through the brownstone. She rarely sleeps at home these days. Elizabeth moves like a caged animal about her mother's bedroom, fussing, straightening bedclothes that will never be used. Claire has Elizabeth in chains, and will until she draws her last breath. And that could take some time.

The rusty lock flips on the sliding glass door and my darling appears in the center of the patio. Her face is bathed in moonlight. She hoists a trash bag to her side and carts it across the lawn to the alley, where I am always waiting for her. Her tired hands fumble with the temperamental latch on the gate, and I stop myself from reaching to hold it open for her. She does not want my help. Not yet. Elizabeth heaves the bag into the waste can. She pauses, her hand pressed to the back gate, holding her breath. The hairs on her arm stand on end.

Call out to me, Elizabeth. Turn and face me. Tell me to come to you—with or without words—and I will. Ask me to take this pain from you. Admit that all this ugliness is more than your heart can bear.

A breeze dances over her bare neck. My fangs descend from my gums and I cover my mouth to keep from claiming her. My legs tremor from the effort to keep still, to maintain my composure. There would be such peace in devouring her, to bathe in her blood inside and out. She would fight, of that I am certain.

Elizabeth straightens her spine, shoulders squared, grinding her teeth. The message is clear when the gate locks behind her and her steady, purposeful tread knocks loudly over the warped patio. She throws the lock on the sliding glass door and extinguishes the kitchen light. *Go away. Leave me in peace. You are not wanted here.* As plain as though she opened her mouth and said it herself.

For weeks this holding pattern, this intolerable détente. The moon hangs swollen overhead, whispering that my time is almost spent. I must feed before the evening's end. But I can be patient, Elizabeth, you will see. Hold Claire's hand, if you must. Sing songs to your mother that she never sang to comfort you. Read her stories, and change the bed. Mother Claire the way you wish she mothered you. I will be waiting, my dove. All I have is time.

* * *

To illustrate just how far I have fallen from his grace, Fane asks Lydia to accompany me to the quarterly meeting. I—being in no position to abstain or refuse—agree with such enthusiasm that Lydia herself appears poised to object. She gapes at me like a beached fish, but never utters a word, despite being fairly certain that I aim to get her alone, to exact my revenge for having been embarrassed in front of our Lord.

I practically have to hold her upright in the elevator. She is pitifully uncomfortable moving about in daylight hours under the herculean weight of the waning sun. Again I curse Andrew for wielding his petty power play so that we meet in daylight hours. I could insist that his father's consideration continue, but rather than admit any weakness, I meet his arrogance undeterred.

"How much higher?" she asks, fanning herself.

"To the top. Mr. Opes prefers a room with a view."

I run my nail over the top of her head to fix the crooked part in her black hair and Lydia swats at me blindly, doubling over with a growl. I hoist her up by her arms with a firm shake and force her wide almond eyes level with mine.

"You will put on your sunglasses, straighten your garments and compose yourself."

"Stela, how are you doing this?" She stares at me openly, not attempting to hide her astonishment.

"This is what you wanted, Lydia. A chance to usurp me and to impress Fane. I suggest you acclimate."

Lydia's honeyed skin grows increasingly ashen, but she stands tall. She leans heavily upon my arm projecting an air of comfortable familiarity, instead of intense physical discomfort. Without a trace of our ever-present animosity we could almost be taken for close friends. But Lydia has never forgiven me for leading her down that alley in Constantinople and into Bård's waiting arms all those years ago.

Lydia was a gift to Bård from Fane. We met her father while searching for a boat that would sail my family to Denmark. Lydia was there, glowing in the sun while she and her mother bartered with a local fisherman. Bård stood beside me as broken in the waning daylight hours as his progeny is now. She seemed an excellent choice of companion, full of fire and life, the scent of myrrh curling in her thick black hair. She looked over her shoulder to her father and caught sight of two pale strangers. Leaving her mother, she walked to her father's side and whispered in his ear. Lydia asked if she could touch my hair. Bård tightened his grip on my arm and I knew this gleaming statue of a young woman was already his.

Who could have foreseen that she would adjust so slowly? Who could have predicted her immense sorrow? Her animosity toward Bård and her almost instant adoration of Fane? The newest addition to our coven, and by Fane's decree our last. The world around us was changing, rushing headlong into a new era. People were not made of the same mettle anymore.

My dear Bård. Still so very alone in this world. Even after all his spilled blood. I see him now in a new light. The pain he carries and has for centuries, that the woman he chose never chose him.

In the lobby, Rachel stands guard at reception, her head hung and a clipboard clutched to her breast.

"Good evening, Ms. Radu. Mr. Opes is expecting you. Right this way."

Rachel rushes ahead with a twirl of her pinstriped skirt and the sharp click of her heels. Beside me Lydia's body lurches forward, eyes fixed on Rachel's bright red hair. I pull her sharply back into step and a miserable groan escapes her parted lips. The sound makes Rachel freeze momentarily, but she recovers quickly. Smart girl, Rachel. I tighten my grip on Lydia's arm and praise the small mercy that we were not made to wait in the lobby. I doubt Lydia could have resisted Rachel for long.

As we round the marble corridor the glass wall of Andrew's office assaults Lydia with blinding hues of orange and pink, courtesy of the blistering sun.

For all our shared hostility, I am truly sorry for her pain. "Quiet yourself," I whisper.

"Mr. Opes, Ms. Radu is here," Rachel announces. "She has brought a...friend?" Rachel turns to me for confirmation with an apologetic shrug and gives me a wide berth as I steer Lydia over the threshold.

"An associate," I amend.

Rachel nods and disappears down the hall.

Andrew rises slowly behind the desk, discarding his staple glass of scotch to clutch the back of his chair instead.

"Mr. Opes, you look well." I shoulder Lydia toward the empty armchair to the right. She collapses in a rumpled, grateful silence.

"Ms. Radu." hHe nods. "And your associate?" Andrew—no doubt emboldened by Lydia's obvious fatigue—moves around the side of the desk to offer his hand. I know I should warn him away, but some lessons really must be learned.

"Mr. Opes, this is Ms. Dilay Sadik. Your *other* point of contact within the family. We thought it was time the two of you met."

Andrew's fixed smile twitches, and it is all the confirmation I need. This worm has been conspiring with Lydia behind my back. "Of course, Ms. Sadik. It's a pleasure to finally meet you." Lydia takes his outstretched hand in her own and the jovial mood sours with the loud pop of his crushed knuckles. Just before she releases him, Andrew looks to me for help.

"Enough, Dilay." I place a hand on her shoulder. Lydia releases him instantly with an empty apology and a warning on her sallow face. Whether or not she truly meant him harm, is hardly the point. She wasted the last vestiges of her resolve just climbing out of the elevator and managing not to murder the receptionist. The woman is a lion in a pen of spring lambs.

Andrew's face pales and he cups his hand to his chest, certain that he is going to die tonight. I step between them and guide Andrew back behind his desk. "Could we trouble you to close the blinds this evening? Ms. Sadik has a splitting headache." Andrew stares at me, silent, uncomprehending. "The windows, Andrew. Now." He wakes with a jolt.

"Yes, of course." Quickly, Andrew darts to the end of the room and closes the blinds with the press of a button. I take the vacant chair beside Lydia and pat her knee patronizingly. She shuffles upright in her seat and crosses her legs primly. As if to underscore her improvement without the sun smacking her in the face, Lydia reaches to remove her glasses.

"Leave them," I warn.

Andrew clears his throat, his gaze darting fretfully between us. His pulse beats so loudly that I can see his carotid pushing away his shirt collar. "Well, shall we get to it then?" He flips open the manila folder. Everything as I predicted. How unfortunate for him.

"Andy, I was hoping you would surprise me this quarter."

"Surprise you? It's all here, every penny accounted for."

Lydia shifts in her chair unexpectedly and Andrew's hand jumps to his throat, unable to conceal his unease.

"Yes, the numbers are exactly what I anticipated." I lean over the desk and close the folder in front of him. "But you have a debt to repay, and I see no significant progress made to fulfill that obligation."

Andrew falls back in his chair. His red face is damp with perspiration as he takes a long drink from his scotch. He holds the glass in his trembling hands and stares down into the murky surface of the lingering ice cubes, searching for strength. The man was given a second chance. He has no idea how rare an occurrence that is with Fane. A forty percent increase or he forfeits his life. Negotiations are closed.

"I just need a little more time, Kathryn."

"The year is nearly spent."

He nods solemnly, and takes another long drink.

It is in this tense moment that the unthinkable happens. Loudly clunking black boots and ripped stockings accompany an iridescent tutu. A shock of purple tangled in her blond head and a silver ring in her left nostril. There are deep black lines drawn over her fair eyebrows. His beloved child, his only heir. Her headphones are so loud she cannot hear Rachel calling out to stop her.

"Christine?" Andrew stands abruptly and buttons his blazer over his bulging stomach. His daughter hovers in the doorway, tapping aggressively on her mobile until she registers Rachel's approach from behind.

"I need fifty dollars." Christine does not glance up from her mobile. Andrew chastises her for the interruption to a meeting. "Yeah, I can see that you're busy. Just need a yes or a no. Ella's waiting downstairs." She cocks an expectant eyebrow, arms crossed imperiously.

The first photograph of Christine on her father's desk was taken at her christening and there was something shrewd in her small round eyes even then. I knew I would be fond of her.

"Yes, fine." Andrew barks, fishing in his pocket for his billfold. He presses a hundred-dollar bill into her palm and tries to rush her back out into the hall. Lydia's eyes are glued to Christine's face, a fact the girl does not miss. I could not have planned this better if I tried.

"Andrew, how rude." I waft past her father and extend my hand to Christine. All the color drains from Andrew's stricken face when she takes it, as confident and fearless as I hoped she would be. He has dreaded this day from the moment she was born, and this distracted, acerbic, beguiling creature is still a handful of years from understanding why.

"Christine, this is Kathryn Radu. One of our more…influential clients." Andrew clasps Christine by the shoulder to keep her from stepping any closer. She shrugs him off without a second thought.

"Pleasure to meet you, Kathryn. Sorry I barged in unannounced," she responds with practiced cordiality. Firm handshake. Steady eye contact. She stares quizzically at my sunglasses, but does not mention them. Good manners, excluding her entrance.

Lydia stands abruptly on frightfully strong legs.

"Not at all, Christine. Have a seat, if you like. We were just wrapping things up." Lydia's own hand hangs in the air untouched, leering at Christine. I slip my arm around her waist, yanking her beside me. Words have completely failed Andrew. He is petrified.

"I've gotta get going. Thanks though. Nice to meet you both," she says, waving over her father's shoulder. Andrew ushers Christine through the door and follows her down the hall.

He returns to find me holding Lydia in place, her body twitching in my arms and her face contorted by an unmistakable snarl. He stands silently in the doorway, barricading it long enough for his daughter to exit the building.

Andrew clears his throat and steps around us. He resumes his place behind the desk, staring daggers at Lydia. "Kathryn. A word alone, please."

"Of course."

Lydia must feed, and soon. Young blood waltzing into the office was more temptation than her weakened body could withstand. "Wait for me in the lobby," I instruct with a firm hand on the small of my sister's back. "And Dilay, if you harm Rachel, I shall have no choice but to inform Mr. Radu." Dazed and famished, Lydia shuffles toward the hallway.

Andrew removes his suit coat and his relief is palpable. "Kathryn, I'm fairly certain this goes without saying, but Ms. Sadik's conduct this evening was—"

"Completely unacceptable," I finish.

"Yes. Unacceptable, and terrifying to be frank. Are her visits to become a regular occurrence?"

I take a seat. "That depends entirely on you, Andrew."

"Kathryn, I am committed to making the estate as profitable as possible. I assure you." His voice quakes, the man is almost to the point of pleading but not for his own life. For all I dislike Andrew Opes, I will admit that Lydia unnerved us both by moving on Christine. We have invested too many years in this enterprise, this family, to see our fortune spoiled for a single meal.

"Ms. Sadik's visit has nothing to do with your performance, or lack thereof." Andrew—shocked by my candor—leans forward on his elbows. "I carry a considerable workload for our mutual benefactor. You know this, better than most. Lately, Mr. Radu has been worried that my burdens are too great. Those concerns were underscored at our last family meeting when Dilay showed a staggering knowledge of our financials, and I did not."

I pause and rise from my seat. Andrew now has a choice, and we have the opportunity to become allies instead of rivals.

I walk around the side of his desk toward the window, parting the blinds with the back of my hand. Sunlight cuts across the top of his desk in a long thin blade of burnished gold—wretchedly painful. Slowly, Andrew turns in his seat, staring at me as though seeing me for the first time. His eyes alight with opportunity. Perhaps he has a bit of his father's fighting spirit after all.

"Suppose Mr. Radu was to learn about Ms. Sadik's conduct this evening? That she behaved unprofessionally, threateningly, and that I feared for the safety of my child." His voice softens when referencing Christine and I know that I have him. I allow myself a small smile which Andrew answers with his own. I remove my sunglasses and look him square in the eyes. For once, he does not cower.

"Andrew." I place my hand on his arm. "Where would we be without your family's loyalty? It was a genuine pleasure to make

Christine's acquaintance this evening, I hope you know that. If Mr. Radu thought for a moment that the Opes legacy was in danger he would have no choice but to act. To protect her, if only for the sake of his own family." I adjust the collar of his shirt.

"I think we understand each other, Kathryn." He rises from his seat and stands taller in my presence than ever before. He takes my chilled hand firmly in his own.

"Careful Andrew," I slide my sunglass over my aching eyes, "I may grow to like you."

In the waiting area, Lydia has curled into the corner of the long black sofa against the far wall. Her eyes are locked on Rachel's every move. Rachel hears my approach and flees the fortress of her desk to press the call button for the elevator.

"Come now." Lifting Lydia by the shoulder, I mouth a silent thank you to the erstwhile receptionist.

"We'll see you next quarter, Ms. Radu."

I shove Lydia inside the elevator and she sinks down the steel wall before the doors have closed. I catch her by the lapel and pull her against me while Rachel pretends to tidy pristine her workspace. "A pleasure as always, Rachel."

Lydia's body is limp in my arms by the time the elevator reaches the cool shade of the basement. Wrapping her arm around my shoulder, I carry her across the parking garage to my vehicle and drop her heavy limbs into the passenger seat. Her head rolls down to her chest.

"What am I to do with you?" I pull her head back by her hair and remove her sunglasses. Her eyes are twice their usual size and completely unfocused. The thirst has her now, and there will be no hunting until she is replenished. I consider taking her to the hospital—the only safe place she could feed in her weakened state—but I remember my promise to Elizabeth not to feed there.

A low moan escapes Lydia's pale lips and she tips toward me in her seat, slumped across the center console.

"Stela?" Her eyes struggle to find my face as I brush the hair back behind her shoulders. I really do not have strength to give, but I see no acceptable alternative. Fane would be furious with me if I delivered her to him half-starved. I bite the skin of my wrist, and hold it to her mouth.

"You must feed."

She needs no further encouragement. The strength returns quickly to her hands, which latch onto my elbow and forearm when the first drop hits her tongue. Just a few mouthfuls and she should be strong enough to hunt. We will find something elderly for her, though Lydia prefers her nourishment nubile and full of exuberance. A young woman is simply out of the question tonight. Lydia does not have the wherewithal for the seduction game. She twists the skin of my arm in her fingers, and I recall Elizabeth's ashen face that night in the alley, crumpled on the filthy ground. Sharing my blood with this ungrateful little beast seems repugnant in comparison. I banish the thought of Elizabeth immediately, and pry my arm free. Lydia reels back with a bellowing gasp, shaking with newfound energy.

She nestles back into her own seat, gathering her dignity in the tense silence that follows such an intimate exchange. She flips the visor down, wiping the corner of her mouth with the cuff of her black satin blazer. I watch her every move. Did she see Elizabeth? How could I have been so careless? But Lydia says nothing. She flips the visor back into place and turns to the passenger window.

"How are you feeling?" Because I cannot ask her what she knows.

"Better."

When it becomes quite clear that we have said all we intend to say to each other, I pull the car from its parking space and adopt Lydia's muteness. Panic will only draw her attention to Elizabeth's significance, and what proof do I have that Lydia had the strength to glean my thoughts while we were entwined? She was nearly mad with hunger.

Lydia places a gentle hand on my arm. "Thank you, Stela." She will not look at me. I doubt she has ever thanked me for anything and meant it.

"Think nothing of it."

* * *

The sound reaches me softly, as though crossing a great distance, piercing the black edge of sleep. Shallow breaths in rapid succession, little more than a tempestuous breeze. My body prickles with the presence of another, spiking action into my limbs while my mind grapples with what I cannot see. My fingers trace patterns on the sheets which are at once familiar—my own bed, thankfully. The frightened breathing—at once familiar—echoes in my ears. Citrus fruit, lemon, and orange peel. *Open your eyes. Open them.*

My body bolts upright. A timid step thuds as loudly as a brick dropped on the floor. Erebus crouches low to the ground, coiled at the foot of my bed. The coarse fur down his spine stands on end. I put my hand out to him and part the bunched burgundy tapestry hanging from the corner of my bedpost.

"Elizabeth?"

Her sweet brown eyes are thrown wide in unmasked horror, locked on Erebus's every move. The delicate veins in the milky skin of her wrist bulge blue and brilliant as she tightens her grip on the bedpost. Erebus edges back on his haunches, prepared to lunge. I throw myself between them. Elizabeth places her hands on my shoulder blades, pushing me toward the hound, and Erebus's answering growl is a warning shot.

"Lie down." I point to his nest in the corner, but the hound stamps one large and defiant paw at my feet. He tosses his head, teeth bared and eyes wild. There is a human in his home, and his only purpose is to ensure that any mortal in the tunnels never leaves.

"Erebus." I crouch in front of him and hold his attention. I reach up and take hold of Elizabeth's hand. Seething, Erebus edges away from me but will not turn his back. He remains low, shuffling backward to his nest, his protest made abundantly clear through a mix of harried growls and high-pitched whines.

I rise unsteadily, expecting the vision of Elizabeth to disappear the second I turn around. But her hands, soft and warm, are as real as her lingering scent. She does not vanish when I face her. She wears the same black dress she donned for her evening out with James, the same simple shoes, hair in long heavy curls. I can scarcely make out the deep purple bags beneath her eyes. She looks beautiful. Rested for a change.

"How did you find me?" I cup the side of her face and she leans into my touch. "Do you have any idea how dangerous—"

She places two fingers to my lips, the blush rising in her cheeks as she presses her body against mine. She shakes her head and silences me with a lopsided, mischievous smile. I curl my hand around the back of her neck and press my forehead to hers. Her fingers slip down to my naked chest. Surely the others heard her approach in the corridor.

"We have to get you away from this place. You cannot stay here."

She slides her hands along the exposed skin of my abdomen and up the sides of my breasts, locking her arms tightly around my neck. She buries her face in my hair. My body is rigid with fear, but her heart beating against my own and the gentle cadence of breath against my ear are my undoing. Slowly and selfishly, my desire begins to outweigh my terror.

I ought to push her away, to chide this reckless disregard. Instead, I wrap my arms around her waist and she presses a deliberate kiss to my jaw, my cheek—and with a challenge in her open eyes—my mouth. Another kiss, this time with her eyes drifting closed and her lips lingering in solicitation of a response. My hands tangle in her hair, and my mouth opens to her intrusion while my brain is still screaming in alarm. Erebus maintains his litany of deep growls.

Elizabeth pushes my sternum, leading me down to the bed and climbing into my lap. Despite our frenzy her smile lingers, her hair curtains our faces, and I resolve to whisk her quietly away as soon as we have finished. She presses her palms to my chest, bidding me back, and the momentary break in contact gives my mind room to wonder.

Has Claire's heart finally stopped its futile but stubborn beating?

Elizabeth trails her mouth along my neck and I pull her up to face me by the sleeves of her gown. The glossy black fabric shreds in my hands. She looks down at her now bare shoulder and smiles back at me. That same satisfied grin I have come to adore.

"I can buy you another…"

She flips her hair out of her face and kisses me roughly. Her hands hold my face with surprising strength. My responses are slow. My fingers trace the frayed stitching, moving down her left shoulder. My hand tightens around her left bicep, her injured arm, but she does not flinch. I can feel the heat of my want evaporating from my skin as a cold dread settles in my bones.

I burned this dress the night she was shot.

"Forgive me, my Lord. I did not recognize you."

The body on top of mine stills and large hands wrap around my wrists. The face in the crook of my neck stalls, and then pulls back. Fane laughs so loudly it drowns out Erebus's frightened whimpering. Fane keeps his hands firmly on my wrists as he leans back and settles between my bent legs, laughing wildly the entire time.

"Oh, my dove. A moment longer and the game would have become much more interesting."

He extricates himself and smacks the side of my thigh so forcefully my legs twist off the side of my bed. A tight embittered smile is my only response as I reach for the sheet to cover myself. Grabbing my hand, he stops me sharply and wraps his arm around my shoulders.

"Stay as you are. You have never been modest." Fane is clothed in dark jeans, and the left shoulder of his white shirt is ripped, dangling down his arm. I try to straighten my back and he tightens his arm around my neck. He gives my head a shake, made to appear endearing or playful, though it is neither.

"We have to get you out of here. It is not safe," he intones with forced fright. "Come now, a human in my home, Stela? With Erebus's pack roaming the tunnels?"

He turns his taunt from me to Erebus, who has crept up to the foot of the bed. "Which is exactly where you belong, old man." He thrusts his finger into Erebus's face, his voice dangerously loud.

Erebus slinks to the service entrance, his hackles still standing on end as he disappears through the narrow passage. I listen to the heavy pad of his steps fade into nothing.

"It was ignorant, my Lord. I was not thinking clearly."

Fane grips the back of my neck and twists my face to his. With my protector gone, he is not hiding his malice, fighting to control his bottomless rage. His clear blue eyes are half crazed with the undertaking.

"That is the most honest thing you have uttered in months." He does not release my neck straightaway. He stares me down, tight-lipped, almost smiling. His anger vibrates in his fingers pressing against the top of my spine. Is this my death? My neck severed in his iron grip? Fane releases me with a shove and his lips curl as he grits his perfectly white teeth. My head snaps back from the force, but I will not shrink from him. I am in a hell of my own making. Besides, if there is one thing he appreciates it is bravery in the face of assured defeat.

I sit straighter, feet on the floor and hands folded in my lap. He looks over my face with what can only be described as disgust.

"I wanted so much to be wrong," he laments. The threatening smile is gone.

He quits the space beside me and begins pacing the floor, his head hung in disappointment, hands clasped behind his back.

"I am loath to anger you, my Lord."

It is a half-truth, but true nonetheless. His disapproval aches like a gaping wound. But I acted knowing full well that this would be the outcome, and I persisted all the same. His footsteps still as he towers over me, peering down into my eyes. His icy glare reaches deep, pulling the strings of truths I can no longer conceal.

"How could you deceive me this way, Stela? Did you honestly think you would not be found out?"

"How could *you?*" My first action is always to placate him, and we are both shocked by my outburst. I had imagined that when this moment finally arrived, I would tell him how desperately I feared his reaction. That I was certain he would find me out sooner rather than later. But it is no use. I barely have time to register the pressure of his hands around my arms, let alone apologize. One moment I am seated, bracing myself and marveling at my own arrogance, and the next, I am soaring across the room.

The writing desk lies in splintered ruin, shards piercing my back, and fragments embedded in the wall. My laptop, largely spared from the impact of my body, is crushed under my foot as I struggle to stand.

I deserved that.

Fane approaches with all the nonchalance of a deadly storm and hoists me to my feet by my hair. His fist tightens, nails scraping my scalp. A trickle of blood oozes down my temple, halts, and recedes back into the wound. "If you dare to accuse me, Stela, say exactly what you mean."

I knock the splintered wood out from under my bare feet as the fragment of a drawer is expelled from my spine. The skin puckers and seals shut again. I stare intently back at him, my rage going much deeper than this charade. "Why match me deception for deception, my Lord? You could just as easily have set fire to the bed while I slept. You could have roused the whole house and had me executed for treachery."

Fane laughs, silently this time, shaking his head. He clamps his hands on either side of my face, nearly lifting me off the ground. He covers my mouth with his, and though this is the same intimacy he has shown me thousands of times, I did not realize how one-sided the act has become. Has his kiss always been distasteful to me? How is that possible?

When he has finished, Fane releases me just as abruptly. I land firmly on my feet. "Public execution of my only child? My blood?" His eyes remain violent, but his voice softens like a song. "Do you think me monstrous?" Fane turns away and stalks around the foot of my bed, disappearing into my washroom. He emerges with my black silk robe draping it over my shoulders and tying at my waist. With his every move my body tenses for attack, waiting for the next assault. He avoids my eyes until I am covered, and threads a lock of my hair back behind my ear. There was tenderness between us once, I swear I remember.

"I had only a suspicion that teetered on the edge of certainty," he says. "Collins gave me a name. Lydia gave me a face. I had to know what this human was to you."

So, the failure *is* mine. When I shared my blood with Lydia, I let myself linger in thoughts of Elizabeth and then Fane seized the image from so many others when he drank from her last night. He showed me my heart's desire to gauge the depth of my affection.

"I will not use Lydia's allegiance to you to mount a defense for myself. I cannot deny my mistakes. And I will not work to deceive you any longer."

Fane tilts my chin up with the tips of his fingers.

"I want the unmitigated truth," he warns.

A fair request. I place my hands on his broad shoulders and stare unobstructed into the pale blue of his incisive eyes.

"As you wish, my Lord."

Scattered images flicker before me, dredged from the depths of my mind by the fistful. Random and unrelated, a toppled box of photographs. Fane reaches through the tangled web of memory as easily as cobwebs, brushing all else aside. One holds his attention:

the image of Elizabeth still damp from her shower, running a towel through her dark hair. Her long legs dancing in the doorway to her bedroom, a knowing smile on her face.

He tugs the string tied to this innocuous moment, and a flood of remembrance surges from within me with such force I rock forward on my feet, against his immovable frame. The sensation reminds me of a buried human joy, waking at first light and stretching into the fragile morning.

The pictures start to knit themselves together in a line. They find their sequence under Fane's direction and animate like a child's flip book. I see the hospital room marked four-twelve and William Moore's graying corpse. Elizabeth in her unflattering scrubs, red-faced and righteous. Her mother Claire taking a spill in the kitchen while Helen stands in the front room on her mobile. A vision of Elizabeth fast asleep. Elizabeth dancing in that crowded basement club with James's hands on her thighs. The single gunshot. Derek pinned to the wall of the crematorium as I altered his memory of the evening. The truths I told Elizabeth that were not mine to tell. Collins, with and without a face. And then like a hailstorm: Elizabeth's hand in mine, my thumb settling in the cleft of her chin, the weight of her ankles on the small of my back.

All the feelings that are beneath Fane, or any other Moroi. He reaches for one more moment, and I am tracing the bloom of a calla lily, wondering if Elizabeth would try to stop me turning off the machines that keep her mother's body anchored to this world.

Fane rears away from me so suddenly that he shoves me hard against the wall. The oak paneling splits against the back of my head as I clatter to the floor. Pain is relative to the organism. But as I begin to straighten my limbs from their tangled heap and my shoulder snaps back into its socket, my stomach turns. I fear that I might become sick before I remember that such a reaction is not possible for our kind.

Fane rages, tossing his head about like a riled horse, as though he can shake the emotions from his mind if he just keeps moving. I thought the same thing. What an inconvenience this must be for him.

I do not get up from the floor. Perhaps if I stay down he will not drag me upright again, this time to my death. But then, I have seen him crush his enemies underfoot. I have no idea where we go from here, and I cannot imagine that I will be going very far. There is a poetry to the moment, a beautiful alluring uncertainty of tomorrow. The thought of never standing again, of an end, seems so much simpler than facing another night, because it requires nothing and handles everything.

Fane's gait has grown steady and purposeful. He brings his hands to his temples and grits his teeth. A sound like fracturing marble fills my ears, and reluctantly, he opens his eyes. He appears almost dazed. He wraps a steadying hand around the post of my bed and perches on the edge of my mattress. The ensuing silence seems eternal. "Why did you hide from me this way?"

Because I knew you would never understand. Because I was terrified that you would destroy her. Because you want me entirely to yourself, and you always have. Because you would never give Elizabeth a place in your home.

Fane rakes his hands up and down his thighs, waiting for my reply. "Did you think I would laugh at you? Refuse you? Have I ever refused you, Stela?" A pleading tone betrays him and he clears his throat.

My eyes dart around the room, everywhere but him. I realize quite suddenly that there will be many tomorrows. The moment is too precarious to jeopardize with careless words.

Fane rises sharply and runs a hand through his flaxen hair. He walks toward my hatch as though preparing to leave, and stalls just short of my legs. He regards me distantly, with the detached curiosity of a stranger.

"You proved your strength this evening," he says. "Lydia herself called your performance at Opes and Sons 'a remarkable feat.' I would imagine it took a great deal for her to praise your actions to me. Andrew was positively brimming with gratitude when he called, that you were able to conduct yourself so admirably in the company of his daughter."

No longer bound to a fate of infinite blackness, I struggle to my feet on wavering legs. I stand tall in his presence and sweep the hair back from my eyes. He leans forward slightly, as if to whisper a secret.

"And how did you find the Opes heir? Our Christine?"

We share a tenuous, satisfied smile.

"She is everything we hoped for, my Lord. Twice the mind of her father, I am certain of it."

He nods his approval, and struck with an afterthought, turns back on his heel. I flinch and hate myself for it.

"Your Andrew insists that he be permitted to continue his work under your eye, and yours alone. I too insist that you be the sole liaison between our family and his."

I know I wear my heart on my face. I can scarcely contain my pride. "If it pleases you, my Lord."

Fane rubs his hands together, as though washing the issue away. My position is intact, my life escaped from his fury, at least for now.

"Stela..." He takes a step in my direction, deliberate and firm. "Killing Collins was an act of treason. He was not yours to take and you ended his life for foolish, selfish reasons."

His eyes fix themselves on mine, the portent of a bargain in the air. I meet his glare steadily, and with my utmost humility. "Yes. It was."

He takes another step closer, crossing his trunk-like arms over his chest. I have to tilt my head up to his face.

"But protecting Christine was an act of loyalty. Aiding your sister home, despite your unyielding rivalry, that too was an act of loyalty," he decides. "I will consider the safe passage of Lydia and Christine as payment for the life you stole from me. On one condition."

I lift my empty palms between our bodies. "Anything, my Lord."

"Bård offered an interesting and lucrative venture with Mr. Collins. You must supplement that enterprise. The details are yours to fret over and arrange, but I expect delivery of an alternative."

Overcome with generosity for his leniency, I kneel before him. I do not know why in light of all that I have concealed from him he would spare me so readily. And I am in no position to question. "I swear it, my Lord."

His lips smooth back into a genuine smile, the smile he reserves for me, and I have not seen it in ages. My chest brims with familiar affection for him as he turns back toward the hatch. But just before he can leave me I remember myself, and without a single thought to how fortunate I am to receive such mercy, I find I have one more question. If he turns and destroys me where I stand, so be it.

"My Lord. The girl…"

He throws his head straight back, staring up at the ceiling as frustration chisels his jaw.

"Stela, do I not always give you that which you desire?"

He twists his head over his shoulder. He is weary of me, he is weary of this conversation. And then his lips spread in a pitying smile.

"All these months you hid her from me. And you hid yourself away from me. But I have never been your enemy, and I am not your obstacle in this matter."

"Of what obstacle do you speak, my Lord?"

"You were once a gifted warrior." Fane grows serious. "Matters of the heart are as bloody as any battlefield, my dove. You must remain stalwart and merciless, until the very last foe. If you cannot see my meaning you must ask yourself: what separates you from absolute victory?"

I close my eyes, and permit his words to sink in. I stand in a field with Fane by my side, blood dripping from my sword. My Lord's hand curls around my shoulder, he whispers his encouragement. James's exsanguinated body twitches and convulses at my feet. The boy cries out for quick death. But against the dark horizon Elizabeth stands unattended. A lone, windswept figure at the edge of the frame. A slip of a woman nearly hidden from sight, blotted out by the top of her mother's silver head.

"Claire…"

My fingers curl into claws and violence floods me from toe to top.

When I open my eyes the hatch has closed, and My Lord has vanished as though he was never there.

Of course, with a general's eye, he is right.

* * *

Elizabeth has gone to unsurprising lengths to ensure her mother is adequately cared for while she "recovers." The exterior doors of the care facility are protected by cameras and no one can enter or leave without buzzing the visitor's desk. More a system to keep patients inside than to keep others out. I would have preferred to stroll gallantly into the first floor, instead of slinking through a rust-sealed basement window, dust and grit nesting in my hair. Needs must, I suppose.

Though the common rooms are closely monitored, the hallways are not. Many of the lights have been dimmed, so moving unseen is no issue. The nurse will not make her rounds for another fifteen minutes. Plenty of time.

The building reeks of decay. The plaster walls sing with the low buzz of electrical currents, sockets powering machines powering people. The hollow light above Claire's bed is on, as though it matters to her whether it be day or night. Elizabeth's discarded shoes are tucked beneath a vacant chair. Her scent is strong in the room, but she is visiting with Helen in the lounge.

"Good evening, Mrs. Dumas."

I lean against the doorframe. Claire's eyes are still as stone beneath sealed, wrinkled lids. Her chest belabors under a mass of immaculately tucked quilts Elizabeth has brought from home. Aside from the whisper of her breath, the room is silent. Claire was taken off the ventilator after her surgery, so the only equipment of concern is the baby monitor Elizabeth keeps on the nightstand when she leaves the room. I switch the radio off and set it back on the nightstand. "Now we can speak in private."

I take a seat on the edge of the bed and Claire's body slides toward mine. "I was certain that Elizabeth's nightmare was a subconscious enactment of her murderous intentions. Wish fulfillment. I see now where I was mistaken. The nightmare was a wish, yes. But it was also a cry for help."

I crane my neck, my face close to Claire's ear. "Does that surprise you?"

Claire's face remains immune to provocation, wearing only the usual amount of irritation she so often exhibited in daily life. Apart from the feeding tube, she looks very much herself.

"Unlike yourself, Claire, I am moved by her desires. However, buried they may be."

I cup the back of her neck in my hand and slide the pillow from under her head, which is soured by sweat. Laying her down gently, I stand beside the body, clutching the pillow tightly between my fists.

"I see no reason you should suffer any longer." A rush of panic, swift and decimating, sweeps over me as I seal the fabric over Claire's accepting face. But the panic is not mine.

My name rings clear as a bell through Elizabeth's mind. A second later I hear her rushed footsteps climb the hall. I release the pillow and conceal myself in the shadows along the wall, infected with Elizabeth's fear and rendered impotent by her outrage.

Elizabeth hurls herself inside the room and with a sock-clad skid, she crashes against the side of the bed. She flips the pillow from her mother's face like an insect she cannot bring herself to handle with bare hands. Unseen, I slip outside the room and flatten myself against the wall.

"I'm sorry," she says, though not to me.

Elizabeth stifles a muffled sob with the palm of her hand, and tucks the quilts down the length of her mother's body. This is not the reaction I anticipated. I should leave this place. Immediately.

But emotions, contorted and atomic, spill from the room in neon plumes. There is a violet anger vibrating around Elizabeth, sharper than usual. Warily, I stand in the doorway, bracing myself for whatever explosion awaits. Elizabeth's spine straightens, and her hands grip the pillow she has retrieved from the floor. She is so still, so impossibly silent that I can barely make out the rise and fall of her chest. Her mother's corpse seems more animated.

"Is this a game to you?" she asks, curiously composed. "Am I a trophy? A pet?"

The quick snap of her neck sends curling chestnut waves spilling over her shoulders. Her face remains fixed straight ahead and menacingly fragmented in the far window's reflection. I cannot read her eyes, which I suspect is her intention. She does not want to be read, or soothed. Neither—I realize too late—does she want to be rescued.

If my jealously were an ocean it would drown me. This is her choice, not mine. Not even Fane's. And she had already chosen Claire, but it did not suit me to believe it.

"I lied to you." Elizabeth knots the pillowcase in her hands. "I asked you what you were called before Fane named you Stela." She holds the pillow over her mother's head. "I told you I heard your mother say the name Ruxandra in my dream." Elizabeth rests the pillow on Claire's chest, smoothing the hair back from her sweaty face with careful hands. She lifts Claire by the shoulders, by the cradle of her skull. "You asked me what else I heard. What else she said." She slides the pillow back, laying Claire softly back down. Elizabeth falls silent.

I take a step into the darkened room. Elizabeth raises her head, but she will not turn around. She stares down at her mother. "Your mother did say something else," she interjects, quite suddenly. "It was in Romanian. I had to look it up. I said it was nothing because I didn't know what to think of it. Such an odd thing for a mother to say when her child is being taken from her…" Elizabeth strokes her mother's wrinkled cheek. Only the thin edge of one eyebrow and the tip of her nose are visible. "*Mulțumesc. Mulțumesc Domnului meu.*"

The words, so long forgotten, transport me. I can feel the cool breeze rolling off the mountains, stinging my tear-tracked cheeks. The soft prickle of new spring grass beneath my toes. Fane's firm hand around my wrist. I see my mother's face clearly for the first time in centuries, and hear her voice quivering beneath the force of her broken sobs. I step back out of the room, and Elizabeth turns back to the window. Her calculating eyes scrutinize my reaction in our shared reflection.

"I'm sure I butchered the pronunciation," she says with a disinterested shrug. "I looked it up the second I woke up that morning, before I'd even dressed. This small skinny child, ripped from the arms of her grief-stricken mother. And her mother just kept repeating those words over, and over again. *Thank you. Thank you, my Lord.*"

Elizabeth reaches beside her mother's head and turns the dial up on the baby monitor. "It's no wonder you can't understand a daughter's love for her mother, Stela. Your own mother didn't want you."

I have never wanted so dearly to inflict horrific physical pain on her. I have never regretted so completely having saved her in that alley the night she was shot. I clench my jaw as my blood surges for action, for recompense, and my fangs descend—their pointed tips making a bloody bed of my bottom gums.

"You're not wanted here either," she whispers, as though she has not made herself perfectly clear. "Leave us alone."

My body, coiled tightly, prepared to spring. I know that Elizabeth can sense every inch of me as easily as I can see her in the shadows hung around the room, but even her pulse is steady, pointedly slow. She does not turn to acknowledge my reaction, she does not bristle with alarm. She has no plans to fend me off, or fight. There is neither welcome nor fear. Just the clear, cool air of perfect resignation rising between us, as insurmountable as a wall of ice.

I turn around and thunder down the hall. The bleached linoleum cracks underfoot, and a frightened nurse rounds the corner only to stumble backward when sees the murderous expression on my face. She appears to be the only witness and she does not give chase. I exit through the basement more violently than I entered.

I deliberate on the sidewalk that runs the length of the facility, radiating with fury and embarrassment, sincerely considering whether or not to rip the main door from its hinges and paint the walls with both their blood. Cameras be damned. Then I hear it: soft and low, a lullaby. Not a song at all. Just a hushed and tranquil tune whispered in hums between her gasping breaths. Elizabeth's overwhelming sadness follows me outside and sits at my feet like a broken-winged bird waiting to be crushed.

Every inch of my body tightens in response. How can she say such things to me, and then immediately wallow in despair? Inexplicably, an apology has already begun to shape in my throat, catching against the back of my tongue like thorn-covered vines. I turn my face to the night breeze and let it stroke my lashes with its chilled breath. I take in the air with its soot-covered hands as it drags me away from her by the lapels.

No more.

I step out into the dark embrace of the vacant street, a wounded animal ready to retreat and lick my wounds. What her venomous words have touched was so deeply buried that I had forgotten it entirely until tonight.

There is only one place for me. I had nearly convinced myself otherwise.

* * *

The lights of his chamber are low, the door shut firmly against intrusion, but not bolted. He has company this evening, which is common of late. Far more so than when I held the mantel of favorite. I wonder if these increasingly regular visits are at her urging, or his, though it hardly matters. The arrangement appears beneficial to both parties.

My entrance is registered immediately. Fane's answering snarl disappears as quickly as it came, his blood-smeared mouth spread into a welcoming smile. Lydia arches up on her elbows from beneath his wide chest. Her thick black hair in tangles down her back.

"Stela. What an unexpected surprise," Fane says. "And where is your Elizabeth?"

I throw the bolt on the door, but I do not answer him. He is not asking out of concern or politeness. He already knows. When I look upon them again, their entwined bodies casting abstract shadows on the floor, Lydia slides out from beneath him. Fane groans from the loss of her and rests with his head in his hand on his side, expectant and intrigued.

Lydia takes careful steps toward me, her body aglow in the flickering flames from the gas torches along the walls that suit Fane's antiquated tastes. She stands before me, black eyes bright with insight. There is a softness in her features I usually see only when she looks at Fane. She takes my face in her hands as though she has touched me this way a million times, as though she did not betray my kindness by sharing stolen memories of Elizabeth with Fane. I reach up and hold her left hand in place against my cheek.

"She refused you." There is no mockery, no teasing. Only Lydia's mild amazement, and a hint of pity. She states the obvious so that I do not have to utter the words out loud. It might be the most considerate thing she has ever done. But more than anything, I suspect she knows how desperately I wanted Elizabeth. When she shared my blood, she felt my affection as though it were her own. I turn away from her, from the weight of my failure.

Lydia's hands slide down my face and neck. She takes hold of the bottom of my shirt. It is not the first time this has happened, the three of us sequestered in Fane's sizeable suite. But it is the first time she greets me with something other than rivalry. She lifts my sweater over my head, and Fane raises himself up on his arm. Lydia does not rush back to him.

With open eyes she places a soft, chaste kiss to my lips, and runs her fingers through my hair—Fane's blood drying fast on her chin in salty flakes. She has no reason to fight or fear me as she takes me by the hand and leads me to the bed. She has everything she has ever wanted waiting for her there—his favor for the first time in her life. She was intended for Bård, but never took to him. No matter what my brother gave her, no matter how much blood they shared their relationship remained complicated at best. I never understood why. I have never been close enough to Lydia to ask and it seemed indelicate to put the question to Bård.

Fane pulls Lydia to him, greedily and doting in his own way. They are quite a sight. His florid pallor in stark contrast to her miraculously golden skin. She kept the gleam of good health even after she was reborn. I think if I were him, I should have favored her from the start. One tiny glittering statue in a hoard of porcelain dolls.

"Come," he says, holding out his hand. Lydia grabs me by the wrist, delicately ushering me down beside her.

Deep in my bones I sense the sun rising on the horizon. The impending heat of it makes my limbs heavy, my movements sluggish despite having gorged myself on my own kind for hours. The obliterating euphoria of Fane's superior blood buzzes through me, brightening the darkened bedroom as though daylight is already upon me. I extricate my limbs and stand beneath the mirrored skylight in Fane's vaulted ceiling. I see only the reflection of a young sky in the slanted mirrors that carry the sunrise down into his quarters. A mauve morning, puffed with pink clouds.

I have spent many mornings just like this in Fane's bed, watching him gaze up at the same sight. I felt such sorrow for him, banished from a world that should be his. A self-mandated exile to protect his children from his obvious otherness, when it became clear that though the myths of our existence remained, all our human allies were dead. A fresh start in the colonies, he said, but in the new world, he was immediately recognized, his inhumanity impossible to mask. The puritanical peasants fled their native lands in search of a new start too, only to find familiar fiends on foreign shores.

With burning eyes, I take a seat on the leather sofa and watch the sky swell overhead. Fane, permanently alert, stirs and stretches his limbs. He never misses first light. It is the only chance he gets to bathe his translucent skin in the warmth of the sun.

Fane runs his hand down Lydia's exposed torso and procures his emerald robe from the foot of his massive bed. His ever-watchful glare roams over my face as he secures the tie around his waist.

"Perhaps it is better this way, my dove."

"I was just entertaining the thought, my Lord."

The first flickering streams of golden light ignite the crown of his head, and though it pains me, I hold his gaze. A witness to his strength, and a testament to my own that I can bear it.

"This world is not welcoming," he says, deep in thought. "It is ever changing, shrinking if such a thing is possible. These humans know nothing of the past. They have no respect for their own history. They rewrite what does not suit them, and deliberately forget what they cannot tailor."

I have said it all to myself. And would Elizabeth—turned—be a delicate evening primrose like Lydia? Spreading her petals only at dusk? Could I knowingly lead someone I value into eternal night, and steal her beauty away? A secret only for my eyes? One last beautiful image for her victims? Would forever be worth the pain?

"Of course, you are right, my Lord." And he is.

The sun streaks across the sky and pulls the final rays of dawn up over Fane's brow, disappearing completely from our sight. The blistering heat lingers in the resumed dark. Fane releases a longing sigh, dredged from the depths of his being. "Whether she submits to you or not, Stela, I have given you the gift of my blessing. I have offered her a place at my side, with you."

"You have, my Lord. I am forever in your debt."

Fane rises and cupping my chin in his hand. "It gladdens my heart to hear you say that, because from this day forward I expect nothing but your gratitude, Stela. Your unquestioning loyalty." Though his words are ironclad his hold on me remains soft. "Exactly as life was, so shall it be again. Am I quite clear?"

"Yes, my Lord."

He holds my face a moment longer, running his thumb tenderly across my jaw. "Get to bed, my dove."

I leave my clothes scattered on the floor and slip out the door before he can list any further requirements. The impenetrable black of the corridor engulfs me. My muscles remember the way. I climb up the ladder built into the divide and crawl through the raised and narrow corridor that houses my siblings. My hand finds the hatch above my dormitory, the light above my chamber snuffed out hours earlier. I do not rush inside those familiar walls. I sit with my back pressed to the cold and unforgiving ironwood wall, letting the darkness permeate every fiber of my being.

Exactly as it was, so shall it be again.

X

Bargaining

Wiped. Clean as a mirror in an empty room, rootless and suspended. Caught in a black bog, paralyzed, severed from past and present—outside of time. If you have no living ancestor, what proof do you have of a beginning? And isn't ambiguity the very nature of eternity?

Everything is more than it is normally, and less than it ever was. I'm not sure how that's possible.

The leaves show their veined underbellies to the dusk-kissed sky. When I was a child, our gardener warned me inside when the leaves danced upside down on their branches. He said it meant rain. Mother said you could sense the storm in the wind, and she was right. She was always right. The evening breeze is charged and chilled, weighed down with dew, knocking the body instead of rushing past.

I should hurry back, I know. But leaving is the hardest part of visiting her. When the last mourner has returned home, who does she have? The only mourner, really.

Helen made the necessary calls, tearing through the yellowed pages of Mother's moth-eaten address book. She stopped updating me on the meager list of attendees after she learned that my mother's only known relative, my great-aunt Nadine, had been dead for almost six years.

I scrape my index finger along the elegant scroll of her name, etched forever in marble.

She was interred in accordance with her will, in her father's columbarium at St. Boniface Cemetery. My father was buried in accordance with his, several blocks north at St. Peter's. Mother found the thought of burial repugnant, so all that rests beside my father in the joint plots he purchased are the insects fat from his flesh. We had the argument only once. I suggested that she could store her ashes in an urn in the plot beside my dad. She stared at me incredulously for all of three seconds and asked where I had placed the Arts and Leisure section of *The Times*.

Even in death she's asking me to pick a side.

Her wishes were more glamorous. I'll give her that. Selfish, but that was always her style. Is it too much to ask that I be permitted to take one train, and grieve for both my parents in a central location?

St. Peter's is hardly a central location Elizabeth. Besides, it would take at least two trains no matter how much of your family was buried there.

"Touché."

How can I be so painfully aware of someone who is no longer a part of this world? Does she know that I'm here, every single night, crying and shivering at her tomb and not at my father's? Picking her over, and over again. Promising myself to visit him tomorrow, but always stepping off the platform three stops too soon?

What do I do now, Mother? Without you to look after, to disappoint? It's what keeps me from going home. You've painted your shadow into every corner of the brownstone you loved so dearly, and it only makes me feel more alone. It keeps me from getting back to work. Who is left for me to appease? To praise or chastise me? What does any of it matter now?

I could do anything. Go anywhere. Instead, I'm stuck between two cemeteries. Pinned down by the promise of another impossible tomorrow. As certain of my failures as ever I was, and without a single acerbic insult to help me along.

Mother died three weeks after Stela tried to take her from me. A second stroke. Nothing I could have done. Or so I've been told. For two days, I sat at the bottom of the stairs while Helen made the tough calls, desperate to throw together some semblance of a funeral. And James, with his nervous hands and timid mouth, puttered around the kitchen looking for things to clean, going so far as to rearrange the expired contents of the fridge.

There were moments when the whole house would seize up with stillness, like the body bracing for a sneeze. When I could feel the three of us inhale in unison, and hold that breath. James with a dishrag pulled tight in his hands, and Helen with her cell phone held back from her ear, the dial tone of another wrong number or dead acquaintance ringing out around us. And I would sit doe-eyed dumb, dragging my nails in the grooves of the baseboard looking for blood.

I don't know why I did that. Why I sat in the spot where her body had crumbled and hunted with my hands for evidence of the catastrophe. A sliver of torn flesh caught in the wood. A bone fragment. Something, anything to prove that the fall was real, that my mother had an accident on the stairs. That my benign neglect and boundless resentment didn't kill her. That she wasn't a casualty of passive aggression. She slipped. She fell, and that's how I lost her. But there wasn't so much as a copper-colored crumb of coagulated blood. There was hardly any dust. My hands came away clean.

Stela was thorough.

Did she feel it when it happened? My immense sorrow? My shameful relief? When I stopped the chest compressions and collapsed at my mother's bedside, wringing my hands and screaming her name? Could Stela sense my grief? And do I have the right to be offended by her absence when I twice demanded it?

I don't. I have no right to be angry with Stela when she has been entirely honest about what she is, and what she is not. No more than I have the right to parade myself around as the grieving daughter, when all I asked of either of them was to leave me alone.

I've visited the Art Institute on two separate occasions since the funeral. Both times I found myself in the Sculpture Court, standing at the frozen feet of *Truth*. I stared painfully hard into her wide vacant eyes, until my vision blurred and I could have sworn she reached for me. It's a strange place to find comfort, and an odd reminder of Stela when I have so many others.

My bicep begins to throb as though conjured by the thought her and I drop my purse at my feet, rolling the limb up and down to shake the ache away. That grip in my gut is gone. The slow heavy drop in my stomach when she's near. The electric tingling that crawls across my skin, making me shiver with goose bumps no matter the temperature. I'm trying very hard to hold on to what she did, what she tried to do, and hate her for it. But the truth is that no matter how misguided and abhorrent her actions, they made a sick kind of sense. It's what she was also trying to tell me at the hospital. I just couldn't accept it. I couldn't accept that my mother wasn't in that body on the bed. That she wasn't waking up, wasn't coming back. I still can't.

What I know is that things hurt less when Stela was around. Being near her, physically close to her, was the only thing worthy of my attention. It was like being submerged in a warm bath, even when Stela herself was cool to the touch. Knotted muscles would relax. Cares I didn't realize I was carrying would quiet. Everything took a backseat to the fact that she was there.

Some nights she would come to me so late that I would feel it happening in my dreams. My body seemed to sink, and I would wake up curled deep into my mattress with her hair tickling my eyelids. Certain of her presence before I ever registered her with sight.

Now this ache in my arm with its puckered scar is the only proof I have that she was real. It's worse with the changing weather, the downward swing of autumn. I would have it examined, but how would I explain a gunshot wound?

I reach up with a grimace and pull the dead flowers from the bronze votive beside my mother's name, tossing them over my shoulder into the stiff grass. I remove a fresh bouquet of white tea roses from inside my coat. They won't last the night, not in this cold. But what does? Flowers wither and die. So do people.

Reason enough to romanticize Stela, I suppose. She was a constant: immovable, unyielding, fixed, unaged, and unchanged. Something you couldn't lose, though I somehow managed to.

James was easier to push away than I had hoped. A few random explosions of anger directed his way, and he disappeared. No more late night takeout deliveries dropped at my door. No magazines, no conversation. One minute he was standing in my kitchen with tears in his eyes, and the next he was gone.

Helen still calls to check in, like she's taking my temperature, like she's walking me through a preliminary exam.

"How are you feeling today?" A stethoscope to the chest. Breathe, and hold it.

"I'm fine Helen." And exhale. Good.

"Have you heard from James?" Another deep breath, and hold it.

"He's busy, I'm sure." And exhale.

"Such a nice young man." Hold it.

Aunt Nadine rests in the top left corner of the columbarium, beside my grandfather. She was his youngest sister, closer in age to his only daughter—Mother—than any of her own siblings. One can only speculate as to the reason two women who were so close would go without speaking for nearly fifteen years. Nadine was a striking woman, tall and poised like my mother, with one glaring contrast—Nadine was warm, personable, and affectionate with everyone she met. Especially my father.

The last time I was in a room with her was just after his funeral. During the wake, she held me close. She cried, a deep, bellowing howl as she rocked us both. My mother clawed me out of her arms with punishing fingers, and I remember the sound but not the sight of Mother's cool thin hand striking my aunt's flushed and freshly powdered cheek.

Strange to think that Mother would rather spend an eternity entombed beside the woman who may or may not have ruined her marriage, instead of taking her place beside my father. But that was the way Mother held a grudge. Forever. I wonder if this is her way of keeping them parted. Her way of keeping tabs on Nadine, and ensuring that my dad is as alone in death as I suspect my mother was in life.

I talk about my mother as though she's still alive. It isn't healthy. I catch myself speaking to her aloud on a daily basis. Sometimes the words don't make it past my lips, but I hear her whisper the answer in my ear. Logically, she has been reduced to a handful of elements: calcium, sodium, potassium, a sprinkling of carbonate, a dash of dental fillings.

What worries me is the overwhelming anger rising at the back of my throat. Suddenly, every living thing becomes an insult. I rage at everything being as it should be, as it always has been, regardless of my loss. With no thought of me.

I'm uncertain as to when, exactly, you became a raging narcissist, but I'm positive your father is to blame.

I wheel around as though my mother is somewhere within reach. But she isn't there. The only person goading me, is me.

I tear the white roses from the votive and crush them underfoot, because it makes no difference. The white petals brown against the concrete in a sickeningly sweet smudge. In my haste to leave and catch the train I kick my purse, and the contents spray up into the air—cosmopolitan confetti. It's the sharp snap of my cell phone smacking the pavement that ends my tantrum and pulls me back to myself. The shatter of broken glass.

I take a breath, let my head fall forward and press against my mother's marble plaque.

When I've recovered, I crouch down on my knees and gather the shards of splintered plastic that once formed my phone case. My battery, though dented, is largely intact. I flip the phone over with a dismal groan, my reflection fractured on the screen. With careful hands, I snap the battery back into place and swipe my finger over the jagged glass to unlock it. Like an addict, I open the conversation history first, frantically scrolling down the threads—well past my mother—until I find her.

S.

Last message received nearly three months ago. I press my thumb over the icon. Then my index finger. I drag my finger. I scrounge through my belongings strewn across the pavement for an eyebrow pencil to use as a stylus. But the texts won't display. I click several other conversations to no avail. The phone falls from my hands, and it's like she's left me all over again. A loneliness and a physical ache in my chest, so pronounced that I clutch the front of my shirt. I quit my crouch to sit on the cold cement, my back pressed to the marble wall.

I picture the door Stela once described, buried in an untouchable place somewhere inside. I can see it in my mind, know this as the space she occupied only by the blankness I find. Intentional nothing where there should be something. Without petulance, anger, or fear I throw my weight against that door. I pull at a handle I know is there, but can't see. I trace the sealed edges with my fingertips, but the door won't budge.

"Stela."

I've stopped myself so many times, it's an odd relief to say her name out loud.

An icy breeze frosts my tear-tracked cheeks. With chilled fingers, I rock forward onto the balls of my feet and set about sweeping my personal effects back into my scuffed purse, grinding to a halt when I smell it, earthen and faintly floral. My heart beats in my throat and I freeze, waiting for her to emerge from the shadows. The wind rushes past my ears, howling in the dark, but the scent is no stronger than before. Something slides beneath my palm, distinctly organic, and I recoil. A pinch of ground petal and pulp, the remnants of my mother's roses.

A nervous, unstoppable fit of laughter barrels through me with the force of a freight train. I should call Dr. Richmond. Explain to Arthur that I lost the referral to the therapist he recommended. I had been through an ordeal before my mother died. Now I can add extreme avoidance of people and responsibilities to my growing list of symptoms. I swear, if there were a pill that could isolate and expunge the last four years of my life, the entirety of this waking nightmare, I would take it without a second thought. Mother would understand.

I sling my purse over my shoulder and take the hand offered to me, rising on stiff legs. "Thanks."

I manage two solid steps, and then the ground falls out from under me.

My legs won't move. I barely remember to breathe. The elongated shadows of the trees, edge closer, stretching toward me. The antique lamps evenly spaced up and down the narrow walkways, threading around graves, burn bright in a sentient way. I wait for her voice because I don't have the courage to turn around. If she's there, what's next? If she isn't, will tomorrow be more of the same?

Something stirs inside me. That familiar quickening, all pulse and nerve endings. A rush of blood—not mine—moving through my veins, surging, remembering where it belongs. A gust of wind, laced with traces of rust or iron, whips the back of my coat up around my tights.

I close my eyes and follow my body, turning around as though commanded. Run, is that what I want to do? My head swims, and I know I'm going to hyperventilate. She must know it too, because two cool hands cup the sides of my face, and the current of her touch wakes every fiber of my being to life. Every hair follicle on my arms stands on end, every cell in my body buzzes. I cover her hands with mine, and when my eyes open my vision is blurred.

"You are too beautiful for tears, my darling."

Stela traces the wet tracks on my cheeks with her thumbs, smoothing the moisture into my skin. Her black eyes soak up the light stolen from the stars, a silver sheen around the edges. She looks nothing like I remember. Her straight curtain of blond hair spills over the tops of her shoulders in heavy tangles. The knowing twist of her lips is subdued, soft and full of the blood of another nameless victim, parted as though she means to say more. Her eyes are as treacherous as ever, but heavy, aimless as they search my face instead of burrowing to the core of me. The front of her blouse is soiled and torn, splotched with crimson fingerprints. She doesn't need to dress for the weather, but normally she prides herself on her appearance.

Never have I wanted or needed to say more. She must sense this, because with a soft hush she pulls me closer and rests her forehead against mine. Her name is a caught breath and little else, but it manages to carry a question and a request. Stela swallows her name, sealing her mouth over mine.

My body trembles with adrenaline when we part, too soon for either of us. The ache in my arm subsides the moment Stela wraps her hand around my bicep, as though she's encouraging her blood to pool beneath her palm as she directs it to the pain. The relief is instant.

"The wound still hurts you."

Her words tickle the corner of my mouth and I try to take a step back to answer her properly, but she wraps her arms around my waist. Her grip is steadfast but gentle, a breakable hold. I press myself against the front of her shirt. "It aches in the cold, and when the weather changes."

Stela brings one hand to the base of my neck, massaging a knot at the top of my spine. I've known these sensations before, but prior experience never lessens them. Yet it's that same knowledge that makes me wary and I pull my face from her tangled hair, to look her in the eyes.

"Why are you here?"

Stela's laugh is weary and she doesn't hide her exasperation. Her fingers are still at the back of my neck. She meets my stare with her onyx eyes, and once again I sense the tempestuous gulf hidden in their alluring depths.

"Why did you call to me?"

My mouth hangs open prepared to reply, but my wit dies on my tongue. She is changed. More demanding somehow, even in her touch. "I needed to see you."

She purses her lips in a thin line and kisses the creased skin of my forehead, her gaze distracted as she studies the darkness around us. Her lack of focus, the tight, coiled stance worries me.

"To what end?" she asks. The question is as abrupt as it is direct. She cradles my chin in her hand, and her restless eyes scour my face for an answer.

"What do you mean?" Panic sours the back of my throat. I'm torn between running away from her, and pushing myself back into her embrace. She registers this new uneasiness, and runs a hand slowly down my back.

"You are no longer a secret I can keep, Elizabeth." A guarded answer, carefully worded. Again, her gaze shifts just over my shoulder, bouncing off the top of my head and sweeping across the sleeping grass. Like a cold fist fear curls itself in the pit of my stomach as I drop my hands quickly from her torso, and seek to become less conspicuous.

"They know about us, don't they? The others."

The smile she gives me is affected, uncharacteristically anxious. She nods and—as if deciding all at once that her presence here with me is already known—she places a hand between the buttons of my coat and closes her eyes, savoring my heartbeat.

"Stela, how?"

Reluctantly Stela opens her eyes and pretends she didn't hear my question.

"Can you feel me?" she whispers. She brings her mouth close to mine, and her fingers inside my jacket part the buttons at my collar until she can slide her palm against my skin. It's an incredibly effective form of evasion.

"Yes." My lips part against hers, but she won't let me deepen the kiss. She moves her lips along my jaw, back behind my ear as her fingers stroke the skin above my breast.

"I could always feel you. Wherever you were, I was there. You were never alone, my darling. Not for a moment."

The words are comforting but also infuriating and I draw away from her, annoyed. "I couldn't, Stela. I couldn't feel anything but the absence of you. Not for months. Not when my mother died. Not at the funeral. Not when they entombed her ashes, or when they set her plaque."

She lets me take two large steps back from her, the hand that touched my heart hovering between us, palm upturned and extended. Even as I step away, fastening my buttons, I want nothing more than to reach out and take it. Her own anger burns brightly between us.

"I gave you exactly what you wanted. Do I not always give you what you desire?"

There's a quick flash of something across her face, like her own words surprise her. She shoves her clenched fists into the pockets of her dark trousers. Her jaw is clenched, but her lips are soft, an almost human pout.

"Do you?" I ask it more for myself than for her.

Stela closes the short distance between us, keeping her hands firmly in her pockets. "Perhaps not. But I can no longer walk this line with you, Elizabeth. It is not safe. For either of us."

I adjust my purse strap and turn away from her "So, you're leaving again?" I would give just about anything to sound less desperate than I feel.

She takes my arm firmly in hers and slides up behind me. "Not this very moment. Take a walk with me."

As always, it isn't a request.

We walk for a few blocks without speaking. Several times I open my mouth to ask her where we're going, but while a part of me thinks it doesn't matter, another part is certain that I already know. She keeps her arm locked around mine with a worried hand clasped over my wrist. She rubs the soft white skin she finds there, stroking the thin blue veins.

"You were out feeding tonight."

Stela's fingers halt and brush lightly over the top of my forearm.

"Yes."

"Why haven't you changed your clothes?"

She arches a bemused brow, but keeps her eyes front, scanning the vacant streets she steers us down.

"There was no time."

"And the body?"

She seeks out my face from the corner of her eye and regards me suspiciously for a second.

"Is in capable hands."

"So you weren't alone."

A knowing smile spreads across her lips as she tugs me around the weathered corner of a tenement. The neighborhood slips as we walk, revealing failed investment, poor planning, lack of funding and crushed unions. I can hear the rats tonight, slinking in the gutters and scurrying ahead just inches in front of my feet. They trample over each other as quickly as they can to get away from her. I should be so wise.

"I was hunting with my brother Bård when you called out to me. I left the cleanup to him. As for my garments, I will burn them before I retire for the evening."

I slip my arm free from hers in search of her hand. She laces our fingers with a squeeze that is meant to be reassuring but she still hasn't told me where we're headed, and the side streets she so deftly navigates look like a B-rated post-apocalyptic thriller.

"He knows you're with me?"

Stela walks on the balls of her boot-covered feet, skirting dark pools of stagnant, foul-smelling liquid that I don't see until I hear it slosh around my shoes.

"I did not seek to conceal the information, if that is what you mean."

An old man sleeps in the warped yellow light of a crumbling back alley stoop, bent over the paper bag tight in his hands. Sharply, I twist my fingers free of her hand and it takes a moment for my feet to stop following her, to start inching back the way we came. If I scream maybe the old man will hear me. Maybe he's not the only person left on this forgotten block. Maybe windows will brighten and open on concerned citizens with cell phones raised. But what good would the police be?

"Elizabeth…" It's only my name, but the way she says it sounds like the start and end of a very long argument.

"Why don't you care that he knows? Where are you taking me?"

My hand reaches out to grope the slimy brick of the building beside me. I would turn and run, but I'm certain she's faster. My heel makes contact with something soft—something that protests with a sharp squeak—and a scream wells up in my throat. But I don't scream. I don't know what she would do if I did, and it's the unknown that keeps me quiet more than any spoken threat. She stalks toward me, step for step as I stumble back. All I can see are the edges of her body, the bright halo of her hair glowing around her head.

"Home," she says with an easy smile. "Where else would I take you?"

My stomach drops and I'm going to be sick. There is something terrifying about her calm, and that she hasn't grabbed me yet, even though she could. Whether she has fed or not, I know she's enjoying this. "Get away from me, Stela."

She laughs, that unsettling, girlish laugh. The sound drops between us like pennies on the pavement.

"My darling, and leave you to what? To walk about the streets alone? To fumble your way back to the cemetery? Have you forgotten what happened the last time you ran away from me?" I can't tell if it's the distance between us now or the fear, but as she alludes to the night I was shot, my arm immediately begins to ache. It quickly grows into pulsating pain, and my arm drops limply to my side. Is she doing this? "Yes, you remember what happened."

Every word she says carries the light inflection of a joke. Tears sting my eyes, and my fear crests into vile disdain.

"Stela. Stop."

My voice is louder and more forceful than I expected. She raises her hands in defeat and stops walking. The throb in my arm radiates to my teeth, but I keep shuffling backward, too afraid to take my eyes away from her. Her image shrinks, less imposing with every step. And I grow more concerned with what is, or isn't behind me.

"Where will you go, Elizabeth?" Her voice is level, devoid of emotion.

My eyes scan the darkness, drifting, glancing behind me only for a moment.

"Away from you!"

I can barely make out her gestures beyond the shake of her head. My foot slips off the crumbling edge of the gutter, and I stall with my heart in my throat.

"This is ridiculous. You are well aware of that, are you not?"

She starts walking again, while I attempt to free my foot from the rusted iron teeth of a sewer grate.

"Stay back, Stela."

"Enough." She waves a hand between us like she can wipe my suspicions away "You are coming with me."

"Where are you taking me?"

Her head falls back and she pushes a forced, exhausted sigh into the night air. "I am taking you home."

"Then why are we going in the opposite direction?"

Stela kneels in front of me and with a swift tug, she pulls my foot loose from the grate. There's more light at this end of the alley, but not much. Shadows stripe her face as she grabs my bicep. All at once with a swoon that threatens my knees, the pain in my arm subsides.

"Because my vehicle is parked not forty yards from here."

My anger simmers, but the fear begins to evaporate. I jerk my arm out of her hold. "Why didn't you just tell me that?"

She makes a small, bemused shrug of her shoulders. "You are never frightened of me. It was rather intoxicating."

I've never struck anyone. Stela's face remains unmoved as my palm begins to throb. I can't stifle the short, pained breath that leaves my mouth, cupping my hand to my chest. I might as well have slapped a wall.

"I hate you." The words barely escape my gritted teeth.

Stela tilts her head with a sad smile, stroking my cheek despite my flinch. "No," she says, shaking her head. "But I deserved that."

The soft curve of her brows, and the concern etched into her forehead soften my stance. Stela leans forward and presses a light kiss to my temple. Our shared, unreconciled anger pushing our bodies apart. "I shouldn't have said that about your mother, Stela."

At first, she doesn't appear to catch my meaning. Then, as though replaying the night she nearly killed my mother and hearing my words all over again, Stela stiffens and stands tall. "Was it the truth?"

She would know if I lied. I wonder if there's some way to soften the blow, but I live with the same truth. My mother never wanted me either. I look her in the eyes and nod. A slow crooked smile curls the corner of her mouth and she shakes her head. Her eyes turn toward the dark alley. She seems smaller.

"I suppose I deserved that too," she says.

It isn't much in the way of an apology on either of our parts. My mother told me once that you never fight with the truth unless you are completely certain it's a fight you can win. I've never really thought about it before. Truth is the one thing you can't take back.

I reach out and take Stela's hand. She stares briefly down at our threaded fingers, and resumes her usual brisk pace. True to her word, not one full street over, her sleek Mercedes beams irreverently in its compromised surroundings. She leads me up to the passenger side and opens my door, but I linger with one foot inside.

"I know why you did it." I don't expect to have to clarify, and Stela doesn't press me to elaborate. She drifts nearer to me, and brushes a hair back from my face.

"I would never ask for your forgiveness. I am not worthy of it."

I lean against the front of her with my hand still wrapped around the door. Every inch of me alive, and every nerve ending firing.

"I'm not offering you forgiveness. I'm just saying I understand."

She runs the pad of two fingers against my bottom lip and I close my eyes, breathing into the sensation. My body drifts forward into hers only to knock flatly against the open door. She's already opening the driver's side door when I turn around.

"Get in."

The ride is unpleasantly quiet, and heavy with emotion that can't possibly belong solely to me. So much left unfinished and unsaid. I can't leave things this way again, but I can't find the words to tell her what she means to me, because I barely understand it myself. She's my every thought. Good or bad, no matter the subject or the mood. Everything leads back to her eventually. She has to know that. But she keeps her eyes straight ahead on the road, and when I reach for her hand she tucks it in her lap.

Halfway down my street she steers the car harshly against the curb, and I instinctively throw my hands up against the dash. Her arm darts out across my chest, keeping me back against the chair as she kills the headlights. Startled by the abrupt stop, I turn my head only to find her half over the console. I struggle with my belt and Stela brushes my hands away and releases it herself. Her impatient hands pull me by my hair, and this kiss makes anything else she's done to me seem gentle by comparison. Rushed and forceful in a way that would be alarming if it weren't so upsetting.

I don't believe she cries. I'm not sure she can. But I can taste her sorrow on my tongue. I don't try to stop her, or talk to her. I pull her as close to me as possible in the narrow space. As soon as my hand finds the back of her head, she pulls away, straightening her shirt with her eyes fixed straight ahead, as though nothing has happened.

"You can walk from here. I will see that you make it safely indoors."

I can't help but laugh. She stares at me incredulously.

"Stela, what the fuck was that?"

Her jaw set, she stares back out toward the open street. I try to turn her head, but she won't move.

"James is waiting for you."

My hands drop from her face. I lean forward over the dash for a better look. His faint outline on my front step is little more than a speck. I turn back to Stela, prop my arm on the leather console between us and stroke the side of her face with the back of my fingers.

"I'll get rid of him."

Finally, she smiles but she's still miles away. And no matter how close I press myself, I can't seem to reach her.

"You should go to him."

I scoff at first, but Stela stares at me in that earnest, beseeching way she has, willing me away from her. I shake my head and she brings my hand to her lips. She kisses my palm.

"No. I want you to come up with me."

She drops her head back against the seat, staring wishfully back at me. She traces my lips with her fingers. "Elizabeth, you know that I cannot."

I grab hold of her jaw and draw her back into a kiss that she will not return.

"Stay with me. Please." I grab hold of her wrist and she hovers above the armrest, letting me pull at her while stroking my hair.

"I do not belong here. But you do, and so does he." Stela speaks with a softness reserved for small children.

I lose all sense of propriety in an instant. I pull at her arms and her shirt rips in my hands. But every part of her that I grab she releases with ease. She's slipping away without moving. She's leaving. Everyone keeps leaving.

"He is a good man," she assures in her softest tone. "A bit of a cad. But he worships you. He would care for you if you would have him. He would marry, and make a mother of you."

I wrap her arms around my shoulders, because she won't reach for me. She lets me press against her. She lets me sob pitifully with my cheek on her chest, her torn blouse tickling my eyelashes.

"Sometimes I dream of that," she says, petting the back of my head. "Of you standing at the kitchen island with a toddler on your hip. She has your eyes, and his nose. Your mother's hair when she was still young."

I rub my face against her neck and all I can say is "No."

"Would that not be a most gratifying life, my love? After this long nightmare. Would it not be wonderful to wake up next to him? With a child curled between your bodies?"

Finally, fitfully, I grab her face in my hands and shout my dissent in her face. Our eyes locked, I beg her to stop over and over again, until I realize she isn't talking anymore. There is no pull, Stela's eyes are distant and empty, and she is still as a corpse in my arms. I press my lips to hers, to her jaw, her throat, her ear, her eyelids. But she retains her marble, stunned composure.

"Take me with you."

She presses her forehead to mine and our lips brush. Nothing on this earth compels me the way she does.

"If not him, then another. This is the most I can give to you, Elizabeth. You have to see that."

When I kiss her she returns my affection desperately. "I want you. You're all I want," I whisper breathlessly into her open mouth. She turns away from me.

"All I can give you is death. Your own, and the blood of others on your hands."

"How is that any different from the life I've been living?"

She huffs and shakes her head as though it's the most ridiculous thing she's ever heard. She must have considered this at some point. She had to know it would come to this.

"It is entirely different to intentionally extinguish the life of a living being. You forget it now, but you felt it acutely this evening. It was the reason you were so reluctant to follow me."

I release Stela's face and slide back down into my seat. James stands with a stretch and takes to pacing under my stoop light. I lock the car door and reach for the seat belt. Stela stares at me, shocked into silence. She slips the car into reverse, watching me, waiting for me to tell her that I've made a horrible mistake and run screaming into the night. When the car bounces down off the curb, Stela reaches for my hand, holding tight as she pulls out onto the deserted street.

It's not until we've barreled past my brownstone that the roar of the engine reaches James's ears. In the rearview mirror, I see him step into the road. Then Stela turns the corner.

* * *

The building appears condemned, which I suppose is the point. Beside the scrolling steel door is a panel that shines like new, with blue illuminated buttons. Stela punches a short code through her rolled down window, and the overhead door rises with a stiff groan. I wrap my hand around the armrest and sweat pearls against the leather.

There are flickering fluorescents but beyond that, the only illumination is from her headlights. The first level of the garage is nearly full. Cars from every country, some of them makes and models I can't immediately identify.

"This is your parking garage?"

She kills the engine and drops her keys on the dashboard, stepping around to the passenger side to open the door for me.

"None of this is mine, Elizabeth. The property belongs to Fane. This vehicle was a gift. They all are."

"Some gift." I let my fingers brush along the body of the black MG Magnette beside us.

"Some are spoken for," she says, unimpressed. "Others just sit in their spaces collecting dust. You can have your pick of the lot when all is said and done."

When I'm dead, I mentally correct. I can have my pick when I'm dead. There's a loud heavy pounding at the base of my skull.

Stela wraps an arm around my waist and leads me to the back of the garage. The only footsteps I can hear are my own, and were it not for the weight of her arm on my hips her presence would be undetectable. My mind races with trivialities: memories of my childhood, my mother's scent, my father's cigars.

She stops in front of a large concrete cylinder rising up from the floor. There is yet another heavy steel door with the same kind of keypad that guards the entrance. Her hand reaches out for the keys and the beating in my head makes it impossible for me to speak. Instead, I shakily push her hand away.

Stela doesn't seem surprised. She enfolds me in a tight embrace, rubbing my shoulder blades. "I can take you home, Elizabeth. Tell me now if this is your wish."

My whole body starts to tremble violently in her arms, my breath fast and shallow. My face is pressed in the crook of her neck, and she rubs my back in slow patient circles.

"No. I'm okay." It's all I can manage, but I want to thank her for lying. We both know the others are already aware of me.

"Perhaps this was a mistake," she says, pulling back to have a look at me. "I should have taken you home first. We could have done this in a more familiar setting. Would you prefer that?"

I think of my mother at the foot of the stairs, the EMTs. Eyes alert, scanning the scene for foul play. The look on Helen's face when she asked me if I had gone home to clean up the blood. I shake my head before I can gather my faculties to respond.

"It can't happen at home. Neighbors would have seen me enter. Eventually Helen or James would come calling. Someone would find something. There would be…" Blood. I've taken a much more active role in my death than I ever imagined I would.

Stela tilts my chin up with one hand and her stare is like water rushing in the dark. My cerebral pounding grinds to halt, and the space between our faces sharpens as the world beyond begins to blur. A deep full breath rushes inside my lungs with ease. "There we are." Stela smiles. "Breathe." Her voice is soft and her fingers press flat against my carotid. The high-pitched electrical drone of the lights above us grounds me.

"Thank you." I savor the momentary reprieve from dread. Stela flashes me a guarded smile, her thumb resting in the dip of my chin.

"I need you present, Elizabeth. Do you understand?"
I take another uninhibited breath. She's waiting on me.
"Tell me what to do."
Stela smooths the hair back from her face and straightens her blouse still open after my tantrum in the car. Somehow the sight of her bare chest still makes me blush. But she is either unaffected, or unaware.
"This chamber leads to the tunnels, which is my greatest concern. They are patrolled by three hounds, including my Erebus, and they hunt together. Erebus's loyalty to me may not outweigh his breeding. Their only duty is to pick off vagrants that find their way into those tunnels surrounding our compound."
I look over at the cold unwelcoming door that stands between us and them.
"They're trained to eat humans?"
Stela offers only a vague shrug, and pushes me aside to punch in the code before I can reason any further.
"Privacy is at a premium in this world, Elizabeth. The door to our chambers is only a couple hundred feet away. I will go in first, and you can follow. If I hear the hounds and pick you up, please do not protest. It will only slow us down."
The small steel trapdoor on the top of the cylinder opens and the smell of moldering earth is overpowering. Stela climbs in first, lowering herself down a few rungs. An expectant look flutters over her face.
"How chivalrous of you to lead the way."
"I knew you would not be able to resist a retort," she says, shaking her head.
"It's a coping mechanism."
"I am well aware, my darling. Now, absolute silence until I tell you otherwise."
The narrow door eases itself shut as soon as I've climbed down far enough into the passage—there must be a sensor in the lid—and the fast-eclipsing darkness swallows the borrowed calm Stela gave me. I didn't realize I had stopped stepping down the rungs until Stela's hand strokes my calf, and I very nearly scream. With great trepidation, I find the next rung with my foot, and then another, fumbling blindly in pitch black. Stela keeps a hand on my ankle the whole way down to let me know she's still with me. I can't see the

rungs, or hear Stela's tread below me. I'm certain only of my own hands, and my shoes ringing dully against the bars.

The tube is dry but I hear the distant rush of water, droplets splashing into puddles. I've never had a problem with confined spaces, but the enclosure is so narrow I keep hitting the back of my heel each time I search for the next rung, breathing my own expended breath.

There's a light below me, shining off the steel rungs. My foot falls into nothing, kicking at empty air, and though I never heard Stela land she must have dropped down. Stela grabs both my feet, pushing up into my weight. Her hands climbing up my legs, holding on as I lower myself into her arms. She sets me down beside her and before I can release a relieved sigh, Stela clamps her hand over my mouth. All I can see are the edges of her eyes, bright with a crescent moon gleam. She all but covers me with her body, tucking me under her shoulder and creeping along very slowly. She leads me down a damp, uneven corridor in a sideways waltz.

Our surroundings brighten the further we go and soon I can see one freely swinging bulb in a metal grate at the junction of this tunnel and another. The penetrating damp, and the unbelievable scale of our surroundings leave me dumbfounded. We're standing in the middle of a kind of intersection, with three tunnels ahead of us. There are tracks underfoot, too small for trains, and pipes that stripe the walls.

I almost ask her where we're going, but she can feel my body shape the words, and she covers my mouth again. I take one full step before her arm tightening around my shoulders tells me that she has stopped walking.

At the end of the passage is another hatch twinkling in the stark light of a single bulb. We're nearly there, not fifty feet away when I hear approaching footsteps, heavy and fast. I understand why she still has her hand covering my mouth. I am absolutely going to scream.

They aren't dogs. The points of their ears resemble German shepherds, and the thick glistening coats remind me of chows, but these creatures are built like skinny bears. They're huge. They walk out of the center of the tunnel, the largest among them in the middle. He's solid black and his eyes glow like Stela's. The other two only slightly less imposing figures on either side of him are both gray with white underbellies. They all move completely in sync.

Stela uses the hand wrapped around my mouth to twist my face to hers. She's frightened, and again my body begins to shake. Slowly, she pushes me behind her, releasing my mouth only when she's forced to turn back around. She grabs my hands from behind and begins to pull me forward, using her body as a shield. I'm not sure how I remain silent, or remember how to walk. I only know there isn't any other option, because the only thing that separates me from these animals keeps pulling me forward.

We inch a few feet farther before the growling, closer to a roar, starts. I have my face pressed into the back of Stela's shirt, and though I'm not a religious person my mind repeats: "Please not like this, please," in the earnest hope that I'm wrong and somewhere, someone is listening.

Stela drops my right hand and raises her free hand like a barrier. I can't help but look over her shoulder to see how she's received. The black dog, the big one, snarls.

"Erebus. Stop!" Her voice is so loud, and so sudden, that I finally release the scream I've been holding. Just one, quick and sharp, unable to stifle it any longer.

The hound tilts his head in a manner that betrays his size, and I can almost imagine him as a puppy. But he presses on.

"Stop, Erebus."

He growls again, low and pointed, stamping a paw the size of a football and baring his teeth. Even I understand that it's a warning. Against my protest, Stela pulls me out from behind her.

"No. Stela, no."

"Quiet." She wraps her arm around my shaking shoulders and keeps her eyes focused on the hound in front of us.

I tug her back the way we came, anywhere but here. She won't budge. She appears oblivious to my presence, immune to panic, until she pets the side of my face with the back of her fingers. I jerk my face away, every inch of my body prepared to flee. Stela holds me in place with her iron grip, staring the animal down while she moves her hand down my throat. She presses her palm just above my breast, and the surge of foreign blood rushes inside my heart. I understand the gesture, and stand taller as the familiar tempo of Stela's heartbeat echoes in my chest.

Erebus isn't looking at her anymore. His eyes are on my face—a frighteningly sentient stare. He stops abruptly with a pathetic whimper. He turns around to the other hounds and barks sharply at them both. I instinctively cover my ears and the two gray dogs heel in unison. Erebus takes a step toward them, growling a new set of orders to his pack. Stela presses her lips to my temple and shoves me toward the wall where she enters another code on a second hatch. The gray beasts voice their objection, but neither moves on us as she opens the door and lifts me inside.

I crawl on my hands and knees and Stela pulls the steel door closed behind us and covers me immediately. Despite her weight on me, my whole body is trembling uncontrollably, and I think to tell her that I can't breathe with her hand over my mouth, but I'm screaming and I can't stop. I don't know how long we lie on the floor, her hand over my mouth and her eyes pushing for calm, before I can quiet myself. Our bodies are flattened in the small dry enclosure, legs bent at the knee. There isn't quite enough space to stretch out fully.

"You are very brave, my angel. It is done. Be still. Be still now, Elizabeth." Her voice is calm and quiet in my ear.

She removes her hand from my mouth, and runs it back through my hair. I push her shirt up, and splay my hands across the smooth skin of her back, keeping our bodies pressed tightly together as I fight to slow my racing pulse. She doesn't rush me to my feet, seemingly content to lie as we are for as long as I need. Her fingers thread themselves in my hair, brushing against my neck. I press my mouth to her ear.

"What were those things?"

"My brother Crogher's non-union, private security team."

I shove her hard with my shoulders, which barely jostles her. Stela's chest rattles with relieved laughter.

"Come now. They are nothing more than large dogs. More intelligent, vicious, but mutts all the same. And we are past them now, are we not? No worse for the wear."

She sits up and balances on the balls of her feet, her forearms draped lazily across her knees. Scooting against the wooden wall, I press myself tight in the corner of this narrow enclave. She cracks her neck sharply, and with a small stretch stands to her full height.

"Where are we, Stela?" I whisper.

"The compound. My chamber is not far. Come. See for yourself."

She extends a hand and helps me to my feet. The walls around us are dry as bone, dark wood, almost black. There are two shallow footholds spaced a few feet apart. The highest sits eye level with me. She urges me up the first step with firm hands and scoots me to one side by the hips. My hands take hold of an opening, equally dry, sanded smooth and flat. Just above my head there is a soft, welcoming glow. I pull myself up and she follows.

"Third candle on the right. Do you see?"

The corridor ahead of us is no more than three feet high, eight feet wide at most, and bathed in yellow candlelight. Each candle is ensconced on the wall above a beveled hatch in the floor, all the same dark wood, and only visible by the variation in grain. The far end of this corridor is much brighter, suggesting electrical lighting, but the corridor appears to drop off well before that, just short of a much larger opening. The overall effect is deceptively welcoming.

"What's down there?"

Stela runs her hand down my spine.

"These hatches open onto separate dormitories, one for each of my siblings. Bård and I sleep closest to the opening, on opposite sides. At the mouth of the corridor there is another drop much like this one, which leads to the main hall. From there you can reach many common areas. And beyond those rooms, Fane's chamber."

She's proud of her place in all this. Proud of her home. Her dark eyes twinkle, like she's waited a lifetime to share it with someone. The low ceiling will force me to crawl on my hands and knees to her hatch. It hits me rather quickly that the corridor was designed with that in mind, the better to slow an intruder down. It would be impossible to stand and fight someone off. That's assuming any intruder made it this far, past the gigantic mongrels in the tunnels, and they were still somehow brave enough to scurry down this ancient passageway, knowing what was waiting beneath those hatches. An anxious shiver shakes me from head to toe and I brace myself with my arms against the lip of the corridor.

"Elizabeth, we go together now. Tread lightly as you can, as a sign of respect more than anything else. They know we are here. But none have risen, and that is a very good sign."

I can't do anything but stare blankly back at her.

"When we reach my hatch I will drop down first, and you must follow the moment I land. You cannot linger in this hall unattended. Do you understand?"

I fumble for her hand, but she plants my arm back on the ledge and lifts me up into the corridor. She's beside me before I can scramble back down the way we came. She leads me alongside her by the collar of my coat. The floor pops and sighs under my weight, no matter how gently I shuffle. Each noise breathes new life into the dimness around our heads, and I can tell from her sidelong glare she fights the urge to scold me.

The chambers below begin to stir. I hear footsteps beneath us and at my back the distinct sound of a door creaking open. I forget how to breathe but not how to move as Stela doubles our pace, all thoughts of quiet and gentle tread abandoned. More doors are eased open, and though I don't look back, I know we aren't alone. As soon as Stela reaches down and lifts her own hatch, the door to my left opens underneath me, pushing me into her. The face that meets mine is nothing like Stela's. Void of tenderness, mouth open wide enough that it could be mistaken for a yawn were it not for the slow descent of fangs curling over the canines.

Stela throws me into the wall behind her, and crouches low ready to spring. Her face is a contorted and furrowed mask. Her fangs extended and glinting against the backdrop of her otherwise unremarkable teeth. The man closes his mouth with a pleasant smile, and he heaves himself into a sitting position with his legs dangling down into the room below.

"Honestly, Stela. At this hour?" He makes the universal symbol of checking time on a naked wrist.

When I turn back to Stela the mask of violence is gone, a bemused expression sweeping over her face, with only the suggestion of mild irritation around her eyes.

"Go back to sleep, Bård."

He combs his fingers through a mane of long silver hair, and secures it behind him with a tie he fishes from his pants pocket. His white chest, distinctly muscled, is the width of both our bodies combined. I try to curl my body beneath Stela's and as far away from him as I can get in these close quarters, but she seizes me by the shoulder and runs her fingers down my spine. I straighten instinctively. She isn't afraid him.

"And miss all this?" he says with a wave of his hand. "Never."
Behind me, I hear the floor settle under foreign weight.
"All of you. Back to bed," Bård instructs. When the last of the
hatches ease shut, he lifts his legs free and sits cross-legged in front
of me. "So, you are the Elizabeth I have heard so very little about."
I stare at his huge hand stretched out to me, but I don't take it.
And I refuse to look him in the eyes. I don't know what waits inside
them.

"Elizabeth, this is my brother Bård." Stela is remarkably calm,
clearly comfortable with this man, despite having hidden her ties
to me for so long. She smiles and gives me an encouraging nudge.

Years of good manners force me to meet his stare and shake
his hand. His skin is exactly like Stela's. Not cold, but just a few
degrees too low, like holding plastic. It isn't that the skin is hard,
necessarily, but it lacks a certain elasticity. His eyes, wide and black
as hers, dance across my face almost playfully and without any
subterfuge.

"Bård, I have heard very little about you as well."

Bård guffaws, a genuine smile swallowing his whole face, giving
him the momentary appearance of a very young man trapped in
the body of an older gentleman.

"Well, that is our Stela," he says. "So secretive."

Even Stela chuckles. And I laugh like it's the most hilarious
thing anyone has ever said to me as cold dread rolls off my body in
nervous waves.

"I will detain you no longer. See to your foundling, Stela. I will
rouse Fane."

He walks on all fours, with the tips of his fingers and the balls of
his feet—impossibly fast—and disappears head first down into the
wider opening at the end of the corridor.

Stela turns me to face her. "Come. Do not linger."

She positions my legs inside the hatch. There's a cluttered desk
below my dangling feet, and an enormous Oriental rug. Wafting
up from chamber is the distinct floral scent I've always associated
with Stela. She slides around me carefully, lowering herself to the
waist and bracing both hands, as though the dead weight of her
entire body suspended in the air is the lightest thing she's ever
carried. She stares at me, and I nod for her to let go. Stela drops at
least twenty feet to the floor below, like a spent shell casing ejected
from a gun.

With far less grace, I grab the lip of the opening and try to lower myself inside. But my arms tremble and buckle with my full weight on them, legs cycling in empty air.

"Just let go, Elizabeth. I will not let you fall."

It's not Stela's mild amusement that spurs me on, but simple fight or flight. A door lifts in the corridor, and the second it does my body drops dead as a stone into her waiting arms.

The hatch above closes automatically, and Stela plants me on my feet. She rushes across to a much smaller door in the corner of the room, twisting the handle up sharply until it clicks into place.

"Locking me in?" I don't see the point. I couldn't fight my way out if I tried. A certainty that does nothing to settle me. I struggle to remind myself that this is what I wanted. This is what I chose.

"Locking Erebus out for the time being," she explains. "He has frequented my chamber of late."

Stela stands at the center of the room with her shoulder pressed to the post of a very large antique canopy bed. The bold maroon tapestries are tied back with thin gold rope. The mattress on a thick-legged frame sits higher than her hip, and the headboard is cluttered with large down-filled pillows in cream-colored cases. Behind her, on shelves to the ceiling, are rows upon rows of books. Some are so warped and crooked on their peeling spines that I wonder if they can even be handled at this point. Between the towering bookshelves there's an enormous fireplace still smoldering with coals from a dying fire, though I haven't the faintest idea where the chimney goes.

Above the mantel, eerily anachronistic, is a replica of *Morning Sun* by Edward Hopper. Beckoned to the hearth by the familiar, strikingly sad image of a woman alone on her bed, hands clasped around her knees, dreading this new day, I drift farther inside while Stela watches. I had the chance to see the original on a school trip to New York but this version is much larger. I trace the bottom of the heavy oak frame.

"I could not get the image out of my head." Stela is transfixed by the painting.

"Did you paint this?"

Stela shrugs.

"It's amazing."

"Given enough time, you can teach yourself just about anything," she says. Stela's hand moves in the corner of my eye, and

I pull away unintentionally. She frowns and reaches around me for a remote on the mantel. We stare at each other, painfully unsure of ourselves. "Sit with me for a moment?"

Stela takes my silence as an answer. She steps behind me and removes my coat, tossing it onto an embroidered bench at the foot of her bed. I let her take my hand and lead me down two generous steps that separate the sleeping area from a small, recessed living room. There is a long black leather chesterfield, a smart black club chair to match though I would date it around the 1950s, and a low-lying mission-style coffee table separates the two.

Stela steers me toward the chair, which faces a wall latticed like colonial windows but is actually an enormous projector screen. Stela clicks the remote and takes a seat on the sofa. The large screen wakes to life, depicting an animated and realistic portrayal of a beach at dawn, complete with the low rush of a lazy surf. The image transforms the entire room, opening the space, and I would swear we were perched at the window of some cliff-side resort.

"You can change the view, if you like. This one has always been my favorite." I look to her in amazement. "I spent many evenings on this sofa, watching the waves roll in. Thinking of you."

I walk on weak legs to the edge of the coffee table. The illusion remains just as convincing. "Something to make you forget the tunnels?"

Stela laughs wearily. "Something to make the isolation bearable."

She reclines with one arm thrown along the back of the couch, the other propped on the armrest. She rests her head in her hand, her ruined blouse parted down to her navel. I take a seat on the sofa, close but not beside her. Not unless she reaches out for me. Which she doesn't.

Though she remains silent, she shows her nervousness in other ways. Stela rarely fidgets, but she plays idly with a loose button on her blouse, dangling on a single white thread. She won't look at me. The atmosphere is oddly reminiscent of an awkward first date. Bodies close but not touching. The air charged with everything that should be said, but isn't. I reach out and take her hand and the corner of Stela's mouth quirks up into a grateful smile.

"Stela...I don't know what to do."

XI
The Beginning

Leaning forward, I cup her flushed cheeks in my hands to press a chaste kiss to her lips, which she does not return. Elizabeth's eyes remain open—all seeing but removed—and they search my own, dulled to distraction by the inescapable conclusion we must embrace. She places her hand through the torn silk of my blouse and flattens her quivering fingers over my heart, listening to the sluggish beat through her pores.

"You are less bothered by what we must do, than how it must be done."

Elizabeth curls into my waiting embrace and her hands press against my chest. Her touch climbs timidly to the nape of my neck, and I do not halt her solemn exploration. She has traced the edges of this scar before, many times, but never with such morbid fascination. Her fingers skirt the aged reminder that I was once as she is now: terrified, enamored, distrustful, mortal, and wholly unprepared for the change, despite the years of quiet servitude I spent in Fane's great company.

"How then?" she asks, ghosting her fingers over the mark that ended one life and gave me another. I cover her hand with mine, holding her fingers in place.

"I will drain you of your blood and, in turn, force you to drink from me. It is impossible to describe exactly what will happen when you wake. That is a very singular experience. It differs for all of us." She pulls her hand from beneath mine, leaning up on one arm, and despite her apparent duress, the tops of her cheeks darken when her eyes glance over the exposed skin of my chest. A quick, pleased smile whispers across my face and Elizabeth brightens for a second, before her face ices over.

"Will it hurt?"

For all her stubborn arrogance, she is little more than a girl. I forget at times just how green the soul is that flowers in her heart. I linger in my own wretchedness, searching for any comfort I can give to her.

"It was several lifetimes past that I was made by Fane. I do not recall the sensation, but I believe I tried to fight him off. The memories of my life before that night have largely faded into shadow. But it is my hope that you will not suffer. I will be as delicate as I can."

A lone tear slips from the corner of her eye. When I reach for her she does not recoil, and permits me to bring her face to my chest. I run my hand through her dark hair as she weeps, softly, barely audible.

"Why did you fight him? Wasn't it what you wanted?"

With a heavy sigh, I cradle her in the crook of my arm as we recline. Now is not the time for stories. Fane whispers to me, urging a conclusion so that the others may rest.

"I was young and very much in love with my fencing instructor, at the time. When Fane saw us together he became wildly angry. He nearly beat the life out of the poor lad right there, on the promenade. I pleaded with Fane to spare the young man's life. Threw myself at his feet in front of the whole household. Fane had him taken to the dungeons at once, and came to me later that night. There was no tenderness in his heart for me at the time, and as such, it was not his aim to spare me pain."

She wraps her body around mine and draws familiar circles against the side of my neck. Her lips brush my ear.

"What was his name? The young man?"

Elizabeth has an exhausting mind. I press my cheek to her forehead and close my eyes, searching for details long since buried to appease her.

"I cannot recall."

She lifts her face to mine with a furrowed brow.

"Did you see him again?"

Her eyes dip down to my lips. I can picture his face as I look upon her.

The first never leaves you. His features dark and sharp. The cuts and bruises on his face blackened with dirt from his cell. With shattered hands, he clawed the calfskin legs of my riding pants, crying tears of joy that I was spared and returned to him.

I gathered him in my arms and kissed the crown of his soiled head as he wept. The scent of his fevered skin filled my nostrils, obliterating everything else. He was the first human I crossed in my first night in the new world. I did not have years of painstakingly manicured control. I was an infant. He kicked, he pulled my hair, and I apologized, spilling more blood than I ingested in the process. When I laid his body back down in the dirt he was peaceful, smiling faintly, while Fane applauded behind me. It was not a full day after that my human blood began to sour Fane's immaculate constitution. The life force of a mortal polluted the meat and muscle of my Lord. He was bedridden for months, raving mad from the pain.

"Fane had him executed."

A carefully worded omission is a lie by any other name, but what good would it do her now to hear such truths? What peace could it possibly bring her to know that his sentence was carried out by one who cared for him so deeply in life?

"Executed? For falling in love with you?"

"It was a different time, my darling. Simpler if you can believe that, which I do not expect you will. If I had been the ward of any other wealthy Lord, the young man's sentencing would have been thus. I was a maiden and I did not belong to myself. My virtue was not mine to give."

In an instant, Elizabeth is out of my arms and planted firmly on her feet. Her trepidation seems to evaporate with an aggravated hair flip, hands resting high on her hips. I sit up with a groan, knowing full well that she is furious, and with a mind to make demands, though she is not in the position.

"I want to talk to you about my affairs before...anything else."

I honestly do not mean to ridicule her, but I laugh all the same. The sound strips the wind from her billowing sails, and she sits opposite me on the corner of the coffee table. Her mouth tight and vexed from the threat of teasing, yet adamant all the same. I must say, I am intrigued.

"What affairs, dear one?"

She squares her shoulders and arches a brow, waiting for the next fit of laughter. Her mother would be proud.

"We need to talk about my money," she says, clasping her hands.

"As you wish." I lean into the conversation. Elizabeth lifts her chin, which earns her a smile. "What of it?"

"My mother left everything to me. The brownstone, its contents. My parents were of better than average means from the day they were born. There was money on both sides. I'm worth quite a bit."

Elizabeth stands, takes to pacing once more, and I am content to watch. I recline on the sofa and watch the wheels turn.

"Most of the money is locked in a trust," she says, deliberating for a moment. "Which will do for the time being. I want the brownstone sold, along with its contents. All assets liquidated and absorbed into that account. Accessible only to me."

Again she rests her hands on her hips, and I am struck by her slightness. How had I not noticed it sooner? The legs of her dark jeans sag at the back of her thighs. She stares expectantly back at me with swollen, sleep-deprived eyes. Gazing into that exhaustion, I accept a bittersweet truth. I know nothing of true grief.

"To what end, my darling? Why is this so important to you, and now of all times?"

She huffs, and gestures wildly around us as though the reason could not be more obvious. "Autonomy!"

My stunned and frankly confounded silence merely serves to enrage her. She storms over to the sofa, towering over me. I take her hand and kiss her knuckles, holding her with a beseeching stare.

"Elizabeth, we are all here, only because Fane permits it. We live because it is his wish. We are kept and cared for by his generosity. You have no idea the fortune he spends in a single month to keep our existence hidden. The bribes, the treaties, upkeep of the infrastructure. We are indebted to him now, and always."

She rips her hand from mine, brushing it on her pants as though she fears infection. "I don't want to be indebted to him. I want my own money, Stela. I don't want to belong to anyone."

I stand up, nearly knocking her over, and steady her by the elbow. "Not to anyone?"

Elizabeth rolls her eyes. "I didn't mean it like that," she whispers. Her pulse climbs and she wets her lips with her tongue. She slips her fingers under my shirt, dragging her knuckles over my sternum as the color rises in her cheeks. "I didn't mean you."

I caress her hair, savoring the light sheen of sweat on the back of her neck and the way it perfumes the room. Elizabeth rocks into me, closing her eyes as our lips brush.

"Yes, you did."

"Stela, I—"

"No." I shake my head, brushing my nose against hers. She takes her kiss by force, wrapping her skinny arms around my shoulders. This will be the last time that I have to hold her like a piece of china, or a paper doll. The last time that I will be forced to reign in my own urge to devour her completely, or that her body will give and bend to me this way. I suppose that is a positive, yet I feel such overwhelming loss. When I cease to respond to her, she pulls away troubled. "Elizabeth…you honor me with your company. That is enough. Your companionship is more than I ever dreamed I would have."

Slowly, Elizabeth smiles, overcome, and nods enthusiastically, perhaps not trusting herself to speak. She swallows harshly and takes a step back. Never one to be derailed, she tilts her head expectantly. Though I am at a loss as to how we would achieve such deception, I could never refuse her.

"This would bring you peace? To retain your trust account, and maintain, at least on some level, your financial independence?"

Elizabeth straightens, the flush of our proximity fading in favor of a more resolute expression. "It would."

I fear this will cost a favor I do not wish to mortgage at present, but what can be done? She knows her own mind, and there is little hope of dissuading her. "Then it shall be so."

"Thank you." Showing her youth, Elizabeth grabs me by the arms and peppers my face with enthusiastic and playful kisses, until we are both smiling. The joviality is short-lived, both of us sobering as though the precipice on which we balance has begun to quake.

This life will hold many challenges for a woman of her intellect. There is a reason Lydia was to be the last addition to our clan. Fane did not like the growing importance the world at large placed on the individual. A trend he noticed early on, and one that continued to grow, as he said it would. He believed there was no room in his family for such modern self-absorption. It took ages for Lydia to acclimate to this life, and she still has much work to do. "Do not thank me yet," I tell her. "And Elizabeth, speak of this to no one. Furthermore, push the thought from your mind entirely. When the necessary arrangements have been made, have faith that we will revisit this matter."

Elizabeth's eyes narrow, and underneath my hands the muscles in her abdomen clench. "Push the thought from my mind? What, like you can't sense everything I'm thinking?"

My lips part but explanation fails me. An empty breath curls from the back of my throat. Did I assume she knew? She must know.

"Not everything, no. But I am not the one to fear, my darling. You must keep this secret from Fane after you are named."

She turns away, taking a deep breath, holding it in her lungs as though it will be her last. "He's going to be inside my head." She is not asking, merely expelling the remnants of some unspoken hope.

"He will." I need to hear the words out loud as much as she does. "Once you have been named."

"I thought..." Elizabeth keeps her back to me, pacing distractedly in an aimless shuffle. She clears her throat. "I hoped there wouldn't be room for both of you." She shrugs, toeing the bottom step with her boot. "I thought you and I would still be...us."

How can it seem as though I have lost her when all I have to do is reach out and touch her? I stand behind her, wrapping my arms around her waist. I have never felt more powerless.

"We will. Of course, we will." Elizabeth leans back against me, and I press my nose into her soft hair.

"But he'll be there. Inside. Like you are now."

"Elizabeth...I can turn you. But I cannot claim you. Fane is the head of this family. It is the power and the responsibility of the Moroi to name their Strigoi." She runs her hands over mine, threading our fingers together and forcing my embrace to tighten around her waist. "This is the price. You knew this. You must have known."

"I didn't have words for what I knew." She turns in my arms, hands falling on my shoulders. Her displeasure is as obvious in her touch as it is in her face. "Just a strong impression I gleaned from your dreams." Elizabeth quietens, deliberating. "He was there though, with you, I mean. Or," she releases a frustrated breath, "he was, is, a part of you. Separate, but distinct."

Elizabeth digs her thin fingers into my shoulders. She stares at the hatch in the ceiling, the small locked door in the corner that leads out to the tunnels, calculating her dismal odds. She dips her head, releasing an uneasy breath and stares up at me. "But you'll be here. We'll be together."

Fane is the only Sire I have ever known, Maker and Master. Lydia comes unbidden to my mind, her near-instant devotion to Fane. Though he is resigned to this affection, the betrayal shows in Bård's face when he watches Lydia fawn over Fane.

"Where else would I be?" I wear my most convincing smile for Elizabeth. After all, what are we without hope?

Her lips purse and then relax. Her furrowed brow softens and the rest of her body reluctantly follows suit. Elizabeth nods once, and I reciprocate. Meanwhile, at the mouth of the hall in the corridor above, my family quarrels. Loudly enough that I fear Elizabeth can hear them, though she gives no outward acknowledgment. She is far more troubled by her emptying hourglass, than she is of their apprehension and distrust. A crowded quiet falls between us, simmering and intense.

"I'm scared," she says, shattering the silence in the worst possible way.

She would be a fool not to be frightened. And while Elizabeth is many things, she is not a fool. She needs reassurance, and so do I, for that matter. I have never born another into this life. Part of me wishes for her sake that I had. The fact that this is new territory for both of us is not helpful.

Though Elizabeth's breathing is noticeably labored she does not cry. Her trembling has ceased and she stares off at nothing, distant and detached. I press my forehead to hers and her fear-battered frame is still. All the fight has left her, replaced by uncharacteristic resignation. She makes no protest when I take her hands and lead her to the sofa, sitting quietly, wide-eyed and completely lost.

Fane whispers into my ear, pushing me to finish. To take her now, while she is compliant and calm. But Elizabeth is not calm.

I stoke the meager remnants of the evening's fire, building it up with fresh kindling, anything to occupy my restless hands and banish the dreadful chill that permeates my chamber. She must be freezing. The budding flames lick the blackened walls of the chimney, smoke rolling up and into the draft rushing through the tunnels. A reassuring heat washes over my face and hands, relaxing a basic part of me. A human part. We are safe. We are kept under Fane's care.

Elizabeth remains on the sofa staring at the surf scene. The distance between us is so much greater than the few feet that separate our bodies. Insurmountable years. I cannot spare her the brunt of death. In her fear-stricken silence, she knows this.

I can tolerate it no longer. My darling girl sits rod-straight on the sofa, her hands folded. My journey concluded so long ago, that I doubt I have words to prepare her for what awaits. What I remember is the blackness, the emptiness of death. Not how I navigated the darkness. Not how I found my way back. What I can offer her is a distraction from her whirling emotions. If these are her last moments as a coherent human, how would she prefer to spend them?

Her heartbeat hammers in my ears. She fidgets on the sofa. I close my eyes and wipe my polluted thoughts clean. The calm swells around us, and I throw my blouse to the fire, watching the flames change from gold to green.

Fondly I recall the moment I first encountered Elizabeth, beautiful yet furious. The hunger, the need, the intrigue she stirred inside me. That complex cocktail does more to heat my chamber than any fire, and Elizabeth, noticeably affected by the change in current, turns to look over her shoulder.

When I remove my blood-soiled trousers, she stares into my eyes with unabashed fixation. I linger, caught in her sights, and permit her to rake her eyes over my naked limbs. I cross the room without a word, our eyes locked, tracking each other, intent upon having one another to ourselves for as long as we possibly can.

From above us, Fane and company have grown quiet, their anticipation as obvious to me as Elizabeth's. Sitting on the edge of my bed in my undergarments, I call to her in a manner she has forbidden in recent months: the innately intimate whisper of her name passed from my mind to her own.

Elizabeth stands, her footsteps solid and decisive. An intriguing guile brightens her troubled eyes, it sharpens the corners of her mouth into amused points. She stalks me like prey, and I should know. Predator to many as far back as I can remember. She positions herself between my parted legs and in one continuous motion pulls my head back to expose my neck. Elizabeth flattens her tongue, licking the pronounced hollow at the base of my throat. My muscles jump and I grip her wrists painlessly.

Bent above me, Elizabeth's face falls as it always does when I resist her. This is not an intimacy I can grant. Not while she is still so fragile, so easily shattered. We have been over this many times, but I suspect it is a point I will be forced to reiterate, yet again.

"Why won't you let me," she pants, breathless and pained.

I release her to explain yet again what I have tried in vain to make her understand. But Elizabeth, under the heady influence of lust, grips my bare thigh, her thumbs pressing into the warm skin. A shudder runs the length of me, and Elizabeth misreads this as she has before. She swallows my protesting growl with a starved kiss, pushing her tongue into my mouth as though the sound is a reward, instead of a warning.

I pull her back by her hair, and she curses at me. Her fear usurped by indignation. Pink cheeks, a flush all the way down to her chest. Heavy in the swoon of my own hunger, I brace myself on the bedpost, lost to the angry, almost desperate tones of her voice as she presses and questions incessantly. "Can't you see that I want you as much as you want me?" Her confusion is earnest, and heartbreakingly genuine.

My vision clears, and the pounding of her pulse in my ears dulls to a manageable drum. She slumps down on the bed, confounded. I cannot immediately face her, not with the face of a feed, the wrinkled snarl of an eternally famished animal. I turn back as the last lines of my brow unfurl and regard her sullen face, her wounded pride.

"Elizabeth, as I have told you many times, we do not want each other the same way. This is something you will understand, presently. Everything I do, I do for you, my darling. Even my refusal to allow you to reciprocate is for your protection, and not any selfish gain."

Still unsatisfied, she wraps her legs around my hips and in closing them, pulls her front flat against my stomach. She reaches for the buttons of her blouse. "Then why do you shiver when I touch you?" She punctuates each word with their unfastening.

Smiling at her petty torment, I curl my arm around her back and extricate her shoulders from their garb. She is pliant and willing in my hands as I hold the back of her neck, and press my mouth to the middle of her throat. A gesture that once made her recoil, now welcomed with a sigh and a tightening in her grip. I lift my eyes to hers. "To keep from tearing you apart," whispering the answer between her parted lips.

For once, the truth.

The ferocity of my desire is obvious in my voice, my face. My eyes widen, ears sharp and ringing with the sound of her heartbeat. Every breath she takes rushes over my skin with blistering force.

The strangled gulp that slides down her throat rushes like water in a drain as I keep her head pulled back. My senses are mired in every physiologic response her body offers. Her heart rate climbs, and the blood vessels in her neck and face swell in rosy blooms. She does not look away or cower. She barely moves. We are both trapped in this cycle of desire, fueling each other's responses: the surge of emotion, the endorphins that render us dumb to the consequences of this special night. The same starved blood thrumming through our veins, begging me to take it back, urging Elizabeth to let herself be devoured.

Her fingertips dig into the top of my spine, and I can nearly register the pain. She drags me on top of her, delirious, half crazed by her need to be touched. No mortal has ever seen my features darkened with blood lust, and lived.

Elizabeth will not be an exception.

I strip her open shirt from her arms and wrap my hands around her waist, pushing her further up the bed. She slides back as I stalk her on my hands and knees, making quick work of her bra. All uncertainty abandons her when she holds my face in her hands. I settle my body atop hers.

Her jean-clad legs encircle my waist, pulling my torso flat. Her skin is fiercely warm. Her short blunt nails make crescent-shaped cuts along my shoulder blades that heal instantly. Transfixed by her ragged breath filling my lungs and the scent of her hair, I wonder if anything could be more satisfying than the small sounds she tries so desperately to contain.

She breaks our desperate kiss to look me in the eye. Her palm warms mine as she slides my hand down the length of her body, and under her waistband. Her eyes drift closed when I touch her. I bury my face in her neck as her hips arch, her pants rucked down to her knees, and any modesty either of us may have regarding the captive audience in the hall is forgotten. Her voice cracks, breath rushing from her mouth in a harsh gasp as a tremor takes control of her body.

The warmth of her invades me and I do not recall ever having felt this fevered. Two hands knot themselves in my hair. Her breath hitches and every muscle in her body tightens around me. My mouth opens just under her ear, her blood singing a song meant only for me. And when my name bursts from the rigid confinement of her chest, it sounds less like a cry and more like permission.

I close my mouth over her jugular—thundering beneath the skin—before my fangs have descended, and there is a moment that precipitates the pain. A wordless exchange that will never leave me: Elizabeth flattens her hand to the back of my head, and presses.

My fangs stretch from their ruby beds, and when the skin beneath them relents, a sound escapes my mouth—so foreign and starved that I wonder if it belongs to me at all. A soft cry fills my ears as her torso tries to extricate itself from underneath my body. But Elizabeth keeps her hand where it rests on my skull, encouraging me to continue even as her baser instincts seek to free her from this fate.

The flood comes fast and coats my tongue. Everything that is Elizabeth fills the roof of my mouth. When that precious life slides down the back of my throat and crashes into the abyss I have become, I open my eyes. The truth in her blood is as devastating as she is.

The empty brownstone echoing her sock-clad steps. Her mother standing on the back porch, as still as stone. Her father's large arms enclosing her against his chest so completely that I fear for her small body. And his arms around her become her arms around me, wrapped in a twisted nest of sheets in her bedroom.

Every inch of her existence belongs to me, until we are one beating heart roaring in my chest. The roar becomes a hum, and her hand rests limply on my shoulder. Her back settles against the bed as a lone last sigh pushes its way between her lips—the single most terrifying sound I have ever heard.

I tear myself away from her with a gasping moan and her body, now chilled, jostles from the force. Her eyes shut peacefully as if in sleep, with the start of a smile curling the corners of pale lips. I gather her in my arms, weighted limbs dangling from my grasp, and reach beneath my pillow for my dagger. I push the tip of the blade into the side of my throat with a twist. The taste of her fills my nostrils as my mouth pools with my own blood.

I bring Elizabeth to the wound and hold her there. Her pulse is a thready suggestion under my fingers as I stroke her neck. My grip on her tightens instinctively, and I can barely reason with myself that I might hurt her. But Elizabeth's mouth does not fix itself to the wound. My blood stains the pillows, streaking the sides of her face crimson. I hold her head in place, rubbing the front of her throat. My blood slides inside of her, yet still she rests motionless in my arms. A bone-weary fatigue knocks me off my knees and all that borrowed heat returns to its source only to cool in her chest.

"Elizabeth." A hollow command that drifts in the air between us.

My vision darkens and my emptiness wells up around me. With my body crumpled over hers, I continue calling to her as the room cools and quietens. No arguments in the hall. No whispers from Fane. Only an image of Elizabeth—a fading silhouette—growing smaller by the second, deaf to my cries, as death pulls me from her with its impersonal hands.

With a mind all its own, my body bolts upright. I finger the jagged edges of the hole in my throat, but as I push and probe, the skin seals the wound in a gossamer layer of fragile new flesh. I pull Elizabeth up off the bed by her shoulders, shaking her violently. Her arms and neck swing back and forth without resistance. I must be screaming because I hear the echo. Who else would be screaming her name? But Elizabeth sleeps undisturbed, her eyelids ashen. I wrap my arms around her too small, too-light body, and her ribs crack.

Somewhere inside me something splinters like wood, and in the darkness of my heart her name rises, knocking wildly like a sparrow on the windowsill. In the deathly silence that follows something moves—greedy, yawning—and Elizabeth's name is swallowed by the darkness. I close my eyes to seek her out, to find her in my mind.

My confusion is cut short by the crushing pressure of a hand around my throat, so swift and strong that I open my eyes expecting to see Fane. But only Elizabeth's calm and vacant face awaits me. I tear at the hand around my throat, but she tightens her grip. And as I struggle to free myself, Elizabeth's body moves with mine. Her fingers dig into the skin of my neck as I try to call her name once more. The pressure stills, but does not abate. She pulls me forward into her frighteningly placid face, never opening her eyes.

Elizabeth releases a scream so shrill I cover my ears to protect them from the onslaught, an inhuman bellow of impossible volume. With effortless ease the hand around my throat closes like a vise, and she hurls me off the bed with such tremendous force my body streaks across the wooden floor. I topple down the steps into my sitting area before I can catch myself.

Weary with blood loss, I stumble to my feet, still cupping my ears to stifle the awful, anguishing sounds. When I reach the bed, her mouth is wide and her cries continue unabated. All the while her brow remains smooth and untroubled. Helpless for the first time in centuries, I rush beneath the hatch, jump and nearly miss the steel rung on my ceiling. I can feel my body's weight as I drag myself up through the small opening in ceiling.

Bård's large hand hoists me up by one shoulder, dropping me just as quickly to cover his ears. "Stela, what is that?"

All my family, save Fane, is crowded in the narrow compartment above my room, their hands cupped over their ears and faces gnarled for a fight. Below us Elizabeth howls as though the hounds of hell have taken her body.

"Elizabeth. Her face sleeps like death but still she screams."

Through the roaring I hear his approach. His purposeful, resonant steps echoing through the hall toward the corridor.

"She is lost, my dove." Fane's booming voice reaches me before he does. "The darkness has her."

His massive body blocks the light emanating from the hall below as he crouches at the mouth of the corridor. I climb across the tangled mess of limbs toward him. Lydia positions herself between Fane and me, forming a shield. I think nothing of it when

I wrap my hand around her neck and throw her into the wall, out of the way. Fane catches my forearm in his crushing hand, twisting my arm away from Lydia.

"If you harm what is mine, Stela, I will be forced to harm you," he warns with a mix of understanding and rebuke.

"My Lord, please..." Words all but fail me. They flood my mouth, a pitiful, pleading, incoherent rush spilling down the corridor. Emotion rolls off me in fetid waves, repulsing and intriguing him in equal measure. I am on my knees before him, begging for a life.

Fane regards me evenly, unmoved. He shakes his head and silences me with an exasperated glare. "This will be the last favor you ask of me, Stela."

"Anything, my Lord. I swear it." Fane narrows his eyes in disbelief. "Please, just help her."

Fane says nothing, moving to the hatch. He drops to the floor, and one by one my siblings slip through the opening, landing silently on their feet. Strong hands take hold of my shoulders, pulling me back, away from the door. Bård cradles me to his wide chest. "I hope she is worth the misery this will cost you, Stela."

I try to pull myself upright but I slump right back into Bård's ready hands. The last threads of my strength were exhausted battling Lydia. "So do I, Brother."

Bård pats the side of my bare thigh, and the smack of skin startles me. I take in my state of undress and Bård chuckles. He offers his pale wrist. "You need your strength."

He has always been the best of us, my unspoken favorite. He welcomed me as a sister the day we met, years before I was made. He has been by my side through countless battles, undeterred by my quiet reserve, my propensity for violence. When I have crossed Fane for the final time, Bård will be there, with the same forlorn look in his eye.

"Thank you." I tear the skin with my teeth and Bård pats my back like a child. Bård's blood reveals little, an impression rather than a picture. His quiet concern for me, the pain he carries. The rest he has learned to block and protect. He grants me several mouthfuls of his aged blood, more than I deserve, before withdrawing his wrist. The skin covering the wound on my neck hardens, my energy rebounding in a rush.

"Shall we?" Bård slinks to the hatch and drops to the ground.

In my chamber, my family stands shoulder to shoulder beside the bed. Fane has seated himself next to Elizabeth. I push into the crush, knocking Lydia and Darius unceremoniously to the side. Darius balances a vellum bound volume—The Record of Births—in his right hand, scribbling ceaselessly with his left. He glances up from the page to peer through the swath of dirty black hair perpetually falling into his eyes, absorbing every moment, capturing our history in ink.

Lydia drifts nearer, craning her head in front of mine to better her view. She catches herself when our shoulders brush, recoiling as though burned, and casts a familiar look of disgust in my direction. The birth unfolding on the bed is the first she has witnessed, which I suspect reminds her of her own.

The room falls completely silent, Elizabeth quiet as the grave though her mouth remains open, the tendons in her neck still strained. Fane places his palm over her heart and closes his eyes. He tilts an ear toward her and beneath his iridescent eyelids, his eyes move rapidly. The quiet is so tense that I wish in vain for Elizabeth to cry out again, anything to shake me from this nightmare.

Crogher shifts restlessly at the foot of the bed. A hulking, gloomy mass, deathly serious with his flawless dreadlocked hair swept behind his shoulders. He plucks a long wiry black hair, courtesy of Erebus, from the sleeve of his dark coat. Security and infrastructure are his domain, and a new member means added exposure—a larger footprint. He remains attentive in his cool, calculating fashion.

Bård places a hand to the small of my back, and I do not need to see his face to know that he has turned away. I turn to Darius, still enthralled by Fane's efforts.

"Brother, what do you know of this?"

Darius jolts as though stirred from a dream, a dazed expression slowly registering my question. Never one for words—at least with me—he clears his throat and resumes his task. "She is not the first to lose her way," he whispers between brisk passes of his pen. "There have been others."

The room swells with Fane's presence. He pushes his palm down on Elizabeth's heart, compressing her chest. Another bone splinters in the sickening quiet. Lydia gasps. Great waves of humming energy roll from Fane, buffeting his enraptured audience. He is the sun we can withstand without pain, the light that bathes our shaded lives.

I return to Darius, who valiantly attempts to divide his focus between my questions and his duty. His fingers deftly flip to a fresh page, trading his pen for a stick of charcoal from his pocket. Furiously, he sketches a rendering of our Lord bent over my darling girl.

"Where did you read this?"

Darius licks his coal-smudged fingers, slicking his black bangs behind his ears. He does not have the face for deception. Narrow cheeks, a weak chin, all long awkward limbs and sharp bones, with no muscle or fat. "In the archives," he says. "Records from our cousins abroad." He leans in as if to confide a secret. "Tomas witnessed a similar misfortune with her Ladyship's eldest daughter." His voice drops, hoping that Fane will not catch any mention of his bitter rival. Darius's eyes flick apologetically to mine, as if to say we can speak no more of this.

What a strange time for her to find me again, with my own child barely clinging to life. I was a fledgling myself, the last time I saw her. The Lady's beauty rushes back to me with such force I can almost sense her eyes upon me, watching the whole sordid affair come to a close as fate will have it. I shake myself free from her memory, finding it in poor taste to dwell on her magnificence, given the circumstances.

"Her Ladyship's eldest daughter is called Antonia," I supply.

"She lives." I have made Antonia's acquaintance more than once. But how did Antonia survive? I cannot ask aloud. Darius's growing timidity suggests that the Lady herself was responsible. Certain that Fane can hear us, I leave the matter. To draw a comparison between him and her Ladyship would be my end.

"He calls to her. She need only reach for the sound of his voice." Darius pauses, closing his eyes. "You can sense him in the air." His blackened fingers drift across the page in front of him, blending the edges of his sketch, casting Elizabeth's face in shadow.

My throat constricts on nothing and I close my eyes if only to erase the image of Darius's fingers darkening her lovely features. The low hum of Fane's penetrating presence grows resonant and rich, but distant, like a voice from the bottom of a gorge. The words lack shape, but their urgency is obvious. I follow Fane's silent call, drawn down, deeper into the darkness at the edge of world than I have ever dared to venture. He repeats a single word into the emptiness.

Rise.

My skin crawls with an electric charge, a pulsating power that rattles my marrow. My fingers twitch at my sides. This energy—though foreign—settles inside me with an inexplicable ease and familiarity. It pours from me like sweat. There is light in the darkness, faint at first, but undeniable. Fane's voice disappears, but the word remains, oozing out of me and into the abyss. The light grows stronger, more defined.

Rise.

The light curls around my ankles, ebbing, flowing, climbing my calves in warm waves. The blissful embrace, something between drifting and being carried away. There are hands reaching for me, arms stretching from the blackness of the pit. They brush the edges of my body with such tender reverence that I find myself reaching back.

An unwelcome foreboding steals my tranquility, shattering the bliss. Something precious and misplaced. A delicate wrist caught in my hand, and then a forearm. And I am no longer grasping or pulling, but being held in a fierce embrace. Hands I know, that tangle in my hair. Lips I remember, brushing my cheeks.

Elizabeth, my love. Rise.

The brilliance surrounding us culminates in a nearly unbearable crescendo. A dazzling chorus of a thousand matches struck in unison, the light invading every inch of me.

When my eyes open, hers are the first I see. Not the eyes she had in life, casually inviting and autumn brown. Eyes as black and obliterating as mine, burrowing to the core of me without hesitation, beckoning me closer as the room erupts with applause and Fane stands up to receive his congratulations.

Elizabeth is everywhere, a current in my blood, a maelstrom of need. Her desperation as naked as the rest of her, and twice as intoxicating. I take a step and her answering smile is blindingly right.

Bård hoists me back, clamping his hand over my eyes. My mind reels from the loss of her, though Elizabeth still courses through my veins. My brother's gentle teasing, his ridiculous laugh in my ear. I want her eyes on me. I would happily drown in her if he would only release me, but Bård has always been stronger. He tightens his arm around my chest, pinning me in place. "Stela, I could mistake you for a newborn yourself," he taunts, the strain evident in his voice. He forces me to face him, a crooked, knowing smile on his lips, smacking me firmly on the back.

Reluctantly, I huff at my own blunder, refusing to join his joyous laughter. Bård nods his head, releasing his hold once he is convinced I have control of myself. Elizabeth's voice is fragmented, clambering around my mind, unintelligible and breathless. I face her, but I do not linger on her eyes again. Her disappointment is a physical thing, an unquenchable urge—rooted in her marrow—and unable to temper her power or her strength, every new surge of emotion spills into me. My head swims with her half-realized thoughts. I delight in the strength that courses through her once frail body. A vitality and exuberance of which neither Elizabeth nor I knew she was capable. Her uninhibited joy is enough to bring me to my knees, but everything moves too quickly. Her wants, her delights, her anxiety all mixed up together and indecipherable.

"Stela, my dove." Fane pries himself from Lydia's worshipping embrace, and extends his hand to me. "Come." He leads me to the bed with a doting smile on his face, and he releases me to Elizabeth.

Her immediate reaction to my nearness is so abrupt it is alarming. Elizabeth grabs me by the neck, the shoulders, willing me closer with unchecked strength until she has all but concealed her body behind my back. Her palpable, enticing enthusiasm to have me in her arms is second to her fear and her budding embarrassment, neither of which are easy to distinguish in the melee of her rapid thoughts. I had forgotten that she was exposed.

"Lydia…"

Lydia, needing no further instruction, dismisses herself from our happy company and disappears into my washroom. She returns with my black silk robe. Elizabeth is not pleased by her approach. A growl escapes Elizabeth's lips, which surprises only herself.

I take the dressing gown from Lydia, and every member of my family except Fane takes a respectful step back. Elizabeth's body is rigid, coiled for a fight even under the welcome attention of my hands. The pressure of her fixed gaze grinds my resolve to nothing, until she returns her attention to the unfamiliar faces assembled around us.

In the congested murk of our joined minds her thoughts begin to clear. Solid words find a foothold, and I can nearly understand her meaning. The whole aching mess of her unfurls inside me like stars in a clear sky. I hear the whirling contradictions, her happiness, her mortal pains, her countless disappointments, her few victories, every quiet moment we shared upstairs in her bed, the loaded silences when I knew she wanted to say so much more, but stopped herself. We need no words any longer. Her thoughts are tangible, tethers binding us together.

Now covered by my robe, Elizabeth settles, curled against me, borrowing my comfort around these beings and recognizing her place among us.

Fane moves closer, slowly at first, not wishing to startle her. But his purpose is clear, and my heart rises to my throat. The love I felt for the woman she was pales in comparison to that I feel for what she has become: as much a part of me as an arm or a hand, she is my blood. Keeping his distance, but determined to meet my eye, Bård steps up behind Fane. How could he stand it? How could he have felt Lydia swimming inside him like this, and relinquish this heaven to Fane?

Fane gives Elizabeth time enough to sit up and tighten the sash tied at her waist, and then he takes her face in his hands. His pale blue eyes plunge to her dark depths, and she reaches out for me in a panic, unable to free herself. She searches blindly for my hand, crushing it to her chest, pleading in a voice that—for now—only I can hear, cursing me and begging me to push him away.

"Stela." Bård calls. He shakes his head gravely, as if he can read my mind as clearly as I can read Elizabeth's.

Fane has made his way into Elizabeth's mind, finding form as a solid partition that separates our bond, which has only just begun to flourish. The integrity of each self intact, but severed from a greater whole.

My hand slips through her fingers, and the swoon hits her. Both our minds are muted by his intrusion. He pushes her head back and lifts her top lip with his thumbs. New fangs, little more than pearls, nestle in her gums, but they will grow deadly sharp within a night or so.

His hands spur a surge of reserved strength and she finds my hand again, shattering my thumb and index finger in her mute protest. Her voice in me is the sound of angry fists pounding on a door. I look to Bård for support and find nothing but warning in his eyes.

Fane settles back on the balls of his feet, appraising her, and not entirely pleased. He takes her pulse, though her heart can be heard as clearly as any in the room. As slow as mine, and just as loud.

"My Lord, your verdict?" Darius's voice is rife with humiliation at the prospect of distracting Fane from his sacred task. He has his pen back in his hand, poised to record Fane's response.

When Fane's hands leave her body, Elizabeth shudders violently. My own sympathetic shudder follows shortly after, as her thoughts once more spill unchecked into mine. Elizabeth wraps her arms around my shoulders, dragging me to her as though a last moment in my embrace will make the rest of this bearable.

She knows now what will follow, and a part of her hates me for failing to capture it with words. But what should I have said? I had no idea what we would become. What we would be forced to surrender. I swear. I did not know. Elizabeth's face contorts with sorrow, and I run my thumb over her cheek as she grapples with another loss—she can no longer cry. The strength of her words redoubles, until I can see them as clearly as I see her, as though they were burned into the back of my eyes.

Stay with me.

Fane claps his hands together sharply, turning to Darius. "One of us," he proudly proclaims. The room erupts in thunderous applause. Fane lifts his arms in triumph, prepared to take a bow.

Elizabeth rests her forehead against mine, squeezing her eyes shut, willing the tears she still needs to roll down her cheeks. She runs her hands over my shoulders, my neck. Her skin is warm under my hands, firm but smooth and far more appealing than I dared hope.

Bård steps forward and embraces Fane, offering his quiet congratulations. "What will you call her, my Lord?"

I could kill him for asking the question. Not that Fane would forget to bind Elizabeth to him, but coming from Bård of all people, the question carries the sting of betrayal. I stare into Elizabeth's face, unfocused, protecting her from my own pain as much as I can manage. What I would give for a moment longer. One night to hold her without an audience, or a few minutes in private before she belongs to him. But Fane's patient hand clamps down on my shoulder, urging me back without forcing me away. For all his failings, he knows that I ache.

"What do you know of her history, Stela?" Fane's voice is deliberately gentle. I kiss her clenched fists and stand beside him, Elizabeth's wordless screams ringing in my ears as she reaches for me. Wrestling free from her grip, I nearly collide with Lydia, who places a steadying hand on my waist. Lydia drapes a clean shirt over my shoulders, our shared animosity shelved for now. Elizabeth moves to stand, to pull me back to her, but with one look from Fane she stops, sitting perfectly straight, hands folded neatly in her lap.

"The mother was a homemaker. The father was an attorney of some kind. Irish and French descent, I believe?"

Fane clenches his jaw, considering Elizabeth. He reaches out and cups her chin in his hand, tilting her face this way and that.

"The trouble with humans these days is that they have no heritage. The bloodlines have all been crossed, twisted." He shakes his head. "Unclean."

A jolt jostles Elizabeth's head, a violent but futile attempt to pull away from him. Fane traces the planes of her face. "Greek, further back," he surmises. He lets her go, tilting his head as though straining to hear her.

Stay.

I start at the sound of her voice, Fane's eyes still upon her. Elizabeth's chest heaving though no breath passes through her lungs, as though the price of that one word was all the strength inside of her. My fists clench when Fane looms over her. He holds her firmly in his giant hands and the heaving stops. Elizabeth dangles limply in his grasp, her eyes blown wide and fixed on his.

"She is quiet," he remarks, curiously. "A mind more placid than her body."

My surprise is difficult to conceal. I would never use the word placid to describe her, and rarely have I encountered a more beleaguered mind.

Fane smiles, obviously pleased with himself. He releases his hold and steps back, placing a hand on her shoulder.

"Welcome, Irina."

The name is a knife to my heart, cutting Elizabeth out of me. She leaves silently, so much more gently than she arrived, and for all my strength, my supposed power, I cannot stop my broken outcry—a desperate wail that sounds as though Fane has cleaved my soul in two. Crogher and Bård are beside me, arms stretched out like ready nets. My brothers engulf me in their arms—holding me in place—and Crogher has the decency to apologize when he covers my mouth, lest I spoil this auspicious occasion for Fane.

When the last remnants of Elizabeth float away from me I fall to my knees. My brothers leave me to sink to the floor in despair, unable to aid me any further. Every thread of understanding, the love we shared made physical—a beating pulse—everything severed and spoiling, as helpless as autumn leaves in the first frost. My body is cold in a way that no hunt will ever cure, empty in a way I never imagined. I touch my chest, surprised to find myself physically unharmed, but certain I will never be as whole as I was for the brief moment that Elizabeth was mine. I plant my hands on the floor and push myself up, finding my family as engulfed in celebration as they were before, utterly enamored of themselves and their newest member.

Elizabeth, however, has not lost herself in their merriment. She sits where I left her, utterly, eerily calm, and staring straight at me. Completely unaffected.

Smiles are exchanged, embraces are shared. My siblings welcome me back to the fold with hands on my back, my shoulders, encouraging little shakes. Darius snaps the volume in his hands shut before the ink of Elizabeth's—Irina's— journey has dried. The sound of it as final as the slamming of a door. I edge closer to the bed, my whole body weak and numb, filled with hostility for the happy, uplifted voices of my family. When will they leave me to hold her and apologize as I should?

Each sibling extends their hand cautiously to Irina, bidding her a quiet welcome, calling her by her new name and introducing themselves. Her eyes never leave my face, she barely regards the person standing in front of her, angling around them with a polite smile, tracking my approach. Against my better judgment, I do not resist her. I open myself to any intrusion she can mount, staring intently into her obsidian eyes.

Stay with me, Elizabeth.

But she sends me no reply, if she can hear me at all. Did I expect anything else? Her senses brand new and her mind racing with Fane? Irina's attention turns to an exuberant Lydia, just as Bård's woeful face drifts into my line of sight. He wraps his arms around me in a tight embrace, one I return with a fervor that surprises us both. He knows. He lives with this heartache every day, and so will I.

There, encased securely against the brick of my brother's chest, a pervasive warmth spreads through me. A meek flicker at first, and then a budding bright flame. The warmth becomes heat, seeping into my blood, crawling up my spine. A sluggish inferno that envelopes everything it touches, filling instead of consuming, spreading out to reclaim every inch she abandoned as though she never left.

Elizabeth.

Her want, her need, almost her voice. Almost a word.

My grip tightens on Bård as I fight the all-consuming urge to cry out in ecstasy, and he steps away from my embrace, regarding me strangely. Elizabeth gasps as though drowned. Her cheeks flushed, head thrown back, and smiling as brightly as I have ever seen. The entire room turns to her, watching closely.

"Sorry," she manages, shaking her head. "It's all a bit much." She stares evenly at their attentive faces. She turns back to me, flicking the hair out of her face with a carefree hand.

Where else would I be?

Elizabeth's voice is as clear in my mind as though she spoke the words for the whole room to hear.

Bella Books, Inc.

Women. Books. Even Better Together.

P.O. Box 10543
Tallahassee, FL 32302

Phone: 800-729-4992
www.bellabooks.com